NICKI'S FIGHT

TWIN PEEKS BOOKSTORE ROMANCE, VOL 2

MELLANIE ROURKE

SYNOPSIS

KAINE

A lifetime of abandonment leaves its mark on a person. So much so that when Nicki left, it made a twisted sort of sense. After all, everyone else I had loved in this world had left me, why should he be any different?

Six years later and he's back in my life. He's still the same Nicki. Still the same sensitive, intelligent, loving and compassionate man he was years ago. Except...there are shadows in his eyes that were never there before. How do I love him again, trust him again? If he disappears now, there's no way I'd survive.

NICKI

I love Kaine Devereaux. I always have. But sometimes love just isn't enough. When my family moved thousands of miles away to chase the dream of a cure for my mysterious illness, Kaine and I had no idea that more than distance would end up separating us.

How do I ask Kaine to trust me again when I almost destroyed him? How do I ask him to love me again, when I'm still haunted by the specter of my past?

Cover Art by Reese Dante

Editing by Ann Atwood

"CrossRoads Gin" and "Sinners Gin" band names used by permission of Rhys Ford.

To my wonderful best friends:
Sue, Jaey, and Amanda.
Thank you for being counselors, cheering section, and ass kickers when
needed!

TRIGGER WARNING

"Nicki's Fight" deals with HIV status, stalking, domestic violence and child abuse. There are first-person depictions of abuse.

If you are sensitive to these topics, please proceed with caution. While I think Nicki's story is important to share, I care about my readers and don't want to cause any of you distress.

NICKI

I COULD TASTE THE BLOOD IN MY MOUTH. COPPERY. SALTY. A GRUNT escaped me as the belt bit in along my back, the end slapping around my side and along the softer flesh under my arm. The sting made my eyes water and I blinked back tears.

"Count, goddamn it," his voice growled at me in the darkness.

I tightened my grip on the rope that held my arms suspended in the barn, refusing to give the bastard the pleasure of seeing me cry.

"*One*," I said, my voice harsh even to my own ears.

The belt whistled through the air and came down again, striking lower this time along much older scars. Not as much pain there, not after hundreds of other beatings like this one.

"*Two*," I continued, taking a breath between strikes. Again, he lashed out, the leather whistling as he struck me again and again.

"*Three*."

"*Five*."

"*Fifteen*."

Sometime after twenty-five, I lost count. Blow after blow rained down, and when my knees finally gave out, I hung with all my weight on my arms, too lost in the pain to care.

I heard him seething in the darkness. The man who should have protected me from pain and anguish. The man who took his anger and frustration with the world out on my flesh and blood. The man who hated every breath I took. The man who was my father.

When I opened my eyes again, he was gone. The only evidence he'd ever been there were the crumbled blue nitrile gloves he wore whenever he beat me. God knew, he didn't want to take the chance of getting my blood on him. He hadn't touched me skin to skin since the day we'd received my diagnosis. I lay crumpled in the dirt of the old wooden barn staring at the blood smeared gloves on the floor, just inches from my face. Just like all the other times this had happened.

I wasn't even sure what had set him off this time. It could have been a word, a look. Hell, it could have just been a memory. I used to try and figure out what I'd done to deserve all the pain he'd dished out over the years. I tried to be a good man, a good son, but nothing I did was ever good enough.

It took me years to realize the pain he inflicted wasn't about me, really. It wasn't the things I said, or things I did, or the way I looked. It was about *him*. His pain. His loss. He'd made it clear by the scars on my body that he was the one who was important. After all, he'd lost a wife *and* a son. It didn't matter that I was still breathing, that I walked, and talked, and flinched at his slightest move. I was already dead to him.

The sole reason for my continued existence was to be a weapon, *the* weapon. The only one that he that could use to wound my mother daily.

Every bruise he inflicted on me, every drop of blood I shed, was damage he *wasn't* inflicting on my mother. So instead of fighting back, I took the hit. Instead of running away, I gripped the rope that held my arms aloft. I was a willing victim in the nightmare that had become my world because it was the bargain I'd struck to keep my mother alive.

I blinked as a stinging drop of sweat dripped into my eye. A muscle in my back began spasming, but I just shut my eyes and tried to breathe through the pain. I wanted to move, to try and find a position that would ease my discomfort, but I knew I'd pass out again if I tried to get up. For the longest time I just lay there, the sharp agony in my back and legs making my eyes water, watching the setting sun throwing soft beams of light through the slats of the wooden walls and along the dirt floor. Motes of dust swam in the sunlight like lazy fireflies.

Time passed and darkness eventually slithered into the barn, the oppressive heat of the day giving way to the chill of the evening. After a time, I felt strong enough to get to my knees. I knew I had to get up, to get clean. If even one of the cuts on my back and legs got infected, I could die from it. My father sure as shit wouldn't take me to a doctor to get antibiotics, and it was too soon for me to beg any more from Dr. Dunwoody, our next-door neighbor.

Once I got to my knees, I was able to get a grip on the sturdy workbench that hugged the side of the barn and drag myself to my feet. I grabbed the shirt I'd been wearing before the beating and crumpled it up in my hands. I had to be careful not to get any blood on it. A stain on a wearable shirt would be just another reason for a future beating, and I didn't think I could handle two so close together.

"Don't rile him up. Get to your room. Get a shower. Get some sleep." It was what my mother had told me, the first night he'd struck either of us. It had become a mantra I repeated nightly as I dragged myself, step by step across the yard and into the house.

As I entered through the back door, I stopped for a moment, listening. I could hear the TV on in his bedroom, then heard the hiss and clink as he opened another bottle of beer. Good. If he was drinking, he was probably done for the night. He'd never take the chance of drinking and driving. He was a sheriff after all. He had appearances to maintain, and a DUI just wouldn't do.

I started across the linoleum floor of the kitchen to the stairs that led to the second story, my bedroom, and relative safety. My bare foot came down on a shard of glass from the beer bottle he'd thrown at me earlier. That's what had started everything tonight... his beer hadn't been cold enough. I couldn't repress a gasp as the unexpected pain lanced through my foot. *Fuck* that hurt.

"*Dominic!*" he roared from his room. Shit.

"Yes, *sir*," I said through gritted teeth, hoping like hell he was done.

"Get your ass in here," he yelled. Dammit.

As I limped toward his room, I felt something wet and sticky on my back and saw the smear of blood on the kitchen tile. My fingers brushed along my side and I winced as they came away bloody. I rubbed my hands frantically on my jeans, hoping that the dark color would disguise the stain. My father hated the sight of my blood. Hated and loved it in equal measure, it seemed.

I walked to the open door of his room and stared at him, keeping to shadows as much as I could. He sat on the mattress, his feet propped up in front of him, the remote on top of the dingy bedspread. His beer sat on the table next to him, right next to his badge and his gun.

My father, Willis Terhune, was the Sheriff of Monroe County, Florida. Our family had moved here from Ohio when I was just sixteen so that we would be closer to the medical specialists in Tampa. I'd suffered from a mysterious chronic immune system disease my whole life that the doctors in Ohio couldn't identify.

The specialist we'd moved so far to see had taken one visit and one vial of blood to diagnose what all my previous doctors hadn't been able to. To be fair, at the time "grade schooler" and "HIV positive" weren't words you'd normally associate. It was always "the gays," as my Dad called us, or drug addicts. Prostitutes, maybe. Not Sheriff's kids. Not Sheriff's wives.

After I was diagnosed, Dad and Mom both got tested. When she tested positive, and he didn't, I watched my father lose his mind.

I remembered that night so clearly. The drive home from the doctors' office was silent. My father drove, his face pale in the evening light. The heat was stifling, the air conditioner in his car blowing full force, but seemingly unable to make a dent in the temperature.

When we got home and out of the car, Mom tried to talk to Dad.

"Will..." she began.

"No! Not here," he'd whispered furiously. "Get in the house."

My mom's eyes had leapt to mine as he stalked inside and she reached out and grabbed my hand with hers, pulling me toward her as we entered the kitchen.

"Mom?" I'd said, my voice questioning. She closed the door behind us and I sat down in one of the kitchen chairs, nausea and fatigue draining me.

"It's okay, Nicki. Just... Don't rile him up. Get upstairs and go to sleep," she ordered.

I nodded, frightened by the tension between my parents. I knew the doctor had told my mom she had the same disease I did. What I couldn't understand why my dad was so angry about it. The doctor had insisted that he thought it was treatable and would someday be curable.

"There are new discoveries being made every day," he'd told my parents as we sat in his office. "I believe strongly that there will eventually be a cure for this disease, maybe even a vaccine. The key is going to be keeping your wife and son alive until we find it."

I hadn't really wrapped my mind around the fact that I had a disease that could, and probably would, someday kill me. Despite the doctor insisting it was treatable, my father had been acting like I'd already died. He'd barely spoken to me in the previous weeks, and whenever I felt his eyes on me, I'd look up only to see pure rage on his face.

"It'll be okay, baby," my mom said, hugging me fiercely.

When she backed away, I saw tears were slowly trickling from the corners of her eyes. She'd worn her hair down that day, her red curls dark and limp in the humid heat. For the first time, I realized that I was almost as tall as she was. She had always been my protector, my advocate. Now she looked... small. Frightened. Like the diagnosis had diminished her, somehow. She tried to smile at me and tucked a stray strand of hair behind my ear.

"Nicki, I am so sorry," she whispered, her voice sounding ragged and low.

"Mom, it's not your fault," I answered. "It... it's a virus. It just is."

She shook her head and I saw her swipe her palm across her face.

"It is my fault... it really is..." she cried. "I... I did something I'm not proud of. I think that's how I got sick. Then I gave it to you... My baby..."

I didn't even know why I was crying really, but we cried together, huddled together in the kitchen, the dying sunlight painting the walls.

"Nicki, I'm so proud of you. You are an amazing young man, and I want you to know how...how very much I love you. You are going to do such amazing things with your life," she whispered.

"Mom, why is Dad so upset?" I asked. "I don't understand... It's not your fault. Neither of us did anything wrong! It's an illness!"

"Tell him, Har," I heard my father bark from the doorway, a beer in his hand. We hadn't heard him come back into the kitchen and my mother and I both jumped.

He'd unbuttoned his shirt and abandoned his jacket somewhere in the darkened house. He usually put his gun in his gun safe as soon as he got home, so I figured that was where he'd gone. His face was like stone and his eyes looked half-dead as he glared at my mother and me. He took another sip of his drink, his eyes never leaving us.

"T-tell me what?" I asked, looking from him to my Mom, and back, confusion flooding me. I was still in shock that my mom had this disease, that we were both probably going to die from it, someday. My mother just shook her head.

"*Tell* him, Harley!" my father demanded.

"Will, don't do this..." She begged tiredly, her head down, her fingers gripping tightly to the back of her neck, her long red hair tangling in her face.

He strode into the kitchen and slammed his beer on the table, jerking my mother's slighter frame away from me and to her feet. He dragged her close, eyes gleaming with anger, he shook her back and forth like a rag doll.

"*Tell* him, Harley! Tell him, or *I* fucking will!" he screamed at her, spittle spraying out of his mouth and landing on her face.

"*Dad*! Stop! You're hurting her!" I yelled, trying to get his attention.

"*Please*, Will..." she begged. The salty tears made her hair stick to her face like ribbons of blood.

"Tell him!" he yelled, flinging her backwards, her body striking the refrigerator, making the pans and flower vases atop it rattle and clank.

"Tell him what a whore you are! Tell him how we hadn't been married a year when you *left* me and decided *you* didn't want to be married anymore," he yelled. "Tell him how you fucked some nameless, faceless guy and *got* this goddamn virus!"

I stared at my parents in shock. I saw my Mom glance at me, the fear and shame that had flooded her face was slowly giving way to something else.

"We were *separated*, Will," she responded, her anger finally sparking. "Things hadn't been working and you *know* it! We *both* knew it *wasn't* working!" She looked down at her hand where her wedding ring encircled her finger. "...*Isn't* working..." she whispered, but only loud enough for me to hear.

"He was nameless to *you*, Will," she answered, her eyes voice growing stronger even though her eyes were still distant, her face sad. Defiance grew and edged her voice as she seemed to refocus on the present and continued, "...but *I* knew who he was. I just never told *you* because I knew what you would do!"

"What the fuck *should* I do, Harley? Tell me that!" He demanded, flinging his beer bottle he'd picked up from the table across the kitchen, the crash of the glass against the wall made me jump. "My wife ran away and slept with some guy and I should just forget about it? Ignore it? Pretend it never happened!?"

"I certainly ignored enough of *your* affairs!" she spat back angrily.

"That was different!" He screamed. "How did you expect me to live without sex, Harley?! Men have needs!"

"Needs? *Needs?*" My mother's voice turned into a mocking laughter. "Is that how you described it to Angela, the server you fucked at our wedding? What about Marilyn, the tour director on our honeymoon? How about Dori? Oh, and how about that skank at the sheriff's office, Ellie?"

My father seemed to deflate for a moment as my mom named the many women he'd had affairs with over the years. He seemed to shrink into himself as she pressed her verbal attack. I'd known, of course, or at least, suspected. Our town was too small not to. My father stood, unflinching, as her words flew at him.

"I could have lived with that, though, Will. I could have lived with you. Then you made me give up everything—give up my family, give up my friends. You even demanded I give up my *writing*," she said. "I had nothing else!"

I knew my mom had written books before I was born, mostly romance novels and other fiction. I'd found a box of them in the attic when we were getting ready to move and had snuck a couple of them into my room to read.

"You're 'writing' was *filth*!" he said, an odd calmness coming over him as he spoke. "No decent woman would have read that crap, much less written it! I should have put a stop to it a long time ago. I was the laughingstock of the station!"

"Of course, we can't have *that*!" she replied, tossing her hair back as she laughed, mirthlessly. "It's always about *you*! You and *your* career!" she said, her chest heaving. "God knows, you can't have your reputation be tarnished by having an *intelligent* woman as a wife! A woman with needs every bit as strong as any man's! My writing was *mine*, Will. The only thing I had until Nicki was born!" she looked over at me, her voice trailing off.

My father's eyes, the odd calmness that had washed over him, had scared me worse than his rage.

"Dominick..." he said, his voice trailing off into a whisper. "He was my son, and you murdered him."

"What are you talking about, Willis?" my mother responded, confused. "You know I'd never hurt Nicki—" her voice was cut off by the sound of flesh against flesh as my father's fist flew out and struck her.

Mom cried out as she was knocked backward against the refrigerator, her hand going to her lip where my father had punched her. She was more shocked than hurt at first, I thought. That would change.

"Dad!" I yelled again, jumping forward, desperate to protect my mom.

"Will, no!" She yelled, but he began striking her.

"No? By fucking around on me, you got sick and passed this fucking *disease* on to him. To my *son*! Maybe I should be glad we haven't slept together since you got pregnant! At least it saved me from catching this filth from you, you goddamn whore! You. Killed. My. Son." He timed his blows with his words and he struck her over and over and over.

I tried to stop him. God knows, I tried! I yelled. Screamed. Pulled on his arm with all my might, trying desperately to get him off of her. Nothing could stop him. The blows rained down inexorably. I begged him to stop hurting her. He didn't hear me. Didn't *see* me. I didn't think he ever really had.

Finally, I did the only thing I could think of doing to protect my mother. I ran to the living room closet to grab an old baseball bat from a futile attempt at little league. I could hear the obscene grunts and wet, slapping sounds from the kitchen as my father continued to beat her. She had stopped screaming. That scared me more than her cries had.

I ran back into the kitchen only to see my father kicking my mother's prone body.

"Leave her *alone!*" I yelled. I swung the bat with all the force my tiny frame had and struck my father on the shoulder. The blow staggered him, but Dad was a big guy, thick framed and broad shouldered, while I was a scrawny fifteen-year-old boy with a body ravaged by frequent illness.

He turned to look at me, that dead gaze scaring me more than any threat he could have mustered. I swung again... and his left hand flashed up to grab the bat with his palm. I stared in shock as his fingers wrapped around it and he whipped it away from me. His other hand flew out and struck me across the mouth, sending me flying backwards into the wall. I collapsed, stunned, feeling the coppery taste of my own blood filling my mouth. More began running down my chin from the split lip he'd given me. My hand flew to my face and came away crimson. I stared up at my father, the man I'd loved, respected, all my life.

"Dad?" I said fearfully, hating how weak my voice sounded in that moment. Tears mixed with the blood on my face and he took another step toward me. I couldn't help it. I flinched.

That slight movement... something about it, or maybe the terror in my voice, seemed to finally get through to him. Life slowly began to leak back into his gaze.

"Nicki..." he began, looking from me to where my mom lay, moving weakly on the floor. "Harley..."

He started to reach toward her, then spied the blood that smeared the back of his hand. He had split his knuckles from hitting one of us, I didn't know which one. When he saw the blood on them, something new entered his eyes, something I hadn't seen there before. Fear.

He stared at his hands for a moment, a mixture of terror and revulsion flashing across his face. He ran to the kitchen sink and began frantically scrubbing at the blood on his hands. I crawled across the floor to my mother. She lay huddled on the ground, blood smearing the floor around her. I pulled her head into my lap and she opened her eyes.

"Nicki..." she whispered hoarsely.

"I'm here Mama," I said, my own tears pouring down my face. "I'm here!"

I huddled over her beaten body, determined to protect her from my father in any way possible, but it turned out it wasn't necessary. After scrubbing at his hands for several minutes, Dad slammed off the water and stormed out of the house. I heard his truck start and he peeled out of the driveway.

When he was gone, my mother lay on the floor, blood smearing her face from a cut on her lip, dark bruises already beginning to purple her arms, legs and face as she lay.

My father had never struck either of us before that night, so far as I knew. The shock of that action was almost worse than the physical pain he caused, to me at least. Mom was a different story.

Her body was battered and bruised. Black and red mottled her face, which was swelling so badly, if it hadn't been for her red hair, she would have been unrecognizable. I got her to her bed and tended her wounds the best I could, but Boy Scout first aid didn't begin to cover this.

I brought ice packs for her wrist, abdomen and back. I brought her water and acetaminophen to help with the pain, but she struggled to swallow the pills. More water spilled down her face and onto the bed than made it into her, I think. Then I heard a hitch in her breathing and only had a moment's notice before she vomited.

Saliva and tears spilled down her face as I held her hair back. She coughed and gagged into the trashcan next to the bed, finally ejecting something solid. When she was done spitting and clearing her mouth, she fell back against the pillows, exhausted by the spasms. On top of the discarded paper towels and the ripped-open bandages lay at least one bloody tooth, and parts of others.

"We can't let him get away with this! We should call the police!" she shook her head and I sighed. "Mom, please let me call *somebody!*" I'd begged, tears running down my own face as I did my best to clean the blood off her face without hurting her...

"You could go to a-a women's shelter—" I began, but she interrupted me.

"-o!" she mumbled, trying to speak, but her mouth so swollen she could barely make recognizable noises. "-an't!"

"At least let me call an ambulance, or Dr. Dunwoody!" I insisted, but she stubbornly refused. I knew why she didn't want to call the police. Our town was small. It didn't have its own police department. All emergency calls went to the Sherriff's office, and Dad... was the Sheriff. It wasn't like one of Dad's deputies would have the balls to arrest him.

"At least let me get you to the hospital!" I pleaded, but she again shook her head. Her blue eyes glittering with tears. Her left eye had burst a blood vessel, so what would normally be the white of her eye was blood red.

"...dan-ger..." she managed to get out from between her battered lips. "-urt 'em..."

I finally understood what she was saying. She was afraid of putting anyone at the hospital or a shelter in danger. While my Dad's service weapon was still in the safe in their bedroom, we both knew he had others.

"-ed..." she wheezed. "-on't -set 'im, 'et s'ee..." she tried to say. She was trying to tell me not to upset him, to get some sleep. My mother was the bravest person I knew. She had just been horribly beaten by a man who was supposed to love her, and she was trying to take care of me.

I sat with her until she drifted off to sleep, then I fell asleep next to her.

She was restless that night, moaning and crying out in her sleep. I debated whether to wake her. I didn't know which would be better... Let her sleep, or wake her to take more meds? She felt feverish to me, and I didn't know what to do.

I fell asleep next to her on the bed.

About 6 a.m. I woke up, terrified because her side of the bed was empty. I tore out of the bedroom, fear suffocating me, only to find her asleep in a chair in the dining room, her head laying on her crossed arms. The receiver for the kitchen phone lay on the floor next to her, an annoying fast busy signal blaring from the speaker.

I didn't know what she had been doing for sure. Maybe she had tried to call someone. Maybe she had just knocked the phone off the receiver. To this day, though, sometimes I'll wake from a nightmare where I hear my mom crying for me from a long way away. In the dream she always calls me by my middle name, Rowen, which she almost never did normally. She'd sob and beg for me to come get her, to save her, but I could never make my limbs move, in that quicksand way of dreams. I would always wake to tears and self-loathing because I hadn't been able to help her.

My dad didn't come home that morning, and I never asked him where he'd spent the night. I was able to wake Mom enough to get her to bed from the dining room. I wanted to stay home with her, but she insisted that she just needed some rest and I needed to go to school.

Before I left the house, I peeked into her bedroom and saw her pained, pale face against the pillows. Her eyes were almost swollen shut, and she had black and blue marks all over her face, neck and arms. Her hair spread out around her head like a bloody halo.

Her forehead was hot, but she was aware enough to insist that I go to school, even though I didn't want to leave her. I refreshed her ice packs, and set more water by the bed, along with the bottle of pain meds. I found some pudding and applesauce in the refrigerator and set it next to her bed with some spoons. It was the only thing I could think of that she might be able to eat in her condition. Then I fled the house like a coward to the relative normalcy and safety of school.

When I got home that afternoon, she was gone. The only sign that I hadn't dreamed the events of the previous evening were the bloody towels and sheets on her bed. To my fifteen-year-old eyes, the amount of blood was frightening. I wasn't sure how someone could bleed that much and not die.

I'd waited up, hoping that maybe she had gone to the doctor or a hospital. Evening came, and she hadn't come home. The next time I would lay eyes on her would be in a courtroom where I would tell her I never wanted to see her again.

My best, and only, friend, Vivian, often asked me why I didn't leave. I couldn't bring myself to tell her about my deal with my father. The shame and fear was just too much. Even though I was doing it to protect my mom, staying made me feel... complicit... in my own abuse. Like I didn't have the right to complain about it.

I wasn't smart enough for college, as Dad reminded me on a regular basis. With my diagnosis, there was no way I could keep up with classes and work a full-time job, which was what I'd need if I had to pay for meds, school and other expenses. The medication made me nauseous. Some days it was all I could do to get out of bed, much less attend school full time.

He made me very aware of how much he paid for the anti-retro-viral treatments that kept me from getting full-blown AIDS. He showed me the bills for the drugs as well as the ones for the specialists who treated me. Without insurance there was no way I'd be able to afford to live on my own. Even with insurance, the co-pays were exorbitant. They cost thousands of dollars every year.

I despised the very idea of owing that man anything, so as soon as I graduated school, I got a full-time job as a server at a restaurant out on the interstate. It didn't offer insurance, but it *was* something. My father demanded most of my checks "for room and board", leaving me only enough money to scrape by. If I hadn't had a job where I earned cash tips that I could hide from him, I don't know how I would have made do. There was no way I'd be able to afford my meds on my own, much less save for an escape plan.

We had a deal, and I would keep my end of the bargain.

The pain in my body brought me back to the present, and I tried to remember how much I had loved him once. How much I had idolized him. I remembered I'd had those feelings once, but I couldn't remember now how they'd felt. They were buried under the years of pain, physical and emotional, that he had inflicted on me.

"What are you lookin' at?" he growled, my thoughts snapping back to the present as he glared at me.

"Nothing," I whispered, hoping my eyes didn't look as dead as I felt inside. "Absolutely nothing. What did you want?"

He glared back at me. "Don't you talk back to me, *boy*, or was one ass whooping not enough for you?"

My eyes narrowed, but I didn't say anything. My mom's gentle voice whispered through my ears. *"Don't rile him. Get to your room. Get a shower. Get some sleep."*

"Make sure you take the trash out in the morning," he growled, before taking another swig of his beer. "I don't want it stinking up the house."

I really wanted to tell him where he could put his trash, but I restrained myself.

"Yes, sir," I said through gritted teeth.

"And clean up the glass in the kitchen," he yelled. I backed away from his door and headed to the kitchen. If he saw my bleeding back it could send him into another frenzy.

My body had started to stiffen, so cleaning up the glass in the kitchen sucked. The climb up to my second story bedroom hurt like hell, too, but at least I knew upstairs I would have a modicum of freedom. I stumbled into my bathroom and turned on the shower. The water took forever to warm up, but at least it gave me time to slowly shed my clothes without too much added discomfort. I climbed under the warm spray and sighed as the heat began to spread through my muscles.

He was going to kill me some day. I *knew* this, as surely as I knew my own name. It was just a matter of time. I had to get out of here, but how?

Vivian helped me hide what cash I could skim from my nightly tips without drawing his attention. I'd learned very quickly not to try to hide too much, he had eyes everywhere, it seemed. The meager income amount I'd saved wasn't enough to pay for even a month of my treatment without his insurance. Plus, unless I found another way to protect my mother, I wasn't going anywhere.

I sighed, the warmth beginning to ease some of the pain in my back. I watched the water turn pink from the blood that washed off. If a few tears fell into the pink swirls, well, at least here, it was safe to cry. No one would know. No one would be hurt. No one, but me.

2

KAINE

I woke to the image of a pair of furry asscheeks and a tiny pink hole pointed straight at me. Not in a good way, either.

"Meow!" demanded Bottles, my cat.

Fuck.

I rolled over, pulling the bed comforter up over my head, forcing Bottles to perform a variety of acrobatics to stay on top of me. She snuck her nose under the blanket anyway and leaned close to my face, her fishy breath blowing affectionately across my cheek.

"Meooooooow!" She yowled,

"Okay! Okay! I'm getting up!" I groaned as I threw the covers off my head and sat up, my head aching from lack of sleep.

Bottles jumped off the bed and onto my desk. She just barely managed to avoid knocking my camera onto the floor, only to hiss and snarl at the squirrels outside the window.

Bottles had an ongoing war with the two squirrels that liked to take up residence on the other side of the glass. I'd somewhat-affectionately named them Sassy and Snark. They *so* deserved the names, too! I could see them outside my window, chittering away at my cat. My fingers itched to take my camera and start capturing their antics, but right now, though, I could have done with a little less taunting, and a lot more sleep. My phone beeped, and a text notification appeared.

SONNY: Are you coming to the opening this weekend?

I stared at the text and yawned, running my fingers through my hair. I opened my calendar and tried to figure out my schedule for the day.

Schedules ran my life. Work schedule. School schedule. Dojo schedule. I practically had to schedule myself bathroom breaks at times. It was the only way I was able to keep my life in order, and juggle all of my many responsibilities.

My brothers were opening a bookstore this weekend in Highland Square. Thus far I'd avoided committing to attending, but I knew I'd probably be there one way or another.

I'd worked the night before at The Belt, a local gay bar and night-club, and when I'd gotten home, I'd been too wired to sleep right away. I'd hung out in the living room for a while and watched television, trying to convince my brain it was bedtime. When I finally started to feel tired, I'd drifted upstairs, but found my feet wandering to everyone's rooms. I couldn't resist checking through the house to make sure my family hadn't disappeared. Old habits did die hard, I guessed.

I'd been around eleven years old when my family had abandoned me overnight, and I still had issues over being left behind.

My heart began racing as the memories of that morning from my childhood began to flood my mind.

I didn't really remember anything remarkable happening in the weeks leading up to their disappearance. It had seemed like a normal summer. Mom and Dad had worked at their jobs, and I'd been enjoying the freedom that came with being out of school.

My mom was a waitress, Dad was a mechanic. They tended to work opposite shifts, so I never had to be at home alone for long, but I'd noticed recently Dad's shifts had gotten longer and Mom had looked more and more tired every evening when she got home. We never seemed to have a lot of money, but I thought that was how all families were. I assumed everyone went to the food banks when the paychecks weren't enough, or took the bus instead of driving, or sometimes went to bed hungry.

For all the things we didn't have, we did have love. I loved working with my dad out in his garage. He would make extra money restoring old cars he found in junkyards. Dad had wanted to be an engineer when he was younger, and Mom had wanted to be a photographer. Then Mom had gotten pregnant, which meant they'd been forced to get married before either of them got to go to college. I knew Dad loved me, but he made it clear he wanted me to do better than him when I grew up.

"You're a smart boy, Kaine. Smart enough to get scholarships and be an engineer someday. If you work hard and keep your grades up, you'll never have to worry about putting food on the table," he'd said as he wiped the grease from his hands and leaned against his work-bench. "You won't have to spend your life slaving away for other people for scraps."

I didn't really realize what he was talking about, because we didn't eat scraps. I had just shrugged and figured it was an adult thing, and maybe I'd understand it, someday.

Maybe my parents had argued a little bit more than usual that week, or been more tired, but nothing really stood out to me about those last few weeks to warn me what was coming. In the years since, I'd gone over my memories with a fine-tooth comb to try and find clues as to what had happened, or where they had gone. Nothing really stood out to me, I just remembered the last night before they disappeared.

We'd watched my favorite movie together on an old VHS tape, ate popcorn, and done all the silly things you did with your family on a Friday night. Right before bedtime, my mom and dad had stopped in my bedroom and Mom said she had something for me. She looked like she had been crying, but when I asked her what was wrong, she had swiped at her eyes and insisted it was just her allergies. Mom's "allergies" acted up whenever Dad and I fought about something, or I got in trouble at school, or there wasn't enough money to pay bills.

I looked at my mother dubiously as she sat next to my bed. The only time I could remember them looking this serious was when we had been forced to move out of our old house and find a new place to live overnight.

"Kaine, I... I want you to have my camera," my mom said.

"*What!*" I exclaimed, my eyes opening wide. I'd been begging my mom to give me her old camera for years, but the answer had always been no. "Is... is there something wrong? Did I do something?"

I glanced from my mom to my dad. Dad's face seemed stiff and his eyes were suspiciously bright.

"No! No, honey, nothing's wrong! I just think..." she paused to clear her throat, then continued. "We... we think you are old enough now to take care of it properly and we want you to have it."

I was over the moon. I bounced out of bed and started hugging my parents, so excited that I could barely see straight. I'd loved photography since I was a little kid. When I was little, I'd follow my mom around when she had a shoot and I'd make clicking noises to imitate the shutter on her camera.

It took a little while for me to calm back down, but once I did, Mom tucked me into bed, then pulled something out of her pocket.

She placed two small, white pills in my hand and Dad set a cup of water on the bedside table.

"We... we need you to take these, Kaine," my Mom said.

"What are they?" I asked, looking at the pills suspiciously. They didn't look like the chewable vitamins I normally took every night.

"It's... It's medicine, baby," I remembered her saying, refusing to look me in the eye. "We love you, Kaine, and want you to have the opportunity to grow up big and strong, so w-we need you to take them."

I looked to my dad in confusion.

"But I'm not sick?" I argued. I hated taking pills, they always seemed to get stuck in my throat.

"Just take the medicine, for god's sake, Kaine," my father had barked from the doorway, before storming off.

My dad was normally a very quiet man. That, more than just about anything was what made that moment memorable to me. My mom and I had stared at each other for a moment without speaking. Her eyes were shiny when she handed me the glass of water, and I'd taken the pills without further argument.

When I woke up the next day, the first thing I remembered noticing was that it was quiet. Eerily quiet. Our house was always loud—Mom playing music in the kitchen, Dad in the garage working on one of the various cars he took in to earn extra cash, the television playing in the living room. Not today.

The second thing I noticed was that I had to pee, badly. I could tell by the light coming in my windows that it was late in the afternoon, and I was really confused. My parents never let me sleep this late, even on a weekend. I rushed to the bathroom only to come to a screeching halt when I opened my bedroom door.

Except for my bedroom, the entire house was empty. By empty, I mean *empty*. All the furniture was gone, not that we'd had much to begin with.

"Mom?" I called. Not hearing anything, I slowly opened the door to my parent's bedroom. "Dad?"

My parents' room was an echoing void. I looked around in shock. The bed my mom had cuddled me in when I had a bad dream was nothing but a dusty outline on the floor.

I wandered through the empty house, my brain full of fuzzy static as I tried to process their absence. How could they have left me?

I walked into the kitchen and froze. On the kitchen counter was my mom's beloved camera and an envelope with my name on it.

I opened the envelope with shaking fingers. Inside I found five twenty-dollar bills, a picture of the three of us that my mom had taken, and a note that said,

"Kaine,
We are so sorry for leaving like this. You are better off without us. We hope you can see that someday.
Love Always,
Mom and Dad."

21

My fingers brushed over the glossy surface of the photograph. I remembered the day she'd taken that picture. Like my dad and his dreams of becoming an engineer, my mom had had dreams of becoming a photographer. Every spare cent my mom had made as a waitress went to film or developing materials.

We'd spent that day at the park together as a family. Mom had insisted she wanted a family photo together, so Dad had lugged her tripod all over the park with us, and Mom carried her camera in its case.

We'd been set up alongside a stream at Wolf Ledges Park. It had been a good day for me. I'd been to the park lots of times with friends, but it was the first time my family had been there with me. There was a place where a stream made a little waterfall that fell into a pool under an outcropping. I'd been raving about it to my parents for weeks, so Mom had offered to take our family photo there.

She had set the timer on the camera and run back to get in the shot with Dad and me. Just as the camera clicked and whirred, Mom lost her balance and we'd all three ended up in the water. It had turned into one big water fight, and it was one of the best memories I had of my parents.

I looked at the money, the picture, and her camera. It had to be a trick, a practical joke, or *something*. My family couldn't just leave me, could they? Maybe if I waited long enough, one of my parents would pop out from behind a door and yell "Gotcha!" or show up and tease me for being so gullible.

But no one did.

I'd been so scared at the end of that first day, I didn't know what to do. I'd searched the entire house, from the basement to the attic, looking for something, some clue, as to where they might have gone. There had been nothing. Every single piece of evidence that my parents had ever lived in that house, other than the contents of the envelope and my bedroom, had been wiped away.

For a while, I figured it had to be a test of some kind, a challenge to see if I could be good without them there every minute. Over the next several days I created a whole fantasy world in my head about my parents, scenario after scenario that explained why they'd been forced to leave me behind. Sometimes I imagined they were secret agents. Other times, I dreamed they were royalty in exile from another country. Or maybe they had stolen sensitive government information, and now they were fleeing for their lives. Where my father, a mechanic by trade, might have gotten government secrets was beyond me, but it didn't keep me from fantasizing.

Regardless of my conjectures, the persistent theme was that they *would* come back for me. They'd be back if I could wait long enough, be good enough, prove myself worthy enough of having my family back. They always came back.

I did everything I could think of to prove myself. I cleaned the house, top to bottom, as well as I could with just water and a few old t-shirts that I tore into rags. I made my bed every day. I did my summer reading for school. I even tried washing my clothes in the bathtub, but without soap it hardly seemed to make a difference.

I'd done everything I could think of to be a good son, but the days passed, one after another, with no sign of my parents returning.

I'd stayed in the house for weeks, walking down to a nearby convenience store to buy food. Luckily, it was summer, so the days were long and even the evenings were warm. I'd go to the local library and borrow books, always making sure to return them on time so I didn't accumulate fines I couldn't pay. I'd asked the librarian for help in making a calendar so that I would know what day it was.

I didn't have a clock, so I had to guess at the time. I'd stay up late eating cereal out of the box and warm soda. All the dishes were gone, and even the refrigerator had disappeared, which didn't really matter to me, because the electricity to the house was cut off a few days after my parents disappeared anyway.

An electrical worker had stopped by the house one day and rang the doorbell, but I was too afraid to answer. What if he called the police? If they took me away, my parents wouldn't have any way of finding me. The worker had posted a disconnection notice on the door and left. I'd read the notice several times, trying to understand it, but it indicated we were hundreds of dollars behind on the bill and I knew there was no way I could pay it. The hundred dollars my parents had left me in the envelope wouldn't have even made a dent in it.

I had a rechargeable flashlight, and when I went to the library every afternoon, I'd charge it in an outlet hidden behind some books in one of the stacks. I thought one of the librarians believed I was trying to steal something, because she would stop by to check on me with annoying frequency. I wanted to yell at her that it was a library, for god's sake! Why would I steal something I could just borrow?

The idea of stealing started playing a prominent role in my thoughts. I was running low on money and was almost completely out of food. The funds my parents had left me hadn't lasted very long, and I didn't know where the food bank was that my mom used to go to.

I started going around to our neighborhood, offering to do chores. It added a little bit of cash to my diminishing hoard, but wasn't nearly enough to feed a growing boy, especially when I was buying all my food from a high-priced convenience store.

It was the hours alone at night, after the flashlight battery would die and hunger gnawed at my stomach, that fear really began to take root in my soul.

I'd sob, asking God—who I didn't really believe in—to send my family back to me. I begged. I pleaded. I bargained. I promised I would be good. I apologized for being so bad that my parents had to leave me behind. I promised I would do anything, *be* anything, just so long as He sent them back to me. They never came.

A part of me knew I should probably go to the police, or tell an adult my parents had left, but something in my mind had become fixated on the idea that if I left the house my parents wouldn't be able to find me when they came back. Irrational, I knew, but I *was* just a kid.

I didn't know how long I was alone. After a few weeks, hunger became a serious problem. My pants weren't fitting me anymore. They were too short, but too loose as well. I'd lost my belt and they kept threatening to fall off my skinny hips, so I found a piece of rope I could use to keep from embarrassing myself. I was rationing every cent I earned. Even with being frugal, though, and adding the cash I earned from mowing lawns and other chores, I soon ran out. I had been to every house in the neighborhood that I could walk to in what seemed like a reasonable length of time, but all the lawns were mowed, all the chores were done.

I'd lie in bed at night, so hungry I'd feel dizzy. I'd drink as much water as I could stand to stave off the hunger pangs, but after a while the thought of plain water just made me even more sick to my stomach. To this day, I hated drinking plain water, because it reminded me of those days alone in the house.

I'd become desperate. Desperate enough to resort to stealing.

I'd been walking back to my house after another fruitless day of looking for work when I saw it—a pizza box sitting on top of my neighbor's trash can.

Our neighbor, Mrs. Rohring was in her seventies, and a feistier lady I'd never known. All the other kids on the block were afraid of her, but I secretly liked her. My mom had said she had lived alone in the house since the death of her husband some fifteen years before. She was short, spry, and her temper was infamous in the neighborhood, but she and I had always gotten along. The number of times she had yelled at kids to get off her lawn and stay away from her prized roses was beyond count.

If a ball landed in Mrs. Rohring's yard, I was always nominated to go get it. I had always been polite and just asked nicely for the return of the wayward toy, and she had always returned the lost items to me.

That pizza box called to me as I stood there, and the mere thought of it going to waste made me almost dizzy. I looked around guiltily. There was no one in sight, and my stomach growled again, demanding food.

I looked around one more time to see if anyone was watching. Still seeing no one, I grabbed the box and ran back home with my prize.

That pizza was one of the best-tasting things I'd ever eaten in my entire life. I devoured two pieces before my brain began to catch up with me. I'd looked longingly at the remaining pieces and my rational side tried to convince me that I should save some of it for the next day. After all, I had no idea when I would get more food. My stomach argued with my brain that the pizza would spoil soon in this heat, so I might as well eat it all anyway. My stomach won. I lay on my bed that night, stuffed full to bursting for the first time in weeks, and I slept soundly.

The next day, revivified, I tried to find someone to pay me for work. I made a couple of dollars for tearing down some cardboard boxes for one of the nearby businesses, but it hadn't been enough to buy a substantial amount of food. I'd learned quickly that candy and sugary treats didn't keep me full for very long. When I bought food, I tried to focus on items that were filling and would keep for a while without refrigeration, such as bread, cheese, boiled eggs, jerky.

One evening, several weeks after my parents had disappeared, I came home to find an eviction notice on the front door. I couldn't understand everything on the pages, but it was clear that I had thirty days to find another place to live.

It was early evening, seven or eight o'clock I'd guess, because I didn't have a watch or a clock to tell the time. Shadows were getting longer, and I had been looking forward to the date on my calendar when I thought school was supposed to start. I knew they gave free lunches to us at school, so I was hoping I could continue to find odd jobs until then. The thought of the once-despised school lunches made my mouth water.

I was using the last of the sunlight to read just a few more pages of a book I'd borrowed from the library before it got too dark to see. The battery on my rechargeable flashlight wasn't working as well as it had at first, and I needed to save it for emergency bathroom breaks in the middle of the night.

I'd been to the library that day and found out from the librarian that I had missed my own birthday. I'd hidden in the bathroom for a while after she told me the date, tears streaming down my face as I sobbed. I couldn't believe my parents had missed my birthday.

I tried to cheer myself up by borrowing a book that had been my favorite story forever. It was about a kid who played drums to send messages for dragons. I'd always loved the character, because he was bullied a lot by the other kids at his school. I identified with him even more that summer, because the other kids in the neighborhood had started picking on me when they saw me.

They had started teasing me because I never played with them anymore. They said I was stuck up, and thought I was too good to spend time with them. Fuck, I didn't exactly have *time* to play after spending the day trying to find work that would let me buy food. Even on the rare days when I had a full stomach, I was usually too tired to play, worn out by physical labor. So, they had stopped asking, and started bullying.

My clothes were looking ragged. I had been out of soap for a while but even before that, I hadn't had much luck trying to wash my clothes in the bathtub. The kids had started calling me names and telling me I smelled. One of them had seen my belt was missing and started calling me a bum. I'd run home. I knew better than to listen to bullies, but it still stung.

I was flipping through the last pages of my book when Mrs. Rohring had come out her back door and stood glaring at me across the lawn.

"You there! Boy!" She hollered at me from across the driveway.

"Me?" I asked, looking around nervously.

"Yes! You! Come here!" She demanded.

I swallowed anxiously and put my book down. It didn't even occur to me to ignore her or try to run away. My parents had ingrained in me a respect for my elders, so despite my trepidation, I got to my feet and walked across the drive.

"Yes, ma'am?" I asked as I stood at the bottom of the stairs leading up to her back porch. Her gimlet eyes looked me up and down, and I flushed slightly. I knew I didn't look the greatest.

My skin was brown and peeling in spots from a sunburn I'd gotten the week before while mowing a yard. My brown hair was shaggy, and far longer than my mother had ever let it get. I hadn't had much success when I tried to wash my clothes in the cold water of my bathtub, so they were pretty dirty despite the fact I kept rotating through them.

"What's your name, boy," she demanded.

"Kaine, Mrs. Rohring. Kaine Monroe." I answered.

"Okay, Kaine Monroe. Take this to the trash can, if you please," she said, stuffing two bags into my hands and nodding toward the street where the trash cans sat.

I looked at the bags. They were white bags, almost see through. I could see in one what seemed to be regular trash. In the other, I saw carryout boxes like you get at restaurants. That bag was warm on my arm, like the food had just been cooked.

I looked up at her in surprise.

"You're throwing this away?" I squeaked. My mouth watered reflexively, and I swallowed hard, hoping she couldn't hear my stomach growling.

"I never did like spaghetti," she said crossly. I could smell garlic and other wonderful odors wafting from the warm bag.

"Go on now! Git!" she growled, turning her back on me and going back inside her house, then slamming the door shut behind her.

I stood there for a moment, confused. Mrs. Rohring hadn't spoken to me in months. Now, she was giving me orders?

Part of me wanted to just leave the bags right there on her porch, but I knew I wouldn't. I walked back toward my house, tugging the two bags with me. We had a number of lilac bushes that grew along the drive, so I was shielded from view of her house when I walked behind them. The bag with the delicious smelling food in it I stashed on my back porch. I figured that with the plants giving me cover, no one would be able to see if I'd kept one of the bags.

I took the other bag out to the trash cans at the street and dropped it inside.

When I got back to my house, I took the remaining bag into the kitchen and stood there looking at it. Was it stealing if you took something someone was throwing away? What if she'd poisoned it to keep rats out of the trash? What if she poisoned it to kill whoever stole it from her trash can?

I shrugged off my outrageous thoughts and tried to be practical. I decided that if someone was throwing something out, that made it free for all. I knew people often set furniture, baby toys and clothes out on the curb that they didn't want anymore. Why not food?

With the dim light of my flashlight I dug into the bag. Inside I found a plastic bowl full of spaghetti, a bag with garlic bread inside, and even a tin with chocolate brownies! One of them looked like it had a bite taken out of it, and I wanted desperately to dive right in, like I had with the pizza, but the last few days of hunger had taught me a lesson. I ate the spaghetti first, because I figured since it had meat in it, it would spoil quickly. I saved the bread and the brownies, figuring that if I rationed them, even if they grew stale, they would last me a day or two. I didn't have any silverware, so I ended up with spaghetti sauce all over me, but the full feeling that let me sleep through the night made it worth it.

That began a strange, but sweet, relationship between me and Mrs. Rohring. She would come out on her back porch most evenings and boss me around a bit. Sometimes she had me watering her beloved roses. Other times it was taking care of her lawn. One night she made me carry a bunch of old paint cans off her back porch to her shed. I could almost swear a few nights later she'd had me transport the very same paint cans from the porch to the shed again, which was crazy, of course. That would have meant she must have retrieved them from her shed herself, and then ordered me to repeat the task. Which didn't make sense to my twelve-year-old brain.

Regardless of what chores she had me do, the night would always end with her giving me a bag or two of "trash" to take to the trash cans. One of those bags inevitably contained food of some kind. Sometimes there was more spaghetti. Other times there was home-made meatloaf. Once or twice there was pizza, or burgers. Usually along with whatever hot food she had "decided she couldn't stand" there was something less perishable. A jar of peanut butter and a loaf of bread one time, that she said she just "didn't like the taste of". Always, there had been something.

More important even than the food to me, though, was her companionship. I hadn't realized how big of a void my family's absence had left in my life before Mrs. Rohring filled it. In the mornings she would walk down to the mailbox wearing a bright pink bathrobe with matching slippers and pick up her newspaper. She was still able to drive, so she was often gone during the day while I was out working or at the library. In the evening, we'd meet up for whatever chores she had for me to work on and dinner.

I hadn't really talked to her about what had happened. I hadn't told *anyone* about my parent's disappearance. I was too terrified that if another adult knew I was alone, they would call the police on me and I'd be sent away from the house. For some reason, I wasn't afraid of Mrs. Rohring telling anyone. She'd often talk to me about world politics, the government, all kinds of things I had real knowledge of. I'd sit, and listen, and occasionally comment on how dumb adults seemed at times. She'd just nod at me. One time, I said something that made her almost fall out of her chair laughing. To this day, I had no idea what was so funny, but it was like we were co-conspirators in a fight against "the Man", whoever that was.

Mrs. Rohring didn't seem to care what I wore, but she encouraged me to share my opinion. She was as regular as clockwork, meeting me every evening for a short chat and her to-do list, always ending with a trip to the "trash can".

One evening, though, she showed up on her back porch with a trash bag that was different. She thrust it at me before sitting down in her rocker, exhaling sharply and looking anywhere but at me.

"You've got school coming soon, and I don't know what your plans are, but you can't go back lookin' like that. I know you're going to argue with me about it, but let's just agree that I'm older and far more stubborn than you, so just take the damn things," she groused.

I'd opened the bag, not quite sure what to make of her statement.

My cheeks burned in humiliation as I realized what it was. Inside the bag was a backpack, several pairs of jeans, packages of t-shirts, underwear, socks and a brand-new pair of tennis shoes.

I felt a flush creep up my face as I looked from the bag to her. I knew I was beginning to look a sight, and though I'd struggled to maintain a relatively normal appearance, I knew it was a losing battle. I'd hit a growth spurt and the shoes I'd started the summer with just didn't fit anymore. I had to have *something* on my feet, though, especially if I was going in people's yards, so I'd cut the toes out of the shoes with a pocketknife. My jeans already had more holes than not, so I had just turned them into shorts. My t-shirts were so tight I was having a hard time getting them over my head, but I hadn't known what to do about that.

I stared at the gifts, and felt tears prickle at the corner of my eyes. I had come to the conclusion that my parents hadn't loved me. If they'd loved me, how could they have left me? Here this old woman was, though, someone who not only cared about me, she had seen me. Something the rest of the adults in the neighborhood hadn't, or hadn't bothered to do anything about.

I threw my arms around her neck and hugged that old woman for all I was worth.

"Whoa! Whoa there, child!" she said, hesitantly patting me on the back.

When I had calmed down, she got me some water and took me into her kitchen. Her house was laid out just like ours was but decorated in muted greens and blues. It was kind of weird to actually be in her house, but it was nice, too.

She sat across from me at the kitchen table.

"So, are you going to tell me what happened to your parents?" she asked, her eyes strangely kind in the twilight.

"I... they..." Sobs threatened to overtake me. "They're gone."

She nodded slowly, as if my few words had been enough to tell her everything she needed to know.

"I take it they aren't coming back, either?" she asked. I shook my head.

"Any family? Grandparents, aunts, uncles?" she questioned.

Again, I shook my head and she sighed.

"Well, alright then," she said, taking a deep breath. "How about you come live with me?"

My mouth dropped open and I just stared at her in shock. Live here? With her?

"I don't got no one in my life, neither," she said. "You've always been such a polite, good-hearted young man. I've seen how you been! I see a lot from my upstairs... Maybe... maybe we can be family for each other." She finished, "At least, until we find your family."

The next morning Mrs. Rohring fed me a breakfast of eggs and toast, and asked me what kind of foods I'd liked.

I'd had some luck and found two houses that needed lawns mowed. I waited outside her door, excited to tell her about my success. The hours grew later and later, and still no Mrs. Rohring. I'd eyed the lengthening shadows with worry. Mrs. Rohring *always* came out before the shadows reached the roses by the porch, and now the shadows were halfway up the porch railing.

I debated what I should do. She had invited me to live with her, but I didn't want to presume on her hospitality. Walking into someone's house uninvited was not something my mother would have approved of. Maybe Mrs. Rohring changed her mind? The doubts and fears swirled in the pit of my stomach as I finally approached her back porch. I could see the screen door was closed, but the inner door wasn't latched.

"Mrs. Rohring? It's me, Kaine Monroe!" I called softly. The only sound was my heartbeat thudding in my ears. I knocked again, louder this time, thinking maybe she had been in the shower or in a distant part of the house. To my surprise, the door wasn't latched and it swung inward.

"Mrs. Rohring?" I called in question. The door had hinges on the right side, so when it swung open, I could see most of the first floor of her house. I craned my neck through the door so I could see the kitchen, a large farmer's sink with a single light fixture overhead off to the left. A set of stairs led to the second story directly in front of me, and a skylight let in light down the stairs. I tried to open the door further, but it hit something on the floor.

"Mrs. Rohring?" I called, looking down to see what the door was catching on.

I saw a pair of bright pink slippers and skinny, pale legs sticking out of a pink bathrobe lying perpendicular to the stairs.

32

"Mrs. Rohring!" I screamed, rushing into the house and kneeling next to the older woman.

She lay face first on the ground, a trickle of blood running from her head. She was unconscious, and from the tiny puddle of blood under her face, it looked like she had been that way for a while. She was still wearing the pink bathrobe she wore in the mornings when she walked out to get her newspaper. I could see she was breathing shallowly, because her back was moving up and down intermittently, but it seemed like her breaths were coming slower and farther apart even as I watched.

I didn't know what to do. I was afraid to move her, remembering stories of people being paralyzed from falls. I knew how independent she was and how much she'd hate being in a wheelchair or having to depend on someone else.

Looking around wildly, my eyes coming to rest on the telephone on the wall in the kitchen. I ran to the phone and dialed 911 with shaking fingers. When the dispatcher answered I'd given her the address with remarkable calm, my eyes trained on Mrs. Rohring's prone body. I watched as she took a breath, an extremely long pause, then another. Then nothing.

By the time the police and EMS showed up, I knew it was too late. I had tried to do CPR on her, paralysis be damned, but I had no idea what I was doing. The paramedics pulled me away from her when they arrived, but only long enough to confirm what I already knew. She was gone.

I'd sat in the back of the police cruiser while they'd taken her body away in an ambulance. The police had asked where I'd lived. When I'd pointed mutely at the house next door, one of the officers walked over to the house and knocked. When no one answered, he came back to the cruiser.

"Where are your parents, son?" he'd asked, not unkindly.

I shrugged. It didn't matter, did it? They'd left me. Just like Mrs. Rohring had left me. Just like everyone left me.

The feeling of tiny claws digging into my thighs brought me back to the present. I looked down to see that Bottles had seated herself back on the bed and was doing that adorable kneading thing cats did for comfort.

"I am not alone," I muttered, knuckling my eyes, trying to chase away the feeling of emptiness. "It's not now. I have friends. I have a family. I am *not* alone."

I repeated the mantra in my head as I struggled with the aching feeling of emptiness that I'd felt for years. I struggled to control my emotions, listening to the sounds of the household as my family woke up.

I hadn't felt this bad in ages. The compulsion last night to check on everyone probably should have clued me in that I wasn't doing well. I didn't usually struggle this much with my feelings anymore, except when I was my most stressed, most tired. That was when I had to battle with my old demons.

I'd been taking on a lot of extra shifts at The Belt, our local LGBTQ bar and dance club. I'd been working there for almost two years now, and it seemed like we were always a little short-staffed. I had started as a bar back, then become a bartender when I'd turned twenty-one. Josie, one of the other two bartenders that worked there had asked me to cover for them so they could celebrate their birthday with their boyfriend. I'd been exhausted, and really wanted to say no, but then I'd seen Sammie giving me heart eyes from her office door, and I couldn't turn them both down.

Sammie, the woman who owned the bar, was amazing. She had started The Belt back in the days when gay bars weren't something people really acknowledged existed - just a dirty little secret that wasn't openly discussed. She had turned The Belt from an oddity to an important part of the local music and entertainment scene. Several bands that got their start at The Belt had cracked top forty music lists. I respected Sammie's business acumen, but even more so, I appreciated the fact that she seemed to care for each and every one of her employees.

I scrubbed a hand across my face and stumbled toward the door as

Bottles meowed at me again. I opened the door and watched Her Highness race into the hallway and down the stairs before I collapsed back onto the bed, tempted to fall back asleep, but I knew I had too much to do.

I was going to school full-time, working full-time, and holding down a part-time job. It seemed like all I did was work, study and sleep. I was enrolled at the University of Akron in their engineering program, but I was struggling with the work and wasn't sure if that was even what I wanted to do with my life.

I winced as I heard an excited bark and Bottles' hiss of annoyance from the first floor, follow by the sound of Mama K's voice yelling "Kaine! *Mijo*, come get your demon cat!"

Fuck, fuck, and *double* fuck! I'd forgotten we were watching Gracie today. Gracie was the service dog of my friend Brannon Eames. We— meaning I—had agreed to watch her while Brannon and his wife Anna visited with Anna's parents for a few days. Anna's mom claimed to have a dog allergy, and while we knew it wasn't true, Bran and Anna had agreed that taking Gracie on the visit wouldn't be diplomatic.

They were expecting their first child in a few weeks and the in-laws were in town for a few days. Bran had called me the night before asking if Gracie could stay with us overnight, as they were planning on staying with the in-laws, but he had wanted to check on his girl. Yes, I'd video chatted so that he and his dog could talk. I'd held the phone up so Gracie could hear Bran talking on the other end, and then painstakingly cleaned the dog slobber off my phone after she got done trying to lick him. It was gross, but the bond between the two of them was awe inspiring. Gracie was such a part of their life, I knew it would destroy him if he ever had to give her up permanently. They had been talking about getting a pet in addition to Gracie—who was very much a working animal—when Anna became pregnant. That, along with the mother-in-law's allergies, was making them unsure if they should even consider another animal.

I wished I could blame my parents for *my* indecisiveness, but they had been nothing but supportive of me and my plans for my life. I mean, at twenty-three I was still living at home for God's sake! Yes, I worked part-time at one of their dojo's to "pay" my rent, but I still felt like my life had stalled. By "parents" of course, I meant my adoptive parents, Diana and Kyra Devereaux.

Mama D and Mama K were a couple of the most amazing people in the world. First, they were a same sex couple who had been together for over twenty years, almost thirty. In my opinion, *any* couple who was together that long was remarkable. Second, they had six (yes, *six*!) kids—all of whom were gay. Some of it was probably genetics: Lee, Weaver, Sonny and Hicks were their biological children. Some of it was because they were just good people who had seen Bishop and I struggling and had given us homes.

Lee was the oldest, and sometimes the biggest pain in my ass. He meant well, but he was struggling with his own demons after losing the love of his life overseas. He'd come back from Afghanistan with a shattered hip and a broken heart. His fiancé had been killed in an ambush there just a few weeks before their tour of duty would have been up.

Weaver was the only girl amongst my siblings, and she was in the Air Force. She was stationed at Wright Patterson AFB outside of Dayton and only had another eighteen months on her enlistment. I loved Weaver. When she was in town, we were the original party children. That was generally the only time I turned down overtime at the bar. If she was in town, we were more likely to be dancing and drinking than doing anything productive. She kept inviting me to Dayton and swore there was a bunch of wonderful clubs I would enjoy, but I hadn't had the opportunity yet.

Then again, who was I trying to kid? I hadn't *made* the time to go. Ever since she'd left to join the military, I'd battled with this tiny seed of resentment that had taken root inside me. Weaver had gotten out. She escaped Akron, Ohio and was making a life for herself out in the real world, while I sat at home and slowly worked myself to death.

Just as that morbid train of thought got started, the alarm on my cell phone went off. I glanced at the clock and swore. I was running late.

I showered quickly then threw some clothes on and ran down the stairs to the first floor. Gracie came trotting over to me but sat at my feet with just a whispered command.

"Good girl!" I said, scratching her ears as I clipped her leash to her collar. It wouldn't be fair of me to expect Mama D or Mama K to walk her when I was the one who had agreed to watch her.

"That demon cat of yours was taunting her again," Mama K said as she stirred a pan on the stove. I wasn't sure what she was making, but it smelled delicious. My stomach rumbled.

"Sorry, Mama. Bottles is just used to ruling the roost," I said with a grin.

"Hrmph. Some day she is going to mess with the wrong animal, *mijo*. Then where will she be?" she asked, a smile teasing at the corner of her mouth.

"I dunno, Mama, but I'd put my money on Bottles any day," I responded, straightening up. "Have you heard from the twins? Is everything ready for the store opening tomorrow?"

The twins, Sonny and Hicks, were my youngest siblings. They were opening a bookstore in Highland Square that week called "Twin Peeks". They carried gaming materials and comic books, as well as niche authors in sci-fi, fantasy, and LGBTQ fiction. They had held a "soft" opening a few months prior, but they had recently renovated the store and were going to be holding a grand opening tomorrow.

One of the twins knew someone who knew someone, and that someone had convinced a well-known graphic novelist, Mason Cameron, to fly out from Seattle and do a special signing. He was also going to be the headliner for the upcoming Akron Pop Culture Festival in a few weeks.

"They are very nervous, but they won't admit it," Mama K answered as she flipped the bacon. "I spoke with Lee last week, and he has agreed to spend the weekend at the store and help them."

"Mama, you know we'd all help them, if they'd let us," I said. "Will they let Lee?"

Mama K nodded.

"*Sí*. He has already spoken to them, and they agreed *he* could come out, since he has already been helping them set everything up," her Spanish accent was stronger than normal. "They said they didn't need any more help, though."

I sighed. My twin brothers were so damn independent.

Mama D wandered into the kitchen, her long blonde hair pulled back into a messy ponytail.

"Is that bacon I smell?" she asked hopefully.

Mama K leaned over and dropped a kiss on her lips. "Yes, *mi amor*. Bacon, eggs, and toast with *extra* strawberry jelly. I had planned on letting you sleep a little longer, though, then bringing you breakfast in bed."

Mama D looked around in mock anxiety. "Did I miss an anniversary?" she teased.

"No, silly woman. I just wanted to remind you how much I love you," Mama K said, setting down the tongs she was using to flip the bacon. She stepped forward and wrapped her arms around Mama D and kissed her again, slower this time. I'd swear, there were little hearts swirling around their heads.

"Ewww. Gross..." Came a voice from the hallway as Bishop walked into the kitchen. "Can't you two be like straight parents and pretend sex doesn't exist?"

Bishop was naked except for a pair of tiny black briefs, his shaggy brown hair a tousled mess around his head. I knew people who paid a shit load of money and spent hours in the salon to attain that look, and Bish did it just by rolling out of bed... His amazing abs were on full display, the muscles looking chiseled to perfection under his tanned skin.

I was more than a tad bit jealous of my brother's physique. I was taller than he was, but he was whipcord thin, and damn fast on the mats, all without ever seeming to spend any time in the gym. His briefs hung low on his hips, his happy trail on full display, his trimmed pubes just barely visible above the material. He hadn't shaved yet, and the stubble covering his face was fucking sexy as hell. Not that I'd ever tell *him* that.

"Gross, yourself, dude!" I said, throwing a dishtowel at him from the counter. The towel hit him in the face, and he completely ignored it. "Put a fucking shirt on, at least! You live in a house full of gay men. You might as well be walking around naked."

"I had a late night. Lemme alone…" he said, scooping some beans into the grinder, its obnoxious noise playing for a minute while it ground the coffee.

"Bishop, go put some clothes on," Mama D said when the noise stopped, a small grin tugging at the corner of her mouth. "I'll start your coffee."

"Thanks, Mama," he said, dropping a kiss on her cheek before turning around to go back to his room. He barely caught himself a second before he ran straight into the wall. He righted his heading, eyes still mostly closed, then left the kitchen.

"Want to bet he falls asleep before he gets his clothes on?" Mama K asked, chuckling.

Mama D smiled in agreement. "He's been studying for his accounting exam. I think they are coming in a week or so. Same as yours, right, Kaine?"

I nodded. Yay, summer session! It was short, but it was brutal to finish a class in five or six weeks instead of the normal semester.

"Do you have time for breakfast?" Mama K asked, raising an eyebrow at me.

"Nah, I need to take Gracie for a walk, then I need to get to school. I have an appointment with Dr. Tate today to discuss my paper."

"How's Natalie doing?" she asked. "How is your class going?"

"Um, fine," I lied, focusing on tying my shoes. I'd learned long ago to never try to lie to my parents' faces. It never went well. "Bran and Anna will be stopping by this evening to pick Gracie up."

Gracie's ears perked up when she heard the names of her owners. I didn't know if I'd ever be ready to have kids, but I'd certainly love a dog like Gracie.

"Here, take this," Mama K said, taking the eggs and bacon she had just cooked and quickly making a breakfast sandwich out of it.

"That's yours, Mama, I can get something—"

"Nonsense, *mijo*! I was planning on making more anyways. Plus, I don't want you to be late for your appointment with Natalie!" She smiled at me and patted my cheek. "You can walk Gracie, and eat your breakfast, too!"

"Thanks, Mama," I said, smiling at her. "You're a lifesaver!"

"Hah! I don't know about that, but I might be a stomach saver! I could hear that belly growling all the way over here!"

I laughed and tugged gently on Gracie's leash, and out we went.

The sun was just coming up over the horizon, but it was already warm out. We'd had an unseasonably warm summer. Akronites weren't used to one hundred-degree temperatures, but that's what we'd been having lately. I waved to some of the neighbors as Gracie and I made our rounds. Being the diligent pet sitter that I was, I cleaned up after her and then deposited everything into the trashcan before making my way back into the house.

I got Gracie settled in her kennel, then headed to school. I'd been attending the University of Akron for two years now, and I was getting antsy. I needed to decide soon about school. My official major at present was engineering, but I wasn't sure anymore that I really wanted to pursue it.

I loved numbers, but I'd been struggling with the summer session of differential equations, and for an engineering degree I would *need* to pass the class. Even worse, the class was taught by my academic advisor, Dr. Natalie Tate. My moms had known Natalie for years, and she had taken me on as her advisee when I joined the university. Every time I'd get a paper back from her with a low grade, I'd see that disappointed look in her eyes, or hear a slight sigh as she handed out the graded assignments. I was failing her class, and I didn't have a clue how to fix it.

I entered the academic hall a little behind schedule and took the stairs two at a time until I reached her floor. The long hallways of the new building positively glowed and were surprisingly quiet. The engineering and polymer science building had been a huge feather in the university's cap, and it had opened just the year before, but since it was summer session, not many people were around. Plus, it was only about seven thirty. No one wanted to be up this early in the summer.

I made my way down the halls to her office and knocked quietly. I heard her voice telling me to come in, so I opened the door and entered. Dr. Tate was seated behind her desk and looked up at me from the paper she was reading. The office was carpeted—not many of the other professor's offices were—and filled with mahogany furniture. It positively glowed in the mid-morning light, and I couldn't help but appreciate the picture of academia she presented.

Natalie Tate was what used to be referred to as a "well-preserved" woman. I couldn't even begin to imagine the amount of plastic surgery she had invested in over the years, but it was obvious she was struggling to remain youthful. Perhaps *too* much so, in my opinion. Of course, my opinion didn't count, just hers, and maybe her husband's. Daniel Tate worked at the university as well, but he was an administrator or something. I didn't know him very well, because he hardly ever came to the cookouts or holiday events.

While I thought wrinkles and silver hair added personality to a woman's face, it wasn't as if I cared if she had bags under her eyes and wrinkles to her knees. *Women* just weren't my type.

"Kaine Devereaux! Good to see you!" she said, standing and offering her hand.

"Dr. Tate," I acknowledged nervously. I shook her hand and took a seat when she gestured toward the two chairs strategically aligned in front of her desk.

"So how are your parents?" she asked as she leaned toward me, her long blonde hair in loose waves around her face.

"Good!" I answered. "Getting ready to open a new dojo in Brimfield, so keeping busy with that."

"Ah! Yes, that area is growing significantly, I hear. How is the rest of your family? All of you were so sweet when you were little, especially you boys. I remember you and your sister playing together in the back yard…" she sighed. "So adorable."

"The sibs are doing well," I said. "Lee is still recovering from Afghanistan. Weaver has about a year and a half left on her enlistment. Bishop is finishing school this year, and the twins are getting ready to launch their next week."

"Yes, I seem to recall that. 'Twin Peeks' isn't it?" she asked.

"Yes, ma'am," I answered.

"Cute play on the name. I seem to remember your parents showing me the bookstore logo. It was the twins, sharing a comic book, right?" she questioned.

"Yes, ma'am," I answered. "They based it on a picture I took of Sonny and Hicks when they were kids."

A funny look seemed to cross her face as I spoke.

"'Ma'am?' Am I *really* old enough to be a 'ma'am' now, Kaine?" she teased, sitting up straight in her chair. "Surely, at least here in my office, you can call me Natalie."

I squirmed slightly in my chair. This was one thing I *didn't* like about having Dr. Tate as an advisor. She had been treating me... *differently* this summer. It was subtle, nothing I could really put my finger on, exactly, just... something. When she looked at me, it felt almost like she was sizing me up for a meal. It made me uncomfortable, but I couldn't say exactly why.

"I don't, um, think my parents would approve of that, Dr. Tate..." I began.

"That's all right, Kaine, I understand... Not *every* student is ready to cut the apron strings," she said, smiling brightly at me. I felt the blush working its way up my neck. *Apron strings?* Really? I *was* a grown man!

"We're not here to talk about your family, though, we're here to talk about you, and *your* future in engineering," she said.

I felt my face growing even redder. The way she phrased her comment made me think this conversation meant I *had* no future in engineering...

"Um, yes, well... I know I've been struggling with your differential equations class, but I'm trying to get extra time in with the tutor, but they generally aren't available the hours I am, so it's been..." I let out a long breath. "It's been tough."

"Challenges..." she said, standing and moving from behind her desk to sit in the chair next to me. "Challenges are what make us..." she laid her hand on my arm, her dark nails gently trailing over my arm. "…or break us," she said, squeezing tightly as her gaze caught mine. "And I know Kyra and Diana didn't raise a young man who would break."

"Um, yeah, I think I've heard my parents say that a time or two in the dojo," I muttered, shifting uncomfortably and trying to laugh off her touch. "I don't mind *challenges*, I'm just…" I ran my hand through my blond hair and let out an exasperated sigh. "It's not a challenge, anymore. It's a grind. I just don't know if I can do this."

"*Do?* What do you mean? You're going to be an engineer, right?" she questioned, raising a painstakingly shaped eyebrow at me. There was genuine concern on her face now, and I felt like I was being dissected under a magnifying glass. I hadn't meant to bring my doubts up to her.

"I'm… I'm not exactly sure…" I began hesitantly. "I mean, yes, that's what I've wanted to do for a long time, but I've kind of hit a wall, and it's just not… not as *fun* as it used to be!"

"I used to do math for fun, run through problems to relax, or challenge other people just to see what we could do," I stood and began pacing. "Now… All I want to do is turn everything *off* and take a vacation."

I stopped pacing, realizing Dr. Tate was looking up at me with an understanding smile on her face.

"It sounds like a classic case of burnout to me, Kaine. You've been working yourself to the bone! It's the end of the second summer session. You have a couple of weeks off before fall classes start. Why don't you just take this time and unwind?" she asked.

"I can't!" I exclaimed, running my fingers through my hair. I was sure at this point the short blond strands were standing on end.

"I still owe you two papers, and my final in art history is next week. If I don't get at least a B on it, I'm going to have to retake the entire class. We've got the twins' store opening soon, inventory next week at The Belt, and the new dojo opening in Brimfield…" I sighed. "It's just… a lot!"

"Kaine," she said, as she stood and walked over to where I was standing, practically pulling my hair out.

"Have you talked to your parents? I know Kyra and Diana would understand if you weren't able to put in as many hours as normal..." she said.

"No," I almost barked. The reproach in her eyes had me muttering an apology. "I'm sorry, I just... they need me to get my instructor's license so that they can move Donell to the new dojo. I have to do a certain number of supervised hours in order to get certified, and I'm behind on that. Plus, we're down two bartenders at the club I work at, and I need to make my payment on fall semester tuition."

She looked at me thoughtfully for a moment, no doubt taking in my harried appearance.

"Why don't we do this? Let's forget about the two papers you were doing for me on differential equations. I think... I think you need to reconnect with *why* you loved math in the first place. Write me a paper about what it is about engineering, or about math in general, that fascinates you. I'll give you an extension on the paper until next weekend," she offered.

I began to protest, but she laid a single, manicured nail on my lips. "I know I said I'd be out of town next week, but I'm just going to be spending time at the summer house while Daniel is out of town. I know! I'm throwing a house party next Saturday! You can stop by then and drop your paper off. I'll read it, we'll discuss it briefly, then you can have the rest of the summer off to relax..."

"Oh my god, Dr. Tate—" She raised an eyebrow at me, so I continued, *"Natalie!* That would be... you're amazing," I finished appreciatively. Again, I felt that odd, vaguely uncomfortable feeling as she looked at me, like she was measuring me in some way. She was a family friend, and I knew she couldn't mean anything... *inappropriate* by it... right? And I *did* need the break.

"My pleasure..." she said, before pulling away and smiling at me.

She glanced down at my chair where I'd set my backpack and camera case.

"Is that yours?" she asked, nodding at the camera.

"Yes, ma'am. I've been doing amateur photography since I was a kid. I'm thinking about taking a class in the spring," I said, blushing slightly. I didn't like to talk about my photography. My mom's camera was the one possession I had managed never to lose or have stolen from me when I was in foster care.

"How... delightful! Do you do anything with it, professionally?" she asked.

"No, not really. I mean, I've photographed a few events for friends, but nothing... you know, *official*," I said.

"Well, electives are all well and good. We all need to have our hobbies," she said, smiling at me condescendingly.

"Yes, ma'am. It's nothing, really..." I said, my voice trailing off as blood rushed to my face.

I left Dr. Tate's office a few minutes later and headed for my class, feeling quite a bit lighter than I had going in. I had Art History class at 8 a.m., and while I loved my professor, I found the subject matter boring. It still had to be done though, as it was a requirement for graduation. I had already managed to skip it for two years, and it was a freshman-level class.

I sighed and made my way through the halls, still unsure of what I wanted to do.

3

NICKI

I WAS MAKING MY WAY THROUGH THE CROWDED RESTAURANT, balancing a tray stacked high with food when suddenly something akin to a koala latched on to my side.

"Nicki! There's my favorite boy!" Vivian yelled in my ear, squeezing me tightly.

Vivian Dunwoody was my next-door neighbor, and the only thing that had kept me sane since I moved to Florida. Viv was five eleven with straight brown hair that hung to the middle of her back and beautiful dark brown eyes. If I'd had any sexual interest in women, I would have married her a long time ago. Those eyes were smiling when she looked up at me, but then she froze as she realized how stiff I'd gotten in her embrace.

"*Shit*, no... Not again?!" she exclaimed, quickly releasing her hold on me.

I took a deep breath, shaking off the pain her hug had caused my still-healing back.

"It's okay," I whispered.

"*No*, Nicki, it's *not* okay!" she exclaimed, then lowered her voice as we drew looks from the diners. "It's *not* okay for him to hurt you, and it's *not* okay for you to do nothing about it."

I knew I had started to blush, and I really felt like shit. Of *course* she felt that way. If anyone ever laid a hand on Vivian Dunwoody, I was pretty sure they would lose it. She always stood up for herself, and for everyone else, too. Bullies in our high school had learned quickly not to attract Vivian's attention. Her payback was legendary.

"I'm fine, Viv, really," I said, shifting the tray to my other arm uncomfortably. Vivian didn't know about my bargain with my father, and I hoped she never would.

Disbelief was evident on her sweet face. Vivian and I had been best friends ever since I moved to Florida from Ohio.

My first few weeks here had been rough, and it only got worse once we had received my diagnosis. I'd loved Kaine Devereaux with all the passion of first love, but in those early days in Florida, I had felt so guilty for being the reason my parents had to move, I would have done anything they had asked me to. Including leave the one person in my life who really understood me.

My parents had uprooted the family and brought us cross country to try and figure out what was wrong with me. That was a lot of responsibility to place on the shoulders of a sixteen-year-old kid. I felt so incredibly guilty for having caused them both to lose their jobs, their friends and even family to move to this miserably hot and humid corner or the world.

While I missed Kaine like you wouldn't believe, I thought my Mom had suffered more. She was a child of the north, loving the cooler climes, the changing seasons. Even though air conditioning was readily available in Florida, she couldn't get outside like she had in Ohio, and her mood suffered as a result. And my god! The *bugs*! Mom was terrified of insects, so Florida was a nightmare for her.

She put up with all of it, though, for me. I knew it wasn't for my father. They hadn't really loved each other in a long time, but my mother would have done anything in the world for me.

When we got the official diagnosis that I was HIV positive, my father had gone ballistic. He was sure at first that I had gotten it from Kaine or another of my "gay friends," as he called them, but I knew that was impossible because I'd never had sex. Dad had just assumed that because I was gay, I must be a slut and that was the only way it could have happened. Then the doctors had insisted the whole family get tested, and we found out Mom was positive, too.

They reviewed all my medical history from the time I was born and determined that I had probably contracted it from my mother during childbirth. Which meant she had been the one to have it first.

As much as I wished I could, I would never forget hearing the argument where my mom had confessed that she had been involved in an affair years ago, when she and Dad were going through a tough patch in their relationship. That was when Dad began beating her.

When Mom left, I went through so many conflicting emotions. I was angry she was gone, hurt she left me behind, furious that she had given me this disease. With all of that, I loved her. She was my mother, always my confidante, always my friend. A part of me was eternally happy she had escaped.

I had loved my dad, too, in a distant kind of way, but he was a man's man. I was a nerd, more bookworm than athlete, the kid who'd rather read comic books than play catch. I had never lived up to his ideal of what a son should be. Mom was always the one I was closer to, but she hadn't taken me with her when she left.

I remember the day Dad had been served with the divorce papers. I had been in the living room watching television when he got home, since I hadn't been expecting him home from work so early. I heard crashing from the kitchen along with a thud so loud it made the floor shake throughout the whole house. Then I heard gunshots.

"Goddammit! You *fucking* whore! You goddamn *bitch*!" he'd screamed.

"Dad!" I'd exclaimed as I'd ran to the kitchen, only to stop at the doorway in shock. He had tipped over the corner hutch that held my grandma's china on display. It had been my mother's favorite possession, something that linked her back to her own mother, who had died before I was born.

I stood and stared in shock at the broken wood, glass and china. My father stood over it all, his revolver in his hand as he repeatedly kicked the splintered wood and stomped every piece of china he could find. I had never seen him so angry... His face was flushed and red, his eyes wide, nostrils flaring like an animal, spittle foaming at the corners of his mouth like a rabid dog. He stomped over and over, taking his anger out on the china.

"Dad!" I yelled again. He swung the gun toward me, his eyes glazed, almost blind as I said his name again. "Dad?"

"You! This is all *your* fault! Dominic *Rowen* Terhune," he snarled, the gun trained on me. "I should never have let her name you that. What kind of fucking name is 'Rowen'?"

I froze, my very breath quiet in my lungs as blood roared in my ears. While I'd never liked guns, my father had made sure that I was trained in gun safety from the time I was a child. I stared into the black hole of his weapon and mentally cataloged that the safety was off.

"Dad? Wh-what happened?" I stuttered.

"Your *slut* of a mother! That's what happened!" he screamed, stomping on yet another piece of china. "Goddamn bitch dared to serve me at my office! As if I was some random *lowlife*!" he screamed again.

"S-serve you?" I stammered again. "I—Wh-what does that mean?"

His eyes remained locked on mine as I tried to make myself as small a target as possible. It wasn't too hard, I hadn't really hit my growth spurt yet, and I wasn't that tall.

"Papers! Goddamn *divorce* papers," he said, grabbing them from the kitchen table with his left hand and throwing them at me.

I didn't dare move to inspect them, but I saw words like "alimony", "insurance" and "child support".

"You want it! Don't think I don't know!" he hissed, glaring at me. "You want to go prancing back to your boyfriend, live with your mom and think you'll live all happily ever after. Not if I have anything to say about it! She never had any room for *me* in her life since you were born. Now she wants to take you away and expects me to *pay* for the privilege!" He practically spat the words at me before continuing, "That fucking bitch isn't getting a red cent out of me. I will put all of us in the ground, including your fucking boyfriend, before I give her the satisfaction!" His thumb pulled back the hammer on the revolver and aimed it at me.

Unnatural calm descended on me in that moment as I realized what he was threatening. My father had always been possessive, a trait my mom and I had lived with good-naturedly. Staring down the barrel of the gun, I knew beyond a shadow of a doubt that, rather than letting us go, he would kill me, my mom, Kaine, and himself.

I had always been good in a crisis, my brain and responses often lauded by my teachers as being mature beyond my years. In that moment, it was like a switch flipped inside me as I stared him down, and I knew there was only one way to stop him from carrying out his threat. I needed to give him a better option for revenge.

I stopped huddling in on myself and stood up straight. My father didn't respect fear. For this to work, he had to respect me.

"Why make it that easy for her?" I asked. I ignored the mess on the kitchen floor and walked over to the refrigerator, opening the door and pulling a soda out.

"What?" he asked, my calm confusing him.

I popped the top of the soda, and took a sip, hoping that he couldn't see the way my hands were shaking.

"Why make it that easy for her?" I repeated, keeping my voice low and quiet. "It only takes a second to pull a trigger. Why be that painless?"

My father looked at me, uncertainty apparent on his face. Intelligence slowly seemed to return as his rage faded, but I couldn't be certain yet. He tilted the weapon slightly toward the floor as I leaned against the counter, soft drink in hand.

He glowered at me, his breath coming in pants as he stood with the gun in his hand. I knew from experience that a one-handed stance wasn't as easy as the movies made it look. In just a minute or two his muscles would start shaking from the strain. I really didn't want to be in front of the barrel when that happened.

"Make her live with it. Make her live… without me. Without… us."

He stared at me for a moment, indecision warring behind his eyes.

After a moment he lowered his aim, though he kept the gun pointed in my direction.

"Why would you stay? What's to keep you from taking off as soon as my back is turned?" he demanded.

I stared down at the can. I hadn't thought that far ahead. I had been hoping that I *could* get him calmed down, then escape. My sneakers nudged one of the papers on the floor, the edges wrinkled where he'd gripped them. A single word stood out to me.

"Insurance," I said, feeling the dust from the damaged walls stick in my throat. I took another drink to clear it.

"Insurance?" He asked.

"Health insurance," I said louder. "She needs health insurance if she's going to live, and so do I. No place will cover either of us with a pre-existing condition like HIV. You agree to the divorce and let her go. Don't—don't hurt her. Give her what she wants—" I saw his gaze harden as he started to raise the weapon again, so I rushed the rest of my offer out. "—except me. As long as she's alive, I'll stay here."

He looked at me speculatively. I considered this a hopeful sign, so I continued, "I'm almost sixteen. The judge will give me the option of choosing what parent I want to live with," I said, my voice gaining confidence. "I'll stand up in court, and say I want to live with you. Between that, and the fact that she's... she's sick, no judge in the world will give me to her."

I could see the wheels turning in his head as he thought through my bargain.

"You know it would hurt her worse than anything you could do to her, physically," I finished. "...and it would last longer."

A slow, dark smile formed at the corners of his mouth as he took in the idea.

"You'd stay here—" he asked, raising an eyebrow in question. "—no matter what?"

I swallowed hard, as I had an idea of what was going through his head. When he'd hurt my mom, she had fled. If I remained, he probably could—would—hurt me. I thought of my mom, and how much she meant to me.

"As long—as long as she's safe... As long as Kaine's safe..." I locked gazes with him, and nodded, swallowing hard. "No matter what. I'll stay."

He slowly holstered his gun, then turned around and left. I'd almost dropped to my knees in relief. That had been the beginning of my own, personal hell.

He gave my mom the divorce. He gave her health insurance, alimony, everything her attorney wanted, everything she asked for.

Except me.

She still fought for custody, though. The day of the custody hearing had passed in a blur, but the time I'd spent at the courthouse still stabbed at me with painful clarity. I'd been called into the court room by the bailiff.

There was no witness stand like there was on television. It was just a room, with a judge behind a desk, a bailiff, and both attorneys. I remembered looking at my mom once, letting myself have that one second to say goodbye, then forced my gaze away. I knew if I tried to say what I had to say while looking her in the eyes, I'd break. And she would die.

Maybe not that day exactly, but it would happen. I glanced at my father and my breathing quickened. Hell, maybe it *would* be that day. He sat in his seat, his gaze boring into me. My dad had walked into the courthouse *with* his service weapon, and no one said a damn thing. I saw him glare at me, and he nodded at me once, his hand resting for just a moment on his weapon. He could have killed us both, right then and there. I had to make this good.

Mom and her attorney had flown in from out of state. I'd remembered Dad complaining about having to rearrange his work schedule. She'd sat in a wooden chair next to her attorney and the judge had started talking to me.

"Mr. Terhune..." he looked down at his papers, then back up to me. "Dominic. Do you mind if I call you Nicki?"

"No, sir," I said.

"Nicki, do you understand that your mother has filed for divorce from your father?" he asked.

"Yes, sir," I answered.

"Do you know why she has filed for divorce?" he asked.

"No, sir," I said, swallowing hard and forcing myself to hold the judge's gaze.

"Your mother says that your father..." he looked at his papers, then back up to me. "She says your father attacked her and beat her badly enough that she required medical attention. Her doctors show that she was in the hospital for several days afterward. She also says your father struck you."

It didn't seem to be a question, so I didn't say anything.

"Has your father ever struck you, Nicki?" he asked.

I looked him in the eye, and I lied like my life depended on it. I lied like *her* life depended on it.

"No, sir," I said. I heard my mother gasp and whisper my name.

"Nicki, baby..." she said. I couldn't look at her. I knew I would break if I did and get us both killed. I held the gaze of the judge and told the lies my father and his attorney had devised.

I told the judge how angry I was with her, how she had basically murdered me by her infidelity before I was even born, and that I'd rather live with my law-abiding, morally upstanding sheriff of a father than with a woman who cheated on her wedding vows. I was hoping he couldn't sense the sarcasm when I called my father "morally upstanding".

A part of my soul broke inside me as I parroted lie after lie, letting fly darts of venom with each lie I told about her. I'd heard my lies strike home, and she'd finally collapsed and sobbed quietly in the chair next to her attorney, but I continued relentlessly. I had to lie if I was going to save her.

I told the judge all the half-truths and outright falsehoods my father made me say. There were stories my father had made up of neglect, excessive drinking, and men. Lots of men. I couldn't look at her as I spoke, so I forced myself to look behind her to a part of the wall where there was a small water stain. I knew to an observer it would look like I was holding her gaze, but I couldn't. I told the stories as if my own life depended on it, because, in a way, it did. If anything happened to my mother, and I could have prevented it, there would be no reason for me to live.

Not surprisingly, the custody judge ruled in my father's favor. That night was the first time my father beat me bloody. It wouldn't be the last.

The mere thought of the pain I had endured over the years at his hands was enough to cause my mood to sour even further, so I just shook my head at Vivian with an exasperated sigh.

"I'm fine."

"I don't believe you, but I also know better than to fight with you, babe," she said. "I wanted to stop by, because I got my co-op, and I've got something for you." She dug around in her purse for a minute before pulling out a cream-colored envelope with a green registered letter sticker on the front.

"You know Mr. Dellen, the mailman? He's been trying to deliver this to you, but he was never able to catch anyone at home, so I went ahead and signed for it," she said, starting to give it to me before realizing I didn't have any free hands. "I hope that was okay."

I nodded. "Probably something for school. Can you put it in my pocket?"

She stuck the surprisingly heavy envelope in the pocket of my servers' apron.

"Thanks, sweetie. You got your co-op!? That's awesome! I'm so happy for you! I want to hear all about it. I have to get this food out while it's still hot. though. You going to be around long?" I asked, hopefully.

"Yep, I figured I'd hang out for a while, then drive you home after your shift," she said, smiling. "I'll wait for you outside."

I loved that smile, but something was off. Viv hated this restaurant —probably because the owners were friends with my dad. A couple of times when I had tried to hide money from my father, he had inexplicably known almost exactly how much I had earned in tips that night. It took me a while to figure out that the owner was reporting my credit tips, but he didn't know about the cash ones. Viv never stopped by to see me here, though it was quintessential Vivian for her to pretend to be in the area to give me a ride. I was twenty-one years old and had never owned a car. Dad said the insurance and upkeep were too expensive, but we both knew that money wasn't the real reason. It was just one more way to control me.

I agreed to meet her outside after my shift ended. I held the tray precariously over our heads as I kissed her cheek, making her laugh as I did so, then delivered the food to the table of hungry guests.

The evening passed quickly enough. I finished my tables, cashed out, then grabbed my things from the back. As I walked out into the parking lot, I saw Viv sitting on the hood of her Honda Civic, her phone out as she texted away.

"Hey, Baby Cakes," I said, carefully stepping up on the hood and scooting next to her.

"Hey, Doll," she said, tucking the phone into the pocket of her jean jacket and leaning affectionately into me.

I reached into my pocket and pulled out a roll of bills - the tips I'd earned tonight. I pulled off a hundred dollars and stuck the rest of the money back in my pocket. As I did, my hands brushed across the envelope Viv had brought me. I pulled it out to look at it while I put the money on the hood of her car.

"Can you put this away for me?" I asked, not looking up as I slid it toward her. I ripped open the end of the envelope.

She whistled as she counted the money.

"Won't your Dad notice this much missing?" she asked worriedly.

"I had two graduation celebrations tonight that tipped in cash, and worked my ass off on both of them," I answered. "I've got enough left to keep him happy."

The sun had long ago set, but the humidity was still high. It had taken only a few steps outside of the restaurant to begin feeling hot and sticky, and not in a good way.

Vivian looked over at me, her eyes gleaming in the neon lights. She nodded and I blushed under her scrutiny. I knew what she would see. I was about five nine, and skinny as a rail. Regardless of how much I ate, I was never able to put on weight. I was pale, but that wasn't anything new. My skin was a legacy of my mom's side of the family, just like the red hair. I kept my hair shorter, but it was always unruly, something that drove my dad crazy. I almost always had to keep it cut short to keep him happy. I'd have to cut it in the next day or two, or it could set him off into another rage, and I don't think I could handle that right now. My mom's hair had been so long it fell to her waist, and he had always resented that my hair was like hers. I'd spent hours when I was a kid brushing her hair. The reminder of better days made my eyes fill, and I backhanded them quickly, hoping to hide from Viv's sharp eyes.

Fat chance. Her eyes narrowed in concern as she reached out to tuck a stray lock of hair behind my ear.

"You can't keep letting him do this to you, Nicki. It's not right," she said softly. "You—you don't deserve this."

I sighed and looked away. Sometimes Viv had a one-track mind, and it was ridiculously sharp. Hoping to distract her, I unfolded the papers from the envelope and began reading.

"I know, Viv. I know! I just need to…"

My voice trailed off as I scanned the heavy-weighted paper, the print cold and unforgiving in the glow of the parking lot lights.

"No…" I whispered, feeling the blood drain from my face as I read the legal mumbo jumbo written across the page.

"What is it, babe?" She asked, her eyes turning to me in concern.

The papers fell from my grasp and a sob tore through me.

"No!" I cried, sliding off the car hood and falling to the ground as if my legs were boneless, the pain and anguish overwhelmed me.

"Nicki!" She cried in alarm, hopping down and dropping to her knees next to me.

I lashed out at the ground, my fists flying over and over into the hard-packed Florida soil, trying to take some of the pain and despair out on the dirt beneath me.

"Nicki, what is it?" She exclaimed, grabbing at the paperwork from the law firm in Ohio and scanned it. The words were already emblazoned on my memory, the cruel, impersonal words informing me that my mother, the woman I had literally bled for, had died.

4

KAINE

I made it through my Art History class, but only because Sonny kept sending me funny memes and texts. Well, that and the probability of an orgasm in my immediate future...

By the time I'd made my way to the lecture hall, I'd gotten about twelve messages from Sonny about minutiae regarding the bookstore opening, and one pic of a hot guy who delivered some packages to them the day before.

SONNY: Seriously, dude! Look at those abs!

A picture accompanied the text of a guy in a UPS uniform, his thigh muscles bulging as he unloaded some boxes from his truck.

ME: He could crack nuts with those thighs...

SONNY: He could crack MY nuts with those thighs...

ME: Shit. WEAVER could crack your nuts with her thighs.

SONNY: Cold, bro...

I smiled and sat up straight. At least Sonny was doing *something* to help me wake up.

I noticed a student sit down next to me as Professor White began his lecture. He seemed inordinately interested in my phone conversation, constantly peering over at my desk.

He looked familiar, but for the life of me, I couldn't remember his name. Rick? Steve? Something normal like that. He glanced at my phone again, then at me. He raised an eyebrow and grinned. I glanced back at the phone and realized the photo had resized and was now full screen... centered on the UPS driver's crotch, of course. *Kill me now...*

I stabbed at my phone quickly, and I knew my face was blazing. *Gary!* That was the guy's name, Gary Jordan. A guy with two first names. We'd been in a study group the previous year for Western Civ. We'd also hooked up a couple of times, but I'd managed to lose track of him over the last few months.

I stabbed at my phone for a minute until I got the picture back to normal size and my blood pressure back under control. Just as it re-set my phone pinged with an incoming text. From Gary. Because of *course* I had given him my phone number. The incoming text showed a picture of a peach and an eggplant. Okay, subtle he was not.

He looked at me and raised an eyebrow in question. Gary was hot, in a jock-ish linebacker kind of way. He had dirty blond hair that was a little too close to a mullet for my liking, but I did recall enjoying his soft, plump lips. He was a little shorter than me but outweighed me by a good fifty pounds. I thought of what it might feel like to have him pin me down and fuck me into a mattress. We'd never fucked, just hand jobs and blow jobs. But shit... the thought of it had me surreptitiously pressing the palm of my hand against my cock to try and tame my erection.

I hadn't had sex in what seemed like forever, and my dick was perking up and making its preferences known. I tried to count backward to when my last time had been, but when I got past four months, I stopped trying. Some things were better left uncounted.

I got another text right after the first.

AIRGORDON: You got time before your next class?

ME: Depends... I have to teach a class at the dojo at 11. What'd you have in mind? ;) Are you faster than a speeding bullet?

I grinned at him before hitting send.

AIRGORDON: I'm *definitely* more powerful than a locomotive....

He sent me the eggplant emoji and the sweat emoji. Yup, I was in...

I chuckled. At least I wasn't struggling quite so desperately to stay awake for the rest of the lecture, as the thought of a quick make-out session with Gary at least provided me with an incentive to stay awake. What in God's name had made me think an 8 a.m. class was a good idea?

When the teacher ended his lecture, we all made a beeline for the exit. Professor White was a great guy and all, but I was only taking the class because it was required, like about ninety percent of the *other* students in the lecture.

We were *almost* to the exit when I heard Professor White call my name.

"Mr. Devereaux? A moment, please."

Shit. I saw Gary look at me, a knowing smirk on his face.

"Tick, tock, Devereaux..." he teased, tapping his watch as he walked toward the door.

I stifled a groan and jogged back down to the front of the auditorium where Professor White stood hoping my shirt was loose enough to prevent embarrassment. The sooner I got this over with, the sooner I could be getting off...

Professor White's hair matched his name, but his skin was unusually wrinkle free for his age. He had piercing blue eyes that looked perpetually surprised, and his hair was wild and standing on end in places, like it did after almost every lecture. He was known amongst the faculty for getting *very* passionate about even the most boring of art topics, often swinging his arms wildly and running his fingers through his hair. You learned quickly that if you wanted to avoid being splashed by whatever beverage he had in his hand you didn't sit in the front row. I slowly made my way back down to the front of the lecture hall.

"Yes, sir?" I asked as I stood in front of the desk. I had a pretty good idea what this was about.

"Mr. Devereaux, you understand that this is a required freshman level class that you have managed to avoid taking for over two years now?"

"Yes, sir," I said, a blush starting to build up my neck.

"The summer session is the shortest, most intense way to 'get Fart History over with' as the students say," he quoted.

I looked at him in surprise. I had no idea he knew the term students used when referring to the class.

"Oh yes! I know very well what the students call this class behind my back, no worries there! Do you know why this class is included as part of our core curriculum?" he asked.

"No sir," I began, but then stopped. "Well, maybe..."

He nodded at me to continue. I took a deep breath.

"The curriculum is designed to help create a well-rounded individual," I quoted. I saw a small smile appear on his face, and it gave me courage to continue. "At least, that's what all the pamphlets say. Some students come in with academic blinders on and feel like they know exactly what they want to focus on, and don't see the value in broadening their horizons. Taking Art History, and Literature, and all the other core classes makes them consider... alternatives."

"Yes! *Yes*! Exactly! Alternatives..." He muttered a moment and glanced through his papers. "So, you are an engineering major, correct?"

"Yes, sir," I answered.

"What *alternatives* have *you* looked at?" he questioned.

"I—I haven't really, sir. Looked at any, I mean," I stuttered, feeling silly for having quoted the pamphlets, but proving myself a perfect example.

"Hrmph. I thought not. Maybe you should, Mr. Devereaux..." He said. He turned to set his coffee cup on the lectern, looking up at the slides of famous paintings that ran on the screen behind us. He began to say something, then paused before asking, "Wait, *Devereaux*? Are you the Kaine Devereaux that won the Diversity Amateur Photography event last year?"

I blushed and nodded. Not many people knew I had won the photography prize put on by the art department of the university. I'd always been fascinated by photography. When I was placed in foster care after Mrs. Rohring died, it was one of the few things I'd been able to take with me. After Nicki's parents moved them to Florida, I'd taken a class in high school with Bishop as a way to distract myself from Nicki's absence and since then it had become my primary hobby. Not that I really had time for a hobby right now, but I'd occasionally taken photos for friends or family events. In many ways, I found I had turned into a kind of family historian, documenting all the important events that happened in our lives.

The picture Professor White was referencing had been of my parents in the kitchen of our home. Mama D's arms were resting on Mama K's shoulders, a dish towel hanging from her hands as they had leaned in to kiss. I had caught them right in that moment before their lips had touched. It was a great shot, but I felt it had been more luck than skill that I'd captured the moment. Anna and Bran had seen the picture on my camera when I went to take some pictures of them with Gracie and had encouraged me to submit it to the contest. I'd done it, more to get them to shut up about it than anything else. To my surprise, I'd won. It wasn't something I put on my resumé or anything, but it *was* something I was kind of proud of. My parents had a framed copy of the photo hanging in their bedroom.

"I've seen many students come through these halls in my lifetime, many *engineering* students, Mr. Devereaux. They had no soul, for the most part, young man. *No* appreciation for beauty," he turned back to me. "You *do*. I see in you a deep appreciation for art. Oh, maybe not this!" he said, waving at the slides of Picasso on the screen behind him, then looking at me contemplatively. "But… something. I can't see you spending your life as an engineer. It's just not in you."

My spirits fell as he said the words that had been percolating in my brain for several months now. I *wasn't* an engineer. I craved the stability that life as an engineer would provide, but I doubted I'd ever live up to my father's goal for me.

"Professor White, may I ask… Did—did Dr. Tate say something to you about me, sir?" I asked.

"*What*! No! That… woman… and I have not spoken for many years," he said, his mouth turned down in an uncommon frown. His obvious dislike of Dr. Tate surprised me. I had thought she was generally held in high regard amongst her peers. Professor White continued. "Hrmph. I should have phrased that differently, that was not at all professional. Dr. Tate and I have not spoken about your performance, and I doubt we will. Our paths... do not frequently cross."

He gathered the last of his materials and came around the low table to stand in front of me.

"I think you should take some time and consider what alternatives are available to you at this university, Mr. Devereaux. The world is in front of you! Pick the path *you* are passionate about! Not just the one you *think* you should be passionate about!"

I stood there for several moments after, thinking about his words. Maybe he was right? Maybe I should consider alternative majors, instead of focusing on only engineering.

My phone dinged, and I saw a text from Gary.

AIRGORDON: You have thirty seconds to get that ass out here, or I'm taking off.

ME: OMW

I sprinted to the hallway where I saw Gary leaning casually against the far wall. He flashed a knowing grin at me.

"Professor White chew you up and spit you out?" he asked.

"Sort of..." I said, shrugging. Gary was backing away from me down the hall, his finger crooked at me in a "come hither" gesture.

"What are you..." I began, but he shook his head.

"No way, smarty pants. It's only ten thirty, and I've *already* had enough lecturing to last me the whole day. No more words..." He reached out and grabbed my hand, dragging me over to a storage room. Gary's dad was a maintenance guy for the university, and he had master keys to just about every door in the new building. Which meant *Gary* had master keys to almost every door in the building.

He swung the door to the storage closet open and flipped the light on, dragging me inside. He closed and locked the door behind us and then Gary was muscling me up against it, his beefy hands gripping my hips and grinding our cocks together.

"You are perfection, Devereaux," he groaned.

"Not so bad yourself, big guy..." I gasped, my own hands finding their way into his hair, tugging gently. I remembered from previous encounters that Gary liked having his hair pulled.

The heat from his body was ferocious, especially when he leaned in and captured my mouth with his own. His kiss was hot and demanding, but it left me feeling oddly... cold and empty. Almost... numb. My body was into what we were doing, don't get me wrong. My cock was hard, and a groan escaped my lips as he palmed my erection through my jeans. It just felt so... so meaningless. He was a nice enough guy, we just didn't care about the same things.

Gary was big on football, and tailgating, and drinking. But that was about all there was to him. Or at least, all *I'd* seen. You could throw "fucking around" just about anywhere in that lineup, and he would be good with that, too, I guessed.

I had already decided that we didn't have enough in common to make a relationship work but fooling around didn't seem exactly like a *bad* idea, especially in the moment. I just felt kind of... cheap... to be fucking with him in a storage closet. It seemed so damn stereotypical. A part of me wanted to make an excuse and walk away, forget that he'd even sat next to me in class. Aaaaaand... then he was unzipping my jeans, and I knew I wasn't walking *anywhere*. He began sucking sloppy kisses along my neck, roughly pushing my shirt collar aside as his hand dipped beneath by underwear and he began fisting my length.

"You like it a little fast and rough, right Devereaux?" he whispered in my ear, his teeth nipping at my earlobe. I jumped at the bite, his teeth causing *way* more sting than I was interested in.

"Ouch! Fuck!" I said, jerking away from him, one of my hands flying to my ear. Who did he think he was, fucking Mike Tyson? I rubbed my early gently, trying to soothe the sting.

"Dude, not *that* rough..." I said.

I saw a shadow pass across his face.

"Shit, Kaine, I'm sorry, I didn't mean to—" I could see the genuine regret in his eyes, and I felt bad for putting it there. Just because he and I weren't meant to be forever loves didn't mean he wasn't an okay guy after all.

"It's okay, babe," I said, turning my attention back to him and smiling. "Let's just go a little easier…"

I saw his face brighten as I smiled at him, and inwardly shrugged. For some reason, people went ape shit over my smile. Hell, if I even knew why. It got me out of a lot of trouble, and into a lot of pants… speaking of which…

I rubbed my palm along his body, gentle kisses playing across his neck and chest.

"Mmmmm…" I groaned. "I do *so* love your muscles…"

I grabbed hold of his t-shirt and untucked it from his pants, bunching up the fabric towards his neck so I could reach his chest. He had small brown nipples that were standing at attention, and I leaned in and flicked my tongue across the stiffened flesh before nibbling gently at them.

"Fuck, Kaine!" He almost shouted. "That feels so fucking good…"

"If you think that feels good, just wait until you see this…" I teased. I slip my hand inside his track pants and gripped his stiff cock. He already had a wet spot at the tip of his dick, and I used the fluid as natural lube to stroke him up and down.

"Oh, god…" he sighed. "You have magic fingers."

I grinned. That was one I'd never been told before.

I teased him gently, my hand caressing the hard length of his dick. He let his head fall backwards and land against a shelf. There wasn't much room in the storage closet to begin with, and with the two of us in here, it was even more cramped.

I stroked him quickly but firmly, twisting my wrist a bit as I wrapped my hand around his cock head. I felt him shudder under my touch, and I felt a little rush of satisfaction run through my veins. *This.* This I knew how to do. I might not know how to run my life, or how to solve all my problems, but I did know how to make a man go crazy with need.

He shivered again, and before I could think his eyes were practically rolling back in his head and he was shooting thick stripes of cum across the enclosed space.

I managed to twist out of the way so he didn't blow his load all over me, but it was a near thing. We stood there for a minute, Gary gasping and me feeling utterly unsatisfied.

"Fuck, I didn't mean to— I should have given you more warning..." he said, looking at me sheepishly.

"It's okay," I insisted. "Really."

The alarm on my phone chose that moment to beep and we both jumped. *Shit.* I was supposed to be at the dojo to help teach a class in twenty minutes.

"I gotta go," I said, glad for the excuse not to have him reciprocate.

"But you didn't—" he began.

"Next time," I assured him hurriedly, before zipping my pants back up and slipping out of the closet.

I made it to the dojo with barely enough time to change into my *gi* and step onto the mats. A *gi* was the uniform that martial arts participants wore for training and competition. It included a pair of loose pants and a jacket-like top that was secured with a belt. Belt colors were symbolic of levels of advancement in martial arts. White belts were the lowest level, those with no experience or training. Colors varied from there, depending on the type of martial art you were learning, but typically advanced from white to yellow, yellow to orange, orange to green, green to purple, purple to red, red to brown, and brown to black.

I bowed to the flag, bowed to the senior instructor, who also happened to be one of my mothers, Mama K, and called for the students to line up.

Mama K was short and petite, which led many of her opponents to underestimated her. Today she had her long, curly dark hair pulled back into a braid at the base of her neck and it hung almost to her hips. She stood at the front of the dojo running the students through their warm-up drills. I was going to be running this class, as I was working my way up to senior instructor certification.

This was a class in tae kwan do. At D&K Martial Arts, everyone started out as a white belt, no matter what their experience was at any other dojo. Advancement was earned based on effort, skill and discipline. This was an open class that mixed varied experience levels. We had everything from newbies to regionally ranked black belts that attended this class.

The familiar forms of the warm ups flowed through me and calmed my mind. The simple patterns, repeated over and over, brought a sense of peace to my jangled brain. There were no decisions to make here, no earth-shattering consequences. If you did a form wrong this time, next time you worked to do it better.

As we started lining up before beginning the warm-up routine, I saw two tall, fit men I didn't recognize exit the locker rooms. One of them had dark brown hair and the other light brown. The one with dark brown hair seemed especially annoyed about something as he finished closing his *gi* and tied his white belt around his waist, but they both laughed and joked as they went to step on the mats.

"Good morning, students!" I called out, getting everyone's attention. In front of me was a sea of white with a rainbow swath of color.

Part of me cringed inside when both of our new students stepped on the mats without bowing. I glanced at Mama K and knew she had noticed it as well. Moira, our administrative assistant, usually vetted transfer students for us before they started a class, as well as doing orientation, but she had been out sick with a nasty stomach bug that week. We always reviewed the rules with new students, but sometimes people forgot.

"Class, I am Sensei Devereaux, and I'd like to take a moment to remind everyone about proper protocol when entering or leaving the mats of the dojo. We always bow to the senior instructor," I turned and executed a bow to my mother, who stood at the front of the room. "Then we bow toward the flag." I demonstrated the bow again, this time toward the U.S. flag that hung in the dojo. I waited for the students to follow suit.

Bowing was a gesture of respect, not just toward the instructor, but toward the training environment itself. It was the student acknowledging that they were there to learn, and that they understood and respected that this was an environment where there were others who knew more than they did but were willing to share their knowledge.

Once they had all bowed, including the two late additions, we continued the warm-up, and the lesson began in earnest. It became quickly apparent to me that the new additions *didn't* respect the learning environment. They were a pair of "those" students. Students who thought they were better than everyone else and didn't need to start at the bottom of the class. Students who felt they were wasting their time learning the basics. Students who were there to show off to their buddies, not really to learn.

I generally worked with the new students when they started in the dojo, learning their skill levels and determining the appropriate class level for them. We usually had students who were transferring from other dojos spend a week or two in an open class or the beginner class before placing them in the class their skills warranted. It allowed me the opportunity to really assess their skill level, as well as their maturity. The more mature students didn't have a problem with spending time learning the dojo *katas* or demonstrating their level of discipline. The less mature students...Well, these two were prime examples.

After the third time Mama K or I had to correct their stance and redirect them back to the lesson at hand, the one man had apparently had enough.

"I don't take orders from some Mexican bitch," he sneered, looking down his nose at Mama K, who didn't respond. "I've got a black belt at Golden Sun dojo. I don't need to be doing this basic crap."

Mama K looked him up and down and smiled calmly. I barely restrained myself at his insult. I know my mom had been called worse, but that didn't mean I had to stand by and listen to it. Where did people come up with this macho, racist bullshit? Maybe there was a class I missed in junior high... We'd dealt with this kind of attitude before, though, and since I was supposed to be running this class, I stepped up.

"Cooper and Addison, right?" I asked, digging through my brain to dredge up their names from their application paperwork.

"Yep," the one with the dark brown hair answered. He should have responded with "Yes, Sensei," but I hadn't really expected him to. Respect didn't seem to be something these two understood.

Mama K clapped twice and without a spoken order, the rest of the class fell into a circle around the four of us and sat cross-legged on the floor. I saw Cooper's buddy look around a little nervously as they were suddenly ringed by the twenty-some seated students. It could be unnerving to see the class move like that when you weren't expecting it, but we'd been working with most of them for at least a few weeks. They understood when there was going to be a lesson.

"Okay, Cooper. Since you have such a high estimation of your skills, I'm sure you wouldn't mind sparring with Laurie, right?" I gestured for Laurie to stand and step forward.

Laurie grinned and hopped up from her cross-legged seat and came forward. She had been attending the dojo for almost three years now, and she was good. She was around average height with short blonde hair that made her look a good deal younger than her eighteen years. She held a second rank brown belt and would be testing for her black belt in the fall. Her father had come to us after she experienced a vicious mugging at a local mall and had been desperate to try and reestablish her feeling of security. Cooper towered over her, and I had a feeling this guy wouldn't be able to resist showing off.

"She's just a little girl," he barked and laughed. "I want a *real* challenge!"

He hopped around a bit on the balls of his feet, making a big show of doing a couple of roundhouse kicks and throwing a bunch of air punches. I almost laughed as he danced around. His stance wasn't solid, and each time he punched he overextended himself. I was surprised he didn't end up losing his balance and falling face first on the mats. I looked at Laurie, who looked back at me and grinned for just a moment before putting on her game face. She nodded solemnly at me. She had seen the same thing I had.

"I'll tell you what, Cooper," I said. "If you can spar five minutes with Laurie *without* her putting you on your ass, I'll let you teach the rest of the class," I offered. "If she lays you out, you will spend the rest of the class quietly observing, obeying the instructors, and being a model student. Agreed?"

I saw him size Laurie up, his eyes pausing on her brown belt. A slow grin crossed his face and he nodded smugly.

"Sure thing, Teach!" he agreed.

"It's 'Sensei,'" I interrupted him as he moved to where his friend was standing.

"Whatever..." he muttered, ignoring me.

Mama K gestured and the class spread out and moved to the edges of the mats to give the sparring partners room. I watched as Addison spoke in a hushed tone to his friend.

"Coop! Knock it off! I already lost my membership at one dojo, I don't want to forfeit my deposit at another one!" Addison whined.

"Fuck off, Addy! I got this! She's just a chick. I'll deck her real gentle like, then teach 'Sensei' Devereaux who's boss," he growled, nodding at me as he continued to dance around on the mats.

If they had been kicked out of Golden Sun dojo, their attitudes made a lot more sense to me. Donny Martin ran Golden Sun, and he generally didn't put up with a bunch of bullshit. Moira usually checked out any transfers, but with her being sick, I was betting something had slipped through the cracks. I stepped back and nodded at Laurie. She bowed to her opponent, who returned her bow sketchily, then they began sparring.

Cooper immediately let loose a volley of feints, punches and kicks, which Laurie blocked easily. I could tell that Cooper had received some good basic training in martial arts, but he certainly wasn't ready for a red belt, much less a brown or black. He was too eager, spent too much time looking around the room to see who was watching him instead of keeping his eyes on his opponent.

I watched with approval as Laurie kept her gaze leveled on Cooper's body, refusing to be distracted by his flurry of strikes. She kept her guard up, her shoulders level, and paid close attention to his chest, exactly like I'd trained her. The chest is the center of gravity for men, and most men will telegraph their moves with their body, as opposed to their fists. Women's center of gravity tended to be in their pelvis and hips. Since their center of gravity was lower, it made them a lot sturdier and more difficult to take down.

Laurie blocked strike after strike, taking her time and letting him wear himself out on her defenses. I could see him growing more and more frustrated as he bounced around trying to land a hit. His face flushed and I could almost see the steam coming out of his ears as he continued sparring without result.

If I had been the one fighting Laurie, I would have stayed back, kept my guard up, and forced her to come closer so I could use my longer reach to my advantage. Instead, Cooper kept taking increasingly risky swings at her that left him open to counterattacks and overbalancing.

We all saw the moment when Cooper let his frustration get the better of him. Laurie had sidestepped yet another round of punches, making him stumble forward, slightly off balance. She hooked her bare foot around his shin and pushed. Cooper landed on the floor with a loud "Ooof!" I made a mental note to downgrade him to a green belt. He didn't even know how to fall properly.

The students applauded the take down, a hoot of congratulations coming from some of the senior students working out in the corner of the dojo.

Cooper scrambled to his feet, anger suffusing his face as he spun and aimed a kick at Laurie as she turned to smile at me. I barely had enough time to step between the two opponents and grab his foot before it could connect with the side of her head.

I stood there, his foot captured between my arm and my torso, and glared at him angrily.

"What the hell do you think you're doing?" I growled at him, my eyes boring into his. With his height and weight, and even his relatively weak skill level, he could have seriously hurt, or even killed Laurie.

"She's a fucking bitch, man! She cheated!" he whined, hopping awkwardly on one foot as I held tight to his ankle.

"Bullshit," I said calmly. "Robin, what's the rule on head strikes during sparring?"

Robin McKinley was about eleven years old and was the newest addition to our class, prior to Cooper and Addison. He hopped to his feet.

"Um, don't?" he began. Mama K cleared her throat and he blushed before continuing. "I mean, no head strikes during sparring, unless both opponents are wearing the appropriate protective gear, Sensei."

"Right. How long have you been in this class, Robin?" I asked.

"T-two weeks, Sensei," he answered. I nodded at him in approval and he took his seat.

"You'd think that a black belt would know more than an eleven-year-old with two weeks of martial arts training, wouldn't you, Cooper?" I said. Cooper flushed even more. I shoved hard and released my grip on his ankle. He flailed his arms in a vain attempt to stay upright but ended up flat on his ass.

I walked over to him as he lay on the mats, fury apparent in his gaze.

"Pack your things and get the hell out of our dojo," I said. He scrambled to his feet.

"You can't do that!" He yelled angrily. "I paid for a year's worth of these classes!"

"I can, and I have," I said calmly. "When you signed up for this class, you agreed to abide by all of the safety rules. Rule number four reads 'I will not strike any unprepared opponent.' Rule number six reads, 'During sparring I will not deliberately strike, or attempt to strike, any opponent above the shoulders who is not wearing appropriate safety gear. If I do so, I will forfeit any and all deposits, and will be banned from the dojo for life.'"

"B-but— But—" he continued, flabbergasted that I was holding him to the rules. "I want to talk to your Manager!"

Mama K walked up next to me and looked down at where Cooper sat on the floor.

"That would be his Mexican Bitch Manager, Mr. Cooper," she said, smiling down at him sweetly. "And I agree with my son. Get out of my dojo."

"C'mon, Addy," Cooper swore as he headed toward the changing room. "Let's get the fuck out of this dump."

Addison didn't move from his spot on the mats and looked around nervously.

"Mr. Addison? Are you ready to return to the class?" My mother asked, her voice soft but with a core of steel to it.

Addison glanced around nervously and swallowed.

"Addy? Get the fuck over here!" Cooper yelled as he headed to the locker rooms.

Addison looked from me, to my mom, to Cooper, then back to me.

"I... I would like to return to the class, if that's all right... Sensei," he said, his eyes on me as he refused to look at his friend.

Cooper shook his head in disgust, yelled at all of us to do a variety of anatomically impossible things then stalked off to the locker rooms. I listened as he slammed some things around in the locker room, then left.

The class continued uneventfully, and I was glad to see that, when he wasn't being distracted by Cooper, Addison was a decent student. Definitely not a black belt yet but I could see him getting there if he gave it enough time and effort.

When I dismissed the class, Laurie stopped to speak with me as I put away the equipment and the other students headed for the changing rooms.

"Sensei?" she asked, pausing respectfully. "Do you have a minute?"

"Of course, Laurie! You did a great job today!" I told her. She really had. A blush rose on her cheeks, her short blonde hair just brushing her cheekbones.

"I wanted to apologize for screwing up," she said.

I automatically started to tell her she hadn't screwed up, but if that blow had landed, she could have been seriously hurt or even killed. Instead, I asked, "What do you think you should have done differently?"

She paused a moment, and I could almost see her mentally replaying the fight.

"...I shouldn't have taken my eyes off him until the fight had officially ended," she said finally.

I nodded.

"Exactly. With guys like him, I probably wouldn't have taken my eyes off him even *after* the fight ended," I said, grinning. "You did good, though! I was really impressed with your strategy. You didn't let his little dance moves distract you from his real objective."

She blushed even more, her cheeks taking on a rosy glow that even an hour of exercise hadn't given them.

"Speaking of dancing, I— I wanted to ask you something..." she said, her voice ending on a high note, as if she wasn't sure she wanted to ask her question at all. I put the last of the equipment away and turned to speak to her. Whatever she wanted to ask me was hard for her, and I wanted to make her feel heard.

"Sure," I said. "What's up?"

She stood there awkwardly and cast a sidelong glance at the locker rooms. I heard some giggling and saw the door to the women's locker room slam shut. Uh oh.

"I-I— We, that is, some of us were going to go, um, dancing, this weekend, and—" She stuttered and stammered, staring anywhere but at me as she tried to ask me out. Fuck.

"Laurie," I started, shaking my head, "I'm flattered. Really..."

Her face was bright red by that point, and I didn't hear any more giggling coming from the locker room. I felt badly for the kid. I'd had a crush on one of my instructors, too. Of course, that had ended up with a blow job in his office. I wasn't going to do that with Laurie... I'd dealt with students having a crush on me once or twice, but it was never a comfortable conversation.

She was looking anywhere but at me, and started to back away.

"No, it's okay, I get it. I mean, I'm just a kid..." She started to say, her cheeks flushed bright pink as her hands balled into a fist that she struck against her thigh in embarrassment.

"Please stop," I said. She stopped striking her leg, but still refused to look at me. "It's not that you are younger than me. I mean, I'm not ancient or anything. If I were into women, I would totally take you up on your offer in a heartbeat."

"Oh." She said, then my words seemed to register. *"Oh!* You're *gay!"* She yelped, then dropped her voice down to a whisper, looking around frantically, like she'd let the cat out of the bag. "I'm sorry, I didn't mean..."

I smiled again.

"It's okay, I've been out since I was thirteen, and I don't care if anyone knows," I said.

"Really?" She asked, looking at me in confusion.

"Yep. I've got two moms. The idea never really seemed foreign to me," I said. "I fell in love with my best friend when I was sixteen."

I chose to completely ignore my history with Vinnie Avery. Vinnie may have been my first boyfriend, but in more ways than I really wanted to discuss, Nicki had been my first love.

"Awww! That's adorable! Okay, I-I guess I better go change," She turned to head to the locker room, then spun back around. "You know, if you'd ever like to join us at the club some time, the offer is always open! See you next week?"

I nodded and waved as I saw her hightail it out of the dojo, pausing to bow to me, then the flag. Mama K stood in the door of her office and I knew she'd seen the whole exchange. My alarm on my watch went off, and I sighed. I was beginning to hate the damn thing.

I showered and headed home. I was hoping that I'd get a nap in, but as luck would have it, sleep was not something I was getting any time soon. I'd just gotten home and gotten out my camera when Anna and Brannon Eames showed up to pick up Gracie. Bran positively glowed as Gracie tore through the house when she heard their voices in the living room. I got some amazing shots of them greeting each other.

Bran was tall and lanky, all arms and legs. Anna was petite, with short brown hair. Well, "petite" except for the fact that she was eight-and-a-half months pregnant with their first child.

Anna sat on the living room couch, her feet propped up on a padded stool as she watched Bran and Gracie roll around together on the floor. She looked... exhausted. She had dark circles under her eyes, her face was unusually pale. I caught her eye over the top of my camera and we grinned together.

"So, have you made your mind up about documenting the hatching?" She asked, teasing me.

They had asked me to take pictures at the birth of their child, and I hadn't decided yet if that was something I could handle. Lady parts were already things I didn't want to be familiar with, much less those of one of my best friends.

"Hatchings I could handle," I said, teasingly, walking over to give her a hug. "I just don't know if I could manage the radiance this child will bring into the world. Any spawn you bear will have to be an angel."

She laughed.

"Don't tell my parents that. They would probably decide it was a fallen one and send a priest to exorcise it!" She exclaimed.

I smiled at her joke, but the undertone of bitterness caught my attention.

"Ouch. That bad of a visit, huh?" I asked in concern.

Bran looked up at me from the floor where Gracie lay with her head in his lap.

"I think they would have been okay if it had just been Anna. With me there, they couldn't pretend it was a virgin birth," he snarked.

I snickered. Anna's parent *really* didn't like Bran, but that was okay, they didn't have to. Anna's Dad wasn't that bad, but her mother would try the patience of a saint. Anna adored Bran and didn't give two fucks what her fundamentalist mother thought.

Anna sighed and said, "Mom was pretty much at her worst. She actually had the gall to tell me that if I ever wanted a divorce, they'd pay for my lawyer!"

"Shit. That's harsh," I said, sitting in a chair opposite the couch.

Bran got to his feet and moved to the couch next to Anna, his hand placed protectively on her belly.

"I asked if you can divorce your parents and that shut her up," Anna laughed. "It was an interesting and uniquely torturous visit, but at least it's over now," Anna said sighing.

"Baby, if you put your feet up in my lap I'll rub them for you," Bran offered. Anna smiled at him, the love between the two making my heart melt. This was what I wanted. Someone to love me. Someone to be beside me for the rest of my life. Someone who would never leave me.

"That is why you win the award for best husband in the world," she said. "But we really can't stay. I want to get home and take a bubble bath before I fall over."

I gathered up Gracie's things and we got her settled in her kennel in the back of their SUV. I hugged them both, waved goodbye, then headed back inside. Before I'd taken five steps, my watch dinged a-fucking-gain. I was supposed to be meeting my differential equations tutor at the university library in ten minutes. Shit. I'd forgotten our appointment when I'd headed back to the house to meet the Eameses. There was no way I was going to be there in time. I texted the tutor, a guy named Mark Verbena, and scrambled to gather my things and get on the road.

Traffic to the university wasn't bad, so I was only about five minutes late by the time I arrived. Just as I parked my car outside the library, my phone rang. I recognized Bishop's number, so I went ahead and answered it, even though I knew I needed to find Mark.

"Hey Bishop!" I said as I answered the phone. "What's up?"

"Hey, K! Whatcha' up to?" He asked.

Bishop was my best friend, and we did almost everything together. When we had time, that is.

"I'm trying to find my differential equations tutor so I don't fail this class," I said, looking around the quad. Mark had told me he would meet me outside the library, but I didn't see him anywhere.

"Cool. Hey, sorry about this morning. I was running on empty," he said. His voice sounding a little odd. Bishop and I had been close before Nicki and I had started dating, but his art studies had made him unavailable during our sophomore year. When Nicki had left, Bishop had become my best friend and confidant. He had convinced me to switch to a photography class the year I had to deal with Nicki moving away, and it was the only thing that had gotten me through it. Hell, he had even encouraged me to pursue my interest in photog-raphy as a career, but I needed something that was more stable. I knew an engineering degree would mean I was pretty much set for life. I'd be able to get a good paying job almost anywhere in the U.S. with it, and financial stability was one of my top priorities. With my history, go figure.

My brother was an amazing artist in his own right. He drew pictures that were so realistic that they had been mistaken for photographs. I had taken a year off school, and then only started going to school part-time, so even though he was younger than I was, he was going to be graduating that year with an accounting degree. Since Bishop was pursuing accounting instead of his own art, he didn't really have any room to criticize my life choices.

"No worries, bro," I said. "I was just worried about you. You seemed a little out of it."

I heard some noise in the background that sounded like papers crinkling, as well as the sound of a bell jingling. I recognized that sound.

"Are you at the bookstore?" I asked.

"Yeah, I came down last night to help the twins unload a shipment they got in for the grand opening," he said. I kept looking around the quad for Mark, but he was nowhere to be seen. "Do you think you are going to be able to make it down this weekend? I'm interested to see if Cameron is as cool as the boys say he is."

"Twelve texts. Twelve texts during Art History this morning, between the hours of eight and nine thirty in the morning. Bish, I swear to God, I'm going to kill Sonny if he doesn't lay off about the store! I mean, I know they have the Grand Opening coming, but for God's sakes! It's all he can talk about," I said, laughing into my phone.

Cameron was like a modern-day Hemingway. He was a notorious recluse. He never did meet and greets or book signings and was rarely even seen in public. The fact the twins had convinced him to come to Ohio was nothing short of a miracle.

"They're just excited, bro. This is what they've always wanted. I think it's kind of nice to have the opportunity to watch someone's dream come true right in front of you," he said.

"I know. And I'm not *really* giving him shit over it. I just have fun teasing him. I think he has a crush on Cameron," I said.

"Well who wouldn't? Did you see his picture? Mm *mm!*" Bishop groaned.

I continued toward the library as we spoke, a strange itching sensation building at the base of my neck. I felt like someone was watching me, but I didn't see anyone paying me any overt attention. A couple of students were walking to or from the buildings around us. I saw a girl with long brown hair getting into a car in the parking lot. Then I saw him: Mark waved at me from a bench outside the door to the library. Shit. He looked pissed.

"Hey Bishop, I see Mark, I gotta run," I said. We said our goodbyes and I headed toward my tutor like the condemned heading for the guillotine.

My tutoring session with Mark did *not* go well. I decided I had some kind of block when it came to the material, and just could not seem to comprehend it. I would be following along with his explanation, then boom! It was like he was speaking a different language. When our time was up I eagerly made my escape and headed home again. I didn't usually make this many trips back and forth to school in one day, but I'd had to run home so Bran and Anna could pick up Gracie.

I sat at my desk in my bedroom and struggled with my calendar. I was scheduled to work the next three evenings in a row at The Belt. Tomorrow was the first day of the bookstore grand opening. I had three two-hour classes at the dojo on Friday, Saturday and Sunday as well. Our weekend classes were extremely popular with our students. My next scheduled night off was Sunday evening because that was D&D night in the Devereaux household. Attendance was mandatory if you were in town, and none of us wanted to risk the wrath of the moms.

I sighed as I glared at my calendar. I didn't see any time on there that I could get any additional sessions in with a tutor this weekend. I blocked myself a mandatory six hours of sleep each night, because I knew without it I would be a complete wreck. Less sleep, and I was likely to do something really stupid... like fall asleep at the wheel when driving, or get the whole party killed during D&D.

I usually headed to the club at around 8 p.m. and didn't get home until three or four in the morning, since we had to clean up after we cleared the last of the patrons out. I typically worked forty hours at the club, plus another twenty at the dojo. I was taking three classes during summer session: Differential Equations, Art History, and a Pop Culture elective. The classes met three times a week for ninety minutes each. Fortunately, I only had the one paper due for Dr. Tate now. I still needed to study for my Art History final, but I'd already turned in my pop culture project so that was finished.

I sighed. I had to start cutting back, but I wasn't sure how or where. I would have a few weeks off once summer session was over. I was thinking of taking Dr. Tate's advice and taking some time off and just having a stay-cation until school started. I'd been hoping that Sammie would be able to hire a new bartender for the club, but so far there had been no movement on that front.

I needed a minute to figure it out. Fatigue weighed on my eyelids, and I struggled to keep them open. Maybe I'd just take a brief, brief nap...

5

NICKI

"...Nicki? Nicki, honey, drink this," I heard a voice speaking to me, as if from far away, but I was having a hard time focusing on it. I blinked and shook my head in confusion, the room slowly coming back into sharp focus.

My brain felt foggy, as if someone had wrapped it in cotton, causing all sensation to feel distant and strange. Dad had given me a concussion once when I was sixteen, and I'd woken up in the hospital after collapsing at school. I'd felt like this back then and was really hoping I didn't have another concussion. I'd hated the nurses waking me up every hour all night long just to make sure I was okay. I didn't want to go through that again.

My eyes began to focus on the cup of coffee in front of me, and I realized suddenly we weren't at the restaurant anymore. We were seated in the kitchen at the Dunwoody's house.

I glanced around frantically, feeling Vivian's arm wrapping around me as I heard murmured words of comfort whispered against my head. Seated in front of me was Vivian's mom, Arabelle Dunwoody, and holding her hand was Vivian's dad, Dr. Isaiah Dunwoody.

"Um... I began, starting to stand. "...I— I have to go..."

"Nicki, you've had quite a shock tonight, I don't think you should go anywhere," Mrs. Dunwoody said, reaching out to take my hand in hers. "We are so very sorry for your loss, sweetheart," she said.

"Loss? What—" Memory came crashing back in tearing a sound from my throat that was part gasp, part sob.

"Oh, god, I— I have to—" I froze with the realization that I had no idea what I had to do. What did you do when your mother died? When the woman you had suffered and bled to keep safe, didn't need you anymore?

"Dominick," I heard Dr. Dunwoody say, and I looked into his pale blue eyes.

"Son, the only thing you have to do right now is drink that coffee. The caffeine will help," he assured me.

I obediently took a sip from the steaming mug, and felt the hot, sweet blend slide down my throat. It was just the way I liked it, which made sense. I'd been coming to the Dunwoody's kitchen for years now. They knew me better than my own father did. He was right, the hot liquid did seem to help clear some of the fog from my brain.

"I— I just... I feel like there's something I should be doing," I whispered. "Someone I should be telling."

"Who? That asshole you call a father?" Vivian asked sharply. "He never deserved your mom in the first place, much less you."

"Vivian Diane Dunwoody!" her mother rebuked her sharply.

"No, he's—" I started to defend my father automatically. It had been my job these last few years to be the perfect son, present the perfect picture.

Literally, at times when he ran for re-election. Anything that threatened that perfect picture threatened the safety of my mother. But that didn't matter anymore. She was safe from my father now. He could never touch her again.

I dropped my head into my hands, tears spilling from my eyes. It wasn't the harsh, tearing pain I'd experienced earlier. It was more like a great, aching emptiness that threatened to consume all that remained of me.

Mrs. Dunwoody squeezed my hand again.

"Nicki, I know this is hard, and seems like the worst possible timing, but there is something we think you *should* be doing," she began.

"Arabelle..." Dr. Dunwoody began.

"She's right, Dad," Vivian interrupted. "He's not going to get a better chance."

I looked between the three of them, confused. I saw Dr. Dunwoody look at me pensively, then he slowly nodded.

Vivian continued, "Nicki, we think... we think it's time for you to leave, baby."

I looked at her, hearing the words she was saying, but lacking the ability to comprehend them.

"...Leave?" I asked, confused.

"Yes, dear," Mrs. Dunwoody answered. "We think it's time for you to leave your father."

My breath hitched in my throat.

"I- Why would I... I mean, I..." I looked around the room wildly, years of ingrained responses forcing me to rush the denials. "I-I can't!"

Vivian sighed. We'd had this argument more times than I could count.

"I don't have enough money, and I don't have any meds, or doctors to treat me if I get sick. Without any insurance, I'll... I'll... I mean, like my mom..." I couldn't say it. I didn't remember the paperwork from my mom's attorney spelling it out, but I assumed it was my mother's illness that had killed her. The same illness that would kill me if I didn't have the very specialized, and very expensive, antiretrovirals that kept full-blown AIDS at bay.

"How much is enough, Nicki?" Viv asked. "You've got a couple of thousand dollars set aside now. It's time to go!"

My eyes went wide when she told me how much money I had saved, because I'd asked her never to tell me. The hope it would cause me could hurt as bad as my father's fists. I'd had no idea I had managed to hide that much cash from him. Then the thought of the monthly cost of my co-pays hit me like a punch in the gut. Not to mention the cost of medication *without* insurance. My hopes crashed, as I'd always feared they would.

"It's not enough, Viv," I said, setting the coffee down. I flattened the napkin on the table ineffectively, its wrinkles returning despite my fingers brushing it over and over. "My meds alone... I mean, assuming I could get away without him knowing, I'd have to find a place to live, plus transportation. Not even counting the cost of a couple of months' worth of my meds without insurance... I appreciate what you're saying, it's just... not enough. And no, I won't take your money!"

"So, to avoid *maybe* getting sick and *possibly* dying, you're taking the chance that one of these days he *beats* you to death?" she answered, her voice dripping with disdain. Shit, she didn't pull punches.

I saw her mom and dad wince as Vivian named the thing we'd held unspoken between us for so long.

"He will go ape-shit on you when he finds out your mom is gone, Nicki!" she exclaimed as she took a seat next to me. "You can't stay!"

"What am I supposed to do, Viv? He's the goddamn *sheriff* of this town. He has deputies and the law behind him. I don't have *anyone*, now. I don't have *anywhere* to go. If I don't have my meds or insurance, I'll never get away from him for good."

"You've got me, Nicki, always," she said, nodding toward her parents. "You've got *us*. You may not be my brother by blood, but you are the brother I would have chosen, Dominick Rowen Terhune."

I winced when she said my full name and sighed. My dad had given me my first name, but my mom had given me my middle name. She'd never explained where the unusual choice came from, but it just highlighted to me that Viv just didn't understand. She came from a loving, two-parent household that was very liberal and accepting. Her Dad was the town physician and her Mom was a teacher at the middle school.

Viv was in school now too, attending the University of Florida in Gainesville. She wanted to be a meteorologist. I remembered her comment earlier about the co-op assignment.

"Hey! You got your co-op assignment, right? Where is it?" I asked.

"Great diversion tactic, jerkwad, but I'll let you get away with it, because it's relevant. Yes, I got my assignment," she said. "But before we talk about it anymore, I need to know, do you have your driver's license and social security card with you?"

"Um, strange question, but yes, I keep them in my wallet. Why?" I asked.

"Well, it was the only part of our plan I wasn't sure of. Yes, I got my assignment. I'm going to be working at Channel 8 News… in Akron, Ohio," she said.

"What?!" I exclaimed.

Akron was where I'd spent the first sixteen years of my life and was the place I always thought of as home. Akron was where Kaine lived.

"You're going to Akron?" I sputtered.

"Yep," she said solemnly. "I applied to the meteorology research program. Case Western Reserve has a great program, and they partner with the local television station. My department advisor knew someone who works there, and she got me in."

"So, it wasn't a random assignment? You wanted to go there? Why?" I asked, confusion apparent in my voice. "And what does my driver's license and social security card have to do with it?"

"Well, you're going to need them if you're going to come with me," she said, laying her hand on top of mine.

I looked around at the three of them in confusion as Dr. and Mrs. Dunwoody nodded at me. Go *with* her? What did she mean? It didn't make any sense.

"To *Akron*? I *can't*! My dad—"

Vivian interrupted me.

"I know what you're thinking. You're thinking he won't *let* you go, but you *are* an *adult* now, Nicki! You're almost twenty-two. He can't keep you from going. Especially if he doesn't know," she said, glancing at her parents nervously.

"…But he'll *know*, Viv! He *always* knows! He has everyone in this town in his pocket," I said.

I'd tried once, years ago, right after the custody hearing to reach out to my grandparents on my mom's side. Dad had arrived before the echo of the "this number has been disconnected" had even faded. I'd made the mistake of asking the librarian for change for the pay phone. Dad had eyes everywhere.

"Not everyone," she said, smiling at me. "I have a surprise for you."

Vivian stood and took my hand, dragging me out of the kitchen toward a small room the Dunwoody's used for storage. I knew this because I'd helped Mrs. Dunwoody clean out a bunch of old Christmas decorations this last January and helped organize the room.

Viv stood outside the door for a minute, a Cheshire cat-sized grin on her face. She threw open the door to the room and took a step back.

Inside the room, on the shelves I'd painstakingly put together for her mom to supposedly turn into a new pantry, I saw stacks and stacks of cardboard boxes.

"Viv, what—" I began.

"Shut up, and open them," she ordered.

I stepped forward and looked at the first cardboard box. It had the return address of a well-known pharmaceutical company. I looked at her in confusion.

"Open. Them." She ordered again. Bossy Viv was out and active. I obeyed.

Inside the cardboard boxes were other white boxes. Hundreds of them.

"Viv, what is this?" I asked, looking from her to the boxes in confusion.

"Look closer, doofus," she said gesturing at the box.

I leaned in and pulled one of the smaller boxes out. All of them were antiretroviral medications or related medication I took to control my HIV. *Thousands* of dollars' worth of medication.

"What did you do?" I looked at her in confusion. "Did you rob a pharmacy? I can't take this—" I began, starting to push the box toward her.

"Yes, you can," she said, interrupting my attempts to hand the box back. "I knew you were going to say you couldn't go without your medications, you've been saying it for years. And I knew you wouldn't let me—us—spend money on you," she gestured to her parents, who had joined us in the hallway.

"You've always been way too freaking stubborn for your own good, Nick. And, no, we didn't rob a pharmacy. Dad and I started contacting the manufacturers back in January and began working with their compassionate assistance programs. The response..." she blushed now, glancing around. "The response was overwhelming. I wasn't sure what medication you might be on, and Dad didn't want to ask anyone to look at your medical records, because he was afraid it would get back to your father. So we had to guess. You have, at minimum, six months of medication to get you through until you get a job that provides insurance. If you need more after that, we can contact the programs again."

I glanced at her parents, fear and uncertainty warring within me.

"She never told me, son," Dr. Dunwoody answered, laying his hand on my shoulder. "I'm not stupid, though. I've known ever since you broke your ankle your junior year."

I shuddered involuntarily as I remembered that day.

I had been cooking dinner one night when my father got home. I hadn't been feeling well the last few days, and was making what we called "brinner", breakfast for dinner. It was something my mom used to make when I was sick, and I hadn't stopped to think how my father would react to it. I was an idiot.

Dad had just gotten home from work and walked into the kitchen. He'd taken one look at the eggs and sausage simmering on the stove, and his face had taken on a blank expression I'd come to know too well. He hadn't said anything to me, and I hadn't even seen the blow that knocked me to the ground. Then he'd taken out his riot baton. The clicking sound of it expanding was one of those sounds that would forever haunt me. He'd taken a single swing at me while I was on the ground, still in shock from his vicious punch. I had reflexively jerked my legs up to protect my face and the baton had connected with my ankle.

The shockwave of pain that flashed through me made me scream and almost vomit, but also stunned me. He had dragged me out of the house to the shed, where the blows had rained down for what seemed like hours. I'd crawled back to the house late that night when I had finally felt strong enough and collapsed into bed.

The next morning I could barely walk and I couldn't put any weight on my ankle. When I looked at myself in the mirror, I barely recognized myself. Bruises purpled my face and upper body. When I looked at my back, there hadn't been any broken skin, but the dark red and black mottling was pretty obvious. *Shit.*

I knew I had to hide the damage from people at the school, so despite the ninety-degree weather, I pulled a long sleeve shirt from the back of my closet and buttoned it up all the way. I had a lot of experience with covering bruises at that point, so I had broken out this cover up makeup I'd ordered on the internet. It was designed to cover tattoos, but it worked just as well on bruises. I haltingly moved through the rest of my morning routine, barely getting dressed and to the first floor in time to make my bus.

He had been sitting at his normal spot at the kitchen table, dry toast and orange juice in front of him. His badge shone in the morning sunlight, the reflected light dancing over the kitchen as he ate and read his paper.

He looked up at me, his eyes narrowing as he watched me limp around the kitchen as I packed my lunch. I was desperate to get out of there before something set him off, but I didn't have any money. If I didn't pack my lunch, I knew I'd go hungry all day.

"You are a worthless piece of shit," he said, his voice deep and rumbling, a hint of a southern accent in it that he'd picked up since we moved to Florida. "If you weren't such a miserable excuse for a son, you wouldn't make me angry like that."

I froze as he spoke. After a few months of his attacks, I knew better than to answer or try to defend myself. After a moment of silence, I threw the last of my lunch items in a paper bag and stuffed it in my backpack. I'd rather starve than stay another minute in that room.

I made my way to the door that led out the back of the house, but stopped as he growled, "How did you hurt yourself?"

"What?" I asked in surprise, looking at him. What the fuck? He knew I didn't hurt myself.

He stood slowly, adjusting his belt over the paunch that had been growing larger and larger since Mom left, causing his gun and other items to shift at his waist. I swallowed as I saw his riot baton sway against his thigh in its holder. A wave of nausea shot through me as he walked calmly over next to me and set his dishes in the sink. I desperately wanted to shrink away from him, but that was a surefire way to draw his ire.

"Are you deaf now, too?" he demanded, his voice low and dangerous.

"No, sir," I said, voice low and eyes downcast. "I... I just don't... understand the—the question," I stammered.

"How did *you* hurt *your*self?" he repeated, his voice strangely calm as he emphasized the words.

Realization dawned on me, and I felt the blood rush to my face. Of course, I had to have a story for the bruises I *hadn't* been able to cover.

"Oh. Um, I was, uh... putting some boxes in the... the attic and the ladder—" I stopped quickly as I saw his hand tighten slightly around his belt. I was going to say the ladder broke, but that might indicate some kind of negligence on his part. Can't have that... "—I mean, I slipped on the ladder, and, um, fell."

He nodded and stepped away.

"You need to be more careful, boy," he said

I bit my tongue and escaped out the door just barely making it to the bus stop in time. I managed to make it to school that day, and the next. On the third day when I got my fourth tardy of the day for being late to a class, I got sent to the Principal's office.

Mr. Lartner was a decent enough guy, but he had five hundred students and not enough staff. I was a kid with good grades from a "good" family. My being late because of an injured ankle was low on his priority list.

I'd given him my story about falling down the ladder and he'd sent me to the school nurse. She'd been certain enough that I had a broken ankle that she'd taken me to the hospital herself, which was where I met Dr. Dunwoody.

Vivian and I had been acquaintances for a while. When Dr. Dunwoody heard my father wouldn't be able to pick me up, he had called his daughter. When her dad realized we knew each other, he had called her from the hospital. She had picked me up from the emergency room and agreed to hide my crutches for me so my dad wouldn't see them. Of course, I hadn't counted on the fact that the hospital would have billed his insurance. But by the time the charges came through, I had healed enough that a few new bruises hadn't mattered.

"I tried to convince Dad this was a project for school, but he didn't buy it," Vivian said, her voice bringing me back to the present.

"You never were good at lying," Dr. Dunwoody said, smiling affectionately at his daughter. "We used to tell her when she was lying the devil jumped up and down in her eyes. It was pretty easy to tell when she was fibbing, because she wouldn't look at us."

She smiled up at her father, and I was so jealous in that moment, and I hated myself for it. Why couldn't my father have been like Dr. Dunwoody? Why couldn't he love me, unconditionally, instead of hating me for something that wasn't even my fault?

I squashed the green-eyed monster back in its closet.

"I—I don't even know what to say," I murmured, looking at these wonderful people.

"You don't need to say anything," Mrs. Dunwoody interjected. "You just need to take this opportunity to make a life for yourself, somewhere safe from that man."

Before I could comment, or allow more tears to overwhelm me, Dr. Dunwoody spoke. "There are antibiotics and pain medication in there, too," he said, nodding at the box. "You are always welcome to call me, though. I know you are a responsible young man, but you make sure you follow the directions on the packaging, you hear me?"

I just nodded as I clutched the box in my hands, unable to comprehend how I had ended up with friends like Vivian and her parents.

Vivian reached out and wrapped her arm around my shoulders as my vision blurred with happy tears.

"Vivian, this is so much. Too much. My god," I set the box down and shook my head, scrubbing at my face as the tears overflowed. "You are the most amazing fucking woman in the world," I said, wrapping both my arms around her and pulling her close.

"Nah, I just love you way too much to let that bastard put his hands on you ever again," she said.

I chuckled slightly and sniffed.

"So, now what?" I asked.

"Now? We head to the airport," she said.

"What? Now?" I exclaimed. This was all happening so fast, I was having a hard time processing it.

"Yep, we have two tickets to Akron, Ohio. I already have an apartment on the Akron U campus, and it has two bedrooms," she said, smiling at me.

"I—what? Now? But my stuff, my clothes…" I began, but Vivian shushed me.

"The only important thing in that house was you," she insisted.

Mrs. Dunwoody handed me a leather backpack that looked well-used.

"This was Isaiah's when he was young," she began.

"I'm *still* young!" Dr. Dunwoody piped up querulously.

"Well, young*er*," Mrs. Dunwoody continued. "There's clothes and some toiletries in there. It's just jeans, sweatpants and t-shirts, but it should be enough to get you through for a couple of days until you two can find a Walmart," she finished.

"I snuck a peek at your sizes," Vivian announced, and grinned. "Or did you think I was rummaging around your gym bag because of my secret smelly sock fetish?"

"Oh my god, I don't know what to say," I sniffed as I hugged her closely. Mrs. Dunwoody took her turn at hugging me, her motherly embrace enfolded me, and for a moment I could almost pretend it was my own Mom. She held me for a moment before whispering in my ear. "Your mother would be proud of you, Nicki."

That set off a whole other round of tears, this time ended by Dr. Dunwoody tapping his watch.

"Arabelle! Let the boy go! Or we'll be late getting to the airport!" He insisted.

We packed Vivian's few remaining items and my backpack into the car, then walked out of the house. Mrs. Dunwoody stood at the door and waved to us as Dr. Dunwoody got in the driver's side.

"So, what do you say, Champ? Ready for your new life to start?" Vivian asked, smiling at me.

I stood there, looking into my best friend's eyes, tears rolling down my face. I knew I could stay here, hope for things to change, hope my Dad would stop hating me. Or I could act. I could escape.

I said the only thing I could, the only thing my mom would want me to say. "Let's go."

The flight to Akron was surreal. I sat next to Viv as we flew through the night, and I could barely believe how quickly my life had changed. I'd gone from terrified prisoner to... what? Hopeful adventurer? I didn't even know the answer to that question.

We'd had a brief layover in Charlotte, then we were on our way to Akron. Vivian shifted in the seat next to me, her head on my shoulder and I wondered again what I had done to deserve her friendship.

Viv had befriended me the first week of school in Florida. I'd been lost and confused, the school building so much bigger than the one I had attended in Akron. Some jocks had cornered me near the cafeteria as I'd tried to find my way around the new school, and they'd been offended that my dad was the new Sheriff.

Thanks to the Devereaux moms, I was no slouch when it came to defending myself, but there *were* six of them. I'd put three on the ground, and a fourth was limping when two of them managed to pin my arms. I was bleeding like a stuck pig from a cut over my eyes when Vivian had broken a cafeteria tray over the head of one of the guys holding me. We'd run, but there were cameras that caught the whole thing, and we'd *all* been suspended for a week because of the school's anti-violence program.

When my father had picked me up, he made a point of telling Mr.

Lartner to have the boys get HIV tested—since they literally had my blood on their hands—in an office full of other kids. Which meant my HIV status was all over the school by the time my suspension was over.

That night had been a pretty memorable beating. Dad must have figured that he could blame any new injuries on the bullies at school, and he'd really let me have it. Afterward he'd dragged my sorry ass to a tattoo parlor and held me down while the artist had tattooed a biohazard sign and plus sign on my wrists.

"No more hiding, you pervert," Dad had said as I'd sobbed. The shame of having essentially a scarlet letter branded on my skin was as painful as the beating. "I won't let you put decent people at risk by hiding. This way anyone who sees you will know what an abomination you are."

I'd begged and pleaded with him not to do it, reminding him that I hadn't chosen this, that being gay had nothing to do with me being positive, but he was deaf to my cries. The tattoo artist had looked scared to death of my father, but to his credit he'd tried to protest when it became clear I didn't want to get the tattoos. My father had threatened him, though, and he'd acquiesced.

"I'm sorry, kid," he whispered to me as his tattoo gun bit into my wrists. The sharp pain made my eyes smart, and I had to bite my lip to keep from crying out. The artist tried to put some anesthetic spray on me to make it easier, but my dad stopped him.

"I want it to hurt," he'd said, his eyes like black holes in his head. "He deserves it for all the shit they've put me through." That was the moment... The moment I realized it didn't matter what I did or said. It didn't matter how hard I tried, it would never be enough. I would never be the son he wanted. It was in that moment that I realized my father, the man I'd idolized, the man who'd adored my mother with uncommon passion, was gone. It was like the HIV diagnosis had killed all three of us.

It was after three in the morning when we arrived at Akron-Canton airport, and the place was deserted. All the restaurants had their gates closed, and the only personnel still working were the rental car representative and the TSA guard at the checkpoint.

I didn't have any luggage, just the backpack that Viv's parents gave me. Dr. Dunwoody had given me the meds to get me through until they could ship the rest to our new apartment. Vivian had more than enough luggage for the both of us. By the time we got the rental car loaded up, we were both exhausted.

We used her phone to find our way to the apartment. I'd left the prepaid phone my father had provided in the parking lot of a grocery store back in Florida. I was pretty sure my Dad had tracking software installed on it, and I wasn't going to take the chance he'd be able to follow us somehow.

I'd learned a long time ago to memorize any numbers that were important to me, because he had a habit of going through my phone and looking for evidence that I was talking to anyone he didn't approve of. Or maybe he thought I was secretly in contact with my mother? I never really understood my father's logic.

So, we found ourselves, in the wee hours of the morning, outside the door of a nondescript apartment building in downtown Akron, Ohio. Viv fumbled in her purse before pulling a key out of an envelope and quickly unlocking the door.

We entered the apartment on the third floor, and I couldn't help my smile. I set the last of Viv's luggage on the floor and looked around.

I flipped the switch by the doorway, turning on the overhead light. The entryway opened up into a living room area. There was a basic sofa and entertainment stand set up in the living room. The kitchen was just off the living room and a small light had been left on over the sink. I could see a small dinette table with two chairs in a nearby breakfast nook. There were large cardboard boxes addressed to Vivian stacked in the living room, along with a variety of Amazon boxes. Vivian *loved* Amazon.

There were two bedrooms with one bathroom off a long hallway. In each room there was a full-sized bed with brand new mattresses, a desk and dresser. It was small, and cramped, and more than a few years old. Overall, it was heaven.

I walked out of one of the bedrooms only to see Vivian lying on her back on the bed in the other room.

I flopped down next to her and took her hand.

"'Thank you' doesn't seem nearly enough," I whispered.

"I'm just glad you're going to be safe now," she whispered back, reaching up to tuck a stray curl behind my ear. The move reminded me oddly of my mom, and for the first time in hours, the hurt seemed to lessen.

We fell asleep like that and didn't wake up for many, many hours.

6

KAINE

Ugh. My "brief nap" the night before had ended up making me an hour and a half late for my shift at The Belt. Luckily, my boss loved me.

I'd made it through that night only to wake the next morning with the household in a tizzy. I wandered down to the kitchen and listened to Bishop growling on the phone to someone.

"...well, where the fuck *is* he?" he demanded.

I rubbed sleep from my eyes and blindly reached for the coffee pot. Mama K and Mama D were seated at the kitchen table, their eyes intent on Bishop. I fixed myself a cup of coffee and sat down.

"Fine. Let us know when you hear something, Lee," he said, then disconnected the call.

"What's going on?" I asked sleepily, looking at the concerned faces.

"Cameron didn't show up," Bishop snarled as he slammed his phone on the counter. "Again."

"Shit..." I answered. It took a lot to make Bishop angry. He was generally the most level-headed of the Devereaux boys. Our parents had taught us, though, you screwed with one Devereaux, you screwed with us all.

"*Bishop McElroy Devereaux,*" Mama D's voice snapped and Bishop looked up guiltily at his display of temper. "Save it for the dojo," she said.

Bishop nodded, a pink blush tinging his tanned cheeks. Our parents had very different ways of dealing with anger, but neither one of them allowed their children to use violence to manage their emotions. Mama D always worked things through logically and calmly, putting any pent-up feelings into whatever project she was working on at the time. Mama K was the one who let her sharp tongue fly. She could cut you to the bone one minute, and make you feel like a million bucks the next. But neither of them allowed us to express our anger with violence. Seemed strange, considering they ran a martial arts studio, but it worked for us.

Cameron had been scheduled to come out to Ohio at least two or three times before this. Once he'd had a scheduling conflict come up. No big deal, right? Then he'd had an attack of food poisoning. Then something else. I didn't remember what happened the third time, but it was becoming apparent that this guy didn't really want to come to Ohio.

"What's the plan?" I asked. This was the Devereaux clan. We *always* had a plan.

"Lee is at the store helping the twins. Hicks is trying to reach the airline, and I'm going to try and reach Cameron's agent," Bishop said.

"I also need you boys to get the box fans out of the attic to take over. I'm calling a friend of mine who's an HVAC specialist, but I don't know how quickly he can get out there. The air conditioning is out at the store," Mama D said.

"Shit! It was supposed to be almost one hundred degrees today!" I exclaimed in sympathy. I glanced at the clock. It was already almost noon.

"That's why I canceled our afternoon classes and *you* are loading up your car and heading out there with ice, a cooler and a couple of cases of water for everyone," Mama K said.

Like a well-oiled machine, we all went about our assigned tasks. I loaded up my car with the cooler and box fans, then hit the local convenience store, stocking up on several cases of water and almost a hundred pounds of ice.

When I pulled up to the store it was almost one thirty. The line for the meet and greet with Cameron stretched around the block. There had to be over a hundred and fifty people in line! Shit. I hadn't really realized how popular this guy was. I pulled around back into the employee parking area, loaded half the ice in the cooler then took it inside.

"Stop your grinnin' and drop your linen! Reinforcements have arrived!" I hollered as I walked in the back of the store.

The heat inside was like walking into a brick wall. I saw Hicks in the back office, his always-perfect blond hair in a neat ponytail, but sweat was dripping down his forehead. Sonny was out front with Lee, manning the registers. The front doors were propped open. There was a table set up near the front windows with banners announcing "Award Winning Author/Artist Mason Cameron" will be signing autographs at 12 p.m. Noon was crossed out with a black Sharpie and rewritten as 12:30 p.m., 1:15 p.m. and now 3 p.m. There was a wall-sized promo print on the back wall touting Cameron's "Dark Angel" series. Black and gold helium balloons hung festively around the store, but even they were starting to wilt in the heat. A few brave customers wandered aimlessly around the room looking at merchandise, but I noticed there wasn't a line at the registers.

As I lugged the cooler in, my oldest brother, Ripley "Lee" Devereaux came up and wrapped me in a giant hug. Lee was almost six foot five and was the tallest of the Devereaux brood. He'd spent several years in the military where he'd met the man he'd thought he'd spend the rest of his life with. He and his fiancé, Mack, had been ambushed while on a mission in Afghanistan just a few weeks before they were due to be discharged. Lee came home with a shattered hip and a limp. Mack didn't come home at all.

I hugged him back then pushed him away playfully.

"Damn! It's too hot in here for you to be that close! What do you have in there, a furnace?" I teased, poking him in the stomach.

"Watch it, hot shot," he growled as he slapped my hand away. "I could have called in dead today, you know!"

We both laughed. When we'd been kids, I'd done a lot of faking to get out of doing chores. As the oldest, Lee would get stuck doing whatever I didn't.

"I would have dragged your sorry ass out of the grave, bro," I chuckled. "Help me get this crap out of my car before it all melts and raises sea levels."

Lee and Sonny followed me out to the car where we unloaded the fans, cooler, ice and water onto a cart they used for deliveries. We dropped the box fans off inside. Sonny went back to his phone call and Hicks began setting up the fans. I sent Lee back inside to help them, then began handing out bottles of water to the waiting customers.

The line of people was even longer than it had looked. It went all the way down to the end of the block and around the corner. If Cameron didn't show up soon, we could be looking at trouble.

When I first walked out, the mood in line was ugly. Between boredom, the heat, and general frustration tempers were beginning to fray. I knew how to handle a crowd like this, though. In my full-time job as a bartender, I often had to deal with angry or belligerent guests. It was amazing how far an understanding smile would go in easing tension.

I started handing out cold water and working my way down the line. About half-way through I spotted a friend of the twins, Jeri. Jeri was a fourteen-year-old trans girl that we'd met the previous year. She was about five foot four with straight blue hair that was only just starting to grow out of a super-short boy cut. The twins had sort of adopted her when they'd met at an LGBTQ support group at the downtown library.

Jeri had discovered comics through the twins and become engrossed in the stories, spending so much time at their original store they'd talked her into taking a part-time position to help prepare for the Grand Opening of the new location. She had come out to her parents as trans only a little bit earlier in the summer. Her boyfriend,

Tobi stood next to her, his arms wrapped around her protectively even in the heat.

"Hey guys! Want some water?" I asked, handing them a couple of bottles automatically.

Jeri grinned at me. "Hey Kaine! How'd you get roped into this? I thought you were working at the dojo today?" she asked.

"It's all hands on deck, *chica!*" I said in response. I looked around, but not seeing any of my family members nearby, I leaned in and whispered in her ear. *"They canceled classes!"*

She looked at me, her eyes wide. My parents *never* canceled classes. We'd had a blizzard last winter with almost three feet of snow and my moms had just loaded up their SUV and headed in.

"Shit! That *never* happens!" she exclaimed.

"I know, right? I think the moms are happy that it gives them the opportunity to surreptitiously help the twins," I guessed.

"Do they need any help inside?" Jeri offered.

"Nah. There's not really anyone in the store right now. Everyone's just lining up for Cameron. I'll let you know if that changes though, okay?"

After confirming I had her cell number, I continued down the line. I handed out water, laughing and joking with the people I recognized in line, either from the store or from working at The Belt. I was pelted with questions at first about what was going on and when Cameron was going to show up. I told everyone, truthfully, that I had no idea what was happening, but that we'd let them know as soon as we knew. I suggested everyone keep an eye on the store website for updates because I knew Hicks would be posting info as soon as we got it.

I had less than a dozen bottles of water left by the time I reached the end of the line. I rounded back and went into the store. I watched Lee angrily stack and re-stack the same boxes of trading cards three times.

"Any luck?" I asked Sonny as I took the cart back through to the back room.

He sighed and answered, "No, nothing. The last we heard his plane was on time, but we've heard nothing since then."

"Are we sure he was even on it?" I questioned.

"His manager, Lizzie, said he was," Hicks called from the back room. The noise of the box fans was making it hard to hear in the store, but it seemed to be helping the heat. "We just don't know why he's not here yet. We hadn't sent him the hotel information yet, so he couldn't have gone there."

"I assume you guys called Lizzie again, right?" I asked.

If looks could kill, the glare I got from all three of them would have killed me instantly.

"Okay! Okay! I had to ask!" I said. My alarm went off on my watch and I glanced at it. It was five o'clock. I had just enough time to get home, shower, change and get to The Belt for my shift.

"I'm sorry, guys, but I gotta go. I'm working at The Belt tonight," I said. "I was late last night, and Sammie will kill me if I'm late again tonight."

I hugged my brothers one after the other. Hicks hugged me first, but kept his phone in his hand as he did so. He was trying to get hold of Lizzie again. Sonny's blond mop smacked me in the face as he almost tackle-hugged me, then Lee gave me a quick squeeze.

"Thanks for bringing the water out, Kaine. Tell the moms thank you as well, because we know they're really the ones behind it," Sonny said, winking at me as he went back to the cash register.

I laughed and nodded. I wished there was more I could do, but I couldn't just wave a magic wand and make the guy appear. Besides, I had to get to work.

I made it to The Belt essentially on time—for me. It was ten after six, and the music was already so loud that I could feel the beat in my feet. I entered through the employee entrance and shoved my things in a locker. I grabbed an apron and went to stow my phone in my back pocket when I saw a text in the family chat.

LEE: I found him!

SONNY&HICKS: OMG Thank you man! We oweski majorly!

BISHOP: You don't owe fucking anything. Cameron does.

WEAVER: Chill, B! It's all working out, right?

BISHOP: Yeah yeah. Sunshine and fucking roses.

KAINE: WTF Dude? You've been crabby for days.

BISHOP: ...

LEE: Do you want me to bring him back to the store?

SONNY&HICKS: Nah. Can you just take him to the hotel? Most everyone has left anyways. We'll plan on starting fresh tomorrow.

LEE: Will do.

MAMA D: RSVP for Devereaux Den D&D tomorrow?

BISHOP: Yes, ma'am!

WEAVER: No can do, sorry Mama Bear! Since I was off last weekend, I'm on duty this weekend.

SONNY&HICKS: As long as the grand opening doesn't do us in, we'll be there!

LEE: Yep, I'm in!

KAINE: With bells on, Mama! You know I'll help you kill the party anytime... Oops? Did I send that to the Fam chat?

MAMA D: LOL

MAMA K: You get us killed, I'll turn you over my knee!

MAMA D: You can turn ME over your knee... /eyebrow waggle

MAMA K: Bye bye kids, TTYL!

I laughed at my family's antics. Well, at least Cameron had been found. That was one less thing to worry about. D&D at the Devereaux Den was a standing affair. I knew I'd have to get some sleep tonight, or I wouldn't be in any shape to play. I had barely stepped behind the bar when Josie's arms were wrapped around me.

"Thank you so much for covering for me tonight, pretty boy!" they said, hugging me tight.

Josie and their boyfriend were gender fluid. They identified as either non-binary or gender queer. Their gender identity could vary and either of them could fall anywhere on the spectrum, depending on the day. Today Josie was wearing a pretty summer sundress with a spaghetti-strap cami under it. I whistled in appreciation and they twirled for me as I admired the outfit.

"The boots pull it all together," I teased, pointing at their hiking boots. They grinned and blushed.

"Mick and I are leaving for southern Ohio as soon as he gets here.

We're driving down to the John Glenn Astronomy Park down in Hocking Hills. We're going to stay a few days at a bed and breakfast down there," they answered, their curly brown hair bouncing with their excitement.

"Look what I got my Micky!" Josie exclaimed, reaching into their pocket. I leaned close as they pulled out a small velvet box. I raised an eyebrow at them.

"Is that what I think it is?" I asked. "You finally gonna put a ring on it?"

Josie nodded excitedly. "It's my birthday, so I figured I'd give myself the best present ever!"

"That explains why Sammie was making heart eyes at me when you asked me to cover for you!" I said.

Josie blushed. "You don't mind, do you? I know you've been putting in a lot of hours to cover for me. This will be the last time I need you to cover for me. From here on out, hopefully we'll be saving for a wedding!" They squealed and bounced up and down again, and I couldn't help but share in the joy.

I *had* been putting in a lot of hours to cover for Josie, but I knew they would do the same for me in a heartbeat. Plus, there was no way anyone could resent Josie. They were too damn cute, and far too loving for anyone to deny them. Josie was a sweetheart. They were so sensitive, they had stopped one time and picked up a skunk that had been hit by a car. By the time they got it to the vet the poor thing had passed away, and Josie's car had reeked to high heaven. All they'd had to do was bat their eyes at us, and my whole family had been cleaning their car with tomato juice.

I wasn't worried about Josie's unexpected proposal. I knew Mick would be onboard as well, because I happened to know they had a similar "surprise" in a box for Josie. I kept my mouth shut, though. No one liked a spoilsport.

"I better get to work, hon," I said. "You two have fun!"

I hugged Josie again, put my earplugs in, and went to work.

Seeing Josie had been the high point of my night. Despite the adrenaline rush I got whenever we had a decent crowd, I was bone tired. I slogged my way through the evening, making drink after drink. The crowd at The Belt was nice enough, don't get me wrong. The music was good, and I couldn't complain much about the company. I'd made plenty of "friends" on my shifts at the club. Sammie, the owner, didn't care, as long as we all got our work done and didn't bring trouble into her establishment. She had met her own husband at the club years ago when she was first starting out. She believed in fate.

Tonight, though, I just wasn't feeling it. I turned down several offers of a trip to the bathrooms, where, Sammie would be shocked —*shocked*, I say!—to hear that more than personal hygiene occurred, and I threw away almost a half dozen phone numbers. Who had time for relationships, after all?

I'd poured my last drinks, called cabs or Ubers for the last couple of lonely patrons, and was flipping chairs on the tops of the tables when Sammie came out of her office.

"Hey, Kaine!" She said. Or, at least I thought that was what she was saying, because I realized I still had my earplugs in. I quickly took them out and shoved them in my pocket. Sammie had her dark-brown hair pushed back from her face with a headband, but the curls framed her smile.

"Hey, Sammie! Sorry about that. I forgot I still had the plugs in," I said.

"No problem. I'm glad I caught you! I need to talk to you about something," she said. She walked around the side of the bar with some papers in her hands and sat down on one of the chairs I hadn't flipped yet. She gestured to the chair next to her. "Take a seat."

"Everything okay, boss?" I asked, pulling the chair up. Between my shift at the bar and helping out the twins earlier, I'd been on my feet for over twelve hours now. I was not passing up the opportunity to rest.

"Everything is fine," she said. "I wanted to talk to you about your schedule."

I groaned inwardly. That usually meant I was picking up more shifts for someone.

"I'm worried about you, Kaine," she said.

"Sammie—" I started.

"Don't you 'Sammie' me," she snapped. She glared at me for a minute until I nodded, appropriately chastened, then her gaze softened. Her grey eyes looked at me fondly as she smoothed the papers out on the table. I realized with a glance that they were the pages from our schedule book.

"You are worn out, Kaine. How many hours a week are you working?" she asked.

"Forty—" I began, but she cut me off.

"You think I don't know you? I *know* you, kiddo. I've been to the dojo website. I see the number of classes you're teaching there. I know what your schedule is like here. How many hours a week have you been working?" she demanded.

"Seventy...?" I began, the saw her glare.

"Seventy-five or so," I admitted.

She shook her head and sighed at me.

"Why in the name of all that's holy are you working so many hours?! You work more hours than *I* do!" she exclaimed.

"I just... Sammie, I don't want my parents to have to spend their money putting me through school, when I don't even know what I want to *do* with my life!" I admitted finally, hanging my head. "They have enough to worry about, what with Lee and the twins' store and everything!"

"Oh, baby boy... You are a good son and an amazing brother. I see how hard you're working. Do your parents have any idea how many hours you've been putting in?" she asked.

I shook my head again. There was no way my parents would have let me work so many hours between the bar and the dojo if they'd known. I'd deliberately downplayed the time I spent at the club, letting them assume that I was there to hang out with friends, not just work. Which was true, from a certain point of view... I considered Sammie and Josie and the other staff members at The Belt to be friends.

"I don't want to worry them, Sammie," I finally said. "There are so many kids in my family, and Mama D and Mama K have already done so much for me... I don't want them to have to pay for my school, too."

"You know it's in the job description, right?" She asked. "Parents worry. Parents help. It's right under 'change diapers' and right before 'provide bail money.'"

I laughed. My parents had done all that for the fam at some time or another.

"I know. It doesn't mean I don't want to do as much as possible by myself. Besides, you need me. Especially with Josie off for a few days," I insisted.

"About that..." she began.

Uh oh, I thought. *Here it comes.* An unreasoning panic tightened in my chest. Shit. She was going to fire me. That's what this was all about. She was going to fire me. Or they were going to close the bar. Maybe there had been a health code violation I didn't know about. Maybe someone had been dealing drugs in the bathroom. Maybe—

"Stop, Kaine! I can see you working yourself into a panic attack right in front of me! This isn't a not a bad thing," she reassured me. "I posted an ad online and I've hired a new bartender. She's going to be picking up some of the weeknight shifts for you, so we should be getting you back to forty hours or under, starting this week."

I stared at her in amazement.

"What—how—" I began.

"She's a student at Case Western and she just moved to the area. I told her I couldn't guarantee her more than twenty hours, because I don't want you losing your benefits, but she seemed more than pleased with that," Sammie said.

"Oh my god, Sammie! I could kiss you right now!" I exclaimed. This position was one of the few jobs that I knew of that provided health insurance even to hourly employees. Sammie had experienced some major health problems in her early thirties and she had insisted the bar carry decent and affordable coverage for all of its employees, even though I knew it had to be financially tough for her.

I didn't have anything going on with me health-wise, but my

parents had ingrained in me the importance of planning for all eventualities. I leaned over and hugged her.

"No kissing! You kiss me, my husband would have to kill you, so let's not go there, okay?" she teased. "The new girl, Vivian, she's starting training on Monday with Aaron. I need you to work Wednesday night, but other than that, I don't want to see your ass in here again until next weekend."

I was speechless. A whole *week* off work? I could sleep in! For days! I didn't think I'd taken that much time off since high school.

Sammie laughed at me.

"Now this! This is priceless! Kaine Devereaux, speechless!" she laughed.

"You are a rotten old woman who will end up a crazy cat lady," I said.

"Yeah, yeah, I love you, too, kiddo," she said, hugging me a final time. "Remember what I said. Unless you are here to drink and dance, I don't want to see you again for at least a week. Now get out of here. My eyes hurt just looking at how tired you are right now!"

I quickly finished up my tasks and headed home. By the time I made it to my bedroom, it was almost 6 a.m. and the sun was starting to lighten the sky. I closed the curtains on my windows, thankful again for the blackout curtains Mama D had insisted we purchase when we redecorated my room a few years ago.

I was snoring before my head hit the pillow.

7

NICKI

I PULLED INTO A CAMPUS PARKING SPOT AND TURNED OFF THE ENGINE, waiting for Vivian to come out of the building.

The days and weeks that followed our midnight run had passed in a blur. We got the apartment set up the way we wanted it. Vivian purchased a new car, since the cost for shipping her old one would have been exorbitant. We found a Walmart, set up utilities, and did all the things you did when you started out on your own. We never really felt alone, though. Almost daily we had boxes and boxes showing up at the apartment door from Vivian's parents. I felt bad for the mailman.

Dr. and Mrs. Dunwoody had included quite a few surprises in the boxes they had shipped to our apartment for us. Primary among them was a brand-new laptop, addressed to me. I'd hated leaving behind the clunky old laptop that had been my Mom's. It had held a lot of photos that I hadn't been able to duplicate elsewhere. The notes that Mrs. Dunwoody had included indicated that it was "an early Christmas present" and that she knew I would make good use of it.

I certainly intended to. I set up accounts online, including a bank account and started job hunting. Vivian cashed out the account that included the money that she had been holding for me. Out of that, I insisted on paying her two months' worth of rent, and my share of the utilities. We'd fought about it for a while, but eventually I wore her down. She did make me promise to at least wait until I had gotten a full-time job before I gave her the money.

So, intent on not being a freeloader as well as mindful of the fact I had a limited amount of funds in my bank account, I found a job as a server at a Wally Waffle restaurant in a nearby town, which I would be starting the following week. The hours allowed me to work mornings, and possibly take classes in the afternoon or evening once my financial aid came through. I had applied to the University of Akron, but it was too late in the summer to be admitted for fall semester. I figured it was just as well, as it would give me the chance to save up some money, apply for student loans, and the rest of the things that went with being a part-time student. I'd contacted the college I'd been taking online classes through. I'd at least be able to continue them from my new home.

I purchased a bicycle to help me get around, but I was currently driving Vivian's car. Vivian was amazing and offered to let me use it whenever I needed to, but I figured it would be best if I limited it as much as possible. I had no idea how I would pay back the Dunwoody's for all they had done for me already.

As I sat in the car, listening to the satellite radio and enjoying the cool breeze of the air conditioning, I watched the people walking around the campus.

It was the second summer session, so there weren't that many people around. A couple of students here and there, a few people who looked like professors, or maybe teaching assistants. This was what I wanted to be. A normal person, doing normal things. Unafraid of saying or doing something that would piss someone off and earn a beating.

A flash of blond hair and the sound of laughter caught my attention as a student walked past the car as I waited. The first thing I noticed was his ass. I mean, sue me, alright? I was a gay man. I liked men's asses. And his was tight, cupped in a pair of jeans that made him look delectable. His hair was brown with lots of light-blond highlights, and his body looked like it was sculpted by God. I swear, I thought my mouth watered a little.

Then I heard his voice. He was standing not far from the car, his back to me. His voice sounded eerily familiar.

"Bish, I swear to God, I'm going to kill Sonny if he doesn't lay off about the store! I mean, I know they have the Grand Opening coming, but for God's sake! It's all he can talk about," he said into his phone.

I stared in shock and a little bit of horror as he walked away from the car. The man talking on the phone had been my best friend. The man I'd come out of the closet for, the man I'd loved with all my heart before I had cut him off without any explanation. Kaine Devereaux.

I froze in my seat, suddenly thankful for the tinted windshield Vivian had selected. I knew it was hard to see inside the car, especially on a sunny day like this one. It gave me a chance to drink my fill of the man I'd fallen in love with five years before.

Kaine's body had grown into the promise it had held as a teenager. I figured we were probably around the same height, but that's where the similarity ended. He was *beyond* toned. I thought his muscles had muscles. He wasn't a hulk or anything, but it was obvious he still worked out. Probably at his parents' dojo? That would make sense.

His face was more defined, more... solid... than it had been as a teen. I couldn't see his eyes because he was wearing dark, mirrored sunglasses. His cheekbones were a little sharper, his whole face a little thinner, I thought. I remembered the day he had come back to school after Vinnie Avery had done a real number on him.

I'd really hated Vinnie. If anyone deserved the title "slut" it had been him. He was well known for breaking hearts in our school, both male and female. He had started dating Kaine when we were fourteen. Kaine and I had already been best friends, but when Vinnie asked him out, Kaine had been beyond flattered.

At the time, I hadn't acknowledged to anyone that I might be gay, not even Kaine. I knew my father would freak out if I told him, and wasn't entirely sure how my mom would react. It was just, my dad was already disappointed in me as a son. I knew that coming out to him as gay would be challenging.

Kaine and Vinnie had been dating for a few days, and we'd all walked home together. Kaine was so gone over Vinnie, I knew he couldn't see the things I saw. The way Vinnie flirted with other people, the way he leered at Cassie McElway, or the way he whispered in Eddie Freeman's ear during PE and made him blush. I just knew he was fooling around on Kaine on the side, but it wasn't my place to say anything.

Kaine and I usually hung out after school, but that night Vinnie had asked Kaine to come over to his house to study. I remembered him teasing Kaine about wanting to give him a haircut. At the time, Kaine had been a little overweight, his hair a little ragged, and he didn't have a very good self-image. Ever since his parents had abandoned him, Kaine had felt like he wasn't worth anyone's time or attention. He had participated in martial arts at his parents' dojo, but like me he'd rather play video games than go running.

I'd always been a little jealous of Kaine's adoptive family. His two moms were the best parents *ever*. Mama D would let me help her make candles, and Mama K would teach me new martial arts moves. I'd secretly wanted them to adopt me for years, only to hate myself for it. I knew that my own parents would have to be dead for me to get new parents. I loved my parents, but I'd always felt—at home, with the Devereaux's.

Kaine and Vinnie had left me at my door and walked the rest of the way home together. I'd stood on the porch and watched Vinnie take Kaine's shy hand in his, and I'd been furious. I had slammed the front door and ignored the sound of my mother calling after me as I threw my book bag down next to the couch before tearing upstairs.

I threw myself on my bed, angry tears welling up in my eyes as I thought of them hanging out without me. What did I have to offer Kaine, after all? Vinnie was popular, gorgeous, and on the football team. He was genetically blessed with good looks and dimples. Fucking *dimples*. While I... I was a skinny kid, one hundred pounds soaking wet, who was sick constantly with one thing or another. What did I have to compete with *dimples*?

I heard a knock on my door.

"Come in," I called, though I knew who it would be.

My mom opened the door and looked at me, taking in my defeated air and the tracks of tears I hadn't had the chance to wipe away yet. One of the things I loved about my mom was that she always wore comfortable clothing. Unlike my dad, who always wore dress pants or khakis, my mom wore jeans and t-shirts. She worked as a part-time secretary at an optometrist nearby. I loved that she was never fussy about what she wore, she just wore whatever was comfortable. That day, I remembered she was wearing a white t-shirt and one of my dad's old green plaid button downs. She had it knotted at her waist and stood in the doorway with her hands on her hips.

"Do you want to talk about it?" she asked softly, her voice gentle as she took in the sight of me staring angrily at the ceiling.

I rolled over on my bed, turning my back to her. She shut the door behind her, then climbed up on the bed, lying next to me on top of the old quilt she had made for me.

"Nicki? Talk to me, sweetheart," she whispered.

I sighed and rolled to my side, mirroring her posture on the bed. I knew she was about as stubborn as I was, and there was no way she would leave without knowing what was going on.

"It's stupid," I said, sniffling and angrily scrubbing at my face.

She reached up and wiped a stray tear from my cheek with her thumb. Her red hair glowed in the fall sunlight, her dark-grey eyes as reflective as silver coins.

"If it's making you this upset, I doubt it's stupid," she said.

I sighed. Mom could read me like a book. I knew I wasn't going to be able to hide anything from her.

"It's Kaine..." I said. She raised an eyebrow at me, and I continued. "Kaine... and Vinnie."

"Ah." She said, nodding in understanding. "You miss him."

"It's so *stupid*," I answered. "I mean, it used to be Kaine, Bishop and I hanging out together all the time and it never bothered me. Now Bishop is all wrapped up in his art projects, and it's just been Kaine and me. But now he's dating Vinnie. I still see Kaine almost as much as I always did, but it's... *different* somehow. How can it feel like I'm missing him, when I see him every day?"

She looked at me a few minutes, her gaze intent.

"Nicki, do you think miss spending time with Kaine, or do you miss spending time with Kaine... *alone?*" she asked.

I blushed.

"I-I..." I stammered, not sure what to say. I didn't really know *what* I felt. I just knew I felt sick when I wasn't with him. That he made me smile and made my heart race in the best way.

"Dominick," she said seriously. "Sweetie. Are you trying to tell me you're gay?"

My heart almost stopped the minute she said it. The thought had occurred to me before, but in the way of most teenagers, I'd avoided looking at it very closely. I mean, considering how open Kaine and his family were, how could I *not* have considered the possibility?

Kaine was my best friend. I loved him as a friend... right? I tried to make myself say that what I felt for Kaine was platonic, then I stopped to think back over the last several months. Thought about how just being in Kaine's presence made me feel physically better at times. Thought about how my heart raced when I would run into him at school, or the special glow I'd feel after we'd done something together. Not to mention the times I'd had to hide my erections when he'd been around. The time he'd spent the night and it was all I could do to make it through the evening without embarrassing myself or him with an obvious erection. Or how I'd rubbed one out in the bathroom as soon as he left.

As per usual, my mom was right.

"I— I think so..." I whispered.

She sighed, her own eyes getting a little watery.

"Are you... are you disappointed in me?" I asked, my eyes searching hers fearfully. I could deal with a lot of things in my life but letting my Mom down was not one of them.

"Oh, baby boy! No! I couldn't be disappointed in you in a million years," she said, wrapping her arms around me and squeezing me tight. "I just wish… wish this could be an easier path for you, sweetie. I know you didn't choose it, but being gay is *hard*."

I nodded and swallowed.

"Are you going to tell Dad?" I asked. I had no idea how my father would react.

"Do you want me to?" she asked.

I nodded. I had no idea how I would even broach the subject with him.

"Okay, then. I'll have a talk with him," she promised me.

We sat there a few minutes. I thought for a while she was going to say something else, but she seemed to change her mind.

"So, let's talk about Kaine," she said. "Why do you like him so much?"

I thought for a minute.

"He's— He's *Kaine*. He's funny, and smart, and really good with math. He's… he's just plain nice, Mom," I said. "The other day Freddie Matthewson, the new kid, was being picked on because his clothes were dirty, and he smelled funny. They were calling him names like piggy and bum. Kaine not only told one of the teachers, he and Freddie became friends. Freddie hung out with us last weekend."

My Mom smiled at me, her grey eyes shining. "You've got it bad, sweetie."

I blushed and pretended I was going to lob the pillow at her. We laughed for a minute before settling back down.

"I do have it bad, don't I?" I said, a touch of wonder in my voice. Being gay just explained so much about how I felt. I started thinking back to all the time I'd spent with Kaine, how he understood me better than anyone—except my Mom.

"Um hmm…" she said. "The question is, what are you going to do about it?"

"I— I guess I could tell him," I began. "…but he *really* likes Vinnie. I don't want to try and break them up or anything, and if I tell him I am gay, I know that's what Vinnie will think I am doing."

"So, what are your other options?" she said.

I took a deep breath.

"I could wait. See how things go with him and Vinnie. The thing is..." I paused a moment. "I'm *pretty* sure Vinnie is cheating on him. I saw the way he was whispering to one of the boys at school in another grade. He was making him blush and I saw him... I saw him... *touch* him..."

I blushed again. I couldn't believe I was telling my *mom* about what had happened!

During PE, we usually had to run laps at the end, then when we were done we hit the showers. I was always among the last ones to get done. I'd been coming out of the showers when I'd seen Vinnie and Eddie Garrett in the locker rooms.

Vinnie was a grade or two higher than we were, and he shouldn't even have been *in* our locker rooms that time of the day. Eddie hadn't been dressed yet, which was odd, because he was on the track team and was usually one of the first kids finished with their laps. Vinnie had been leaning against the locker, kind of boxing Eddie in with both his arms. Eddie was standing there, wearing just his underwear and socks, with his hands at his sides and a bright blush on his face.

It was easy to see that something had gotten him excited, because his cock was tenting his briefs in obvious fashion. It was part of the guy code not to comment when someone popped a boner, especially in the locker room. We were all teenagers, and we all got hard at the drop of a hat. It happened.

I'd come around the corner and froze seeing the two of them standing there. Vinnie had looked over his shoulder and smirked at me, then deliberately leaned down and whispered something in Eddie's ear that made him blush all the way down his neck. Then Vinnie turned to go, and he brushed his hand across Eddie's crotch. I might have thought it was a relatively innocent contact, but I could swear I saw his hand squeeze Eddie through his briefs. The thought of how hurt Kaine would be if he'd been the one seeing this, had me seeing red.

I'd hightailed it out of the locker room, the blood roaring in my ears. When I passed him in the hallway a short while later when we switched periods, Vinnie grabbed my arm and said, "Just remember, Carrots, nobody likes a tattletale."

That, on top of everything else, had me seething by the time I got home.

"Yikes. That's a tough one, baby," Mom said as I gave her the edited version. What happened in the locker room, stayed in the locker room.

"I know," I sighed. "I want to tell him so bad, but I know it's just going to hurt him! And I *don't* want that! I mean, Kaine will probably figure it out on his own, eventually, right? It just makes me mad that Vinnie would do this to Kaine! Why does he have to cheat on him? Hasn't he been hurt enough?"

Mom sighed again and seemed to be weighing her words carefully.

"People have... people have different reasons for cheating, baby. Some people... some people cheat because of the thrill. Some people cheat because they want to hurt someone. Other people—" she stopped a second. "Other people cheat because they were never meant to be with that person in the first place."

I looked at my mom curiously. Her eyes had a faraway look to them, like she was thinking of something a thousand miles away from where we were. Then she smiled at me, refocusing on our conversation and she continued.

"When Kaine finds out, he's going to need you, Nicki. He's going to need a friend to love him and help fix his broken heart. It won't be easy," she said, smoothing a stray curl back behind my ear. "But waiting and being there for him when the time comes could be the best gift you ever give him."

Mom had been right. A few weeks later when Vinnie had dumped him, Kaine had been devastated. Vinnie had given him a list of all the things wrong with him. A god damned *list*! Kaine had disappeared from school for a week. He wouldn't even talk to me when I came over and pounded on his door. I'd spent Thursday and Friday evening and all day Saturday and Sunday camped outside of Kaine's bedroom door. He wouldn't open it while I was there, but I kept up a running commentary about what was happening at school. I read him all the notes from all our classes and had even read our textbooks out loud to him.

His brothers had given me loads of shit over it, especially when I started reading the geometry textbooks out loud, but I wanted Kaine to know I was there for him.

I'd had to go back to school the next day, but Monday night when I came over to see him, he'd opened the door to his room when I knocked.

I'd looked at him in shock. Gone was the mop that usually sat on top of his head. In its place was a chic looking haircut. The sides were cut close, the hair long on top. The dirty-brown color was gone, replaced by vibrant-blond highlights.

We had looked at each other in shock as he'd opened the door. It wasn't just the hair, there was a little bit of attitude change as well. He'd smiled shyly at me, his eyes a little uncertain, as if he wasn't quite sure what I would think. I'd stared at him, and my mouth must have fallen open, because he laughed.

"Careful, you might start getting flies in there," he'd teased.

"Wow!" I'd exclaimed. "You look…"

I paused as I collected my thoughts as I took everything in. His eyes started to lose that beautiful, confident glow as I took too long to finish my sentence, and his hand came up to brush nervously through his hair.

"Um, if it's that bad, I could get my moms to shave it, I think—" he started to say, his face turning bright red as he stepped back from the door.

"No!" I almost yelled, and he halted. I didn't usually raise my voice, over anything. I stepped forward slowly, reaching my hands out tentatively to stroke across his new highlights before whispering, "I think… I think it's perfect—"

He looked at me strangely, as though he was seeing me for the first time as my fingers played across his hair.

"—just like you. You're perfect just the way you are."

It felt as if someone else possessed my body at that moment, because I couldn't stop myself from leaning forward and laying a gentle kiss across his lips. At first, Kaine stood there unmoving, stiff and frozen under my touch. I started to back away, thinking I had screwed up royally, my eyes flashing to his. Then his hands had flashed out and gripped my arms, pulling me back into him. Then... then he'd kissed me back.

That kiss had to be one of the most passionate things that had ever occurred between two mortal beings. Or, at the very least, two *very* horny teenage boys. By the time we came up for air, we were both a mess. Hair disheveled, shirts askew. Kaine looked at me with a kind of wonderment in his eyes.

"Um..." he'd said as we sat next to each other on the edge of the bed. I wasn't even sure how we had made it there. Kaine looked at me shyly, his cheeks bright pink as he rested his hands on his knees. "...Is there something you wanted to tell me?"

"Oh, yeah," I said, a laugh burbling up from deep inside me. "I think I'm gay. Would you go out with me? Also, want to play video games?"

We'd gotten through the aftermath of Vinnie together, but it had been only a few months afterward that my parents had announced we were moving to Florida so we could be closer to the specialists.

I watched Kaine walk away from the car. I had known, at least theoretically, that I could run into him or a member of his family now that I was back in Akron. I mean, there *were* ten of them... I still had his old phone number and had even driven past his home once since I'd been back in Akron. I just hadn't gathered the courage I needed to stop at the house or try and contact him. And here the Universe was putting him right in fucking front of me.

I stalled, though. I mean, what did I say? "Hey, sorry I dumped you, but it's because I agreed to let my dad use me as a human punching bag so he didn't hurt my mom?" Who would even believe that?

Kaine had called me every week without fail, but since my mom had left, I'd started avoiding his calls. I knew he would know that something was wrong, and I didn't know how to tell him about the devil's deal I'd made with my father.

Dad and I had just finished dinner one evening when the phone rang. We both knew who it was, because Kaine always called me on Friday nights at seven o'clock. I'd stood to go answer the phone when my Dad stopped me.

"Tell him to stop callin'," he commanded, his eyes glued to his paper.

"What?" I'd asked in surprise. My father's hand had flashed out and slapped the side of my head hard enough for tears to spring to my eyes. It was only a few days since he had first started taking his frustrations out on me, and the blow scared me as much as anything.

"I'm sorry!" I called out, trying to back away from him, but he grabbed me with his other hand. I hadn't learned yet that running from him didn't offer any refuge.

"I said, tell him to *stop* calling. I don't want him and your rainbow-y friends calling the house all hours of the day and night," my father snapped.

"He—he doesn't! He only ever calls on Friday nights at seven because of the long distance—" I started. Another blow landed, even harder this time.

"You *listen* to me, boy! You do *what* I say, *when* I say. That was our agreement, right?" My father stood and pulled me up until my feet were almost dangling off the floor and I was having a hard time breathing. The phone stopped ringing.

"You call him back, right now, and you tell him you don't ever want to hear from him again, *got it?* Or I'll be making a trip back home and make sure he never calls *anyone* again. "

I nodded, my heart pounding with fear. He'd released me and I'd walked shakily to the phone. I didn't want to do it. Kaine had been my lifeline, and I'd been his. Some part of me had hoped that maybe we'd be able to find some way out of this, together. I was also terrified about what would happen to him if I broke things off with him. I knew how fragile Kaine's emotional state could be.

I could feel my father's eyes on me as I picked up the phone. I knew I had to do it. I couldn't put Kaine's life in danger, not when I could prevent it. This was the only way I could protect him, as well as my mom. I was afraid of how he would react when I told him. I knew he would think he was being abandoned again, and I swallowed hard as I picked up the handset. I didn't know for sure what would happen to Kaine if I called, but I did know what would happen to him and my mother if I didn't.

"Hey, it's me," I said as he picked up, my voice shaky. Dad sat back down at the table, but he kept his eyes glued to mine.

"Dude! I just tried to call you! Where were you?" he asked. I could hear the smile in his voice and my stomach sank. I could hear the Devereaux clan in the background, the sounds of dishes clinking and kids arguing. I figured Kaine must not be on dishes duty this week, which meant he was staying out of trouble.

"I— I couldn't get to the phone in time," I said hoarsely, my eyes flitting to my father nervously.

"It's okay," he answered. "You sound like you've got a cold. How are you doing? How was your week? You're not sick again, are you?"

"Um, it was okay," I said. I could hear the worry in his voice, and my mind was racing as I tried to figure out what to say to him that he would believe. Kaine noticed my hesitation and his cheerful patter paused.

"Nicki, what's wrong?" He asked, his voice filled with concern.

"Um, nothing," I said, keeping my eyes on my father. Fuck. "I— I just need you to stop calling."

Silence met my words but even five states away I could his heart break. The man I loved, the man I had to protect from the shit show that my life had become.

"Kaine— Kaine I love you. I will always love you. I just— I can't love you... right *now*," I managed to get out.

"That makes *no* sense, Nicki," he sobbed into the phone.

"I know..." I whispered. "I'm sorry."

My father had gestured at me to end the call, so I did. I hung up the phone and broke both of our hearts.

Back in the present, I watched Kaine walk away from the car. It wasn't until Vivian got in and asked me what was wrong that I realized I had been crying.

123

8

KAINE

WHEN I WOKE MONDAY MORNING IT WAS TO THE FISHY BREATH OF
Bottles puffing away against my face, but even though I was exhausted
I couldn't get mad at her.

Bottles and I were besties. She had lived with us for almost six
years and had been a literal lifesaver for me.

I'd never told my family all of the details of the night Bottles came
into my life. It had been just a few weeks after Nicki had cut me out of
his life without warning that I'd almost ended my own.

It was my birthday. Nicki and I had planned this celebration for
months before we found out that his family was moving to Florida. I'd
turned eighteen, and instead of celebrating by finally slaking our need
for each other's bodies, Nicki was in Tampa, and I'd just worked a
long, soul-sucking shift at a downtown restaurant where I was a
busboy.

Nicki had turned eighteen a few weeks earlier, but it had been
almost two years since I'd spoken to him. I hadn't heard a word from
him since the night he had called me and ended our relationship
without explanation.

When we were younger, sex had seemed like some huge, life-
altering event. Nicki had wanted it, but I had wanted to wait, to at

least fulfill our contract with our parents. I had told him I was afraid of doing something to hurt him, but I'd been lying to both of us.

I had really just been afraid that if we took that step, I'd lose him. If I gave him that last little bit of me, the universe would swoop in and tear him out of my hands. I was right to worry but holding back didn't halt anything.

I regretted my decision once we found out that he and his family were leaving. I thought back to all the wasted opportunities we'd had where we could have lost ourselves in each other... I shook my head, trying to pull myself out of this funk.

I had been putting in a *lot* of hours at work since Nicki had left. It was the only thing that kept me from poking at the aching void where my heart used to be. Instead of working through my feelings, I just *worked*. At the dojo, at the restaurant, at school, wherever. It didn't matter, as longer as I didn't have to think about the empty spot in my chest.

My shift had ended, and I'd just walked out the back door to the employee parking lot of the restaurant. My phone dinged, and I looked at it automatically.

My cell phone calendar app chimed happily, "Kaine's Birthday!" I stared at the screen, my breath caught in my throat, and I stared at it numbly. My eyes felt hot and dry, heavy with tears that I could no longer shed. There was nothing more to wring from my heart.

The Terhunes had packed up everything and headed south one year, six weeks, twelve hours and thirty-two minutes prior to the end of my shift that night. Then Nicki had called me a few weeks later and asked me not to call him again. Even after he'd promised. *Promised...*

I looked at my cell phone. Nicki's number was still at the top of my contacts list. I couldn't bring myself to erase his number. Fuck, even if I had, it was carved into my heart. I hadn't called him, not in all the time since he'd broken up with me. I'd been tempted so many times. I wanted to know, to understand. Demand an answer. Promise him anything if he would only tell me what I had done to drive him away. But I'd never called.

I thought about his laughter. His smile. The way his freckles made a little star on his cheek. I used kiss him on that cheek, telling him it was my heart's targeting system. I was so fucking cheesy. *God*, I missed him. It would be so easy... Something inside me twisted and broke. Without thought about the time, I hit send.

"...Hello?" I heard a sleepy male voice on the other end. Shit... It was his dad.

"Mr. Terhune?" My voice squeaked. *Goddamn it*, I should have thought about the time. I should have thought about the fact that his Dad might not want me calling at all hours of the night...

"Devereaux?" he asked sharply. "Why are you calling, boy? It's late."

I swallowed hard, eyes flashing around the dirty alleyway, trying to think of something to say.

"I— I'm sorry for calling so late, Mr. Terhune. I was just... I *really* need to talk to Nicki. I was just hoping I could speak to him for just a minute?"

I could feel the hope pounding in my chest as adrenaline raced through my veins. If I could just *talk* to Nicki, get him to listen to me, I knew I could get through to him. I'd make him realize that we were meant to be together. Let him know I could change whatever had made him back off from our relationship. Make him realize—

"I'm sorry, son," Mr. Terhune said abruptly. "He's— he's out on a date."

I stopped breathing. My vision narrowed to a tiny dot, everything else around me fading away into blackness.

A date.

He was on a *fucking* date.

I was alone, heartbroken and miserable. And. He. Was. On. A. *Date*.

I don't really remember what I said to Mr. Terhune, but I think it included an apology for calling, then I hung up.

I doubled over against the brick wall, trying desperately to drag air into my shattered chest. The winter wind blew across my skin, its icy shards sliding beneath my shirt to send a chilling numbness into the pit of my stomach. I'd never felt so much pain while also feeling so oddly numb.

Of *course*, Nicki was with someone else. He was beautiful, smart, funny. His family's decision to move to Florida had probably been a relief for him. At least there, he didn't have to deal with me. He'd only gone out with me because he felt sorry for me. I'd run into Vinnie Avery a few weeks ago at school, and he had suggested much the same, but I hadn't believed it. Or hadn't wanted to, maybe. A part of me, deep down, though, absolutely believed it. Embraced it. Because it fit my reality better than the belief that someone as special as he was could love someone like me.

Sonny and Hicks had found me huddled under the bleachers at the end of the school day and we'd walked home that afternoon in unaccustomed silence. In the ensuing weeks, I'd distanced myself from my family, avoiding my parents and brothers. I didn't really have any friends anymore, anyway. The only member of my family I could stand to be around was Weaver, but that was only because she didn't push me. She didn't try to fix me. She just let me know she was there.

I never knew what the twins had done to exact revenge, exactly, but I heard it had involved super glue, itching powder and a jock strap. Vinnie Avery had been walking funny for a week. I'd been distantly amused at the time, appreciating my siblings' show of support, however misguided. Now, though, all I felt was bleak hopelessness.

I listed against the rough brick wall, struggling to drag air into my lungs. I turned away as some of my co-workers came out, walking away from the restaurant doors to their waiting rides, my body hidden by the darkness. I saw my own car sitting in the parking lot. It was a beat-up old Dodge that Nicki and I had worked on for months to get running. We'd finally figured out what was wrong with it, and we'd had just a few weeks of freedom one summer to enjoy it before he left.

Everything about the car was a reminder of Nicki and our time together. I thought about getting in and just... driving. Drive to Florida, to demand he explain why he had cut me out of his life. I considered just driving off into the darkness, letting the car drift off the highway and strike a bridge support, ending this freezing pain with fire and blood.

The idea was just a little *too* damn attractive. I was terrified, but strangely attracted to the idea of letting it all just...end. I was so tired all the time. Tired of fighting. Tired of hurting. I wanted it to all just...end.

I heard more noise in the entryway to the restaurant, and the urge to get away was overwhelming. Without thought, I ran, away from the car and cacophony of the restaurant.

I don't know how long I ran. Sweat beaded down my face and soaked my shirt. My skin was freezing, but felt too hot, too tight, and each thundering beat of my heart ripped through me, Vinnie's words eating at me.

"You're such a fucking loser, Kaine. I'm not even calling you a Devereaux, because you know you're not *really* one of them. Your own parents didn't want you. Your boyfriend didn't want you. You're ugly. Stupid. Unwanted."

Ugly. Stupid. Unwanted. Ugly. Stupid. Unwanted. *Ugly-stupid-unwanted.*

The words pounded in my head in time to my foot falls. Even when I couldn't run any further and had to walk, they haunted my every footfall.

Ugly. I still felt overweight. Even though I looked at the scale and saw a normal weight, looked in the mirror and saw a normal looking guy, in my mind's eye I was fat, and ugly and loathsome.

Stupid. My grades were slipping. Hell, who was I trying to kid? I was failing *all* of my classes at that point. I knew my parents were worried about me. They had even signed me up to see a therapist, but her schedule was so packed I hadn't been able to get in to see her yet. If anyone ever tried to tell you there was no mental health crisis in the United States, they hadn't tried to get an appointment with a therapist in less than three months.

Unwanted. Everyone left me. My parents. Vinnie. Nicki. It was only a matter of time before the Devereauxs left me, too.

Unwanted. Unwanted. Unwanted.

I saw a bridge up ahead, the pedestrian walkway a sloping curve over my horizon, the winter darkness creating a dark gray emptiness where the sky should have been. The opposite side of the bridge was swallowed up in darkness, and I wondered at the metaphor that was for my life. I kept going, and before long, I found myself at the apex of the bridge.

I remembered the name of the bridge: the All-America Bridge. Sounded cheerful, right? Made me think of parades and little kids waving flags. It spanned the Little Cuyahoga River and was a known site for suicides. I remembered my parents talking about a petition that had been circulated to get a fence or a net, or some fucking nonsense, put up on the bridge to deter jumpers, but it hadn't gone anywhere.

I found myself standing at the middle of the bridge, looking over the side of the bridge and the pain and emptiness was overwhelming. I wanted to cry, but tears wouldn't come. I was so damn... tired. I just wanted it to stop. The pain, the fear, the loneliness. I just wanted it to *end*.

I didn't even remember how I ended up sitting on the edge of the walk, my feet dangling over the side of the bridge. I was on the wrong side of the rail, and the only thing holding me in place were my arms, which were wrapped around the railing as I leaned over the side. I remembered thinking about how easy it would be to just shift my weight a little bit, to let go, free fall, and end all my problems. Cars rushed by in the night, their headlights just flashes of brightness as they flew by. There were no streetlamps on the bridge and I was wearing my dark busboy uniform. No one could even see me, which didn't feel all that unusual. I'd become invisible to everyone, without the joy Nicki brought my soul.

I looked down and had to swallow hard at the tiny splashes of light I saw below. It took my eyes a minute to adjust, but I realized the area of light beneath me was someone's security light for their house. I thought about how awful it would be to come out one morning and find someone dead on your driveway. Or worse, your car! What a mess it would make for the person who lived in that house... I wanted everything to end, but I just couldn't do that to them, those nameless, faceless people. I pulled myself back behind the railing and walked a few yards further north on the bridge, pausing from time to time to look over the edge again to make sure I wasn't over a house. I mean, come on! I might be hurting, but I wasn't *rude*. If I was going to end it all, the least I could do was be considerate of the people who lived below the bridge.

I sat on the rail again, this time looking down and not seeing anything below me but darkness. I stared into that darkness, mesmerized. It would be so easy, just to—

A gust of wind from a passing tractor trailer hit me, and I lost my balance.

As I teetered on the edge, I realized suddenly I was so, *so* wrong. As I started to fall all I could think of was that I was *such* an idiot! Mama D and Mama K would be devastated if I killed myself, not to mention my brothers and sister. And Nicki would be so disappointed in me. He'd always believed in me. And even if he wasn't *my* Nicki anymore, I knew he wouldn't want me to end my life. I missed him desperately, yes, but there was more to my life than just him. There was more to *me* than our relationship.

My arms flailed, but my fingers latched on to part of the railing, and I stood there, my fingers white as they held on for dear life. I desperately wanted to get back on the other side of the rail, back to relative safety, but I was suddenly terrified of moving. Gone was the earlier numbness, replaced by pure terror.

Just then, I heard a car slowing as it neared my section of the bridge. I could have cried in relief as the car headlight approached and washed over me momentarily. I didn't care who saw me or what they thought of me. All I could think of was that whoever they were, they would help get me off that fucking bridge.

Instead of stopping, though, I saw the passenger's side window of the car roll down and some dark objects came flying out of the window of the car, silhouetted against the amber and red lights in the interior. I heard some glass break against the concrete, then the vehicle sped up and drove away into the night. *Shit!* No help there. Just some idiot tossing his empties so he didn't get busted at a sobriety checkpoint.

I was still frozen, my heart racing as I tried to convince my body that the safest thing to do was to get me to the *other* side of the rail when I heard something. It was the tiniest of squeaks, barely audible above the rest of the noise from the freeway. I looked around, but with no light I couldn't figure out where the noise was coming from.

Another semi drove by, but this time I saw it coming and was able to brace myself for the back draft. As the truck passed me, I heard the sound of metal and glass scratching against rock. I heard that tiny squeak again, but this time I could see where it was coming from.

Tilted precariously at the edge of the concrete was what looked like a couple of old mayonnaise jars. I could just make out something moving inside the one container, but in the dim light I wasn't able to tell what it was.

I dragged myself over the railing, ignoring my terrified heartbeat and focusing only on that container. Another car came by, and I watched in horror as one bottle vibrated off the edge of the bridge, free-falling into the darkness. The other jar rolled to the edge and started to tip over. I sprang forward, barely snagging it before the wind from another passing car hit.

I held that little jar to my chest, barely breathing and unable to move, much less stand up. Then I heard the sound again, a tiny, plaintive "Mew!"

I was too afraid to stay on the bridge to open the container, so I shoved it inside my jacket in hopes of keeping whatever was inside the jar warm. I glanced around but couldn't see any other containers on the bridge. I made my way, shaky step after shaky step, to the other end of the bridge. Just as I reached the relative safety of land, my knees collapsed out from under me.

I don't know how long I stayed there. It could have been minutes or hours, but the plaintive mewing began coming from the jar again, so I forced myself to my feet. I walked to a nearby gas station and stood under one of the halogen lamps that lit up the whole parking lot. I pulled the jar out of my coat and it was, indeed, an old mayonnaise jar with holes punched in the metal lid. I unscrewed the lid carefully, angling it so the light of the gas station would hit the bottom of the jar. The last thing I needed to find was a baby skunk or something.

Inside that container, it's eyes barely open, was a tiny white kitten with patches of fur that looked like a tiger cat. It was hard to tell in the light, but its eyes still looked blue. The tiny thing was grimy, and the smell coming from inside the jar made me suspect that the glass had been in the trash for a while before being used as an improvised kitten grenade.

"Awww! Poor baby!" I muttered, tilting the jar gently so I could slide the kitten out of its prison.

The poor thing tried to scramble away from me, extending its tiny claws to catch hold of the glass, but the inside of the jar was slick, and it fell out onto my waiting palm.

The sweet little girl (and yes, I checked, she was a girl) mewed plaintively at me, her tiny little eyes never leaving mine.

"Sweet thing..." I whispered, petting her shivering body, then tucking her close to me.

She snagged her itty bitty claws in my t-shirt, then a tiny little motor inside her began vibrating. She mewed again.

"Shhh! Poor little thing! Sweet baby! I've got you!" I whispered, saying all the nonsense words and sounds you said to babies and animals. She was shivering, so I tucked her inside my t-shirt and snuggled her up next to my skin, hoping my body heat would be enough to help. I wrapped the jacket around us both and hoped it would warm her. It wasn't that cool out, but the wind around the bridge was pretty strong. I was already shivering myself, so I couldn't imagine how this poor baby was feeling.

I made my way to door of the gas station. I debated whether I should try heading back downtown and trying to find my car, but thought better of it. I wasn't sure where I was, and something told me the kitten in my coat wouldn't last very long without help. I took a deep breath and looked at my phone.

When my parents had given my brothers and I the underage drinking talk, they had told us that if we ever needed them to help us out of an unsafe situation, all we had to do was call. There would be no judgment, no punishment, as long as we called. This... this wasn't underage drinking, but for me, I thought it was just as much of an emergency.

I dialed my parents' number and it rang a few times before I heard Mama D answer the phone, sleep and confusion in her voice.

"Hello?" she asked quietly. She must have looked at the caller ID, because she asked, "Kaine? Are you okay, sweetheart?"

I couldn't talk for a minute as her concern washed over me. Tears began rolling down my face as I just listened to her voice.

"Di?" I heard Mama K ask sleepily in the background. "Is everything okay?"

Cars flew by the intersection, their noisy passage making it difficult to hear. I thought again how easy it would be to end everything, just to step out into traffic. I didn't want to hurt them anymore, or make them feel like any of this was their fault. I just wanted it to end. If I just took that step, it would be over so quickly—

I must have made some kind of movement, because tiny little claws dug into my neck and I felt the rumble of the little kitten's motor start back up. That tiny touch, that trusting little vibration broke through the walls I'd been trying to build around my heart and the crying began in earnest.

"Mama..." I began, then started sobbing. "Mama, I need you."

"Baby boy, what's wrong? Where are you?" she asked, the fatigue fogging her brain evaporated under the adrenaline rush of one of her boys in trouble. I sobbed for a minute as I stood there, phone pressed to my ear and tears running down my face. I tried to explain what had happened, and she listened quietly as I babbled until I was able to tell her my location. I could almost hear the gears of her mind slide into overdrive as she understood where I was at, both literally and figuratively.

"Kaine... Kaine are you on the bridge?" she whispered. Despite her efforts to remain calm, I could hear the fear in her voice, and I heard Mama K gasp in the background.

"No, Mama. Not— not anymore. I just... I just need someone to come get me," I managed to sob out.

Mama D stayed on the phone with me while Mama K and Lee drove out to pick me up. She kept me talking the whole time, asking me to tell her what I saw, who was around. At one point, I shifted the kitten because her claws were digging into my neck. She mewed at me in complaint. Mama D heard her and started asking me about her. A part of me understood she was just trying to keep me from thinking too much until help arrived, but the rest of me welcomed the distraction.

As I talked to Mama D, I heard a car pull up and saw Lee behind the wheel of his new Jeep. His jaw was clenched, and I could see his white-knuckled grip on the wheel of his SUV. I knew it was dark green, but it looked almost black in the dim light. He'd nicknamed the car "Hound" after an Autobot in the Transformers universe.

Before the car was even in park, Mama K was out of the vehicle and wrapping me in her arms as if she could physically reach through time and space and drag me away from the precipice and make it so I never even considered ending it all.

"Kaine, *mijo*, are you okay? What happened? Why are you here?" she asked, question after question rolling out of her as she pulled me to her. I could see her looking around the parking lot fiercely. "Did someone try to hurt you? Who—"

"Mama! No, I'm okay, now! Really!" I sniffed. Lee had parked the car and was standing next to us by then. He took the phone from me and started talking to Mama D. Then the plaintive mew began again. I saw the consternation on Mama K's face as she registered the noise but didn't immediately understand where it was coming from.

"What the—" she began, then saw the tiny little head peek out of my shirt. "Awww! Who is this *pequeña dama?*" Mama K asked, her Spanish sneaking in, as it always did when her emotions ran high. She caressed the silky soft fur of the kitten.

"Bottles," I said, almost without thinking. "I mean, that's what I would name her if I was going to keep her, because she was in this bottle, and it almost fell off the bridge..." My voice trailed off. Our parents had always said they didn't want any pets in the house, because with six children in the household, that way lay chaos.

"It did, hmm?" she asked, her dark eyes considering the animal, then me. *"Botellitas.* I think the name for our newest addition is *perfect."*

Bottles and I had been best friends ever since. She was fiercely protective of me, and her favorite pastimes were sitting in sunbeams and hissing at the squirrels outside my window.

I didn't like to think about the next week I'd stayed in the psych ward of the local children's hospital. It hadn't been fun, but it had, at least, set me on the road to recovery. I'd gotten a jump start on counseling and had started taking anti-depressants and anti-anxiety meds. I knew medication didn't necessarily work for everyone, but for me it had been a lifesaver.

My family had taken care of Bottles for me until I got out of the psych ward. Just knowing she was waiting for me gave me the encouragement I needed to start working through some of my issues. The hospital had connected me with a fantastic counselor who I still saw every now and again. Kelly had really helped me start dealing with my abandonment issues.

The alarm on my clock beeped at me and I jumped. It was after 1 p.m. I wanted to check in with the twins to see how the second day of the Grand Opening was going.

ME: Hey twinkies! How's biz?

I waited patiently for a response but didn't see any. I tried again a few minutes later, but still nothing. I took a shower, and checked my phone again after I got dressed. Oddly, there was still no response, so I tried again.

ME: Hooligans! What's going on?

I ran downstairs and made myself a sandwich and grabbed a soda to take up to my room.

Still no response. That was very unlike the boys. Usually one or both of them would respond immediately to a text, regardless of the time of day. I lay back on my bed and sent another text. If they didn't respond this time, I was going in search of them.

ME: Seriously guys? Are you okay?

When I finally saw the little dots indicating someone was typing a response, I let out a breath I didn't know I had been holding. My little brothers meant the world to me, and I wanted to make sure everything was going well.

SONNY&HICKS: We are seriously slammed, dude! I mean, lines around the block crazy busy! Bigger than yesterday!

ME: I take it Cameron's a hit, then?

HICKS&SONNY: Big time!

ME: So what's he like?

SONNY&HICKS: ...Completely unlike what we expected.

ME: Really?

SONNY&HICKS: Yep. And he's got a certain older brother of ours wrapped around his little finger... He's acting like he's his personal bodyguard or something!

Well, that piqued my interest! I sat up abruptly from my bed. When Lee came back from Afghanistan, he had been a total wreck. We'd been more worried about his emotional wounds than the physical ones, in truth. Lee was one of the best people I knew, and the loss of Mack had hit him hard. I still didn't think Lee knew that the whole fam knew about the night he tried to kill himself.

The twins had found him passed out in his room with an empty bottle of painkillers and a fifth of Scotch by the bed. They had rushed him to the hospital where he'd had the oh-so-pleasant experience of getting his stomach pumped full of activated charcoal... Served his dumb ass right.

The twins didn't think it had been a deliberate attempt to kill himself, but no one but Lee could answer that for sure.

To say that he hadn't been emotionally stable for a while was an understatement. He hadn't expressed any interest in anyone, really, since Mack had died, so the fact that he was being all protective of our unreliable visitor was a hopeful sign.

ME: I'd pay good money to see that, but I have to finish this paper for Dr. Tate before D&D tonight.

Within a minute, my phone beeped with an incoming picture. It was a photo of the inside of the twins' store, Twin Peaks. In it, I could see Lee standing outside a small alcove that the twins were using for gaming events. A table was set up and a young man with curly black hair was seated behind the table, his head down as he signed something. Lee was standing with his arms crossed over his impressive chest, his muscles standing out under his Twin Peeks t-shirt. He was glaring at something just outside the frame. He looked like he was just barely restraining himself from taking someone's head off.

ME: OMG! That is priceless! What does Cameron think?

Another pic popped up momentarily. It was the same shot, but it looked like Lee was moving off screen. His body was just a blur, but Cameron was in the background looking up from the table, a blush staining his pale cheeks and a sweet smile on his face as he looked at Lee.

ME: Fuck! They've got it bad!

SONNY&HICKS: Looks like. Gotta run! See you tonight?

ME: Wouldn't miss it! Can't wait to hear how everything went!

I sighed as I put my phone down. Something about those two photos just made me fucking delighted. I loved my brother and he deserved to be happy. I just hoped this Cameron guy felt the same. I got off the bed and settled in at my desk, powering up my laptop. I had been debating exactly what I should do with my afternoon of relative freedom and decided I really should work on my paper for Dr. Tate's class. I could figure out the rest of my day from there. I turned on some music and stared at the blank screen.

Dr. Tate had said to write about what I enjoyed about math. How did you put into words how formulas and numbers brought order to chaos? That they were reliable, dependable, unchanging. Two plus two *always* equaled four, no matter who was solving the problem. There were no grey areas, no ambiguity. It was, literally, black and white.

I began typing, trying to put my feelings into words. A little while later I heard a knock on my bedroom door and heard Bishop call my name. I looked up as the door opened inward. My brother stuck his head in the door but held his hand over his eyes.

"You aren't naked, are you?" He called out, his nose scrunched up in disdain.

"Not hardly," I laughed. He cautiously peered from between his fingers before dropping his hand.

"Oh good! Brain bleach is expensive!" he teased.

"Like I'd dare walk around this house like you do!" I said, grabbing a piece of paper from my desk, crumpling it and throwing it at him. He snagged the missile easily.

"You should be buying us all brain bleach after yesterday!" I exclaimed.

"Well, if you had a body like mine, you'd want to show it off, too!" he preened.

"Ass!" I laughed, closing the laptop.

"You coming downstairs for D&D? Lee should be here soon," he said.

I nodded. I had gotten so involved in my paper I'd lost all track of time. I had re-read some of what I had written and was pretty pleased with it. I certainly thought Dr. Tate would like it.

I stood and stretched, my muscles aching at the extended writing session. I rarely got so lost in my schoolwork, unless it involved photography. I loved bringing my photos into everything I did.

"Yeah, I'll be down in a minute. I just finished the rough draft for my paper for Dr. Tate's class," I told him.

"That was fast. You just started that today, right? I thought you sucked at differential equations?" he questioned, his honey brown eyes looking at me in confusion.

"I do. She let me write my paper on a different topic," I answered. I didn't really want to explain the topic to him. Bishop always seemed to see through everyone's bullshit. If I explained the topic to him, he might start questioning why I was struggling with choosing engineering as my major. Bishop paused, a divot appearing between his eyebrows.

"How did that come about, exactly? Isn't that... I don't know, kind of weird?" he asked.

"What do you mean?" I responded defensively.

"Well, the whole class is on differential equations," he said, raising an eyebrow. "How can she let you do a paper on a different topic? How does that show you've mastered the material?"

"She's the head of the department, I guess she can do whatever the hell she wants," I shrugged.

I followed Bishop out the door to the hallway where he paused at the top of the stairs.

"It just smacks of favoritism, bro," he said softly, his eyes searching my face in concern.

I felt an uncomfortable knot in my middle. I knew he was right, but it still kind of pissed me off he was calling me on it.

"I didn't *ask* her to do it!" I exclaimed, anger simmering in my chest.

"I know," he said placidly. "...because I know you. You make Clark Kent look like a hellion. Bet you didn't have to ask for anything... She just offered."

"Yeah, and?" I demanded. "What's that supposed to mean?"

He shrugged again. "Just... be careful, bro. Dr. Tate has a... a reputation."

"What the fuck is that supposed to mean?" I asked. Now he was really starting to piss me off. Natalie Tate was just being nice about my overwhelming schedule. Why did he have to turn it into something negative?

He held his hands up in defense. "Nothing, Kaine! I know you'd never do anything on the shady side," he said. "I just don't want you to get into any kind of trouble. Our moms would *kill* you if they ever felt you were taking advantage of their friendship."

I felt a little better when he said that. He was right, our moms *would* kill me if they thought I was imposing on Dr. Tate.

We made our way downstairs. Mama K and Mama D were already in the dining room clearing off the table for D&D. A fire had already been started in the hearth, and Mama D was getting the table set up.

"I'll get that, Mama," I said, reaching past Mama D to grab a pile of textbooks off the table.

"Such a sweet boy!" Mama D said, smiling at me as she headed to the kitchen to help Mama K. Her hair was pulled back into a long braid, the honey-gold color glinting under the light.

"Sweet, my ass!" Bishop yelled as he walked in from the kitchen, a box of D&D Player Manuals in his arms. "He's just trying to get in your good graces in the hopes you don't kill him tonight!"

We laughed and started setting the table with a dry erase mat and dice. I heard the front door open and had just turned to see which of my siblings arrive when I heard Lee call out in his best drill sergeant voice.

"Hey guys! This is Mason!" he yelled.

Silence fell for a moment as we all turned to look at him and his companion.

Cameron—Mason, apparently—was almost as tall as Lee, but a lot thinner. His skin was pale and seemed to get even more so under our scrutiny. His blue eyes were wary as he stood under the foyer light, and he looked like an animal that was about to bolt.

"Mason, huh?" Mama K walked out of the kitchen as we all stared at them. She was wearing an old Iron Man t-shirt, which showed the muscles in her arms to her advantage.

She walked over to him, wiping her hands on a kitchen towel. She looked him up and down, her eyes piercing.

"So, you're the comic book expert, right?" she asked, her voice still carrying a bit of a Spanish accent, even after all these years in Ohio.

I looked at Bishop and grinned. We knew what was coming.

"Graphic novel," Mason answered her automatically, like he'd been asked the question a lot. "...But, yeah."

I felt sorry for the poor kid. He looked kind of terrified. For someone who was famous, he certainly didn't seem very confident. He looked like he thought Mama K would chew him up, spit him out, and ask for seconds. Which, okay, maybe she could...

Mama K looked up at him and smiled that devious smile she had when she was up to something. Her hair was a dark brown, its curls barely restrained by the headband she wore. Mama K's family had been from Mexico, and though she'd been born in the United States,

Spanish had been her family's primary language, so her accent was strong, even now.

"Maybe you could answer a question for me then," she paused.

"Kyra, don't you drag that boy into this!" I heard Mama D call out from the kitchen.

Mom glared back over her shoulder at her partner.

"Hush, D! I'm just asking him for his *expert* opinion. I'm allowed to ask questions, right?" she said, turning the full force of her innocent smile on him.

"Um... Yes?" Mason answered, his voice ending on an up note, like he wasn't sure if it was a question or an answer.

"Good boy!" Mama K said, linking her arms through Mason's and smiling, walking him into the living room. "So, who do you think would win if a villain made them fight: Iron Man or Captain America?"

I heard Mama D sigh and saw her shake her head, her hair swaying back and forth as my other mother tried to drag yet another unsuspecting bystander into their longstanding feud over which of the Marvel badasses would win in a fight.

"Um, neither?" Mason ventured, carefully extricating his arm from my mother's under the guise of setting his backpack down next to the door. "I mean, think about it. As smart as Tony Stark is, he still has tons of flaws - alcohol addiction, women, etc. But his abilities with tech are almost magical."

Mason's eyes started shining as he began talking faster, obviously feeling more confident on a subject he felt comfortable with.

"Captain America, while all he has is the shield, can strategize way better than Tony can. So he can make use of all kinds of tools if needed to battle Tony, plus he's got lots of friends," he continued, "but the thing is, they wouldn't ever really fight each other..."

I went to interrupt, arguing with him. I mean, the *had* fought before. He held his finger up to stop me.

"...Not for long, at any rate," he continued. "They are both *really* smart guys. If anyone tried to get them to fight each other, they'd probably figure it out pretty quickly, and then work together to turn the tables on the villain who caused it in the first place."

The room when silent, and I saw Mama D smile as Mama K stood there, dumbstruck. Seeing my tiny, dark-haired mother without words for once was epic in and of itself. Mama D walked into the living room and smiled, her hand outstretched to shake Mason's.

"I'm Diana. Welcome to the Devereaux Den. I think you'll do just fine."

Shortly after Lee and Mason arrived, the twins had called.

I answered my phone and stepped away from the living room, which was entirely too noisy to carry on a conversation at that point.

"Hey, where are you guys?" I asked. The twins were already almost an hour late. D&D nights in the Devereaux household were sacrosanct. One did not just "run late" to D&D.

"We're at the apartment," Hicks said.

"Why the fuck aren't you here yet?" I asked. "Didn't you guys leave when Lee and Mason did?"

"Yeah, we did, but we had to hit the bank and make the deposit and we wanted to come home and shower before we came over..." Hicks' voice trailed off.

"What's wrong?" I asked.

"Sonny's asleep on the couch," he said, chuckling. "He took his shower first. When I came out, he was sound asleep. Now I can't wake him up."

My youngest brother was known in our family for his deathlike-sleep. If Sonny fell asleep, you might as well just wait until morning. He had slept through tornado warnings, drum playing, and even cold water being dumped on him.

I laughed.

"Better let him sleep it off, then. I'll let the 'rents know you aren't going to make it. From Lee's account, it sounds like things went really well today."

"Yeah," he answered. I could hear him walking into another room. Up until a few months ago the twins had lived upstairs, two doors down from me. They had decided that they wanted their own place, and since they had the money for it our parents had reluctantly agreed. I think it was rough for the moms to let their babies grow up.

They had privately shared the concern that the boys were taking on too much at once. First the apartment then the new store. Being a business owner was hard, and most businesses were touch and go for the first several years. We had wanted them to continue living at home so they would have one less bill for a while, but when they turned twenty-one, they had argued it was time for an apartment of their own. We'd moved them into their own place at the start of summer.

"Can you give the moms love for us?" he asked.

I agreed, wished him a good night, and hung up.

The evening flew by, and despite the fact that Mama D did, in fact, kill off the party, it was well worth it to watch the interactions between my uptight older brother and the famous graphic artist.

We finally called it a night and I dragged my body back upstairs. I was asleep before my head hit the pillow.

9

NICKI

IT WAS MY THIRD WEEK WORKING AS A SERVER AT THE WALLY WAFFLE. Tips weren't bad, and I was starting to recognize some of the repeat customers who came in every day. I'd been a server back in Florida, so the work was familiar. It wasn't very stressful, the menu was straightforward, and most of the customers were nice.

One cute senior couple, Jay and Joy, came in almost every morning for coffee and to watch the people roaming the Circle.

Tallmadge Circle was a historic area, and they would sit for hours watching people drive around it. The Circle was, literally, a circle of land that had an old church and former town hall that had been built back in the 1800s. It was frequently used for weddings during the summer months, and it had little walking paths traversing it. All I remembered about it from when I was a kid were the Christmas decorations the town put up during the holiday season.

It was a tiny bit of green space, and on its own wasn't anything special, it was the traffic around it that caused problems. There were at least eight streets that led on and off the Circle and navigating them all safely was a challenge.

Jay and Joy were adorable together as they watched people walk in and around the Circle. Jay had been an electrician at Goodyear, and

Joy had been a pharmacy tech. They had only met and married a few years back, but they were so in love with each other, it was delightful to watch.

Jay had kind of thrown me the first time I served them. I'd walked up and introduced myself. He looked up at me a twinkle in his faded blue eyes and asked "So, young man, do you mind who gets the check?"

I could tell I was walking into *something* because when I glanced at Joy, she was rolling her eyes at him, but still smiling affectionately.

"Um, no, sir. I don't mind who gets the check," I said.

"Great! Give it to the next guy that comes in the door then!" he quipped before the two burst into a fit of giggles. It took me a minute, but when it finally registered what he said, I couldn't hold back a bark of laughter.

It began one of the best relationships I'd managed to build since I'd started working at the restaurant. The couple came in daily, sometimes with one of their family, sometimes just them. They had both been married previously and had children who lived in the area.

That day, I had the late shift, which meant I was working from 7 a.m. to 3 p.m. and had been rushing around like a chicken with its head cut off. My trainer, Mary Beth, had called out sick, so we were shorthanded and there was still a lot of things I didn't know. Erika Carmichael, our Manager, was taking Mary Beth's place as hostess, but I wasn't exactly comfortable asking her a ton of questions.

Business had finally started to slow down and I had just cleared out a table of six middle school teachers who had stopped in for lunch. They were having one last hurrah before summer ended and were heading from here to the pool. As I'd bused the table, I saw Erika seat two men in my section. Shit. It was after three o'clock, and I groaned. I was used to being on my feet all day, but I still had my prep work to do before I could cash out. I couldn't really complain, though, I needed the money.

I saw Erika had gotten them their drinks, and given them their menus, so I finished busing the six top before heading over. As I put the last of the dishes in the bus tray, I saw the one man wad a napkin up and throw it at the other man. It flew right past his ear to land in the booth. Great. I knew who was going to have to clean *that* up. I figured if I went over to get their order in, I might be able to head off bigger messes.

As I walked up, I heard the one man tell the other, "Again, with the no thank you," he said, "…but if you keep bringing it up, I might just have to find you a blind date."

The man facing me was tall. Like, six two or taller. I couldn't tell for sure with him seated, but he looked all military-like. His hair was blond, long on top and short on the sides, like a grown-out buzz cut. He was handsome, in a bark-orders-at-you kind of way. Not really my type.

I couldn't really see the other guy's face, but I'd seen his body from where I'd been busing the table. He was almost as tall as his friend, but where his friend was all muscle-y, he was just… yum… My mouth had watered at the sight of his ass as he'd slid into the booth. His hair was cut similar to his friend, short on the sides, but a lot longer on top. It was brown with the coolest highlights to it. I had to force myself to look at my order pad as I walked up and hope like hell that the semi I had growing in my pants wasn't visible.

"I don't need a blind date," he said. "And you can tell the moms that I'm fine. Nothing a little sleep won't solve."

"I'm so sorry for the wait, guys, what can I get you?" I said in a rushed, slightly out of breath voice.

"Just coffee for me, please," the taller man said.

The other man was busy looking down at his menu.

"I think I'd like the…" he looked up at me, and time seemed to stop as eyes as familiar to me as my own caught on my face. His skin went from tan to a sickly shade of grey in less than a moment as he gasped.

"…*Nicki?*"

His voice was soft, almost reverent. I froze.

"*Kaine,*" I whispered finally, feeling a blush spread across my face.

His companion moved, and it finally got my brain functioning. He was obviously older than Kaine by quite a bit that meant this could only be…

"...Lee?" I asked, lifting an eyebrow in question. He stood, reaching his hand out to shake mine while Kaine remained frozen in his seat.

"Good to see you, man! How've you been?" Lee asked.

"Um, good, I guess?" I mumbled.

Though I was talking to Lee, my eyes kept flitting nervously to Kaine who still sat in the booth, dumbstruck.

"When did you get back in town?" Lee asked, as he sat back down, his worried glance hopping back and forth between Kaine and me. Kaine sat in the restaurant booth, still as a stone, his face pale as he stared at me in shock.

"Um, a while now," I said, nervously shifting from foot to foot. *Fuck!* This was so unfair of me. After seeing him the other day at the university, I'd at least had the chance to get used to the idea of running into Kaine or his family somewhere. This was like a bolt out of the blue for him.

I saw Erika glance our way curiously, so I struggled to get back on my server script.

"What... What can I get you guys?" I asked, looking around the restaurant nervously. I couldn't bring myself to lock eyes with Kaine again. I couldn't breathe when we did.

"Just coffee for me," Lee answered. "Kaine, what did you want?"

Kaine finally stirred when Lee said his name, his eyes dropping to his hands as they gripped the menu. His knuckles were white, and I saw the conscious effort he made to relax them and lay the menu down. *Shit*. This was not going well. I recognized the look on his face. He was about to run. They sat there for a few seconds.

"Kaine?" Lee asked again, softly.

"I... I'm sorry. I can't..." Kaine paused, taking a deep breath. "I can't do this."

He slid out of the booth suddenly and bolted for the door. Lee stood quickly and threw some cash on the table and ran out after his brother.

I whipped around and watched as Kaine tore across the asphalt toward the Circle. A low stone wall was all that separated the parking lot from the traffic on the Circle. His hands were buried in his hair, and I could see him fisting his hands to tug hard on the strands.

I ran to the door and was about to run out after them when Erika called me.

"Everything okay over there, Dominick?" she asked. *Shit.* I hated when people used my real name.

"Um, yeah, fine," I said, unable to tear my gaze away from where Lee raced out to where Kaine was pacing.

"Eat and run?" she asked, coming over to stand beside me. I shook my head quickly.

"No. Just... just someone I used to know."

I heard Lee call out to Kaine as I closed the door and stepped back inside. Erika went back to the hostess stand and began rolling silverware up in napkins.

I hesitated at the door for a moment as I watched Kaine and Lee talk. I saw Kaine shake his head at something Lee said. I couldn't hear what they were saying, but I could guess. Kaine looked...lost. Devastated. Angry.

Lee leaned in and wrapped his arms around his brother and pulled him close. I saw Kaine's chest heave as he started sobbing.

I wanted to do nothing more than run to them and comfort him, but just as my hand landed on the door handle, Erika called me. "Dominick? Shouldn't you be doing your prep work?"

I swallowed and looked from her to my ex and his brother. I saw them talking, Lee murmuring to him like he had when he'd been a kid and Kaine had experienced a nightmare. Kaine would often wake up crying, and the only two people who could calm him were Lee or me. At least he was in good hands.

I went into the back and grabbed the items I'd need to prep for the next crew and loaded them on to a tray. I debated for a moment what I should do, whether I should reach out to Kaine or not. I'd almost thought he'd be better off without me, but when I went back out to the hostess station something made me grab my order pad. I ripped off the top ticket and wrote a quick note on it and scrawled my new cell phone number on the back.

Kaine - Please give me the chance to explain what happened. It's not what you think. —Nicki.

I started loading the salt, pepper, sugar, jam and honey containers and ran back out front. I could see Kaine sitting on the low stone wall. Lee had walked up and was getting his keys out as he was standing next to a dark green Jeep Wrangler with an Autobots sticker on it. I looked around anxiously for Erika, but not seeing her, I stepped outside.

I walked up to where Lee stood.

"Is he okay?" I demanded as soon as we were in speaking distance.

"Not really," Lee said angrily. I could see the fury boiling in his eyes, and I knew I deserved every bit of it.

"I'm… I'm sorry," I whispered, my eyes fixed on Kaine where he sat on the retaining wall, facing away from the restaurant so he wouldn't have to see me. I wished I could have gone back in time, found another way to keep my mom safe. Found some way to let Kaine know that I had never stopped loving him.

"You should be," Lee said angrily.

I nodded. He was right. I still had to try, though. I thrust my hand out toward Lee and offered him the folded-up square of paper in it.

"I know… I know I don't deserve his forgiveness," I began, the paper trembling in my hand.

Lee's eyes jumped from my outstretched hand to my face, then back to my hand. Shit. Not my hand. My *wrist*. Where my uniform sleeve had ridden up, and the biohazard sign was there in all its scarlet glory.

His eyes flew to mine, widening in alarm. I grabbed the sleeve of my uniform and tugged it down in shame.

"Please don't tell him," I whispered. "I-I need to t-tell him myself."

Lee held my gaze, the note still extended to him.

"Do I need to make sure he's tested?" He asked angrily.

I jumped in shock.

"What? God, *no!* We never…" I stammered a moment before continuing. "We were just… kids. I wanted to… but he wanted to wait…"

I blushed and forced myself to stop. TMI much, Nicki?

"Please, just... just give him this," I asked, again thrusting the scrawled note toward him.

Lee held my stare for a minute before finally relenting and taking it from me. I went back inside the building just in time, as I saw Erika coming out of the back office. I finished my prep work at the front table and watched Lee drive his car over to pick up Kaine. As they drove away, I couldn't stop the tears, but I finished my work quickly so I could clock out and get the hell out of there.

I had been riding my bike for a good twenty minutes before I realized I had no idea where I was. The tears were slowly drying in the sunlight and I looked up and down the street trying to catch my bearings. After a minute or two I gave up and got out my cell. I pulled up the maps app, and realized I'd been riding in the opposite direction of our apartment. *Sigh.*

I was exhausted, and I knew there was no way I'd be able to make it home like this, so I reluctantly texted Viv.

NICKI: Hey babe, I need a favor... or twelve... or a million... or something...

VIVIAN: Sure thing, Baby Cakes! Need a ride?

NICKI: Is it too much like begging if I say, "Pretty please"?

VIVIAN: LOL Where are you? I'm OMW.

I gave Viv the address and waited. I started walking my bike in the direction I figured she would come from. After a few minutes I saw her new Civic pull up in front of me.

"Hey baby! Looking for a good time... Oh *shit!*" she exclaimed when she got a good look at my face. She slammed on the brakes and turned her emergency flashers on and jumped out of the car.

"What is it, Nicki? Did something happen?" she demanded, rushing over to wrap her arms around me.

"I— no, I, it's—" I started sobbing in earnest as I felt the warmth of her arms surround me. I really didn't know what I'd done to earn a friend like Vivian. I finally gasped, "...I saw Kaine."

"Oh, shit..." she murmured, glancing up and down the street. The road wasn't busy, but it also wasn't someplace she could leave her car indefinitely. "Okay, let's rack your bike, and we can go talk."

I sniffed and nodded. Vivian had insisted on purchasing a bike rack for her car. She'd claimed it was "Just in case...", which had become almost daily. Most days, Viv would let me bike to or from work, but almost never did she let me do both. I appreciated it, especially getting picked up at the end of a long shift.

We drove for a while in silence. After we pulled into our parking space at the apartment building, she turned off the car and turned around to look at me.

"Okay, Nicki, spill. Tell me what happened," she ordered.

I told her about Kaine and Lee coming into the restaurant, barely managing to hold it together as I did so. I even told her about seeing Kaine a few days prior at the university.

"I don't understand why you didn't tell him," she said, after I finally got it all out.

I'd never told Vivian about my deal with my father. I couldn't. I was too ashamed for participating in my own abuse. I didn't deserve the sympathy of her, or her family. I didn't deserve *anyone's* sympathy. I'd known what I was getting into with my dad, and it was my own fault for not doing anything to stop it. Or him.

I especially didn't deserve anything from Kaine, not after the way I had ended things with him. There were so many times that I could have told him about my dad, could have told him what was really going on, and I knew he would have moved heaven and earth to help me, but I hadn't. Why? Because I knew we didn't have a future together. I was going to die.

I had never told him I was positive, or that my mom had been as well. Hell, I didn't even know if he knew my parents had gotten divorced. Or that my mom was dead. I thought back to the times when we were younger and had wished his moms could have adopted me and choked back a feeling of guilt. My mom was dead now, and my father was dead to me. Being a part of the Devereaux family couldn't have been a more remote possibility.

As I thought about all the things Kaine didn't know about me, I remembered Lee's angry glare. I'd have to tell Kaine at least part of the truth. If I didn't do it, his brother would.

"I— I just couldn't, Viv," I said, swallowing back a sob. "Not after I…" I cleared my throat and continued. "…not after the way I broke up with him. And— and everything I said…"

"Oh, Nicki! Sweetie, I don't know what happened, exactly, but I can *guess* your dad was behind it," she said, her eyes catching mine. "He's a vindictive son of a bitch."

I sighed. I should have known she would figure it out on her own.

"It's just… so much time has passed. He's going to want to know why I didn't call. Why I didn't tell him…" I began.

"Makes sense," she said. "That's what I would want to know."

"…He doesn't know I'm positive," I whispered.

"Then you have to tell him," she said firmly.

"I can't! I can't— can't risk him. He'll want to know what happened, and why. He'll want to know why I didn't—*couldn't*—tell him," I said. "And God, what if he wants to try again? I can't risk his life!"

"Nicki, I'm going to tell you something, and I want you to know it is said with all manner of love in my heart," she began. "You are normally one of the bravest people I know. But lately, and especially right now, you're being a whiny bitch."

"Wait… *What?*" I exclaimed in shock, reeling at the attack from such an unexpected quarter.

"You are being a whiny bitch, and you need to knock it the fuck off. *Yes*, you won the lottery for worst father in the world, and for that I am so sorry! You've had a shitty life and it's even more shitty that you have this illness to deal with. It makes my heart ache just to think of everything you've gone through," she said, reaching out and grasping my hand tightly, forcing me to look into her eyes. "But that is in the past. It's over. *Done*. Your dad can't hurt you anymore. He doesn't know where you are. Your illness is treatable. You have a job. You have people who love you. You need to start living your life for *you*. Not for your mom. Not your dad. Not even for Kaine. *You*.

"In order to start doing that, you need to take a chance on Kaine. If he has half a brain and is a quarter of the man you've told me he is, he's going to want to try again, and you need to talk to him."

I looked into her eyes, so different from my mother's, but the words sounding like something Mom could have said.

"I'm afraid, Viv," I said finally.

"I know, baby," she answered. "You can't *be* brave without fear."

Resolve settled in my stomach. I had to tell Kaine the truth. The whole truth. If I didn't, someone else would.

"Viv," I said. "I need to use your car…"

KAINE

MONDAY MORNING FOUND ME TEACHING ANOTHER CLASS AT THE DOJO. Again, I hated myself for scheduling myself for early mornings, but I managed to power through it.

This class managed to pass without any drama, at least. I saw Mama K gesture for me to come see her as I was wrapping up. After I dismissed my students, I bowed out of the mats and headed to her office.

I stood at the door and knocked. Mama K was seated at her desk and Mama D was standing behind her, looking at something on her computer screen.

"You needed me, Moms?" I asked.

They both smiled and Mama K gestured towards the chair.

"Shut the door, please," Mama K said.

Uh oh. Mama K almost *never* closed the door to her office.

"Something wrong?" I asked as I took a seat.

"Not exactly," Mama D said, and sighed. "We're just... worried."

I remembered my conversation with Bishop the night before. Surely, he hadn't said anything to our parents?

"Worried? Why?" I asked.

"It's... Lee," Mama K said, and I almost laughed in relief.

"Lee? Why? He seemed to be doing pretty well last night..." I said, grinning. "He and Mason were getting along really well."

"That's exactly the problem, *mijo*. He *just* met this boy! And he's obviously smitten," Mama K said, shaking her head.

"Neither of them are boys, Kyra," Mama D said, laying a gentle hand on her partner's shoulder.

"I know, *mi querido*. It's just— I haven't seen him as happy as he was last night since before Mack died," she said. "I'm worried it's too fast."

I nodded. My brother had seemed different last night. Lighter, almost. *Definitely* happier.

"Mason seemed like a good guy," I said. "A little shy, maybe. The twins think the world of him."

"He seems to be a nice young man, but there is something... *broken*... about the boy," Mama D said, her moss-green eyes sad. I hadn't noticed anything unusual about Mason, other than he was a little quiet until you got him on a topic he was comfortable with. My parents had both worked with plenty of men and women who had been hurt or abused, though, so if Mama D had seen something there, it was there.

"Watching the two of them yesterday *was* adorable," Mama D said.

"Yeah, he really seemed to be enjoying Mason's 'company' last night," I said, waggling my eyebrows salaciously at them. "And I'm sure it's *just* a coincidence that Mason's hotel reservation was lost, and he has no other option than to stay at Lee's house way out in the woods? Sounds legit to me..."

They both laughed.

"Yes, well, none of you boys have ever been very good at hiding how you feel. You *all* wear your heart on your sleeve," Mama D teased.

"Kaine, would you feel comfortable talking to him? About Mason, we mean?" Mama K asked. "We just want to make sure he's not going to get hurt. He was devastated after Mack died."

I nodded and got out my phone. I scanned through my schedule for the day.

"I was supposed to work tonight, but Sammie gave me the week off," I said, looking at my calendar. I had scheduled myself for a nap after this class. "I could see if he wants to get together for a late lunch?"

"Oh, thank goodness! It's about time she cut back your hours!" Mama K exclaimed. "We were planning to have a talk with her this week. Working sixty hours there, part-time here, *and* school? It was *far* too much, *mijo!*"

"We were just trying to figure out how to cancel all your classes by 'accident'!" Mama D said, smiling gently and nodding towards the laptop. "You have been working yourself to the bone! Your mother and I were really beginning to worry about you."

"I— it's not— I mean, I haven't—" I stammered in surprise, trying to come up with some explanation for the hours I had been spending at The Belt. Mama D quelled me with a look.

"Please! We are your *parents*, Kaine. We know the difference between you coming home after a night of partying and a night of working," she said. Mama K just nodded in agreement.

I blushed. Of *course,* they knew. My parents seemed to know everything.

"I didn't want you to worry..." I said.

"We know, baby," Mama K said, reaching across the desk to take my hand in hers. "You have always been so independent. But you are working far too hard, at everything! We want you to take some time off too."

I was shaking my head before she was even finished with her sentence.

"I need to work, Mama," I said, insistently. I had my tuition bill coming due soon, and I refused to be one of those kids who graduated with a hundred thousand dollars in student loans.

"We know," Mama D said, holding her hand up to silence me. "— but that doesn't mean we can't help, Kaine."

"You are our son, *mijo,*" Mama K said, squeezing my hand tightly to get my attention. "Just as much as Bishop, Lee, or Weaver, or the twins. Each of you may not be our blood, but you *are* our children. It is a parent's prerogative to help, and you have been exceptionally difficult about us helping you. So we have resorted to being sneaky and devious."

Mama K grinned at me, then glanced at Mama D, who placed a crumpled piece of paper in front of me.

"What—?" I asked, picking up the paper and looking at it. The page was from a university bill that I had thrown at Bishop the previous night. There was a date stamp on the bottom, along with the words "Paid In Full" in red marker. Attached to the page was a computer printout that showed my account with the school, which also showed a healthy credit. They had paid for an entire year of school.

"What did you— You can't—" I stammered again.

"We can. We did." Mama K said, sitting back and grinning at me smugly.

I stared at my parents in amazement. I knew how my family was, and I had taken steps to prevent this kind of thing from happening. I'd hidden my account numbers and put passwords on my accounts. I didn't want to owe them more than I already did.

I felt tears welling up in my eyes. My family was not rich by any means, and I knew the amount of money they had spent on me was not easy to come up with. It was one of the reasons I had insisted on working and going to school part-time. I already owed my parents so much. Without them, I would have had a much tougher time of it growing up. They had loved me, supported me, and given me everything I ever needed.

"I'll— I'll figure out a way to pay you back," I insisted, tears choking my voice.

"Oh, baby boy! That's not the way family works!" Mama D insisted, coming around the desk to wrap me in a hug. "We're your parents! We love you! Being able to do things to help you is one of the joys of parenthood."

Mama K came around the desk as well and together they wrapped me in their embrace. I thanked the universe for having brought me to this wonderful family. I didn't know how I'd ever repay them, but I would figure out a way.

After more sniffles and hugs, the tears finally stopped.

"So you think you can meet with Lee today?" Mama D asked.

I nodded. "I'll text him a little bit later and see if we can get together."

I'd headed home after that, taken a shower and a nap. True to my word, I sent my older brother a message when I woke.

ME: Hey, slacker! Whatcha' up to?

LEE: Just dropping off some kids. Why?

ME: You want lunch?

LEE: Dude, it's 3 o'clock!

ME: So? I just got up. Be glad I didn't call it breakfast.

I could almost hear Lee's laughter on the other end. He didn't need to know that I'd been up and taught a class already.

LEE: I could do coffee, if nothing else.

ME: Swing by the 'rents?

LEE: See you in 10.

I wandered downstairs and decided to wait for Lee outside. I sat on the front steps leading up to the porch and just enjoyed the sunshine. I'd been so busy the last few weeks, I hadn't really had the chance to spend any time outside, other than walking to and from classes. Working nights at the bar meant I tended to sleep late, and by the time I got moving, I was generally too late for something to spend much time in the sun.

The crackle of the gravel under the Jeep's tires caught my attention and I couldn't help but smile at my older brother. Lee was behind the wheel of his Jeep, his blond hair just starting to grow long enough I figured it had to be driving him crazy. Ever since he had been in the military, he had kept it in the military "high and tight".

Lee and I had been close when we were growing up, but he'd decided to join the military when I was a sophomore in high school. Nicki and I had only just started dating when he went off to basic training and he had been deployed overseas by the time Nicki had left for Florida.

I grinned at him and ran around to the passenger's side, throwing open the door to the Jeep.

"Is this seat taken?" I asked, lowering my voice comically

"Are you on 'roids again?" he laughed, raising an eyebrow at me.

"Fuck no! You know I don't do that shit. This body is one-hundred percent *au naturel!*" I answered, smoothing my hands down my chest as if showing off a new car.

"Pity the same can't be said for your hair..." he snarked as he turned the car around.

"Hey!" I exclaimed in mock outrage. "No fair! Lay off the locks!"

"So where to?" he asked as we got to the end of the driveway.

"How about Wally Waffle?" I suggested. "They just opened their new place on Tallmadge Circle."

He groaned.

"You just want to get me killed on the Circle," he said. Tallmadge Circle was a historic area in a nearby suburb. Some places called them "roundabouts." It was a circular intersection that surround an area of green space that held the original town hall and church buildings.

There were at least eight streets that led on and off the Circle and navigating them all safely was a challenge. You took your life in your own hands when you drove there. It wasn't bad for people who knew the area and knew how to merge on and off it, but if someone was from outside the area, it usually caused problems.

"Dude, you have lived here your whole life," I said, shaking head at him. "How could you not know how to drive the Circle?"

"*I* know *how* to drive it," he said peevishly. "It's all the *other* idiots in the world who don't know how to drive it. Did you hear they have so many accidents there they've turned it into a 'no fault' area? You get in an accident there and the cops won't even ticket you."

"Is that what you and all your Uber driver friends talk about?" I teased. "What areas you can have an accident and not get in trouble for?"

"No, we sit around and talk about our asshole passengers," he said, eyeing me pointedly.

"Fucker," I said, laughing. "Good thing you're driving. Otherwise I might have to hurt you for that."

"As if you could," he snorted at me.

I looked at him and grinned.

"You really think you can take me, old man?" I taunted.

We were stopped at a red light and he'd slipped the car in park and held me in a headlock before I even saw him move.

"Uncle! *Uncle!*" I said, tapping the armrest in surrender.

He laughed, releasing me right before the light turned green.

"Guess you're buying lunch," He said.

"Joke's on you," I grumbled, embarrassed he had gotten the best of me. "I was planning to, anyway."

"Yeah, right..." he snorted. "I can't remember the last time you paid when we went out."

"That's different," I said, one hand running through my hair to fix the damage his shenanigans had caused. "I act as your wingman when we go out. Can't have our nation's veterans go too long without getting laid."

"I *so* don't need your help in that department," He growled, as we pulled up to the Circle.

"Really? Then when was the last time you got laid?" I asked, smirking at him.

"None of your goddamn business," he said as he turned off the roundabout.

"That long, huh?" I said, mock-pity in my voice. "Poor baby."

"Fuck you," he said, but without much conviction.

"Nah, even if I wasn't your brother, you're not my type," I teased, looking him up and down appraisingly. "Though you are in pretty good shape, for an old guy."

"Again, *fuck you,*" he growled as he parked the car.

I watched with concern as he got out of the car more slowly than normal, his gait uneven as he walked toward the restaurant doors. Lee's hip had been replaced following the ambush. I suspected he had stopped going to physical therapy, another item I intended to grill him over today.

There wasn't much business at this time of day, which was one of the reasons I had suggested it. They were primarily a breakfast place, so were at their busiest first thing in the morning. I absolutely loved their waffles and came to the restaurant a lot. Admittedly, I hadn't been in for a few weeks because of my work schedule, but it was one of my favorite places to eat. The hostess who seated us looked familiar, but the other waitstaff wasn't. She took our drink orders, gave us menus, then told us our server would be over shortly.

I studied my brother as he looked at the menu.

"So, how are you doing?" I asked. "For real, I mean."

"I'm fine," He said, his jaw stiffening. "How have you been doing?"

"Uh, uh. This talk isn't about me, it's about you," I said, gesturing at him.

"This 'talk'?" He asked. "Who said we were having a 'talk'?"

"Um, well..." I squirmed a little in my seat. I finally decided I needed to just come clean. "Mama D might or might not have asked me to get in touch with you today..."

"Uh oh," he said, and sighed. "What now?"

I looked at him from across the table. He looked tired, like he hadn't been sleeping. I knew from experience his nightmares were scary. One night he'd fallen asleep on the couch in the living room. I'd been coming home late from a shift at the bar and heard his pained moans and gone in to check on him.

He'd been tossing and turning, the blanket someone had tossed over him wrapped around his legs and body, twisted and tangled. He'd been moaning and calling for Mack and other members of his team who had died.

I'd tried calling his name, but he didn't respond. So I'd leaned over and touched his shoulder, thinking I could shake him awake. Big mistake. Before I'd known it, he flipped off the couch and pinned me to the floor. There had been no one home in his eyes as he wrapped his hands around my neck. His fingers were biting into my throat and cutting off my air supply. I'd struggled to unseat him, using every trick in the book to get him off me, but things had been going grey before I'd finally resorted to punching one of the areas that I knew he'd taken a gunshot wound. I hadn't wanted to really hurt him, but I also didn't want to die. He'd grunted and collapsed sideways, his personality slowly bleeding back into his face. He'd apologized, repeatedly, and never seemed to really accept that I understood. I had my own nightmares.

It had been right after that he had insisted he wanted to move into the house he and Mack had designed, but never gotten the chance to live in together. I felt that he had been worried he would hurt someone else in the family if he didn't.

"Mom's worried about you. She thinks you aren't sleeping..." I fibbed. It was true, from a certain point of view. I knew she *would* be worried about him not sleeping, if she knew. "...And she wanted me to ask you what's going on with this guy, Mason."

He glanced at me, and I saw it. A tell-tale blush started up his face. This was going to be fun!

"I don't know what you mean," he said, trying for nonchalance and failing miserably.

"I call bullshit," I said, looking into his eyes. "You know *exactly* what I mean. The whole fam saw the way you guys looked at each other last night. It was hot enough in that room to start a fire."

"Nothing is going on between me and Mason," he said again. "The twins screwed up his hotel room, so he's staying with me while he's in town. That's all."

"Oh, I see," I said, enjoying the opportunity of teasing my oldest sibling. "You just *happen* to meet this smart, funny, talented guy, not to mention rich, who also has an ass you could bounce quarters off and he, *coincidentally*, doesn't have anywhere to stay and *has* to sleep in your secluded cabin in the woods? Yep, sounds legit to me."

"Fuck you," he said and threw a wadded-up napkin at me.

"Again, with the no thank you," I said, "...but if you keep bringing it up, I might just have to find you a blind date."

"I don't need a blind date," he said. "And you can tell the moms that I'm fine. Nothing a little sleep won't solve."

I was debating whether to keep arguing with him when our server walked up from behind me. I pretended to read the menu while stealing glances at my brother's blushing face. Wait until I told Bishop…

"I'm so sorry for the wait, guys, what can I get you?" our server asked in a rushed, slightly out of breath voice.

"I think I'd like the…" I looked up at him, and everything froze. That face. I *knew* that face. I knew it like I knew my own heartbeat, which was currently pounding in my chest so hard I thought I was going to pass out.

"…*Nicki.*" I whispered.

The roaring sound that filled my head kept me from hearing anything after that. I stared at him, his red hair tousled, his blue eyes wide as he took in my face.

Dominic Rowen Terhune. The boy who had stolen my heart, promised he would always be there for me, then left me. Just like everyone left me.

We locked gazes and I saw his pale skin go practically white, before starting to turn a bright pink.

"Kaine," he whispered finally. That look seemed to last an eternity and a split second, all in one. I could have studied his face for hours.

He'd gotten taller, if the sight of him next to Lee was any comparison. Despite his growth, though, he looked like he had lost weight. He was wearing a long-sleeved shirt with the restaurant logo on it. His hair was longer than I remembered him ever having it, almost covering his ears. His dad had always made him cut it short whenever it got this long.

Lee kept sending me concerned looks as he talked to Nicki, but I couldn't bring myself to say anything. I could barely hear them talk over the roaring sound in my ears. Here he was, the man I had loved for years, in the flesh. He must have been back in the area for a while now, to be working here. He'd never called. Never written. Fuck, never even sent up a goddamn smoke signal to let me know he was back. As I sat there, I couldn't look away, but I couldn't respond, either. I was so… angry. Furious. It was all I could do to keep myself from throttling him right then, I was grasping the menu like it was a lifeline. Like the guardrail on that bridge. If I wasn't cautious, I was going to free fall into oblivion. There was no tiny kitten to save me this time.

I finally heard my brother speak.

"Kaine, what did you want?"

It was like saying my name had broken some kind of spell. The roaring stopped, but left a ringing in my ears that was almost as bad. I was not going to strangle him. He wasn't worth it.

I forced myself to relax my grip on the menu and set it down on the table. My grip had been so tight, my hands hurt. The pain was helpful, though. It let me focus on the here and now, and not the feelings I'd had for the last six years.

"Kaine?" Lee asked again, softly.

"I… I'm sorry. I can't…" I paused, taking a deep breath. "I can't do this."

Nausea ripped through me and I was suddenly glad we hadn't eaten yet. I slid out of the booth and bolted for the restaurant door.

I ran across the lot until I reached a low stone wall that separated the parking area from the Circle. I had just stepped up on it when I heard Lee calling my name. I froze. The wall was only a couple of feet high, but it reminded me too much of that night on the bridge. I paced back and forth across it until my brother got there. He climbed up next to me, reaching out to squeeze my shoulder gently.

"I take it you didn't know?" he asked.

I just shook my head numbly.

"Nope," I finally answered, my voice bitter even to my own ears. "Last I heard from him, his family was living in Tampa. About a month after he moved, h-he asked me to stop calling him. He said it would be… better… if we made a clean break."

"Fuck," Lee said. He wrapped his arms around me and tugged me close.

I couldn't move. All the strength, all the energy, all the will had suddenly fled my body. The pain in my chest hurt so bad, I couldn't see, I could barely even breathe. I took a breath, and it came out as a sob.

"He left me, Lee," I said, my voice muffled against his broad chest. "He left me. Like everyone leaves me."

The tears let loose, standing just outside of traffic, the breeze of each car's passing tugging at our clothes like errant children. I cried, heartbreak pulling at me. He'd left me, and even when he'd come back, I hadn't even been worth a phone call.

Lee held me until the sobs slowed, speaking into my ear a string of nonsense words and phrases he'd used to comfort me when I woke from my own nightmares as a kid, before the terrified compulsion I'd have to check on every member of our family to make sure they hadn't disappeared.

"It's okay, Kaine. We'll figure this out. It'll be okay," he said, but I didn't believe it. It was never going to be okay. I knew that.

After a while, I calmed, the emotional storm passing as I struggled to rebuild my shields.

"Um, suddenly, I'm not that hungry. Mind if we head home?" I asked, wiping my face uselessly with my hands.

"Sure thing, bro," he answered. "Stay here, I'll get the car."

Lee picked me up at the end of the parking lot and drove me home in silence. When he pulled the car up next to the house, I reached to open the door.

"Wait," he said, stopping me before I could jump out.

"Lee, I don't really think I can handle a lecture," I said, looking away from him.

"I'm not lecturing you," he answered. He dug around in his pocket for a moment before pulling out a crumpled restaurant check and held it out to me.

I raised an eyebrow at him.

"Really? The check?" I croaked.

I could almost see the word "asshole" in his eyes, but instead he said, "Nicki gave me this for you. I figured it should be your choice, if you read it or not."

I took the folded piece of paper out of his hand and stared at it for a minute, like a snake that was about to bite me. Which I knew was exactly what it was, something that would just bring me more pain. I felt like wadding it up and throwing it away, but instead shoved it into my pocket.

"Thanks," I whispered. Before he could say anything else, I was out the door and heading inside.

I ran upstairs to my room and paced back and forth. I hadn't spoken to Lee on the drive home, and the car had barely stopped before I was out and heading to the house. I'd been extremely rude to my older brother, and I knew it. I also knew he'd forgive me. He understood exactly what I was going through.

My hand searched out the crumpled paper from my pocket and stood staring at it. I remained like that for almost an hour, the green and white paper taunting me as I debated whether to read it or not.

I was terrified of what it would say. I just knew it was going to be a list of my shortcomings, details of all the ways I had fucked us up, and why I wasn't worthy to be with him. It had happened before.

The first boy who had ever asked me out had been Vinnie Avery. He'd been funny, gorgeous, and a member of the football and softball teams. He'd also been my first date, my first kiss, my first make out session. So it hadn't really been a surprise the morning at school when someone had passed me a note from him.

I'd opened it eagerly, expecting it to be plans for after school or that weekend. I'd been excited and horny and couldn't wait for the end of the class period to open it. I knew Mrs. Lawton was pretty strict, but I figured I would just glance at it really quick, then put it in my binder without her being the wiser.

Instead, I'd stared at the words for what seemed like hours.

Kaine -

I'm breaking up with you. Here's my reasons why. I generally only tell myself I need two, but for you I might run out of room!

1) You suck at making out.

2) You have shit brown hair that looks like a rat's nest.

3) You're fat.

4) You dress like an orphan. Oh wait! You aren't even an orphan - your parents just didn't want you anymore! Surprise surprise! Neither do I!

I can't believe I ever wasted my time on you.

- *Vinnie*

P.S. I want my Mortal Kombat game back. Eddie Garrett and I are having a sleepover this weekend.

I remembered hearing the tick of the second hand moving around the face of the clock at the front of the room. I felt like the sound had replaced my heartbeat, since I was sure my heart had broken as I'd read the note. My sight had blurred and my vision telescoped down until all I could see were the cold listing of my failings. He'd given me a note, just like my parents...

"...Devereaux? *Mr.* Devereaux!" I heard a sharp voice call me from the front of the room where our teacher sat at her desk looking at me. I jumped and the other kids snickered.

"Y-yes, ma'am?" I choked out, trying to shove the note into my binder.

She lowered her glasses and looked at me over the rim.

"Let me see it," she demanded.

I paled. Reading it myself was bad enough, but to have someone else read it... I found myself shaking my head no and her face grew red with anger.

She stood and walked over to my desk and took the note out of my hands. I trembled as she read it, then set it back down in front of me.

"Now stand and read it," she ordered. The kids around us started laughing. I shook my head, she couldn't mean...

"No, please..." I begged, which just made the kids around me laugh harder.

I glanced at Vinnie, desperate for help, but he just smirked at me.

"Now, Mr. Devereaux! Or do I need to call your... mothers..." she asked disdainfully. Again, the class snickered. Mrs. Lawton was very traditional and had never seemed to think well of my parents. I'd always tried to be a good student in her class, but that hadn't seemed to impress her much.

I felt vomit roiling at the back of my throat as I dragged myself to my feet. This was her normal punishment for passing notes in her class, but I didn't think even she could be so cruel as to make me read this detail of my failings.

I thought desperately for a moment about making something up, but my mind was blank. Besides, she had already read it and would know I was lying. I prayed to the Universe to let the ground open up and swallow me, but nothing happened.

"Please, Mrs. Lawton..." I began, but she interrupted me.

"Now!" She barked, and I jumped again, igniting more hilarity in the students around me.

"K-Kaine—" I began. My eyes swam with tears as I read the note aloud. The kids hooted and hollered as I read the part about me sucking at making out and heard a few whispered "Awww! Poor baby got his little rainbow heart broke..." and "Ooooh! Buuuurn!" as I read the other insults. When I'd finished, I'd dropped back into my seat, my head in my hands, trying desperately not to sob out loud.

The Universe finally seemed to take pity on me at that point, at least, because the bell sounded and all the kids had jumped up to head to their next classes, my humiliation forgotten for the moment.

I'd sat there for a few minutes trying to get myself together, anger and shame burning through me. Mrs. Lawton had returned to her desk and taken her seat. She'd looked up at me and smiled primly.

"Perhaps that should be a lesson to you. There is punishment for engaging in an... unnatural... lifestyle," she sniffed.

I'd looked up at her, my humiliation forgotten for a moment as angry tears spilled down my face. She sat primly at her desk, her hands clasped in front of her. I'd never felt hatred for a person before, but I felt it then.

I'd stared her straight in the face and said, "You. Heartless. *Bitch*."

The shocked look on her face was something I would cherish the rest of my life. She looked like a dead fish, her mouth gaping open, her stained dentures bouncing up and down.

She began yelling at me after a moment, saying she was giving me detention, that I should go to the Principal's office. I'd stood up and gathered my things, walked out of her room, out of the school, and straight home. I'd gone to my bedroom, and I didn't leave it for almost two weeks, and refused to speak to anyone.

The same room I was standing in right now.

I looked down and found I'd crumpled the note up in my hand, the knuckles of my clenched fist white. I took a deep breath and forced myself to relax and think through my fear and anger instead of letting it get the best of me. Go, therapy!

This was *Nicki* I was thinking of. *My* Nicki. The Nicki who had sat outside my door for days trying to get me to speak to him after Mrs. Lawton had humiliated me. The Nicki who had invented countless ways we could get even with Vinnie. The Nicki who had come out to his parents and the entire school for me. The Nicki who—

I stopped myself, crushing down the seed of hope that flared inside me. This was the Nicki who had lied to me. The Nicki who had cut off our relationship without warning, and without explanation. The Nicki who I'd grieved over for the last six years.

I glanced around the room, the urge to hurt myself or someone else overwhelming me. I needed to get out of here. I was not going to let him put me back in this room, or back into a psych ward. Fortunately, I had the evening off from, well, *everything*, so I had the time to clear my head.

I tied my running shoes and headed downstairs. My parents' seven-bedroom farmhouse was set back from the road, the gravel drive leading down to the street. We didn't have many close neighbors. I headed toward the street so I'd have a level path on which to run. As I made the turn, I saw my parents arriving home and I waved at them blindly before turning the corner. They beeped the horn at me in response and pulled into the garage.

I didn't stop. I knew now was not the time for me to have a heart-to-heart with them. I could do that later, after I had decided what to do about Nicki being back.

I wasn't sure how long I ran, but it was almost dark by the time I made it back to the house. I walked down the gravel drive to cool off and noticed a strange car parked in front of the garage. I saw Bishop's car sitting next to it, so I figured it must be a friend of his.

I walked inside without knocking. I mean, I lived there after all. Maybe I should get my own place, but with trying to pay for school, I didn't know how I could manage it, even with the help my parents gave me. I saw my parents sitting at the barstools at the counter that separated the kitchen from the dining room. I could see Bishop on one of the bar stools opposite them. The fourth stool was out of sight, but I figured that was for the best. I was sweaty and gross, and definitely in no shape for company.

"Hey guys!" I yelled, turning to head up the stairs. "I'm gonna go shower—"

"Kaine—" I heard Mama D call, then saw the fourth person walk around the corner from the kitchen.

"Kaine," he whispered.

Nicki.

Fuck.

11

NICKI

I REMEMBERED THE ROUTE TO HIS HOUSE ALL TOO WELL. ROUTE 76 TO Market Street, turn right on Prairie Drive. The street hadn't changed much since the last time I'd seen it.

I'd gone to say goodbye to Kaine the night before we headed to Florida. I'd been sick, of course, but I hadn't let it stop me from going to see him.

His parents had told me he was out on the roof of the garage when I arrived. The two-car garage had been added to their property after they had inherited the house from their folks. Because of the way the addition was completed, the bathroom on the second floor opened out onto the roof of the garage. Kaine and I had spent many nights hanging out on that roof. We used it as a makeshift patio, somewhere his younger brothers weren't allowed to go. We'd spend hours staring at the stars or, later, making out under the moon.

As I folded myself in half to squeeze through the window, I saw that Kaine had brought out our normal blanket and some pillows. The tiny grains of asphalt from the shingles were a literal pain in the ass, and the blanket made it more comfortable. Lit candles glittered across the rooftop and I stared in wonder at the display.

I knew he'd heard me step out onto the roof, but he stayed where he lay, his face to the sky and his back against the sun-warmed tiles.

"I can't believe this is really it," I said after a minute spent trying to memorize the picture he made. His hair hung back and away from his face, the soft, golden light of the sunset caressing his skin.

I stepped carefully around the candles as I walked across the tile to where he lay, setting my backpack down next to the blanket. The sun was almost set, the sky turning indigo as stars began to twinkle behind us.

"It's not," he said as I sat down next to him. "It, I mean. It's not the end. You promised, right?" he asked, his voice quavering slightly. I watched him glance at me out of the corner of his eyes.

I scooted down the angled roof, unable to take my eyes from his face, even to watch the gorgeous sunset. I'd be able to watch as many sunsets in Florida as I wanted. I wouldn't be able to see my best friend every day. I lay down next to him and he automatically held his arm out for me. I snuggled my head against his chest and sighed.

"It's not the end, I promise. Before you know it, I'll be all better, and we'll start planning our college escapades. The doctors in Florida are *way* smarter than the ones here. They'll run some tests, I'll take a pill and be back before summer," I reassured him.

We both knew I was making that shit up. At the rate I was going, I'd be lucky to *live* to graduate high school. I'd had pneumonia four times this year already, and I suspected I had it again. I'd been coughing like crazy the last few days and I was exhausted all the time. Mom had called me on it that night right before we left to come over and say good-bye. I'd been stifling a cough as I stopped to get a jacket from the hall closet when my Mom had called my name. It was still summer, but I was freezing.

"Sweetie, are you breathing okay? Your lips look kind of blue..." she asked, reaching out and tilting my head from side to side in the early summer evening. She laid her palm on my forehead in the time-tested method of temperature checking of mothers everywhere.

I wasn't about to give up my last chance to see Kaine for ages, so I'd convinced her it was just because I had eaten some blue colored ice pops a short time earlier. She gazed at me doubtfully, but she let me get away with it.

I had already seen some really good doctors in the area, but none of them had been able to figure out why my immune system didn't seem to be working right. This move was a last-ditch effort by my parents. There was a specialist in rare infectious diseases in Tampa, but Dad's insurance in Ohio wouldn't cover it. If he took the job in Florida, not only would the insurance cover me, it would be a hell of a lot closer to the specialist.

Kaine and I both knew that moving cross country was not an endeavor my family took lightly. It was highly unlikely that, even if they did figure out what was wrong with me, we'd ever move back to the area. Failing to find an answer, though, was not something any of us were ready to accept. Including me.

Kaine pulled me tighter to his side, and I snuck my arm under the small of his back.

"You'll keep sending me pictures, right?" I asked. "Tell me all the latest gossip. I don't want everyone to forget me."

Kaine's stormy green eyes looked at me somberly from a few inches away before he leaned forward and kissed my forehead.

"How could anyone forget you, Red?" he teased. I poked him in the ribs, making him jump and laugh.

"I hate that nickname, you know that, right?" I demanded.

"Why do you think I use it?" he teased.

"Bastard," I whispered, but my words were without heat. We sat and watched the last light fade from the sky. As the stars began to appear all over, I rolled to my side and looked at Kaine.

"You're really warm," he said, looking at me with concern. "I think you have a fever."

"I'm fine. I'm just— I'm afraid," I admitted finally, ignoring his comment. I'd had more fevers than I cared to count. Right then, I didn't give a shit.

He studied my face in the dying light, then nodded.

"I know," he said, turning on his side to look at me. "Me, too."

We were quiet for a while, staring at each other in the falling darkness.

"You, first," I said. "What's that preacher say? 'Name it and claim it'? Name your fears. What are you afraid of?"

The gathering darkness made Kaine's face seem pale, his bleached-blond hair brushing against my forehead.

"I don't think that means what you think it means. I think you're supposed to talk about the things you *want* to happen, not the things you don't..." he teased.

"Don't care. I'll start my own church someday if I have to, if nothing else than to counter all the bullshit out there," I said defiantly. "So fess up."

"For me, I think it's the obvious. Being... alone. Never seeing you again. Never getting to talk to you. Hug you. Never getting to—" he blushed and looked away a second before looking back at me. "Never getting to have sex with you."

I blushed then, too, suddenly thankful for the darkness. I would have been okay with us fooling around, but Kaine was so vigilant about my health! He had been super worried that anything we did might exacerbate my mysterious illness, or that he would do something to hurt me in some way. Bullshit, maybe, but I also think a major part of Kaine's reticence was that he was afraid I would leave him, just like his family had. Willingly, or not.

Despite his nonchalant façade, Kaine's fear of abandonment ran deep. After what happened with both his parents, his neighbor and with Vinnie, I didn't exactly blame him. Which was why I knew that, even if I *did* have to move away, I couldn't ever let him go. I had to make sure he understood that.

"I am, too," I said, rushing to reassure him. "I love you, and I'm— I'm terrified that I'll never see you again. Afraid that my parents will move us to the ass end of nowhere and I'll die far away from the only man I ever loved—" I stopped, realizing I had just used the "L" word for the first time. And twice in one sentence. *Fuck.* "Um...."

Kaine watched me in confusion as my stilted confession halted. Then I saw the slow realization of what I had said dawn on him. It was like someone had taken one of the candles that flickered on the roof around us and lit it inside his soul. When he smiled at me, the glow was blinding.

"Me, too. You—" he stammered. "I mean, I— I love you, too, Nicki."

We sat there on that roof, looking into each other's eyes, grinning like fools. Or lovesick sixteen-year-olds.

"I promise you, Kaine," I began. "I promise I will always be there for you. You won't ever be alone."

It was a promise I'd intended to keep, but when it came down to it, I hadn't been able to. I'd had to make the choice between my happiness, and my mother's. Of my life, the life Kaine and I might have had, and hers. I couldn't even claim that I'd do things differently, if given the chance. I would have done it again in a heartbeat.

The thought of that, more than almost anything, was what killed me about seeing Kaine again.

I stood at the Devereauxs' front door, trying desperately to make my hand knock or ring the doorbell. Something. My breath was coming in fast pants, and I think I was hyperventilating, because I started getting dizzy. I could feel the tears building up in my eyes, and I tried so hard to move.

I had to do something. I couldn't leave things the way they were with Kaine. I had to make sure he understood that I hadn't wanted to cut him out of my life, but it was the only choice I had.

I'd borrowed Viv's car and driven to the Devereaux Den. I stood outside their door for what seemed like forever. I realized I was at a crossroads. I could knock, go in, talk to Kaine and his family, or I could run away—leave him, for real this time. I realized then that while I hadn't really had a choice when my father was involved, I did now.

I rang the doorbell.

The door opened and in front of me stood Mama K. She stared up at me, her eyes calm as she took in my face. I realized with a start that I was taller than she was now. That hadn't been the case when I'd left for Florida.

"Mama K..." I said, then sniffed, trying desperately to keep from breaking down. "...Is Kaine—"

Before I could even get the words out of my mouth, I felt her arms wrapping around me.

"Oh, niño..." she said, those two words filled with such love and acceptance. I felt the strength in her arms, that hug so like my mother's hugs, and I lost it.

Next thing I knew I was in their kitchen, seated on one of the barstools they kept around the kitchen counter. Mama D was setting a mug of hot chocolate down in front of me. I'd always loved their hot chocolate. She did something more than just add cocoa to it, but she always refused to tell me her secret ingredient. Mama K was sitting across from me and Mama D joined her.

"Nicki, what happened, child?" Mama D asked gently.

I took a deep breath. I knew I'd have to tell them at least some of my story.

"You— you knew we moved to Florida, to find out what was wrong with me..." I began shakily. They both nodded.

"I... I'm HIV positive," I confessed.

"I've wondered if that might have been it," Mama D said, glancing at her partner.

"How...?" I asked, trying to wrap my brain around the idea that they might have guessed the diagnosis that I'd struggled to find for years.

"We have several friends who are, or were, HIV positive," Mama K said, before pausing for a drink from her water bottle. "It's not uncommon these days."

I nodded.

"You and Kaine—" Mama D began questioningly, but I cut her off.

"No, we never," I said. I had to let them know I had never endangered their son, though it might have been a close thing a time or two.

Mama K laid her hand on mine. "That is not what she was asking, nino. She was asking if you and Kaine had talked yet?"

"Oh," I said, my voice almost dropping to a whisper. "No. I was hoping he would be here this evening so we could talk."

"He is out running, but he should be back before too long," Mama D said. "Did your parents move back with you, Nicki?"

I shook my head emphatically. "Mom... Mom passed away last year, apparently. She and Dad had divorced, so I just found out about it a few weeks ago."

I saw surprise on their faces then.

"You stayed with you father?" Mama D asked.

I nodded again. "It... it's a long story." I said simply. I didn't think I could go into all this with them right now. They exchanged a glance. I focused back on the hot chocolate and took another sip.

I heard the side door slam, and footsteps coming up the stairs from the garage. My blood froze in my veins. I wasn't ready to face Kaine yet. I couldn't—

"Mamas? I got your nine one one? What's up—" I heard a voice yell as someone came through the door. I looked up from my hot chocolate to see Bishop Devereaux, Kaine's younger brother, standing in the doorway.

"Hey, Bishop," I said, swallowing nervously.

His face remained frozen for a moment, taking in the tableau the three of us made around the kitchen counter.

"Nicki?" He said, his voice slightly unsure.

"Would you like some coffee, *mijo?*" Mama K asked, standing and moving toward the cupboards.

"Nah, Mama, I need to put in some beans to roast for this week," he said, smiling at me. "Want to help?"

We all lent a hand as Bishop got fresh coffee beans out of the cupboard and set up his roaster. Before long, the sounds of coffee beans cracking, and the pungent smell of roast coffee filling the kitchen.

Working together with the three of them helped me refocus on the here and now. I excused myself for a few minutes to get cleaned up in the bathroom. When I walked back out, Bishop's parents had stepped out of the kitchen.

"Where'd your moms go?" I asked.

"Mama D wanted to show Mama K some video she'd seen today," Bishop shrugged. "I try not to ask too many questions with those two."

I chuckled. "Yeah, I remember the time I asked Mama K about the food assistance program at the middle school. It was called the After School Snack Program, or A.S.S.P. for short. She thought I asked her about eating *ass*, and I got way more information than I ever thought a lesbian would know about that kind of thing!"

Bishop snorted and we both laughed. I remembered his family had always been very open and frank about sex. He was scooping the roasted coffee beans out and letting them cool before grinding them.

"So, you've been doing okay?" He asked me. I looked into gorgeous brown eyes and nodded.

"I'm okay now," I said truthfully.

"I saw you the other day," he said, his eyes dropping to the countertop.

"What? Where?" I responded. "Why didn't you say something?"

Bishop stood and walked back over to where he had the beans cooling, stirring them unnecessarily.

"I saw you at Walmart. You were there with some girl with long brown hair," he said.

I nodded. "That was Vivian, my roommate. She and her family helped me move back here."

Bishop scooped some coffee beans into the grinder and turned it on, the grating noise annoyingly loud for a moment. Once it was done, he pulled the container of ground coffee out and sniffed it appreciatively.

"Why didn't you say anything?" I asked. "It's obvious you didn't tell Kaine. He was gobsmacked when I ran into him and Lee."

Bishop started the coffee maker running and sat back down.

"I... I didn't know what to say," he answered.

"That's a first!" I exclaimed, teasingly. "You are always the brother that knows the exactly right thing to say or do!"

"Not this time," he said quietly. "Nicki, I know you had your reasons for doing what you did. I figure they have at least *something* to do with the tattoos on your wrists."

I tugged the shirt down self-consciously. I wasn't ashamed of being HIV positive anymore. *I wasn't.* It wasn't my fault. I'd done nothing to "deserve" it. It was just a disease, but whenever I saw the tattoos, I still felt the harsh grip of my father's hands on my wrists, holding me down as the needle bit into my skin.

"I just... I want to make sure you're okay. And that Kaine will be, too," he said. I stared into his eyes, and for the briefest of moments I remembered the summer when Bishop, Kaine and I had gone hiking at the park. I'd been... *interested...* in Bishop, back then. He was gorgeous, smart, and always seemed to know so much more, be so much wiser than any other kid our age. I'd wondered, sometimes, if his class schedule had been different, if he hadn't started taking all the fine arts classes, if it might have been *him* I'd fallen in love with instead of Kaine.

"I'm okay, now," I insisted. "...and I want to make sure Kaine is, too. Even if he never wants to see me again, I at least want to make sure he knows I never wanted to leave him."

Bishop and I stared at each other a few minutes longer. He seemed to be searching my face for something, some reassurance or acknowledgment. I wasn't sure if he found what he was looking for, but after a few minutes he nodded at me.

"Okay, then," he said.

"Okay," I replied, holding my breath. For what, I wasn't sure.

The 'rents chose that moment to come back into the kitchen, laughing about the video they'd just watched.

We had just sat back down around the island counter, Bishop sipping on his first cup of coffee while the rest of us drank our bottles of water. Then we heard the front door open and the sound of footsteps in the foyer.

I didn't even remember standing, much less heading to the living room doorway. That's where I was when Kaine walked in the room. He was wearing a pair of track shorts and a sweat-soaked t-shirt that had a camera on the front. His shirt read "I can freeze time. What's *your* superpower?"

I drank in the sight of him, just enjoying for a moment the opportunity to take in the way he had changed over the years. He'd gotten taller, as expected. His short brown hair had blond highlights throughout and currently clung to his sweat-covered face. His eyes were the same dark green they had always been. He looked tired, though. Not just the "I-just-ran-a-marathon" tired, but like he hadn't been sleeping well for a long time. There were dark circles under his eyes and wrinkles on his forehead.

He was Kaine. *My* Kaine. Okay, well, maybe I didn't have the right to claim him, but we'd belonged to each other. I stared into his eyes for a long time, finally forcing a hoarse greeting out.

"Kaine." Smooth, Nicki. Real smooth.

12

KAINE

I stared into Nicki's eyes and noticed almost absently that they were red-rimmed and swollen. Apparently, I wasn't the only one affected by our meeting earlier today. Well, maybe that was being egotistical. He could have allergies.

"Hi…" he whispered hoarsely.

"Hey," I responded, trying to remember how to breathe.

Until today, I hadn't seen Nicki for almost six years. His skin was still pale, but not the sickly pallor it had been as a teen. Probably all that Florida sunshine.

Fuck.

"I need to take a shower," I said, turning tail and heading up the stairs.

"Kaine, wait!" I heard Bishop call after me, but I kept going.

I made it to my room and slammed the door behind me, resting my back against it. I slid to the floor, my elbows resting on my knees, my hands fisted in my hair.

What the fuck was I supposed to do?

I felt, more than heard, Bishop's feet pounding up the stairs behind me.

He knocked softly on the door.

"Go away," I said. Of course, no one in this family ever did what they were told. I heard the knob turn and felt the press of the door at my back.

"Kaine, let me in," he said quietly.

I sighed. I knew Bishop wasn't going to go away. He was stubborn like that, so I got to my feet and pulled the door open.

Bishop stood there and looked at me, his shaggy, dark-brown hair a halo around his head.

"You going to invite me in?" he asked, raising one eyebrow at me.

"What, are you a fucking vampire now?" I asked, stepping away from the door and throwing myself down on the bed. "You need an invitation?"

"No, but I do suck..." He said, waggling his eyebrows and grinning at me salaciously.

I threw a pillow at him, which he ducked easily.

Bishop, like the rest of my brothers, was gay. That was pretty much where the similarities ended. Bish was a little shorter than all the other Devereaux boys, but he was easily the match of any of us in the dojo. Being the shortest just meant that he'd had to be the best if he wanted respect. He moved with a cat-like grace that I envied. I had power, sure, and skill. The result of many hours of practice in the dojo. Bishop was a natural. Watching Bishop on the mats was like watching an Olympic-level skater or dancer. Pure magic.

He flopped down next to me on the bed and wrinkled his nose as he watched the blades of the ceiling fan rotate.

"You stink," he commented.

"It's called sweat. I was *running*," I responded. "Hence, the whole 'I need a shower' comment."

Silence fell for a moment, then he turned and looked at me, his golden-brown eyes searching my face.

"You want me to tell him to go away?" he asked after a while.

My eyes burned and I sighed, trying to figure out what the hell I wanted to do.

"I don't know," I finally admitted.

"Talk to me," he demanded.

I sighed again. Dammit, at this rate, I was going to hyperventilate.

"You know what happened between us, Bish. He promised he'd keep in touch, and he wasn't gone two months before he cut off all contact. He promised *not* to leave me, but he did anyway. Just like everyone else in my life leaves me. End of story," I said angrily.

"Hmm. I wouldn't say *every*one," he said gently nudging me with his shoulder. I broke his gaze and sighed. Goddammit, I had to stop sighing like a fucking teenager over Edward Cullen. Fucking sparkly vampires.

"You really think there's nothing more to his story?" he asked as he studied the ceiling of my room.

I sat up.

"What do you mean?" I asked.

"Think about it, *Special K*," he drawled. I rolled my eyes at the nickname. Bishop had called me Special K since we were kids. He'd dubbed me partly because of the spelling of my name and partly because it had been my favorite cereal growing up.

"You know Nicki. *I* know Nicki. The three of us were best buds for years, even before he came out. Do you *really* think he would have stayed away from you all this time if he had a choice?" my brother asked, continuing to look around my room.

I took a deep breath and considered his words. It was *not* a sigh, goddammit!

Bishop *did* know Nicki almost as well as I did. We had been the three musketeers. We had done *everything* together, up until our sophomore year. It was the end of our freshman year that Vinnie Avery had dumped me, and Nicki had come out in front of the whole school to ask me to prom.

Bishop had helped him plan it.

We'd been dating for a few weeks, but we'd kept it kind of on the down-low. No one knew that Nicki was gay, and since we always spent time together anyway, we really didn't have to change our behavior.

It was prom season, and all week, people had been coming up with creative, hilarious methods of asking their crush out. Over the lunch periods, the school PA system would be co-opted to play music, make announcements, and do the occasional prom invite. The PA system was run out of a little glass booth in the cafeteria. One door opened into the cafeteria, the other opened into the office area.

We always listened with rapt attention to those invites. Even the teachers seemed to enjoy the show put on by some of the funniest and most talented students as they would ask their crush to the dance. And of course, everyone was on pins and needles to find out if the person would say yes.

It was the Friday before prom, and Nicki and I hadn't made plans to go. I shrugged it off. I mean, it was just a stupid dance after all. Nicki wasn't out to the school, so I hadn't wanted to make a big deal of it.

Prom invites were the last item of the lunch hour, and the DJ would always make a big production, teasing out who the big invite of the day would be.

That day, there were more than the normal number of prom invites, since it was the last chance anyone would have to extend an invitation. Nicki had excused himself to go to the restroom after he ate, and I was finishing my lunch when the announcements started. I was listening just like everyone else around us, only to realize the normal DJ had been replaced by Vinnie Avery. I'd felt the blood drain from my face. I was putting on a good act at school, but Vinnie was still able to hit me where it hurt.

"Hey there, Akron High School! This is Vinnie Avery with your invite *du jour* for prom! We all know this is the last chance for all those wallflowers out there to have any kind of social life this year! So hold onto your hats as we begin the Loser's Awards for Worst Possible Date for the Prom!"

A lot of kids tittered and laughed. I glanced around and realized there weren't any adults in sight in the lunchroom. Of *course*, Vinnie would take this one chance to humiliate people even more. I ducked my head, just wishing that the moment was over and we could go back to important things. Like comic books.

"We all know *this* Loser who shared how gross he is with the whole ninth grade history class!" It felt like my stomach dropped to my feet. Oh no, *please*, not again. But Vinnie began re-reading the note he had sent me, listing off all my negative traits.

"So—the winner for Worst Possible Date for the Prom goes to—" There was a piercing squeal and I saw my brother, Bishop, standing next to the PA booth.

"Oops! Did I do that?" He asked, smiling around the cafeteria innocently, the power plug to the PA system in his hand.

I saw Vinnie standing inside the glass booth, and I could distantly hear him yelling at Bishop while yanking at the door that, coincidentally, seemed to be stuck shut...

Then I heard the sound of the piano playing from the corner of the lunchroom. Some seniors from the arts and drama group walking down the main aisle of the lunchroom, grouped around someone in the middle, hiding them from sight as they began humming. They were humming a tune, and I realized after a moment it was a popular love song, but with a twist... We all watched with rapt attention as they completed some choreographed moves, just as they got to the chorus the singers spread out and we were able to see the person in the middle.

"...cause you're amazing... just the way you are."

I froze in my seat, chocolate milk clutched in my hand, as I realized the singer in the middle of them, dressed in a tux and holding a bouquet of red roses, was Nicki.

My Nicki.

I had been dumbstruck. I literally couldn't think, or move, or say anything as the group had finished their song, and Nicki had knelt down in front of me.

"Kaine Devereaux, you *are* amazing, just the way you are. Would you go to prom with me?"

All I could do was nod frantically, and then he was kissing me. The cafeteria erupted into cheers and catcalls. I felt like I was in an eighties rom com.

I'd found out later that Nicki had overheard Vinnie and his friends talking about his plans to humiliate me in front of the whole school.

Nicki had some friends in the choir group and they had concocted the whole plan with Bishop's help.

The three of us had been inseparable before Vinnie had come along, and we'd expected to have the same friendships again our sophomore year, even planning out our schedules so we could all three maximize our school time together. Then Bishop had started dating a senior and made the last-minute decision to switch to taking more fine arts classes. That had left Nicki and I together.

"Well?" he demanded.

I grumbled. Bishop was good at making me admit hard truths, whether I wanted to, or not.

"I don't know!" I lied. He glared at me until I huffed. "Okay, fine! The Nicki we knew wouldn't have. At least, I didn't think he would. But he still *did*!"

I stood abruptly and started pacing. I could feel my anxiety ratcheting up, my heart racing, my breathing coming in angry pants. *Fuck!*

"I can't let him do it again, Bishop! I can't! I've fought too long, too hard to get over him to go through it all again!" I said emphatically. "I can't let him hurt me again. I'm *over* him!"

Bishop looked up at me calmly. I really hated when he pulled this Zen "nothing-you-can-say-will-rattle-me" crap.

"*Are* you?" he asked.

"Am I *what*?!" I exclaimed as I continued pacing. I really wanted to punch something right now.

"Over him?" he asked.

I froze in my tracks and just stared at my brother. *What?* Of *course*, I was over him! It had been almost six years!

"What are the symptoms of abandonment issues, Kaine?" he asked.

"Oh *fuck*, don't make me go through this right now..." I whined and rolled my eyes.

He raised an eyebrow at me expectantly.

"Fine! Clinging to bad relationships. Cycling through multiple relationships. Sabotaging relationships," I rattled off. "Avoiding intimacy, feeling unworthy and difficulty trusting."

"When was the last time you went out with someone?" he asked.

"Luke Stephens," I said quickly.

"When?" He demanded relentlessly.

"I don't know... a month or two ago? We went to that new action movie," I said, fumbling to recall. Things had been a little crazy lately, and I didn't have a lot of time to date. How was this even relevant? I dated.

"That was almost eight months ago, bro," Bishop said softly.

"No way! That was..." I stammered, trying to recall when I'd taken Luke out.

"...that was in December, right before Christmas," Bishop finished for me. "Your car got stuck in the snowdrift and Lee had to come pull you out with his Jeep. And you ended it because, and I quote, 'Luke deserved someone who could be a better boyfriend'."

"Well, he did!" I exclaimed. "He was awesome! Smart, good looking, funny... he volunteered at animal rescues, for God's sakes! He'd started growing a purple horn out of his head and farting rainbows... He deserved someone who could be a better boyfriend than I was."

Bishop looked at me and said, "Why couldn't that have been you?"

"I— I didn't have the time—he deserved better than—" I began, but Bishop interrupted me.

"When was the last time you had a relationship that lasted more than three dates?" he asked.

I paused, trying to remember.

"When was the last time you had a 'relationship' that consisted of anything more than getting off with someone at The Belt?" he demanded inexorably.

"...Fuck you," I said without heat after several long moments of thought. I dropped down into the chair next to my desk, my heart rate slowing as we spoke. He was right.

"No, thanks. Even if you weren't my bro, you're not my type," he snarked. I looked for something else to throw at him, but nothing replaceable was in reach, dammit.

"...So, what do I do?" I asked, digging my nails into my scalp.

Bishop got to his feet in one smooth movement, showing off that catlike grace I envied.

"That, my brother, is up to you. Personally? I need coffee," he said.

He held his hand out to me, and I eyed it warily for a moment before grasping it. He pulled me to my feet and wrapped his arms around me in a tight hug.

"Just remember, Kaine, you aren't alone. *Ever*. No matter what happens with Nicki, or anyone else for that matter, you've got the fam. We are *all* here for you," he said. "And any man you end up giving your heart to better be fucking worthy of *you*, not the other way around."

I hugged him tightly and nodded.

I took a few minutes to shower and change my clothes, then headed downstairs. My parents had disappeared, probably to the basement where we had a separate entertainment area, or to their rooms, I wasn't sure. I glanced at the clock and noted it was after ten p.m. They had most likely called it a night.

Bishop and Nicki were seated at the bar stools around the kitchen counter. Nicki had a bottle of water in front of him and Bishop looked like he had just made a fresh pot of coffee, the first cup steaming in front of him.

I swear, my brother could drink coffee any time of the day or night without it affecting his sleep patterns. I think he had some method of transubstantiating the caffeine out of his blood. He was super particular about his coffee, too. He went to some fancy beanery downtown and bought the beans fresh. He even roasted and ground them at home. He was a coffee *aficionado*.

I grabbed myself a bottle of water from the fridge, put a flavoring packet in it and walked to the seat opposite Nicki. Bishop was seated between us, and the silence grew loud.

Nicki looked nervous, his eyes glancing from me to Bishop and back to me again. I bought myself time by taking a long gulp from my bottle of water as I looked at him.

His dark-red hair was a messy mop, just the way I'd always loved it. He looked like he was a little overdue for a haircut, the ends a little ragged and uneven. His dad had always made him keep his hair short, but I loved it like this.

He was thin. Too thin, maybe. He was wearing a long-sleeved Sinner's Gin band shirt that looked new, and a pair of jeans that looked like they'd been painted on. That was a new look for Nicki. In high school he had tended to wear khaki's and polos, though I thought that was more his parents' style than his own. Maybe he'd had the opportunity to begin making his own decisions. I had to admit I liked it.

"Hey," I said eloquently, finally breaking the silence as I set the water bottle down on the counter and took a seat.

"Hey," he answered back. His dark-green eyes raking my body, taking in everything about me in one glance.

"Three heys! Now all we need are some horses," Bishop snarked sarcastically, taking a sip of his coffee and making a face. Bishop's tone was unusually sharp, more biting than was normal for my brother. Something had seemed to be bothering him the last few days, but I didn't know what.

His tone had Nicki and I both glaring at him, which Bishop completely ignored.

"How long have you been back?" Bishop prompted Nicki.

"A few weeks," Nicki answered. He swallowed nervously, looking back and forth between us.

"Did your parents come back, too?" I asked.

"Um... no," Nicki answered, his face seeming to pale. "...My-my mom passed away. My dad's still in Florida... I think."

"I'm sorry," I said, a pang striking me in the chest. I knew how close Nicki and his mom had been. The way he spoke made me think something must have happened with his dad, but I wasn't really surprised. Nicki's relationship with his father had always been challenging. His dad wanted a son who was into sports or business or whatever. Pretty much, he wanted a son who was the exact opposite of Nicki. At least, he had six years ago. Who knew how much had changed? Nicki's mom had always played mediator between them. She was the grease that kept them from clashing too much. With her gone, I'm sure the sparks would have flown.

"...Thanks..." he whispered, looking down at the water bottle in front of him. The bottle was three-quarters empty, and he'd started peeling the label off, a habit that he'd begun in middle school.

"...How—" I began, but Nicki interrupted.

"I'd rather not—"

"Okay," I said, running my fingers through my hair. I looked at Bishop in desperation. Talking to Nicki was his idea, he could figure out how to salvage this.

"Well, I don't think there's any way this could *be* more awkward," my brother volunteered, taking a large drink from his coffee and capturing Nicki's nervous gaze in his own. "...and I care about both of you, so if neither of you are going to really start talking, I will. Since neither of you has the guts to speak up."

I glared at him again, but he completely ignored me. Bishop turned to Nicki and said, "Nicki, Kaine still loves you and hasn't managed to have any real relationships since you've been gone except some random hookups in clubs. So, if you still love him or want to give this relationship thing a try, you better have one hell of a good reason for ditching him when you went to Florida, because you fucked him up. If you don't kiss and make up, I'll have to kick your ass for hurting him."

We both stared in shock as Bishop continued his rant.

"Kaine, you need to give Nicki a chance to explain. That's what friends do when friends screw up, much less people who claim to fucking love each other. They give them the chance to explain, apologize, and make amends. So shut the fuck up and *listen* to him, or I'll kick *your* ass for hurting *him.*"

Bishop made a face at his coffee cup, and said, "Damn it, I think I burned my coffee beans."

He stood, dumped the rest of the coffee in the kitchen sink, then turned his back on the both of us and headed into the living room and upstairs.

Nicki and I looked at each other, shell-shocked by Bishop's rant and abrupt departure. We stared at each other for a long moment, the tension thick between us. Then our eyes caught, and I'm not sure which of us snickered first, but in seconds Nicki and I were both doubled over, howling in laughter, tears leaking from the corners of our eyes.

We were just starting to recover when I heard Mama K shut the door to her bedroom, but not before saying something about her "niños locos," and that set us off on another round of the giggles.

"Oh my god," I groaned, wiping the tears from the corners of my eyes. I grabbed a couple of paper towels from the holder and handed some to Nicki. He reached out to grab them from me, sniffing as he did so.

My gaze snagged on the inside of his left wrist as he reached toward me and I froze, leaving his hand outstretched. Tattooed on his left wrist was a red circle with a plus sign inside of it.

13

NICKI

SHIT.

Kaine's hand flashed out, grabbing my wrist and pulling me towards him. I'd forgotten how fast the fucker was.

His eyes widened and his gaze flew from my wrist to my face. His thumb traced my tattoo gently. His touch felt so nice against my skin that, despite the situation I reveled in the feel of him after so long.

"...When?" He asked, his expression bleak. I took a deep breath.

"They think I've had it all my life," I said. Slowly pulling my hand back from him, despite my reluctance to lose the contact.

"That's— that's what's been wrong all this time? You have AIDS?" he asked, his voice cracking as his normally-tan face turned pale.

"No, not AIDs. I'm HIV positive, but my viral load is undetectable right now," I said. It felt strange talking to him about my disease. I'd never really discussed this with anyone except Viv and her family before and the conversation felt awkward. Dr. Dunwoody was a physician, at least. I wasn't sure how much information to share with someone who wasn't a medical professional.

I watched Kaine's jaw clench and unclench as he processed my words.

"I'm sorry to hear that," He muttered, finally releasing my wrist. "Not about it being undetectable but about you having it at all."

"Thanks," I mumbled, breaking eye contact.

"So, you got it from your... mom?" he asked.

"That's what the doctors think," I responded.

"Is that how she..." he paused, realizing I think, that I might not want to talk about it.

"I don't know for sure," I interrupted. "I haven't talked to the lawyers yet, but I assume so."

He stared at my hands for a while, and I began to get uncomfortable. I knew he wanted, no needed, answers, but getting them past my lips was something else.

"Lawyers? Why— How—" he started, then stopped. Some thought seemed to occur to him, and he withdrew from me. I could almost see him pull back into himself, the brief connection we'd felt over Bishop's abrupt departure evaporating like it had never been. "No, it's none of my business. I don't need to know."

When I looked at him, the gulf between us seemed a mile wide, his formerly glittering eyes going dead and dull, the pain I saw there making it hard for me to breathe. It was worse than the pain I'd seen on his face earlier. Worse than anger. He just... didn't care.

"Kaine—" I began, unable to bear that emptiness but he held up a hand, stopping me.

"Nicki, I appreciate that you came here. I know it couldn't have been easy, after all these years," he said. "But I can't do this. I can't play a polite game of twenty questions. I'm glad you are okay, really. I'm sorry about your diagnosis. I just have to know... why?"

His voice cracked on the final word, and I nodded, looking away. I got it. I couldn't blame him, really. My excuses rang hollow, even to my own ears. At some point in the last six years I could have tried to get word to him. I could have reached out for help or advice or just to tell him what had really happened, but I'd chosen not to. I was a coward. I knew that if I told him about my dad, he'd get himself, or his parents involved, and that would threaten my mom's safety. I'd chosen my mom over our future together. I had loved Kaine, but I didn't blame him at all for not trusting me now.

I stood, putting my empty bottle of water in the recycling bin, which was in the same spot it always was. I turned and faced him.

"I had to see you. I couldn't leave things the way they were between us. I just— I just wanted to say... I'm sorry, Kaine." I said, struggling to control my emotions. "I know I really screwed things up between us, and I can never fix that, or make amends. But, for reasons too long and involved to go into right now, I couldn't— *couldn't* make a different decision."

His head was down, staring at his drink, pain and emptiness etched into his face. I had put him through enough, hadn't I? Six years was long enough. I'd come here tonight in a selfish attempt to make amends. Selfish because I had done it for me, to clear my conscience, without thinking what it would do to Kaine.

"I'm sorry," I said, then headed toward the living room. I knew the way out. I'd walked about half the distance to the front door when I heard him behind me.

"That's it?" He demanded in question, astonishment apparent in his voice. I turned around to look at him. I knew there were tears glittering in my eyes, but I didn't make any move to dash them away.

"What's it?" I asked tiredly.

"You waltz back in here after six years— six *fucking* years, Nicki— and you tell me it's 'too long and involved' to explain? That you *couldn't* make a different decision? What the *fuck* is wrong with you?" he demanded.

Kaine was standing now, his hands gripping the back of his chair, knuckles white. I froze. I didn't think Kaine would ever willingly hurt me, but I'd thought the same about my dad at one time, too. The signs of his anger were there, and I was all too familiar with rage.

"You left, Nicki. You *left*! You *swore* you wouldn't let the distance separate us. You swore you'd be there," he yelled, tears spilling over his cheeks. The eyes that had looked so dead a moment ago now sparked fire. "I almost jumped off a fucking bridge, Nicki! I almost killed myself because you couldn't keep your word."

His words hit me like a blow to the chest. Kaine had been *suicidal?* When? *How...?* But of course, I couldn't ask. I had no right. None at all. I had been the *cause* of his pain. I had no right to pry. He was crying so hard now, it was hard to even make out what he was saying, but I would *always* understand Kaine. *Always.*

"You should have just told me you couldn't do it, couldn't handle a long-distance relationship. It would have been easier. But you told me that I could count on you. Even though we'd be apart, you'd never leave me. That we'd be together forever. You promised. You *promised!*" His last words were almost sobs, and they broke my heart.

I *had* promised. I'd also been a kid, faced with an impossible choice, and I had no idea what kind of evil could be hiding in even the closest of families.

"I know, Kaine. I'm sorry I couldn't be there for you. I'm sorry I broke my promise," I whispered. "We can't— we can't always do what *we* want. I wanted to be here with you, *for* you, but I— he—"

Movement out of the corner of my eyes made me stop as I was about to share my shameful secret. The yelling had brought Mama D and Mama K to their bedroom doorway and Bishop was standing at the top of the stairs. They watched us silently, their eyes accusing me, and rightly so. Kaine's pain was a result of my mistakes, my choices.

"This was a mistake," I whispered. "I'm sorry."

I fled the Devereaux household like all the hounds of hell were after me. I drove back to our apartment and felt lucky that there wasn't much traffic at that time of night. When I got home, Vivian was asleep already, for which I was forever grateful. She had looked so hopeful when I had left for the Devereaux's, I didn't want to explain to her how badly the day had gone. I was able to crawl into my bed and pull the covers over my head and try and block out the world for a while.

Sleep came reluctantly, but I did sleep. At least some. My alarm went off all too early, though. I had the breakfast shift that morning, and I wasn't looking forward to it. Vivian needed her car that day since she had to drive up to Cleveland for a class and needed to leave before I even got up. I dragged my sorry butt onto my bike and made my way to the restaurant.

The shift passed relatively quickly. Everyone seemed crabby today for some reason. I'm sure it had nothing to do with my own mood... It was hot and muggy out, again. Jay and Joy didn't come in and my tips were depressingly low. I was grateful for a while that I didn't have a car, because on days like this, I didn't think I'd make enough to cover gas money.

It was almost 4 p.m. when I wrapped up and cashed out. We'd had another call off, so I had stayed later than expected. I was appreciating the mindless work, because I hadn't had to think about what had happened with Kaine the night before.

I walked out back to where I chained my bike, only to find someone sitting on it.

Bishop had his back to me, a pair of sunglasses covering his eyes and his hair tucked up into an Indians baseball cap.

Shit. I did not need this.

"Please get off my bike, Bishop," I asked, tiredly.

He didn't turn to look at me right away, just sat staring off into space for a while longer.

"My brother is an idiot," he said finally, dismounting and turning to look at me. His sunglasses were the opaque kind, with round lenses that made me think of John Lennon.

"That's a pretty broad range to choose from," I sighed. "Can you narrow my choices down for me a little?"

He laughed.

"I think you know which one I mean. Let's get some pizza," he insisted. "I'm starving."

So that's how we found ourselves in Mogadore at a tiny Italian place looking at menus. The restaurant was new to me. When I'd lived here before, it had been a salvage place, but Bishop told me that store had burned down. Instead of demolishing it, the owners had saved what they could and turned it into a restaurant.

I like the place. It had a casual feel, but had a nice area upstairs that had some beautiful stained-glass work over the bar.

"What's good?" I asked as I glanced at the menu.

"Everything I've had here has been good," Bishop answered. "The pizza is awesome though."

"You know I'm a sucker for good pizza," I said smiling.

Bishop smiled briefly, too, but he seemed to be... nervous? He kept glancing around the room, as if he were watching for something. Or someone. *Shit*, tell me he didn't—

Just then I heard Kaine's voice rising above the din of the restaurant and I froze in my seat.

"Bish! I've been looking all over for you, man—" he started. I could almost feel the moment he realized I was seated in the booth.

"Fuck, Bishop—" Kaine said, turning to walk out the door.

"How you going to get home?" Bishop called.

I saw Kaine freeze at the doorway. He halted, then dropped his head back in defeat. He turned around and came back to the booth.

He stood for a moment glaring down at us.

"I could just call an Uber. I'm sure Lee would *love* to get out of the Scrabble competition with the moms," he threatened, his eyes focused on his brother.

He was so angry, he had spots of color high on his cheeks, and his hands were fisted.

"Where would the fun be in that? Besides, he's got Mason with him. If you call him, you'd have to sit in a Jeep rife with awkward sexual tension for forty minutes, when you could be eating pizza," Bishop said, ignoring his brother's looming presence.

Kaine glared at his brother a moment longer, then sighed and slid into the booth next to him.

"Kaine, I didn't know—" I began.

He held his finger up, interrupting me. He turned and glared at his brother.

"*You* planned this?" he demanded.

"I had help," Bishop answered placidly, scanning the menu.

"*Who*?" Kaine demanded furiously.

"The 'rents. Who else?" Bishop answered, chuckling.

Kaine swatted his menu down on the table.

"I should have known better than to trust Mama K when she offered to drop me off on her way to her reading group," Kaine sighed.

"Yep. Her reading group ended last May," Bishop answered.

"Last— no..." Kaine muttered, obviously trying to figure out how long it had been. He sighed after a moment. "Fine. I'm a little out of touch. Just remember, paybacks are a bitch."

"Yeah, yeah..." Bishop answered.

The waitress showed up and took our orders, then silence fell at the table. After it had lasted for a few minutes, Bishop sighed.

"Shit, really? Again?" He asked. "Fine. Apparently, this time I have to stay and referee you two, because you don't know how to have an adult conversation."

Kaine and I both bristled at Bishop's assessment of us, but I had to admit he wasn't wrong. He turned to me.

"Nick, what the hell happened?" he asked, his golden-brown eyes pinning me to my seat.

Kaine looked at me angrily, but expectantly, too. I sighed again, wishing suddenly my soda was something with a much higher alcohol content. I owed him a better answer than I'd given him the night before.

"When I was diagnosed, my Mom admitted she had cheated on my dad years before. That was how she got HIV. My parents split up. To get my dad to agree to give her the divorce she wanted, I had to agree to stay with him in Florida," I said.

I saw Bishop and Kaine both taking in the partial revelation. It wasn't the whole story, but I thought it was enough for now. I didn't want to go into all the sordid details in the middle of a restaurant.

"He— he made me cut things off with you. Kaine. If I hadn't —" I looked at Kaine. I didn't want to tell him about my dad threatening to kill my mom and me. It seemed so out there. I mean, who *did* that? It certainly didn't happen around here, right? "If I hadn't, he wouldn't have done what she needed him to do."

I dropped Kaine's gaze to stare at the tabletop. I had my hands clasped in front of me, and this time it was my turn to have white knuckles. I forced myself to relax, taking a deep breath.

"He— he made you—" Kaine sputtered. "That sonof*abitch*!"

Kaine's face was flushed and his eyes glittered dangerously. His voice had risen about the noise of the crowd and drawn the attention of some of the diners.

"Kaine! It was my choice. I'm so sorry, but it was the only choice I could make," I said. I reached out hesitantly and placed my hand over his. "But it's over. He can't control me any longer. He doesn't have any more power over me."

Kaine stared at where our hands touched, and I saw him visibly struggle to release his anger. It took a few moments, but his fury slowly seemed to drain away. I withdrew my hand under the guise of taking a drink of my soda, and my skin tingled where I'd touched him.

Bishop gestured to the waitress and ordered a round of drinks for all of us. She eyed me for a moment. Before she could even ask, I got out my ID. I still had my Florida ID, and she stared at it for a while as if trying to find a counterfeit stamp on it. I looked a little young for my age, and I got carded regularly. My supposed friends both snickered at me as I put my license away. By the time she came back with the drinks, we had all relaxed a little.

"He... he's why you cut things off?" Kaine asked. "That's why you said what you did?"

I nodded.

"There was some— some other stuff, too, but that was the most important reason," I said, glancing in Bishop's direction. Bishop was watching his brother with a satisfied smirk on his face, and I really wanted to dump his drink on him. I might have to tell Kaine about what happened with my father, but I wasn't ready to share it with everyone yet.

Kaine stared at me. I knew he'd seen my glance at Bishop, and I hoped he'd realize there were things I didn't want to say in front of his brother.

The waitress brought our food a few minutes later, and conversation started to flow more naturally as we began to catch up. We talked about school, jobs, friends. I told the brothers about Vivian and her parents, and how much her friendship had meant to me.

"The Dunwoody's... I don't think I would have survived all this without them," I said.

Kaine smiled, and for the first time since I'd been back, I saw a hint of the old Kaine in his face. Just a touch of that smile, that glow that made him so amazing.

I told them about the time Vivian had broken the lunch tray over the head of the bully my first week of school, and they laughed. I didn't tell them the whole story, or about my father's forced tattooing following the event, but I figured it was a good introduction to Vivian's protective nature.

Bishop excused himself to use the restroom and I saw Kaine staring at my wrist, lost in thought.

"What?" I asked gently. I wished I had the right to touch his face just then, to trace his jaw with my fingertips and bring him back to the here and now. I'd given up that right, though, when I'd chosen my mom over him and there was no promise that I'd ever get it back.

"Vivian," he answered.

"Vivian?" I responded, confused.

"Yeah, I think I'm a little... jealous," he said, smiling wryly. "She got to be there for you. Help you. Protect you. That... that was my job."

I could feel the tears welling up in my eyes, and I cleared my throat to try and hold back some of the emotion I was feeling.

"It wasn't exactly a picnic for her, believe me," I said teasingly. "I'd really like you to meet her, though. I think you'd like her."

Kaine nodded and smiled. "I'd like that."

We ate for a minute longer, Kaine's eyes lost in thought. Then he said, "Shit. I have to know, Nick. Do you love her?"

I stared at him in shock. Love... Vivian?

"Of course, I love her," I began.

"Oh. Okay." He responded. It was like the light inside him had been snuffed out, and I realized I'd fucked up.

"Like a friend," I insisted, reaching my hand out and taking his. "Like a sister."

"Oh!" he said, a small smile on his face. That glow he'd had earlier seemed to rekindle in him and he squeezed my hand back before saying, "Okay."

Bishop came back a few minutes later and we finished our meals and paid the bill. Outside the summer sun was setting and stars were beginning to twinkle across the sky.

"Did you drive?" I asked Kaine as we walked to the parking lot.

He glared at his brother. "No, Mama K dropped me off. She told me Bishop wanted to talk about something."

Bishop chuckled.

"There is no one in the world who is a better co-conspirator than Mama K," he insisted. "We'll put Nicki's bike in the back of my SUV. I'll drop him off on our way home."

I gave them directions to the apartment.

"You're right around the corner from the twins' store," Kaine said glancing around.

"Really? Can we drive by it?" I asked.

Bishop drove to the store and I wanted to slap myself in the forehead.

"Good grief! I ride past here every morning! I just didn't make the connection," I said.

"You need to stop in and see them, then. They'll be excited that you are back in town," Bishop said.

As we drove by, I saw a poster in the window and almost squealed.

"They had a signing with *Mason Fucking Cameron*?" I exclaimed. "And I *missed* it? Dammit! 'Dark Angel' is one of my favorite graphic novels!"

"Well, you're going to love this, then!" Kaine said excitedly. "Mason is going to headline the Pop Culture Festival next weekend, and he's staying with Lee until then. Remember the person I mentioned as playing Scrabble with the moms?"

I nodded.

"Mason Fucking Cameron," he declared.

"No way! That is fantastic!" I exclaimed. I was fanboying hard.

"We also suspect there may some hanky in the panky between Mr.

Cameron and Lee," Bishop teased. Kaine handed me his phone and I got a look at the pictures from the signing.

"I hate to say it, but I think you guys are right! That is *not* an innocent blush on those cheeks," I remarked.

"We can probably get him to sign something for you," Bishop said. "He's in town until next week. You should come to D&D Sunday night with the fam."

I was glad for the darkness as I bit my lower lip, trying to decide if I should accept. We three had enjoyed a good time that evening, but I was under no illusions that one meal would fix the six years of grief that I'd caused Kaine.

"You should come," Kaine said softly from the backseat. He'd insisted on sitting in the back when we left the restaurant.

I glanced toward him, but it was far too dark for me to make out his expression. I had to just go with my gut.

"Okay. I'll check my schedule, but the restaurant closes early on Sundays, so I don't think it should be a problem," I said.

When we got to the apartment building, Bishop couldn't find a parking spot, so he double parked for a minute while Kaine and I got out.

I noticed almost absently that the security light over the entrance was dark. We'd found a lot of little things like that around the building that needed to be fixed so I added it to my mental list of problems for the landlord.

Kaine opened the hatch, then lifted the bicycle out of the back like it weighed nothing. I wasn't exactly a ninety-pound weakling, but manhandling the thing was a struggle for me. Not for the first time in my life, I envied Kaine his physical abilities.

He rolled the bike over to me and handed it off. I smiled at him in thanks.

"You'll— You'll really come, right?" he asked shyly, his hair flopping in his eyes a bit. He tossed his head back almost automatically, a move I remembered fondly from when we were kids.

I nodded. "I wouldn't miss it."

He grinned, and despite the darkness, I could almost feel the warmth of Kaine's smile when I agreed.

He started to head back to the car, then stopped and ran back.

"Quick, I need your number," he said by way of explanation. "I left the note you gave me at home, and I want to add you to the group chat."

We traded cell numbers, and I grinned again when he almost bounced his way back to the car. Bishop turned the emergency flashers off and I watched them drive away.

I locked my bike up at the bike rack and walked in the front entrance. Glass crunched on the concrete under my feet as I used my key to enter the building.

I took the stairs up two flights to our floor. There was an elevator in the building, but it was slow, and I didn't feel like waiting. I walked in and turned the lights on.

"Hey, Viv!" I called. I didn't get an answer, but I saw light glowing from under her bedroom door. I knocked and entered when I heard her call to come in.

"Hey lady!" I said, walking in and then bouncing on her bed.

She was sitting on top of the covers, the television on and her laptop on the mattress in front of her. She had some textbooks and notebooks scattered around the bed and a highlighter in her hand.

"Hey there, lover boy! A little late, isn't it?" she teased.

"As if I haven't been texting you all evening, lady," I teased back.

"Yeah, but texting isn't details, so spill!" She demanded as she piled her school things on the floor. "I'm sick unto death of low pressure zones and wind speed. I need some good old fashion *love* drama!"

"Well, not much love drama. It went surprisingly well," I said. "And apparently Mama K and Bishop make for a devious team…"

"Yeah, well, from everything you've told me, I wouldn't want to go up against them," she said, reaching back and pulling her hair out of an elastic band. She batted her eyes at me in question. "Pretty please?"

I laughed. "You know all you have to do is ask."

She reached to her bedside table and grabbed a brush, handing me it and the elastic.

I ran the brush through her hair several times, the movement soothing to both of us. When Viv found out in high school that I knew how to do a French braid, I had become her insta-bestie.

I brushed through her long hair one more time, then began dividing the strands up to make the braid. I used to braid my Mom's hair for her all the time. I wasn't sure why it was exactly, but all the women I knew who had long hair had trouble doing a French braid on their own heads. They all said it just never seemed to come out right.

"So, are you going to see him again?" she prompted. I blushed as I braided her hair.

"...Yes...I guess. I mean, they invited me to Sunday night D&D. That's a good sign."

"Nice! I have to work Sunday night, anyway! It should be one of my first non-trainee nights. You'll have to tell me how it goes!" she insisted.

"Who else would I tell? You're my best friend," I insisted, tying off the braid.

She turned around and hugged me.

"What's your schedule tomorrow?" I asked. We tried to plan our schedules out on the days we might both need to drive somewhere. She began pulling up her calendar when my phone pinged.

We looked at each other in shock. Viv was the only one I ever got text messages from.

I unlocked the phone and looked at it, only to laugh. It was a picture of a t-shirt with the saying "I have red hair because the universe knew I should come with a warning label." A text followed immediately.

KAINE: Hey Red! Thanks for being duped by my brother. See you Sunday. :)

I blushed and shared the photo with Vivian.

"I think he's a keeper, Nick," she said.

I nodded. I couldn't agree more. I just didn't know if I had the right to keep him.

The next day dawned bright and cheerful. Ugh. Weather shouldn't get the chance to have a mood. I rolled out of bed and looked at the clock. It was 11 a.m. already. I wasn't working today, but I still had things I needed to get done.

I yawned as I padded out to our kitchen in my bare feet and pajama pants. Sunlight streamed through the window and I paused to leaf through the mountain of junk mail that had accumulated on the kitchen counter. We'd only lived there a few short weeks. How we got on all these mailing lists was beyond me.

I sorted through it, disposing of the offers for car loans, credit cards, and the occasional bill. I set the bills down in the divider that I was using for everything we needed to follow up on. I had just pinned a couple of the bills to a cork board near the phone when my eyes fell on the heavy paper of the letter from the attorneys notifying me of my mother's death.

I had been putting off contacting them for weeks, now. After the initial shock of her death, I had only skimmed the documents they had included. I wasn't sure why, exactly, I was just reluctant to call them. Part of it was the fear my father would be able to trace me through them. Part of it was that it would make her death too real. I was afraid that finding out more about how she had died would stir up all the guilt, pain and loss that I had felt that night.

The paper was a heavy, cream color. I unfolded it, my fingers brushing across the gold-foil print of the letterhead. Alexander R. Young & Martin L. Zachary , Attorneys at Law. There was a phone number and email address that followed.

I thought about it for a few minutes, then made the decision. I picked up my phone and dialed the number. I held my breath for a moment, then hit the dial button. I looked at my fingers and realized absently that they were shaking. I squeezed them into fists, then put the phone up to my ear and listed to the ringtone.

"Zachary and Young, how may I assist you?" I heard a woman answer on the other end.

"Um, hi…" I began. "I'm calling about a letter I received from your firm."

"May I ask your name, sir?" she asked.

"…Before I give it to you, I need to ask, um, if what I talk to you about is, uh, private?" I felt like an idiot stammering over my words. "I mean, whatever I talk to you about, it's can't be shared with anyone else, right?"

"Well," the woman began, "I think you may be referring to attorney-client privilege. That generally protects you in the event that we are representing you for something. Are we currently representing you in a legal matter, sir?"

I nodded, then realized I was an idiot and she couldn't hear the rocks shake inside my head.

"I— I think so. I mean, you represent… represent*ed* my mom," I managed to get out, but the next sentence came out in a whisper. "Or rather, her estate."

"And what was her name, sir?" she asked, her tone softening.

"Um, Terhune. Harley Terhune," I said.

I could swear I heard a gasp on the other end of the line.

"Is this… Dominic?" she asked gently. "…Nicki?"

"You— You know me?" My voice was shaking even to my own ears, and my finger hovered over the end call button.

"I knew your mother well, Nicki," she said. "My name is Rhiannon. I worked with your mother for several years."

The room started getting blurry, and I realized with a start that tears were filling my eyes. *Fuck.* I had to keep it together. I sat down on the chairs at the kitchen table.

"I haven't talked to anyone who knew her for a long time," I said. "I mean, except for my dad."

"Does your father know you are calling, Nicki? May I call you Nicki? I heard so much about you from Harley, I *feel* like I know you," she said.

"Um, yeah, sure. I don't mind," I answered. "And— no, he doesn't even know I'm— I mean, he doesn't know where I'm at."

"From what your Mom told me, that— that's probably wise, Nicki. Xander— Alexander Young is the attorney representing your— your mother's estate," she said, her soft voice kind as she spoke. "I know he would want to meet with you as soon as possible. He's in Maine this week, but he is scheduled to be back in Akron next Wednesday. Could we set up an appointment for you to meet with him then?"

"Sure," I responded. We scheduled an appointment for 9 a.m. Wednesday and she gave me directions to their offices in downtown Akron. I scribbled everything down on the back of the legal notices and couldn't keep myself from sniffling.

"If you have time, I'd love to meet you myself if you are available before then," Rhiannon said. "Maybe we could have lunch one day?"

"Th-that would be nice," I said, knuckling my eyes to clear my sight.

"Your mom was a special lady," she said. "She was a good person. I can't wait to meet her son."

I hung up the phone and the tears began in earnest. It took a little while, but I eventually got my emotions under control. I had a lot of things to do that day, but I already felt exhausted.

I finally pulled myself together and made my way outside. We needed a few things from the grocery store, and I'd told Vivian I'd pick them up. There was a small mom and pop store not far from our apartment building, and we tried to buy from local stores whenever we could.

I checked my pockets to make sure I had my keys, wallet, and phone, then took the stairs to the first floor. I was stepping through the doorway, reading through my notifications on my phone when my feet crunched on glass. I looked down to see a scattering of glass on the concrete porch. It looked like light bulb glass...

Shit. I looked up at the light over the porch and realized that was where the glass had come from. I forgot I was going to call the building owner and let them know that the light was out, but if the problem was just the bulb, I could get a new one at the store.

I was just adding the light bulb to my grocery list when I stepped on something else and realized I had a bigger problem. The item I had stepped on had once been a piece of reflector from my bike. The same bike that now sat in the parking lot, completely destroyed.

I stared at the cracked bones of my bike, dumbfounded for a moment. My mind couldn't seem to connect the dots and make sense of the whole picture. The tires were slashed, the inner tubes pulled out of the rubber like intestines. The spokes on each of the rims looked like fingers that someone had crushed with a sledgehammer. The handlebars were mangled, and the frame looked like it had been run over by a truck.

I was staring at the remains when I heard someone come up behind me.

"*Shit*, dude. Was that yours?" I heard a voice ask. I turned and looked at the source of the voice. Next to me stood a smoking hot guy in black jeans and a black tee. If I hadn't been so flabbergasted at the destruction of my primary means of transportation, I might have been turned on by him.

He had shoulder-length dark-brown hair held back from his face with a pair of mirrored sunglasses. A jacket was slung over one arm and the part of my brain that Vivian was trying to take over made a mental note to try that kind of outfit on my own, because he looked damn attractive.

He was the same height and build I was, but that's where the similarities ended. He looked over at me over the rims of his glasses, and I noted he appeared to be in his late twenties. His silvery gray eyes had a decidedly Asian cast to them, and his lush pink lips were framed by a dark goatee. If I wasn't still in knots over Kaine, I think I would have really wanted to see what those lips tasted like...

"Um, yeah, it was my bike," I said. Fuck. Of *course*, it was a bike. Like, who couldn't have seen that? Points for the obvious, Nicki...

"Wow... who did *you* piss off?" He asked, whistling as he surveyed the damage. "This looks personal. Hey, I'm Micah. Micah Asano."

He stuck his hand out to me, and I stared at for a minute without moving. He looked at me and raised an eyebrow, a half-smile lurking at the corner of his mouth, as if daring me to take it.

"Nicki," I responded, finally taking his hand in mine. "Nicki Terhune."

"You and the girl with the long brown hair moved into 3B a few weeks ago, right?" he asked.

I nodded, unable to tear my gaze away from the remnants of my bike.

"Hey, are you okay?" I heard him ask, and it took me a moment to realize he was speaking to me.

"Yeah," I said, shaking my head as I stared at the wreckage. "Yeah, I just... I'm surprised, is all."

"Have you called the police to report it yet?" he asked, something approaching concern in his eyes.

The question had me automatically backing away.

"No! I—" I stopped myself. Of course, I should report it. I wasn't in Florida anymore. I didn't have to hide from my father here. "I hadn't thought that far ahead yet."

"Why don't you sit down, and I'll call it in. Is there anyone I could call for you? You look a little shocky..." he offered.

I shook my head, but just as I started to insist I could handle it, the world seemed to tilt and spin a bit. Before I knew it, I was sitting on the concrete stairs leading up to the front door while Micah made a call. I realized almost absently that he was making the call with my phone.

"Here, drink this," I heard a voice command. I looked up to see Micah holding a water bottle out to me.

I took it and opened it, taking a long drink automatically. The cold water seemed to help clear the fog from my brain.

"I... thanks. I'm not sure what's wrong with me," I said, blushing.

"It's okay. People react to violence in different ways," he answered. "Some make it a tit for tat, return violence with violence. Other people shut down. Others run."

"Guess I'm in the 'shut down' category..." I sighed, taking another drink.

"I've seen worse," he said, a sardonic grin pulling at the corner of his mouth.

A police car pulled up in front of the building.

"Wow, that was fast," I said to Micah in confusion. "Or was I spaced out longer than I thought?"

"Nah, we just take care of our own around here," he said, a brief smile playing across his lips.

My breath caught in my throat. Surely, he couldn't mean... I glanced at his belt and saw for the first time the Glock holstered at his hip, a detective's gold badge next to it. I hadn't seen it before because he had been carrying his jacket on his arm.

"Oh... you're a cop," I said, my voice sounding thready and weak even to my own ears. I could feel the blood draining from my face.

"Yep," he said, flashing me a reassuring smile. "Hope you don't hold it against me."

"I'll... I'll try not to," I responded honestly. I had to remind myself that not all police officers were like my father.

What seemed like just a few moments later, a black SUV peeled around the corner and into the parking lot of the apartment building. The noise had Micah's hand dropping to his weapon and the two police officers standing near my bike ducked, seeking cover behind the cars.

I recognized the vehicle from the night before and was kind of expecting it when I saw Kaine jump out of the SUV, but I was surprised to see Bishop jump out of the driver's side next to him and making a beeline for us.

I glanced at the detective as they got closer, raising an eyebrow in question and he shrugged.

"It was the last number you entered in your phone," he said, amusement on his face. "And I had to see if it was..."

His voice trailed off as Bishop and Kaine jogged over to where we stood.

"Nicki! Are you okay?" Kaine demanded as he knelt in front of me. I just nodded and next thing I knew he was wrapping his arms around me. I melted into his embrace, my hands gripping his back and pulling him close, a shudder running through my body as I realized I didn't have to deal with this all by my fucking self.

I didn't know how long we remained like that, but I thought I could have stayed in Kaine's arms forever. He finally pulled back a little so he could run his hands over me, confirming I wasn't hurt.

"I'm okay, really," I insisted, my voice much steadier now that he was there.

His green eyes raked over my body, like he couldn't relax until he had confirmed I hadn't been injured.

"Fuck, Nicki..." he sighed.

He suddenly seemed to notice the officers standing around us and he stepped back a little, giving me a bit of breathing room, but leaving his arm wrapped protectively around my shoulder. Bishop stood next to his brother, his eyes locked on the detective. Something seemed to pass between them, and Bishop broke the standoff to examine me, his golden-brown eyes assessing me quickly before locking glares again with Micah.

Kaine was dressed in cutoff shorts and a t-shirt, but Bishop was shirtless, wearing only jeans and sneakers and his hair was still wet, as if he'd jumped out of the shower and into his car. I couldn't help but compare our bodies. My skin was pale, white, and scarred while his golden skin rippled in the sunlight. Fucking *rippled*. I sighed. No wonder the detective was staring at him.

"I'm fine!" I said, a little testier than I intended when Kaine started asking me more questions. I was tired of being afraid, and now that I was getting my second wind, I really didn't want to look weak in front of my two friends. When Kaine looked at me dubiously I insisted, "Really."

Bishop leaned forward, not so subtly shielding Kaine and I from the detective. I saw the detective hide an amused smile at the protective gesture, but he allowed it to pass unremarked as he turned away to speak to the uniformed officers.

"How did this happen?" Bishop asked quietly, looking down at me, his eyes searching my face. "Were you hurt? Did someone hurt you?"

"No, I'm fine. I don't know what happened. I just came out to go to the grocery store. Vivian said we needed milk and bread, so I was going to run down to the corner store. I came outside, stepped on the glass and saw— this," I said, waving at the wreckage that remained of my bike.

"Glass, huh?" I heard the detective's voice say. I looked over and he was giving the porch ceiling and broken light a considering look, then asked "Any idea when that happened?"

My forehead furrowed as I tried to remember. "I think it was working yesterday morning. I work the early shift at a breakfast place, but when I came home last night, I remember the light wasn't on."

"I remember it was out when we dropped you off last night. I had a hard time seeing the building number," Bishop said. "Maybe it was just some kids?"

"Kids wouldn't think about taking the light source out so they couldn't be seen," the detective answered, walking back to the stairs. "At least, not most kids. Why don't you guys take Nicki inside and let us take a look around out here."

I walked the guys back into the apartment building, electing this time to take the elevator rather than the stairs. I thought my heart had endured enough action for one day.

We sat in my apartment, not really saying much. One of the uniformed police officers came up with the detective and asked me some questions.

No, I wasn't involved with anything illegal. No, I didn't have insurance. Did I know of any reason anyone might want to hurt me, or threaten me?

"No, no reason," I whispered and shook my head. I avoided looking the officer in the eyes while I answered his questions. There *was* no reason anyone would want to hurt me. No logical reason, at least.

I saw Kaine pause at my prevarication. He knew my tells, and knew I was lying. I didn't think the detective believed me either when I answered, though, because I saw his eyes narrow slightly at my response.

The uniform had just finished taking the report and given me a piece of paper with the report number on it.

"Nicki, let me take you over to the house," Kaine offered. "You could stay with us for a couple of days."

"What? No, Kaine, I'm fine. It's *nothing*! Really! It was probably just a bunch of kids with too much time on their hands," I insisted. It's what I wanted it to be. *Needed* it to be. "We moved here sight unseen. Maybe it's just not a great neighborhood."

"Well, *I* live here, it can't be *all* bad," The detective teased, and I found myself smiling. I saw Bishop snap his eyes back to the detective, and it reminded me of a cat who had their tail stepped on.

"You certainly didn't prevent this from happening in the first place," Bishop growled in response to the lighthearted teasing.

"I was working a double, Devereaux. I just got home a few minutes ago. I may be multi-talented, but I can't be *everywhere* at once," the sexy detective answered sharply.

"Wait, you two know each other?" Kaine asked, looking in confusion from his brother to the detective.

The two locked eyes again, with neither saying anything and the tension ratcheted up. Enough was enough. As fun as it was to see someone get Bishop riled up, *someone* needed to act like the adult.

"Thank you, detective, I appreciate your help. Kaine, I appreciate the offer, but Vivian, my roommate, is due home this evening. I wouldn't want her here by herself," I said. "Especially after this."

"I understand your concern. Well, as luck would have it, I'm off work the next couple of days, so I can keep an eye on you... both, and the place," Micah offered. I could swear he was baiting Bishop deliberately, because he took the time to look me up and down in what I could only describe as a lascivious manner. Which was utterly laughable, I mean, c'mon! I was no competition for Bishop. There was some definite history between the two of these guys, though!

Bishop took the bait, though. He glared defiantly at Micah for a moment, and I couldn't help but see something more in their interaction. Something beyond Bishop's normal protectiveness was in that gaze. The look between the two of them was hot and cold, like fire and ice. They acted like Kaine and I didn't even exist.

"You could both come stay with us, Nicki. You know the moms have enough room..." Bishop started.

"Oh, you still live with Mommy?" the detective snorted in derision. "Classic. Is your bedroom in the basement with your video games?"

I saw Bishop's eyes narrow.

"At least it's not in the closet," Bishop snarked back.

I saw his barb hit home, and the detective froze, the grin on his face disappearing and the life drained from his eyes.

"Fuck you, Devereaux," Micah said, stalking out the apartment door.

I could have sworn Bishop muttered, "Been there, done that..."

Okay, it was obvious now that the two knew each other, and from the sound of it, they didn't like each other much. I could have chalked up the interchange to a hookup gone wrong, but there was something in Bishop's gaze as he stared at the detective. Something... ravenous, but distrustful. He looked at Micah like a man dying of thirst who wasn't quite sure if the water in front of him was a mirage.

The detective paused at the doorway and turned back around, his gaze licking over Bishop's body and there was an answering hunger in his face. There was definitely more to this story than either of them was telling.

"Good night," he said, then shut the door calmly, but firmly, behind him.

"What the hell is your problem with him?" I asked Bishop as I tacked the business card up on the cork board near our phone.

Bishop was sitting in the recliner and Kaine was seated on the couch. I sat down next to Kaine and sighed as he put his arm around me again. That small touch seemed to make everything so much better...

Bishop just glared at the coffee table, his face like a thunderstorm. I could almost see little bolts of lightning flying off here and there.

"Seriously, Bish, you were really being an—" Kaine began.

"*I know*! Okay, I just— I know," Bishop exploded. He stood and began pacing the living room.

Kaine and I looked at each other. This was looking very interesting indeed...

"I've known Micah for... well, a while now," Bishop said, running his hands through his hair in obvious frustration. "He makes me *so* fucking crazy! It's like he knows what I'm thinking and feeling, and he knows exactly how to—"

Bishop stopped himself, realizing we were both avidly following his rant. Kaine had a soft, knowing smile on his face as he looked at his brother, and I could feel an answering one on my own.

"Oh, fuck you both," Bishop said without heat, and dropped back into the recliner.

It took me a while, but I finally convinced Kaine and Bishop to go home, which had been no mean feat. I thought only the fact that Bishop had an 8 a.m. class and Kaine was supposed to work that night got them to budge.

"Come with me," Kaine whispered as we stood in the doorway. Bishop had gone out to the car to give us a minute to say goodbye. He'd been tight lipped over the sexy detective, and we hadn't been able to get any more information out of him. "You can hang out in the bar, and we can talk between customers."

"Yeah. Talking and a dance club. Those go together *so* well..." I teased.

"Well, you could dance for me..." he said, waggling his eyebrows in what I assumed he thought was a sexy manner. I wasn't going to tell him it just made him look silly. Okay, silly *and* sexy. Sillily sexy? I didn't think that was even a word.

"I— No. We have a lot to talk about, I know," I said, stopping him from interrupting. "And I *want* to talk. But I'm not going to let Vivian come home to an empty apartment when there's someone messing around in the neighborhood."

I could see that Kaine was angry with my decision, but it was *my* decision. Okay, not angry. Furious. But one thing I'd learned in dealing with my father was to deal with someone who was angry, and I refused to run from things anymore. I'd hugged him and walked him out to the car. I'd at least understood his anger came from a place of concern, not control.

It was around eleven that night that I heard a knock on the door. I'd texted Vivian and she was due back in about twenty minutes. I had told her to call me when she got close and I'd wait for her outside. I didn't want to take any chances with my friend's life.

When I opened the door, I saw Micah—Detective Asano—

standing in the hallway. His coat was over one arm again, his sunglasses were back in place and he looked a little embarrassed. Which he should have. Sunglasses at night were *so* nineties…

"Hey," he said eloquently.

"Hey yourself, Detective," I said. "Want to come in?"

"Nah, I just— I just wanted to say, I'm sorry about earlier. As you might guess, your friend and I have some… history," he said, looking anywhere but at me.

"Yeah, I kind of figured," I responded. "I'm glad you came back, though. I didn't really get a chance to thank you. For calling the report in, everything."

"No problem," he responded. "You were in shock. It happens to everyone at some point."

His eyes became a little distant, as if he was replaying some scene in his own head.

"Bishop just— he gets under my skin, you know? Like I'm not sure if I want scratch my arm or cut it off…" he murmured. I grinned inwardly and thought about how similar the descriptions were that he and Bishop gave of each other. I realized he was talking mostly to himself, and I think he realized it, too, because he seemed to shake himself.

"Anyway, I wanted to give you this," he said, holding a business card out to me. "It has my cell on the back. If you run into any problems, just call me. Despite what Devereaux might have you think, I'm not a complete asshole."

Ah. Back to being "Devereaux," hmmm? *Someone* was trying to distance himself… I chuckled.

"Takes one to know one?" I asked.,

He smiled. "Maybe. Seriously, though… be careful, you and your roommate, both. Make sure you're aware of your surroundings, especially when entering or leaving the building. I'm in 1A, if you ever need anything, just pound on my door."

14

KAINE

I SLAMMED AN EMPTY GLASS INTO THE BUS TRAY AS THE MUSIC POUNDED out around me.

What the hell did Nicki think he was doing? I couldn't believe he'd made Bishop and I *leave*. I was so freakin' angry I couldn't see straight.

The club was dark, loud and had that scent of alcohol and sweaty people all kind of rolled into one that every club I'd ever been to possessed. It wasn't a terribly busy night, which gave me even more time to be angry at Nicki for being so damn stubborn.

"Whoa, Kaine! What'd that glass ever do to you?" Sammie said as she stared at me from behind the bar.

I bit back a growl. It wasn't Sammie's fault that I was in a piss-poor mood right now.

I dragged the tray full of dirty glasses and dropped them off in the kitchen before heading back out front. It was late, after midnight, and things had started to wind down.

My phone buzzed in my pocket, but I ignored it, then felt it buzz again. And again. I grabbed it angrily and swiped my code to open it, then froze.

MAMA D: Kids, there's been an accident. The twins are being

taken to City Hospital. We're on our way there now. Will text when we know more.

WEAVER: Is it serious??

MAMA D: We don't know yet. The police just called.

BISHOP: OMW

WEAVER: God, I wish I was there! Let me know what's going on.

BISHOP: Did anyone tell Lee?

MAMA K: I called him. He's on the way now.

I typed a hurried note and ran to the front.

"Sammie!" I yelled, waving down my boss.

"What's up?" She asked, concern on her face as she noticed my grave expression.

"I have to go, the twins have been hurt," I said, waving to the bar. "Can you..?"

"Go! Go! I got this," she said, reassuringly.

Luckily the hospital was located downtown, so I didn't have far to go. I paced the ER waiting area, anxious for some news. Mama D and Mama K had arrived before me, as well as my brother and, to my surprise, Mason Cameron.

My wonderful parents sat huddled together on the uncomfortable chairs of the waiting room. Mama D had her arm around Mama K, and Mama K's eyes were closed, her lips moving in a silent prayer.

Lee and Mason sat together, their fingers laced together. I was too worried about my other brothers to even wonder. Just as I was joining them, I saw Bishop walking in, his eyes wild.

"What happened?" he demanded as he barreled into the waiting room. Lee stood and hugged our brother.

"We don't really know yet. Someone from the police called the moms," Lee said in a calm voice. I'd never seen my oldest brother look so... so *helpless*, before. He stood in the waiting room, his hands gripping Bishop's shoulders as he tried to reassure him. "The doctors are working on them now."

"Here's what we know. They were found outside the store by a passerby. It looks like they were hit by a car when they were leaving," Mama D said from her spot next to Mama K. Her arm was wrapped around my other mother, pulling her close. Mama K was the physically stronger, more wiry of my two parents, but this was the first time I realized that her strength could be brittle.

"Sonny is in surgery. He has a compound fracture of his leg. Hicks..." she choked for a minute before continuing. "Hicks has bleeding on his brain. They are doing surgery to release some of the pressure in his skull."

Fuck.

I knelt down at Mama K's feet and took their hands in mine.

"They're strong, Mama. Both of them. They are fuckin' ferocious when they want to be, and neither of them would leave us," I whispered, staring into their tear-filled eyes. Mama K looked into my eyes for a moment, her normally strong spirit seeming lost and fragile. Then she closed her eyes and nodded, tears spilling from the corners. When she opened them again, I saw some of her normal strength returning and she tried to smile. I hugged them both and had just stood back up when I heard another pair of footsteps approaching us.

I turned and saw Nicki enter the waiting room, his hands clenching and unclenching with nerves, as if he wasn't sure of his welcome. I was still so angry at him for making us leave when we weren't sure whether he was in danger or not. We glared at each other for a moment, and I saw something shift in his gaze.

Mama K and Mama D had stood when I did, and I remembered one of the family mottos we'd been taught growing up—You mess with one Devereaux, you mess with us all.

Nicki looked around the room for a moment, then his eyes met mine. I felt that familiar spark, the piercing feeling of the other half of my soul connecting.

He held my gaze for what seemed like forever, until it seemed like he couldn't stand being apart a moment longer. He rushed forward and wrapped his arms around me.

I sighed as his arms circled me. It just felt so fucking good to have him there. As a friend. As something else. Whatever he was going to be to me, I was just happy he was there.

"How did you know?" I whispered.

He looked up at me, his blue eyes glittering in the waiting room lights.

"Bishop accidentally texted the group text we set up when we shared our phone numbers," he said. I glanced at my younger brother.

I saw Bishop watching us, something pained in his gaze, and it tore at me. Something… hungry. Hurt. Lonely. Which was ridiculous, because Bishop was probably one of the most social members of the family. I still couldn't deny the look in his eyes.

I looked at Nicki. He had followed my gaze and now stared back at me, and I think he saw the same thing I had, because although he looked puzzled, he nodded slightly at me and we both held our arms out to Bishop at the same time. Bishop sighed and stepped into the circle, which quickly grew to hold all the Devereaux clan. Soon only Mason now stood outside the circle, as if he wasn't sure what to do. Then Mama K opened her arms further and gestured him in.

"*Mijo*, you belong in here, too," she said, waving him forward, her eyes glittering brown with unshed tears.

He walked forward reluctantly, his head bowed, like he felt out of place, but he was soon embraced into the circle, Mama K on one side, Lee on the other.

Mama K's voice began whispering a prayer in Spanish. My Spanish was a little rusty, but I could understand most of what she'd said.

"Lord, you love our sons as You love all children. Please stay by their side in their hour of need. Comfort them and help them heal. Keep them ever mindful of Your loving presence. Bless us with Your powerful healing and comfort us also…"

It was a mother's prayer for beloved, injured children, a voice thick with the fear of loss.

I looked around that circle of chosen family. My eyes staring into each face. Lee, his face strong and powerful, but tight with his own remembered loss. Mama D, her gentle eyes red, her blonde hair in a messy pony tail. Bishop's hair was its normal, wild mess. Mason, whose face looked frightened, but somehow defiant at the same time. Nicki... Nicki just looked beautiful to me. His eyes were closed, his own lips moving in a silent prayer. I remembered his mom used to take him to church with her when he was young. I wondered if he still went.

We broke apart a few minutes later, all of us wiping away tears. Mason offered to fetch coffee from the cafeteria, and we all laughed at the face Bishop made at the thought.

Twelve hours later, we were still waiting. Hicks' surgery had been completed and he had been transferred to the ICU. Sonny was still in surgery. A nurse had come out to speak to us a few hours before just to let us know it was going to be a while before we got another update.

We found out from the EMS workers that somehow Hicks had managed to get his belt around Sonny's leg and create a tourniquet before passing out. They said he probably saved Sonny's life, because the broken bone had nicked his femoral artery. Unfortunately, they weren't sure whether he'd had enough blood flow to keep the cells in his leg from dying. They had taken him in to try and repair as much of the damage to his leg as they could, but we didn't know yet if they would have to amputate.

We were all bone tired from a night in the waiting room. People came and went, some sick or injured, their families rushing in to check on them. There was an ebb and flow to the traffic all that made it seem almost surreal. The faces behind the check-in desk changed, the doctors and nurses that came out to speak with us, but through it all a terrible fear of loss gripped my chest that only eased when I was close to Nicki.

Mason had been kind enough to bring back food and gallons of the horrible cafeteria coffee. Bishop was right about how bad it would taste, but we drank it anyway. The food mostly went untouched, though.

Nicki, Bishop and I had stayed close to my parents, with Lee and Mason on the other side of them. There was definitely something going on between Lee and Mason. I watched Mason hand my brother's phone to him, and saw Lee place a gentle kiss on his hand as they smiled sadly at each other.

It was around noon and we were still in the waiting room. Hicks had been taken to the intensive care unit where he wasn't allowed visitors yet. Sonny was still in surgery. The surgeon had come out once and told us things weren't looking good. He asked my parents for permission to amputate his leg if necessary. I'll never forget the anguished look on Mama D's face as she signed the papers.

"Just save our son," she whispered as she looked at the doctor. "We can handle anything else."

I had watched Lee as the doctors had spoken to Mama D and Mama K. His face was almost white with fatigue. I knew that being in the hospital couldn't have been fun for him, not after all the time he'd spent there after he had been injured in Afghanistan.

The noise in the lounge was fucking annoying. There were televisions set up all around the waiting area, and it was driving me crazy.

I glanced over at Nicki, trying to find something to distract myself. He was pale, too, his red hair falling over his eyes. He brushed it back automatically then grinned at me as he caught me watching him.

"How are you holding up?" I heard Nicki ask me.

"Okay, I guess," I said. "I'm starting to fucking hate these chairs, and if I have to listen to cartoons for five more minutes…"

Nicki laughed and looked around the waiting area. Seeing no one else paying attention to the set, he walked over and turned it off.

"Problem solved," he said, coming back to sit down next to me.

I grinned at him.

"My man of action," I teased.

He blushed.

"I don't know about that, but I was done with the cartoons, too," he said.

We looked up as a man in a white coat approached us, standing next to one of the nurses we'd been getting updates from.

"Devereaux family?" I heard him call.

My parents stood, and the rest of us joined them as he walked over to the grouping of chairs we had claimed.

"I'm Dr. Walgate, the attending physician for both of your sons," he told my parents, sitting down next to them.

"The neurosurgeon, Dr. Parker, will give you an update in a little bit as well. Hudson is still in surgery, but Hicks is settled in the ICU and can have visitors, but only two at a time right now. Once Hudson comes out of surgery, if you want to move to the central lounge area, we can get you updates a little bit faster."

"Do... do you have a prognosis, yet?" Mama D asked.

The doctor looked at her, his brown eyes gentle as he looked at her. "I'm sorry, it's too soon to tell, really," he said. "With Hudson, we're still waiting on the orthopedic surgeon to give us an update. He should be out soon. For Hicks... it's just too early. The blood clot on his brain is causing him problems. The body's natural response to injury is to swell, which is what happened to him. Unfortunately, when it swells, it puts pressure on other parts of the brain, and starts to cause even more damage. To relieve the pressure, we had to remove a portion of his skull to keep his brain from causing further damage to itself. It's called a decompressive craniectomy."

I heard one of my parents sob, but I didn't know which one.

"Will he have to have a plate inserted or something?" Bishop asked, his eyes glued to the doctor.

"No, but I'm going to be very straightforward with all of you," he said, looking around at the circle of family and friends gathered. "Both of your brothers have experienced serious trauma. Barring further complications, even if the orthopedic surgeon decides he doesn't have to amputate, Sonny is going to need a lot of support to allow his body to heal. Hicks... Hicks is going to have a more compli-cated recovery, we just don't know *how* complicated until we are able to assess him after he wakes up."

"What should we expect, Dr. Walgate?" Mama D asked.

"The area of the craniectomy was along the back of his head and is a very small area. He's not going to be shrouded in bandages like you might see on television, but we also don't want him injuring himself further. Please be aware, he could have some paralysis, speech or memory problems. We won't know exactly until he wakes up. You can go back to see him two at a time, but when he wakes up, we'll need you to do everything you can to keep him calm. It's common for people with a traumatic brain injury to be frightened and confused."

Dr. Walgate excused himself and the nurse who came out with him offered to take two of us back to see Hicks. He answered a few more questions, then the nurse offered to take back the first visitors.

"Moms, why don't you two go back and see him first?" Bishop suggested immediately. They both nodded and stood hastily, following the nurse.

I sat down with a sigh, and Nicki sat down next to me. I must have looked as bad as I felt, because he wrapped his arms around me again.

"They're fighters, both of them," he said. "They're going to make it through and be putting corn starch in your hairdryer before you know it."

A smile tugged at the corner of my mouth. The twins were the practical jokers through and through. They'd pulled the "which twin is it?" joke multiple times throughout our lives. I'd always remember the look on Bishop's face when he'd turned his hairdryer on one morning before school and gotten a face full of cornstarch. That had earned the twins dish duty for a month, as well as having to replace Bishop's hairdryer.

"Well, I guess if they have to amputate, we won't have a problem telling them apart anymore," I said, sighing.

Lee reached over and smacked me along the back of my head. I winced and rubbed the spot.

"Too soon?" I asked.

"Smartass..." he whispered.

Mama D and Mama K came back a few minutes later, their eyes still red. It was obvious they had both been crying again.

Lee wrapped them both in his arms, and the contrast threw me for a minute. Lee was tall and broad, blond, but with short hair that was long on top, like a grown out military cut. Which it was. He'd never gotten out of the habit of keeping it short, even after he was discharged. Mama D was almost as tall as he was, and just as blonde, but Mama K was much shorter. She was wiry, and wicked fast on the mats. I hated when she decided she wanted to spar with me, because even now she could knock me on my ass.

After a few minutes they stepped back, sniffling and making use of the tissue boxes scattered around the waiting area before taking a seat in one of the chairs. Lee sat next to them, with Mason next to him.

"Lee, why don't you go in and see him?" Mama D said, her arm wrapped around Mama K. "The... the doctor said his CAT scan showed more bleeding in his brain. He said they have to wait a few days to do an MRI, but right now they are going to keep a very close eye on him. You're the only one of us with any real medical experience. Can you go take a look at him, then tell us what you think?"

Lee nodded. It didn't escape anyone's attention that he and Mason went back to the ICU together.

I looked at my parents.

"So, Lee and Mason, huh?" I said, smiling.

"Shush! Don't jinx it, *mijo!*" Mama K said, a smile peeking through her tears.

"He seems like a nice guy," Nicki said. "Really down to earth. Not at all what I expected."

"What were you expecting?" I asked.

"I don't know. Someone more aloof maybe? Or stuck up, or something?" Nicki said. "I mean, okay, this is weird, but... I know he's this famous writer and artist, right? But he's just a normal guy. A little shy, maybe. Not at all what I expected of Mason Cameron, famous artist. Here, he's just... *Mason.*"

I nodded.

"I know what you mean. He has this reputation for being reclusive, like Hemingway, or something. Never giving interviews or press conferences, or whatever. Now he's here, being this normal guy. Holding my brother's hand for God's sake..." My family laughed at that. Lee wasn't exactly the kind of guy who did a lot of public displays of affection. To be holding Mason's hand, he might as well have put a ring on it.

"Maybe it was love at first sight," Nicki said, shrugging.

"You trying to say Mason is like Bacon?" Bishop teased. "Because that's the only thing I love at first sight."

Bishop and the moms started talking. Nicki leaned against me, his head resting on my shoulder.

"I still need to get his autograph," Nicki sighed.

"I don't think I like way you're looking at him," I said abruptly, narrowing my eyes and looking at him seriously.

Nicki looked up at me, his eyes wide.

"What? Why?" he asked, a slight wobble to his voice.

"You've practically got little hearts coming out of your eyes," I teased.

"Shut up!" He said, shoving my shoulder as he realized I was hassling him. "Like you're any better! You're telling me if that was Nathan Fillion in there, you wouldn't be the same way."

"I wouldn't!" I declared, totally lying. "But if it was Tom Hiddleston, we'd totally be fighting to the death over him."

"I'm glad it's not Tom Hiddleston, then," Nicki said. My breath caught in my chest as I looked at him. Our eyes locked, and the room seemed to fade away into the distance. Then I was leaning forward and brushing my lips across his. My tongue swiped gently over the seam of his lips, then he was opening his mouth to me.

I groaned as the taste of him exploded on my tongue. I'd missed this so fucking much. Missed *him*. I leaned into him, bringing one hand up to grip the back of his head and tipping my head to perfectly align our mouths.

His tongue met mine, dueling me for control of the kiss. That... was new. In the past, Nicki always let me be the one to lead, and put on the brakes when necessary. Now... now he met me, stroke for stroke, his tongue exploring my mouth with equal intensity.

I didn't know how long we were like that, but I heard a coughed, "Get a room," from Bishop, and we jerked apart just as the doors swung open and Lee and Mason walked out.

I saw my brother send a knowing smirk our way as Nicki and I both straightened up and turned to hear his update.

"What do you think?" Mama K asked, her normally cheery voice thick with emotion. Mama D looked up at him as well.

"I think... I think it's serious," he said. "He's awake, but he seems to be having trouble forming new memories. We had to tell him about the accident four times."

He sighed and I saw Mason's hand squeeze his. I felt a squeeze on my own hand, and glanced at Nicki, who nodded at me reassuringly.

"They will keep him in ICU to keep a close eye on him, to make sure the bleeding in his brain stops. From there, it's kind of a waiting game. We have to wait to see how well his body heals from the trauma of his at—" Lee paused and cleared my throat. "...his accident."

Both our parents nodded. Their hands were clinging tightly to each other and Lee reached out, wrapping his large hand around their smaller ones.

"He's young. He's strong. He's adaptable. We will just have to wait this out," he reassured them.

They both nodded.

"Thank you, sweetie," Mama D said. "It makes us feel better knowing that you can check on him."

We settled back in to wait for news from the orthopedic surgeon and I felt my phone vibrate.

I got it out and saw I'd missed several texts, including the one Bishop had accidentally sent the group we'd set up the night before.

There was a message from Sammie, asking if there was any news and if there was anything she could do to help. Then I saw a message from Weaver.

WEAVER: Goddammit, somebody better give me an update, or I'm fucking going AWOL and coming up there to get some fucking answers!

You know the saying "cuss like a sailor"? Yeah, my sister swore like an Air Force pilot.

ME: Calm your jets, sis. Nothing you can do here but drink bad coffee and have your ass go numb in these chairs.

WEAVER: No word?! WTF are those doctors doing? Eating donuts?

ME: I think it's the police with the reputation for eating donuts, Little Bit.

I'd called Weaver Little Bit since we were kids, having picked it up in some book or another. She was the shortest of all the sibs, and she normally hated it, but she didn't object right now.

WEAVER: Seriously, no news?

ME: We just talked to the attending. Not sure what "attending" means exactly, but he's given us the most news so far. Hicks is out of surgery and transferred to the ICU. Sonny is still in surgery, but he thinks the ortho surgeon should be out soon to give us an update.

WEAVER: ...Were they able to save his leg?

I could almost hear Weaver's voice, tiny and lost. She was so much like Mama K, small, but strong.

ME: We don't know yet. We should hear something soon.

I filled her in on the details and promised to call her as soon as we had any more news. She had been texting with Bishop, but he'd apparently taken too long to respond to her.

We settled back into the routine of waiting for more news, but only a few minutes had passed when I saw a police officer enter the lounge. He was probably in his mid-to-late forties, about Lee's height, but he many pounds heavier. His face was bruised, his eyes both sporting a raccoon mask of bruises indicating a broken nose.

I watched him scan the room, lazily playing with hair along Nicki's neck. That kiss had gotten me more than a little hard and was hoping I didn't have to stand up anytime soon. It occurred to me in surprise that the kiss from Nicki, even though it had been just a kiss, had made me more aroused than any of the men I'd fucked in the last six years.

A glance at Nicki in the seat next to me confirmed that he was having a similar problem. I couldn't help but let a smile tickle the corners of my mouth.

Nicki followed my gaze and I heard a whispered, "Fuck you, Devereaux," as he shifted uncomfortably in his seat. I almost laughed, but the sound of the police officer's voice interrupted the quiet of the waiting area.

"Devereaux family?" He yelled, in what seemed like an unnecessarily loud voice as he walked toward us. Mama K and Mama D looked up and nodded. I felt Nicki freeze in the chair next to me. I glanced at him, and his face had gone white. I watched him swallow nervously, before visibly forcing himself to relax.

"Yes, officer?" said Mama K.

"I'm Sergeant Dowling. John Dowling," he said, his gaze roaming over all of us, like I would normally assess an opponent before a match. I watched him look at each of us in turn, until he got to Mason. Then his gaze turned positively predatory.

"I'm investigating the *hit and run* that involved your sons last night," he said.

"Have you found anything yet?" I demanded.

"Nothing yet, and probably won't, to be honest. No security systems, nothing documenting the attack," he responded, scanning a notebook he'd pulled from his pocket. "Fucking idiots if you ask me. That area of town and no security? They were practically begging for something to happen."

Lee and I were both on our feet and headed toward the officer before he'd finished his sentence, but Mama K beat us to him.

"You watch your tongue, young man!" She said, her eyes narrowed, her voice low and deadly. "My sons are not idiots, and you will treat them, and us, with respect, or I will be having a conversation with your Lieutenant."

The officer looked like he'd been punched, and he backpedaled away from the tiny woman. People always underestimated my moms, especially in a fight.

Anger suffused his face as he realized he had just backed down from a woman literally half his size. He looked back at Mason again, and that predatory look was back.

"Are you Cameron?" the officer asked.

A short, jerky nod was all the response Mason made.

"May I have a word with you, privately?"

Mason and Lee followed the officer to a group of chairs by the door. Dowling glared at Lee me as he began to speak. I couldn't hear what he was saying, but Mason had gone pale as a ghost. I saw confusion register on Lee's face and an animated discussion started.

My eyes landed on Mason's face. The kid looked terrified. When the hell had I started thinking of Mason as a kid? He was older than I was! Still, there was something... vulnerable... about the man. I could see where it would trigger every single one of my older brother's protective instincts.

Then I heard raised voices, Lee's rising above the others.

"My parents' hearts are breaking, and you're going to fucking lie to me?" he demanded.

The drama was interrupted just then by a young man in a white lab coat over scrubs.

"The Mrs. Devereauxs?" He asked.

It drew all of our attention back to my parents.

"Kyra and Diana is fine," Mama K said, her hand reaching out and grabbing Mama D's.

"I'm Dr. Watley, the orthopedic surgeon who operated on Hudson," he said. The surgeon's short hair was plastered back against his face, bits of it dry but looking like hay. Or like hair that had been stuck under a surgeon's cap for hours.

"How is he?" Mama D asked, fear and hope warring on her face.

"We were able to save his leg," Dr. Watley began. There was a collective sigh of relief as he answered. "...but you need to be aware, the chance of infection is high."

He looked around the little circle.

"Sonny has what we call an open comminuted fracture of his right femur. That means the bone broke into multiple pieces and there were a lot of bone fragments, including the one that nicked his femoral artery. We were able to repair the damage to the artery quickly and put pins in place to secure the bone together."

"So what's the bad news?" Bishop demanded. "Because the look on your face tells me there's more to it."

Mama D sent a quelling look toward Bishop, but the surgeon nodded.

"Any time you have an open fracture, you have the risk of infection. EMS told us Sonny was found lying in some mulch along the side of the building. There is a very high probability that he's going to get an infection from the bacteria introduced into his system from his wound. Once we repaired the damage to his blood supply and determined he had adequate perfusion to his lower extremities, we spent most of the time in surgery just cleaning out his wound and trying to remove all the bone fragments we could find."

My parents' faces were pale, their eyes fixed on Dr. Watley's face.

"We've already started him on antibiotics, but we will need to keep a close eye on him. He is going to require rehab to regain the use of his leg," he told my parents, his hand covering their clasped fingers.

"…Is he going to be able to walk again?" Mama K asked.

"It's going to be a long road to recovery, but your son is strong. If he wasn't a fighter, he would never have made it to my operating table," the doctor nodded at them reassuringly. "That, and the fact he has such a good support system, leads me to believe he is going to make it through this."

My parents thanked the doctor, and before we knew it everyone was hugging. It was such a relief to know that Sonny was going to be all right. Whatever happened from here, we'd tackle it together.

I turned and looked for Lee and Mason to tell them the good news. I could see them in one of the consultation rooms, the door shut and the cop standing outside the door. Lee and Mason seemed to be arguing about something. I could see anger and hurt flitting over Lee's face as he talked with Mason. The cop stood outside the door, his arms crossed. I made my way over to the room

I walked up to the door and the officer stepped sideways, barring my path.

"…Excuse me?" I said, my voice calm and low.

"They're talking," he said, trying to stare me down.

"I can see that. I need to speak with them," I said. The officer just stared at me.

"Please step aside, I need to speak with my brother," the cop just grunted at me, his hands balling into fists. I could hear Mason and my brother easily through the door.

"...I'm sorry, Lee," he said. He sounded like he was about to cry. "I can't stay. I can't... endanger you, or your family, any further. Just ship anything I left at your place to Lizzie. She'll get it to me."

I'd heard enough. I sidestepped the cop and shouldered past him.

"Hey guys!" I said brightly, ignoring the cop's muttered curse. "Everything okay? The doctor just came out. He said he thinks Sonny's going to be okay. They think they were able to save his leg."

I saw both Lee and Mason sigh in relief.

"Good. That's... I'm really glad, Kaine," Mason said softly, his blue eyes darting from me back to Lee. His face was so fucking... sad. It looked like his heart was breaking.

"Thanks, Kaine," Lee said, his eyes blank, never leaving Mason's face.

I nodded at the two of them, confused as hell by the tension in the room. It was their business, though, so I left the room, stepping around Dowling again.

"Some other time, punk," he said as I passed him.

"You name it," I snarled. Who the *hell* was this asshole?

I went back to where my family sat. Mama K and Mama D looked up as I dropped down into the chair next to Nicki.

"What's going on?" Nicki asked, looking across the waiting area to the room I'd just left.

I saw Mason walking down the hall with the cop, and Lee just sitting in the consultation room, his head bowed.

"I'm not sure..." I said truthfully. "But I think Mason's leaving."

"What the fuck?" Bishop demanded. I shrugged.

"I don't know, just heard Lee arguing with him. Plus, that cop was a dick," I said. I generally had a great deal of respect for anyone who wore a uniform. That guy, however, was like all the worst stories you ever heard about people in power.

"I better go check on him," Bishop said, jumping to his feet.

A while later, we all knew Mason had left. He was gone, without a real explanation to anyone, including, it sounded like, Lee.

We visited with Hicks, briefly, but when Nicki and I went back he was asleep. The nurses said he had been really agitated about Sonny, and he wouldn't stop trying to get up and go search for him until they finally brought Sonny down from recovery and placed him in the bed next to him.

I realized, belatedly, that I hadn't messaged Weaver, so I took care of that once we came back from seeing the twins.

ME: Hey, Lil Bit. Both the boys are out of surgery and resting in the ICU. They were able to save Sonny's leg, and Hicks is resting.

WEAVER: Thank goddess!

I chuckled. Weaver never did things the easy way. Not even her swearing.

ME: They are going to take a while to heal. Hicks... It sounds like he's having some memory problems. Lee had to tell him about the accident three times, and he still wasn't remembering.

WEAVER: Shit. There goes the fifty bucks he owes me... Or maybe I can convince him he owed me a hundred?

I laughed. Trust Weaver to bring some humor into the situation.

WEAVER: I'm trying to get emergency leave, but not sure how quickly I'll be able to get there. Give them my love, will you? And let me know if anything changes!

ME: Always.

Once we got the news, we relocated to the central lounge of the hospital. The moment I did so, I sank down into one of the cushioned seats and swore, wishing we'd done it sooner. The chairs up here were *much* more comfortable.

Once we'd found the waiting area, though, Mama K and Mama D insisted we go back to the house and get some sleep. We decided we'd take turns at the hospital, making sure the boys were never left alone. It made it a lot easier that they were in beds right next to each other.

Nicki had apparently been dropped off by his roommate, who had gone to stay at a friend's house for the night. I drove Nicki and I back to the house. Bishop insisted he was fine and headed to the dojo to run a class that afternoon for Mama D. Lee decided to stay with the moms at the hospital, which I thought everyone felt better about. None of us felt like he should be alone right now.

We were all stunned at Mason's abrupt departure. He and Lee had seemed so... *right*... together. I guessed that'd just go to show you. Appearances were deceiving.

We pulled up to the house and I had the car in park before I even registered the fact that I had brought Nicki home with me.

"Shit, I'm sorry, Nick," I'll take you home..." I began, starting the car back up.

"No, seriously, this is fine," he smiled at me. "It's not like I haven't slept here a million nights before this."

I chuckled. He wasn't wrong. Nicki and I had alternated staying at each other's houses when we were dating. At first, his parents and mine had been "concerned" about us becoming intimate during a sleepover. They'd not so subtly begun eliminating our opportunities to spend time together, which had driven us both crazy.

So one night, without telling either set of parents what we were doing, we invited them all four "out to dinner" at the tree house.

Nicki's dad hadn't been able to make it, but his mom had come, and so had both of mine.

We'd escorted them up to the tree house, where we had set out pizza and a two liter or soda. For sixteen-year-olds, it was *haute* cuisine.

They could have laughed at us, but they didn't. We'd eaten pizza, laughed, and enjoyed the meal. The last piece was finished and the trash picked up, and I saw Nicki look at me and nod, and I knew it was time.

"Moms, we'd... we'd like to talk to you guys about something," I began.

We sat in a loose semi-circle in the treehouse, both my moms seated on a pile of pillows under one window. Nicki's mom, as our "guest" sat in the one folding chair. All eyes fell on me, and I could feel my face getting red, but Nicki smiled in encouragement. He moved over and sat down next to me on the floor and took my hand in his. He flashed me a grin and squeezed my hand.

"You... you guys need to stop trying to keep Nicki and me apart," I said in a rush. "You've been working overtime to keep us from spending the night together, and we want it to stop."

"We're sixteen, and practically adults, and if we wanted to have sex, there are lots better places to do it than surrounded by family!" Nicki exclaimed.

Mama K's eyes were dancing merrily as she glanced at Mama D and Mrs. Terhune. Mama D was glancing around the treehouse thoughtfully, seemingly just beginning to understand the potential for trouble in this very private spot.

"While you are almost sixteen and 'practically adults', you are still our children," Nicki's mom said, her face appropriately solemn.

"We don't want you doing something... something you might regret later, muchachos," Mama K said.

Nicki nodded in understanding.

"We know, but we love each other. We don't intend to have anything to regret," he said, his cheeks turning pink. "...But we also know neither of us is ready to... to have sex."

He glanced at me nervously, and this time it was my turn to squeeze his hand in encouragement. We'd talked about this ahead of time. Mama K and Mama D always said that if you were not mature enough to talk about sex in an adult manner, you weren't mature enough to be having sex. We desperately wanted to prove to them how mature we were, so...

"Since we already know that, and we aren't planning on having sex, it's driving us crazy that you guys are trying to limit our time together so much!" I exclaimed.

"Mom, you and Dad are talking about us moving to Florida," Nicki continued, catching his mother's thoughtful gaze. "If that happens... I might never see Kaine again. Or... or I could get sick, and... and die before we ever move back."

Silence fell in the room. We'd all contemplated the possibility, how could we not? Nicki's illness was so damn unpredictable. But I think it was the first time that any of us had ever confronted stated it quite so baldly.

"I'm not trying to be dramatic about this, but if that was to happen... I would want to enjoy every second I could possibly have with Kaine before we go," he finished.

"Nicki and I have been best friends for years. If we wanted to sneak around behind your backs, we could have done it already. We're trying to be mature about this," I said. Despite the embarrassment that came with talking to my parents about sex, I did my best to convey how seriously we were taking this.

"We promise to stay out of the X-rated zone," I continued.

"It's easy to promise good behavior when there is no temptation, boys," Mama D said. "It's quite a different thing to behave when no one is watching."

"Yes, but we're always watching!" Nicki said. "Kaine and I want what's best for each other. Even with us moving to Florida, Kaine wants me to do it if it can help find out why I'm sick all the time."

I leaned forward, hands on my slightly grubby knees.

"Nicki doesn't want us to have sex because he's worried I'll catch whatever he's got. He didn't even want to kiss me at first, until I convinced him I'd already be sick if he was contagious. We just... we want you to trust us," I finished.

Nicki nodded and dug around under the table.

"So, we created a contract," he said, proudly passing the somewhat-worse-for-wear piece of paper to his mom.

She stared at in bemusement as she began reading. We had done so many revisions of it that at this point, I had it memorized.

The page read, "We, Kaine Devereaux and Dominic Terhune, promise our parents that we will not have sexual intercourse with each other until we are much, much older (at least eighteen), or maybe even REALLY old, like twenty-one!

In exchange for our solemn vow, our parents will STOP trying to keep us from having sleepovers and spending time together! When we do decide to have sex, we will treat this experience with the serious-ness that it deserves, and we will be responsible.

Sincerely, Kaine and Nicki."

"P.S. When that happens, we also promise not to get each other pregnant."

Nicki's mom passed the paper to my parents, who read it solemnly, but I could see a twinkle of laughter in Mama K's eyes. I was pretty sure in that moment we had made our case, but I still held my breath. While our three parents looked at each other, Nicki and I had held each other's hands tightly, waiting for their verdict.

Finally, Nicki's mom nodded.

"I trust you, Nicki," she said. Then she looked at me. "And I trust you, Kaine. I know how much you love my boy. I know you would never do anything that would put him at risk."

Mama D and Mama K looked at each other for a moment, and it was one of those times when I knew my parents were reading each other's thoughts. They both looked back at us.

"Okay, but when the time *does* come," Mama D said. "You promise to be responsible."

We had both nodded happily.

Those last few weeks had been almost heaven. Just "almost" though, because we'd quickly found out that Nicki's parents had, indeed, made the decision to move the family to Florida.

The slamming of Nicki's door made me jump and brought me out of my reverie.

I climbed out of the car and walked over to the front door. I unlocked it and stepped inside, Nicki following close behind.

The house looked just as it had when I'd left earlier in the evening. The couch in the living room had a crocheted afghan thrown haphazardly across it.

"Do you want something to drink?" I asked, my own throat suddenly dry as I walked across the room, suddenly hit by a major case of nerves. What the heck was wrong with me? I'd had Nicki here a million times as a kid.

Maybe that was the issue? We weren't *kids* anymore.

I turned around and saw Nicki hanging his jacket up on the coat rack. He lifted it to hang it on a hook, his shirt riding up just a bit to show a mouthwatering strip of skin between his low-slung jeans and the hem of his shirt. I could just see the band of his briefs sticking out from under his jeans. It was dark, but as I looked at his back, I could just make out what looked like... a scar?

"Hey, what do you think—" he began, then froze as his eyes tagged mine. For a moment we stood still, our gazes locked on each other. His skin was the color of light cream, his dark auburn hair like heated copper in the light. His eyes... his eyes were like ice, so cool and beautiful, sucking me into their depths.

I swallowed, and watched his eyes drop to my throat. I could swear his whole body shuddered as he looked at me, and I couldn't hold back anymore.

I moved toward him, my skin suddenly feeling too tight, too hot, like the only thing keeping me from exploding was the cool light in his eyes. As I moved closer, I saw his tongue flick out to lick across his lips nervously, and with that one small gesture, I was done for.

Our lips were clashing together before either of us could blink. My head tilted slightly so our mouths could slot across each other. He stumbled slightly, and only then did I realize I had reached out and gripped his hips, dragging his body against me. I was only a little bit taller than he was, but that inch seemed to be just enough to make us fit together perfectly.

I felt his arms go around me, his fingers digging into my back like it was a lifeline. We kissed for long moments, tongues tangling with deep, drugging touches. My cock, which had been good all day at the hospital, had suddenly sprung to attention and strained against the confinement of my jeans. As we ground together, I could feel an answering hardness in Nicki's pants. *Fuuuck...*

Nicki was the one who pulled back, slowly, from that amazingly hot kiss, but never let go of me completely.

"Kaine," he whispered, his voice a velvety caress on my skin. It almost felt like his voice was reaching inside me, winding around my heart like a cat would wind around its favorite human's feet.

I found myself staring at his lips, so enchanted by his mouth that I couldn't look away.

"Kaine," he said again, more insistently. My eyes flew to his. I blinked slowly, more than a little lust drunk by the nearness of him.

"What?" I asked, my eyes drinking in the sight of him.

"Can we... Can we go somewhere... private," he asked. The air whooshed out of my lungs like I'd just hit the mat.

15

NICKI

"WOULD THAT BE OKAY?" I ASKED. "CAN WE GO SOMEWHERE PRIVATE TO talk for a little while?"

"Um, sure. We can go to my room?" he said, his voice ending up on an up note, as if in question. I nodded, my body all too eager to agree if it meant spending more time exploring his.

"Lemme grab us some water real quick," he offered, finally letting go of my waist and darting into the kitchen.

I almost stumbled again when he let me go. We'd kissed when we were kids, but it had never been like that.

Kaine came back to the living room and handed me one of the bottles. Before he led me up the stairs, he turned and offered me his hand. I couldn't help but grin foolishly at him as we went up the stairway hand in hand. I felt so dorky, but so... right at the same time.

His room had changed a lot in the last six years. Gone were the majority of the comic books, though a couple were still framed or on display on the walls. The twin bed was gone, replaced by what looked to be a king size one. Which made sense. Kaine was a tall guy, the many hours he spent to keep fit reflecting in his athletic figure. I figured he would probably need a lot of room. Plus, I was sure anyone who'd slept over would have...

I shut that shit down immediately. It was none of my business who he had or had not slept with in the intervening years we were apart. I had no right to be interested in details of his sex life.

The bed was covered with what looked at first like a layer of t-shirts. I did a double take when I sat on the bed, because I recognized the shirts. Or rather, what used to be shirts.

The entire quilt was made of blocks of soft cotton fabric. The fabric had been taken from t-shirts that I clearly remembered Kaine wearing when we were kids. One block in the middle of the quilt in particular caught my attention. It was a t-shirt from the television show "Serenity". It had the words, "I Aim To Misbehave" on it. I'd bought the shirt for Kaine for his sixteenth birthday.

I had planned on flying up to see him for his birthday using the money I'd made tutoring. Of course, I'd gotten sick, and hadn't been able to take the flight. I'd sent him the shirt as a poor substitute.

I ran my hands over the smooth cotton and looked up at him in question.

"Mama D made it for me," Kaine said, sitting down across from me on the bed and toeing off his shoes. "I really hit a growth spurt the year after you left. I wore that shirt until it was too tight and too short to be decent. She knew I didn't want to get rid of it, though, so she took all my shirts with sayings on them that I liked and made them into quilt blocks. She gave it to me for Christmas the following year."

He ran his hands over the much-used quilt, his fingers tracing the stitches lovingly. Mama D was super crafty, and always had some kind of project or another going. She made her own soaps and lotions, too. She had made each of her kids their own signature scents and named them after the character traits she saw most in her kids. She sold stuff online and at craft fairs, in addition to co-managing their chain of dojos.

"She's pretty amazing," I said, the breath catching in my throat. "Both your parents are."

Kaine gazed at me, his eyes soft and kind as I tried to catch my breath.

"Nicki... What happened?" he asked. "I can't help but feel like there is something major you haven't told me. Something more than just your parents breaking up."

He cocked his head and looked at me, his blond hair flopping sideways a little. He made me think of a sparrow trying to figure out how to get the food out of the bird feeder. Only he was trying to get my secrets out of me.

I shook my head, my shame choking me like it was a living creature, its slimy fingers slipping beneath my skin, strangling the words in my throat. I heard a voice in my head, the all too familiar crack of the belt and the sound of my father's voice as he'd beaten me.

"Weak. Useless. Disgusting. Count, goddamn it! Good for nothing. Why didn't you just die and save me from the humiliation of having a son who's a fucking fa—"

I jerked away from Kaine and headed for the door. Why had I thought I could do this? He deserved so much better than me. He deserved someone stronger, someone who would have fought, who would have found a way to escape. Someone who wasn't sick, who wouldn't die and leave him, like so many other people had left him…

Through the dark storm raging in my head, a little voice tried to convince me that I could tell Kaine the whole story, that he'd understand what I'd done to protect my mother. That voice sounded suspiciously like my mother's, but it was drowned out by the flood of vile words I'd absorbed from my father like a sponge.

I had made it to the door before I was able to force myself to stop running. I leaned my forehead against the door shaking it in the vain hope that I could shake off the sound of my father's voice. I saw my palms flat against the wooden door, those hated tattoos staring at me.

How was Kaine going to react when he found out about the deal I'd made with my father? Would Kaine agree if he knew my dad hated me? What if he thought being sick was some kind of punishment, that I was an abomination? A worthless waste of human flesh, who had caused my parents to split and humiliated my father…

I felt like I was standing on a precipice. To either side of me a yawning chasm that threatened to swallow me whole. My terror of Kaine's judgment made the breath in my lungs freeze and I stood leaning against the door. Then I felt it... a touch, feather light, gently running over my back. I tried to pull away. I didn't want him to feel my scars, to know... *Fuck!*

To know how fucking weak I was.

Goddammit, this was *Kaine* I was talking about! My first love, my best friend. Even though we had been apart for years, spending time with him came as naturally as breathing. I'd slid right back into my spot with him, with his family. A spot he'd been holding for me in his heart for six years.

He had shared with me the stories of the weeks he'd hidden in the abandoned rental house, slowly starving as he tried to find a way to survive. He'd told me about his fears, his terror of waking up to find his family gone, again and again... And he'd faced his fears. How could I do less?

I made myself turn back around and I took a deep, hoarse breath that turned into a cough that rumbled through my chest. Nausea swirled in my gut as I tried to get the words out, to tell him what had happened...

"I—My dad, he— he was—" I saw Kaine's eyes narrow and his jaw clench. I'd tried to choke out an explanation, but the words still wouldn't come. I felt the censure in his gaze. *"Fuck, Kaine! I'm so sorry..."* I doubled over with a sob, my hands grabbing my hair in a punishing grip, the pain anchoring me in the midst of my emotional storm.

I couldn't speak. I shook my head wildly in frustration as Kaine tried to talk to me, but the words were just noise roaring in my ears. I couldn't get the words out to tell him, so I did the only thing I could do. I showed him.

I stood up quickly and ripped the shirt off over my head and turned my back to him, head bowed. I could feel my whole body flushing with humiliation, my face scarlet as I faced the closed bedroom door. A full-length mirror hung on the back of it, and I could see the look of horror on Kaine's face. I knew what he'd see, and the shame of it stung through my body like a million angry bees. I'd seen it hundreds of times in my own mirror.

The scars crisscrossed my back, varying in length and width. They started around the middle of my back and moved downward from there. My father had typically used his leather belt to beat me, but he certainly didn't restrain himself if it wasn't at hand. I had gouges out of the flesh along one hip from the belt buckle and more shiny pink and angry red stripes that dipped below my waistband from the time he'd used an extension cord. I knew Kaine couldn't see below the waistband of my jeans, but it felt like I could feel his eyes moving over my body, feel him see the scars that continued down across my ass, stopping just above the backs of my thighs.

Sound seemed to return, and I heard him gasp as he saw my back, then a whispered, "What the *fuck*..."

I just shook my head as I showed him my secret, my shame. The only other person who had ever seen any of my scars was Vivian, and even she hadn't seen them all.

I flushed further at the thought. I couldn't blame my father for all of it. I was the one who provoked him, he'd certainly told me that often enough. I knew there were times when he was just looking for some peace and quiet and I pushed and pushed and pushed. If I'd just done better, been better, he wouldn't have done it. If I hadn't been gay, I could have been a better son, a better man, and he wouldn't have been pushed to this extreme. It was my fault.

Dad's frustrations with Mom had primarily come because she was always interceding for me. Their life had been fine before I'd come along, this undersized, sick freak of a son. Everything that had happened since then had been, essentially, my fault. My mom dying, my father's rage, marriage ending, all of it.

Maybe if I had been more like my mom, more understanding of my father's moods, more of a peacemaker or just generally a better son to him, he wouldn't have felt the need to take his anger out on me as often.

I finally realized there was silence in the room, broken only by my harsh breathing as I sucked in air through my mouth. I realized I'd lost track of time and hastily pulled my shirt back on over my head. It was only as I did so that I realized my face was wet with tears, again.

Fuck. I heard my dad's voice in my head telling me I was such a fucking crybaby.

I'd just gotten my hands through the armholes and was pulling the shirt down over my head when I was slammed forward against the door. I tried to brace myself before I hit it, but I didn't have to. Kaine's arms had circled around me protectively, his chest to my back. I felt his body shaking against mine, but it took me a minute to realize it was because he was sobbing. For me.

"Who? Who did this to you, Nicki? *Who?* Some guy in Florida? Someone else? Because I swear to God I am going to find whoever did this, tear their fucking arm off and beat the living shit out of them for laying hands on you..." he growled, his hands racing up and down my sides protectively, almost reverently.

Tears blinded me for a moment, and a sob of relief wracked me. Part of my brain scolded the other part smugly. I should have known this would have been his response. Kaine had always supported me, always had my back. I should have trusted that he would continue to do so, even after everything that had happened in the last six years.

I tried to answer him, to respond in some kind of way, but the words just came out as an incoherent, broken babble.

"He—I—My—My mom—He—"

Kaine gently turned me around, his fingers tracing over my face until I quieted. It took me a moment to realize he was wiping away my tears.

"Shhhh... It's okay, baby, slow down... Take it one step at a time..." He whispered.

The tears finally ran dry and I was able to stop my babbling mouth, and just stared into his eyes. Kaine's eyes were a different kind of green from his brother's. Lee's were like emeralds, all shiny and glittery. Kaine's were like a deep, warm, mossy green, with flecks of brown and gold surrounding the pupil. I could stare into their depths for hours. I realized, suddenly, they reminded me of my mom's eyes. Not the same, exactly, but the same warmth and compassion were there.

We were mere inches away from each other. I could feel the hot puffs of air as we breathed and I started to calm.

"Feeling better?" he asked after a while.

"Yeah," I managed hoarsely and nodded.

"Good," he said, his eyes still scrunched in concern. "Why don't you sit down."

We sat back down on the bed, Kaine reaching down and untying my shoes before sliding them off. That simple gesture almost caused a new swarm of tears to burst, but instead of sitting across from each other, we sat next to each other at the head of the bed, and Kaine's threw his arm protectively over my shoulders as we snuggled against the pillows.

God, I'd missed this. Missed the feeling of having someone in my corner, someone I could trust and rely on. I'd been so alone over the past six years. Vivian had tried to help, but there was a limit to what she or her family could do. My father was just too powerful.

I felt a part of me I wasn't even aware of begin to relax and unwind in his arms. I knew Kaine would never hurt me, or let anyone else hurt me, ever.

I sighed, my head sagging against his shoulder, exhaustion from the night at the hospital and the emotional tide we'd inadvertently been sucked into taking its toll.

"Tell me what happened, Nicki," he said, his hand running through my hair soothingly. It was a move he'd always done when we were kids. He'd been obsessed with my hair and always loved running his fingers through it.

Finally, slowly, I began to get the story out. I haltingly told him everything, from the time we'd gotten my diagnosis, my mom's confession of infidelity, the beatings, everything up to the point where we left Florida.

Through parts of my story he'd held me tight, and I could feel his simmering fury radiating throughout his body. When I'd told him about my Dad holding me at gunpoint, he had frozen. As I finished my story about Vivian and her stockpile of meds he chuckled.

"I have got to meet her," he whispered, laying a gentle kiss to my temple.

"You will. She is pretty awesome, even if she is a girl," I teased. "We might have to make her an honorary member of the Tree House Club."

We both laughed. When we were kids, his brothers and I had built a tree house in the land behind the Devereaux home. We'd spent many, many hours building on to it and making it something we thought was special. We'd tried to exclude his sister, Weaver, at one point, but his parents had made it clear in no uncertain terms that keeping her out was unacceptable. So we'd make her an honorary member of the Club. She'd come to one meeting, looked around and at our lame decorating attempts and told us we could do so much better.

We'd come back out the next day to find snacks, blankets, pillows, covers for the windows and battery-powered lamps. We had quickly amended our charter to allow females. No one had regretted letting her join us.

"I look forward to meeting her," he answered, his other hand stroking my wrist where the tattoos lay. "Did he do this, too? When we were kids you always swore you'd never get a tattoo," he said, continuing to stroke my skin.

"I was always terrified of the pain," I admitted. "Turns out, there's a lot worse things out there. H-he forced a tattoo artist in Tampa to do it. Threatened to put him in jail for something."

"Nicki..." The simmering fury was back in his gaze. "Why didn't you report him?"

"That's the first question they asked me, too," I said, shaking my head. "Vivian and her parents. My father was the Sheriff of our county. The town was so small, there was no local police department. All reports of domestic abuse went to his office. Dr. Dunwoody, Vivian's dad, reported him when he broke my ankle. Dad just shredded the report in front of me and beat me again."

Kaine's hands tightened on my wrist. It didn't hurt, but I could tell he was pissed.

"When I found out my mom had died, I felt so— guilty. Her death meant my freedom. I knew I could finally escape, that he couldn't hold her life over me anymore. He couldn't hurt her, anymore," I said. "Her, or me."

Kaine turned his face to look at me and smiled gently. "You did all this—endured all this—to keep your mom safe? She didn't even know, did she?"

I shook my head. After that day in court, I'd never seen my mom again.

"Shit, Nick. And people say I have a protective streak…"

I elbowed him gently in the ribs.

"You do! Remember when those guys in junior high were talking smack about Weaver? You scared the shit out of them," I said, smiling.

"Well, she's my sister, I'm supposed to be protective of her," he responded.

"It's always been one of my favorite traits about you," I said, turning to look at him.

He smiled again, but his face became serious.

"How did your mom die?" He asked gently.

"I-I don't know, for sure," I began. "I hadn't really thought about it."

"You never called the lawyers who contacted you?" He questioned.

"Yeah, I did. Just yesterday. I just didn't really ask about it. I— I've just assumed she passed from some kind of complications from AIDS. She'd had it for a long time, and most of her life she had been untreated for it. I have an appointment with the attorney handling her estate next week. I didn't contact them at first because I was afraid Dad would find a way to track me through them, somehow."

"Well, there is that whole 'attorney-client privilege' thing," he said, squeezing me reassuringly.

"I know, it's just…I'm so used to him being the only one with power and influence in my life. I know we moved six years ago, but I'm scared there are still people around here who owe him favors. I just don't want to take the chance," I finished.

Kaine nodded.

"I get it. So, what are your next steps?" he asked.

I paused and thought for a few minutes. What were my next steps?

"School, I think. I-I want to write, like my mom did, back before she met my dad," I said, surprising myself. The idea had just been a nebulous thought in the back of my mind that crystallized at his question. "I don't know if I'll be any good at it, but I think it's something she would like," I finished.

I felt a tiny breath escape me as I thought of writing and sharing stories with others. It terrified me and made me feel horribly vulnerable, but ecstatic at the same time.

"I think you'll be a fantastic writer," he said, smiling at me sweetly. "I remember the stories you used to tell me at night. But, I also think you should do what *you* want, not what your parents would like."

I nodded in agreement and Kaine continued. "So, um... what about... us? What do you want to do about this... this thing between us?"

I looked at him, but I didn't need to be staring into his eyes to feel him next to me. I was hyperaware of his presence. It was like he was a live wire, and I could feel the electricity humming in his presence just by concentrating. My eyes roamed over his face. His skin was flushed with embarrassment, his blond hair falling across his face, hiding his eyes from me just like he'd done when we were kids.

"Do you want there to be an us? After everything?" I asked, my heart choking the words in my throat. I desperately wanted him to say yes, but I also wasn't sure I was the right person for him. I had so much baggage... My dad, my illness, our pasts... everything.

"I hurt you so much, Kaine. I didn't want to, didn't mean to, but the reality is I still did it. And, given the same situation, I don't know what I'd do differently..." I said.

Kaine turned and looked at me full on. He smiled at me again, that same smile I remembered from when we were kids, the one that looked like his soul was shining out of his eyes.

"That wasn't your fault," he said. "I'm just...furious at myself for not seeing it. I was so blinded by my own pain that I wasn't able to see yours. If I'd noticed, maybe I could have...I don't know, prevented it? Ended it, maybe?" he shook his head in frustration.

"There's no way you could have known…" I began.

"I should have! If anyone should have known, it should have been me," he insisted. "It doesn't matter how many times you say it, I'm going to blame myself for a while. What it boils down to though, is that you were doing what you had to in order for you, and your mom, to survive. I don't blame you for that decision, Nicki. How could I? But to answer your question, do I want this thing between us? Yes. My answer to you will always be yes."

He leaned in and laid a gentle kiss on my lips, and I sighed melting against him as he took control, his tongue teasing the seam of my lips until I opened for him. He plundered my mouth as if it was the most delicious thing he had ever tasted, his arms wrapped around me, his hands sliding up under my shirt and dancing along the skin of my back, his fingers stroking each scar lovingly.

I gasped lightly as we finally broke apart, my hands clutching at his hips to keep me stable.

"You taste just as fucking good as I remember," he whispered.

"You, too," I said in response, realizing suddenly I was grinning like a fool. "You taste like sugarless Bubble Yum."

Kaine laughed, his head thrown back as we lay entwined on his bed. "They just stopped making it. I have to find a new brand," he said.

"Oh no! It took you years to find a brand you loved! I hope you have some stockpiled…" I answered.

He grinned and rolled over setting his camera aside and opening the drawer on the bedside table to show me its contents: Inside the drawer was what looked like an entire case of sugarless Bubble Yum. Right next to lube and condoms.

I'd started to laugh, then my gaze caught on the supplies. My eyes jumped to his and my breath caught in my throat. I could feel my facing turning a bright red as my pulse began to race. This was something we'd talked about when we were kids, about how we wanted to have sex "someday". But, someday hadn't come soon enough, and we'd lost our chance. Or so I'd thought. Kaine obviously hadn't been celibate in my absence.

Kaine seemed to realize suddenly what else was in the drawer other than the gum, and he slammed it shut.

"Shit, Nicki, I didn't mean—" he began.

"I know," I said. "I— I didn't expect that you had been a monk all these years."

His eyes searched my face for confirmation and eventually seemed satisfied with what he found there.

"Have you ever...?" He asked tentatively, his fingers tracing the collar of my shirt.

I shook my head. "I— I didn't dare. At first, I didn't want to take a chance at doing to someone else what my mom did to me, even though she didn't know. Not many people would have been interested anyway, what with my diagnosis and all. Even in this day and age, people are still so scared, and I can't exactly blame them. Plus, with my dad... I didn't have a way to hide the— the bruises when he— when he beat me. So it was just... easier, just to be alone." I sat up in the bed, pulling my knees up and wrapping my arms around them. "I think that's the first time I've said that out loud. He beat me. My father... beat me..." I whispered.

I felt tiny and fragile, like a breath of air would shatter me into a million pieces. Kaine sat up next to me, wrapping his arm around me and pulling me against him again.

"I swear on everything precious to me, Nick, that he will never lay another hand on you," he promised.

We sat there quietly for a few minutes. Somehow, having Kaine there, his arm around me, felt like he was coating my heart with a protective layer of steel.

"So, you never got to date? At all?" he asked.

I shook my head.

"I did go out with Vivian to a couple of clubs and was shocked —shocked I tell you!—to find out that club bathrooms weren't always used for personal hygiene..." I teased.

Kaine chuckled.

"I'll have to take you to The Belt," he said.

I raised an eyebrow at him.

"It's a local gay nightclub. I work there as a bartender," he said.

"The Belt... Downtown? That's the place where Vivian works!" I exclaimed. "The owner got some kind of small business grant that let her hire students and still provide health insurance, right?"

"Yep... And guess who wrote that grant request?" he laughed.

"That is amazing," I said. "Wait, I thought you were working at your Moms' dojo?" .

"I do that, too. And go to school..." he said.

"Bar, school, dojo? That's a lot," I said. Kaine looked at me oddly, his skin suddenly going pale.

"That... asshole..." he whispered, shock washing over his face.

"What?" I asked, suddenly frightened.

"The... the night I almost—that I... that I... found Bottles—" Kaine took a deep breath. "I called you. On my eighteenth birthday. I had tried to do what you asked, tried to let you go, but that night... It just *hurt* too goddamn much, y'know? I *had* to speak to you. I knew if I could just talk to you, we could figure everything out. It was late, and your Dad answered the phone. He told me you were out... on a date."

"*What?*" I exclaimed, jerking around to look at him. "You... You called me?"

He nodded.

"I was sick," I said, running my fingers over the backs of his knuckles. "I was so upset about not getting to be there for your birthday, Vivian had wanted to take me to some stupid rom com to cheer me up, but I got sick. I was in the hospital with a bout of pneumonia."

The feelings as I considered all the pain my father had caused ripped through me. Shock. Anger. Betrayal. Sorrow. I had thought my father's hatred had at least just been targeted at me. He had to have known what he was doing to Kaine. I never thought he would have hurt someone else. I shook my head, trying to chase the fog from my head. Then the reality of his words came into focus, and I swallowed hard, my mouth suddenly dry with trepidation.

"The night you almost... what?" I asked.

Kaine closed his eyes and tightened his arms around me.

"It... it was a long time ago, Nicki," he said.

"Tell me," I insisted.

He sighed and squeezed my hand.

"I was... I was suicidal. I almost jumped from the All-America Bridge downtown," he said.

"Oh my god, Kaine," I whispered, staring at him in shock.

"I'm doing better now," he rushed to reassure me. "I take medication, and I've been seeing a counselor regularly. We've actually cut my visits down to only once every month or so. It's really just an opportunity to touch base, and make sure my meds are still working."

I reached my hands out and traced his lips with my fingers, still horrified at the thought that I could have lost him when I was too far away to have done anything. That my own father could have triggered his attempt. Fury boiled beneath my skin. If you were going to hurt me, fine. I'd deal with that. But, when you went after someone I loved... I felt Kaine's eyes on me, and I looked at him.

"Whoa..." He breathed, the word a kiss of wind on my face. "I don't know what you were thinking just now, but I pity the fool that pissed you off."

"That fool is my father," I said, fury simmering in the back of my head. Guilt hid there, too, though. It was my fault this had happened to Kaine. My fault for leaving, my fault for allowing my shitty father to run my life. I tried to shake myself free of the anger. I'd seen what it had done to my Dad. I didn't want it destroying my life. I tried refocusing on Kaine.

"Bar, school, dojo? That's a lot," I said finally.

"It is, but up until now, I didn't really have anything else to do, so I kind of threw myself into work and school," he said.

"Up until now?" I teased.

"Well, now that my boyfriend's back in town, I'm sure I'll need more time to do other things..." he grinned.

I froze at his words.

"Your b-boy—" I sat up suddenly and moved to the edge of the bed. What the hell had I done? Of course, someone like Kaine was seeing someone. Wait, Kaine was as loyal as the day was long. How could he have kissed me, if he was seeing someone? Maybe it was a pity kiss? That was out of character for Kaine. At least the Kaine I knew...

"I-I should go—" I said abruptly, sliding away from his grasp.

Arms wrapped around me and stopped me before I could stand and escape. I felt Kaine's body pressed up against me from behind, and I could feel the hot pressure of his erection as he wrapped himself around me.

"I can hear your brain churning from over there. I was talking about you, doofus," he whispered in my ear. *"You* are my boyfriend. The man I love. Always have been. Always will be."

"Oh," I said, my brain taking a moment to register his words. "Oh!" I turned and looked at him.

"Seriously? I mean, before you make that decision, we need to talk about, well, everything..." I began babbling. "I mean, we should discuss sex, I guess, and PrEP and—

"I know *all* about sex," he nodded at me reassuringly. "Our contract with the moms expired a long time ago."

He grinned at me, the boyish, heart-stopping smile that made my mouth go dry and my lips tingle in anticipation. I thought my favorite thing about Kaine was his smile. Well, his smile, and the way he would run his fingers along the nape of my neck. And... *wait,* where was I?

"Um, yeah, I know," I said, trying not to blush. I was a grown man, dammit! If I couldn't handle talking about sex...

"PrEP," I declared, avoiding Kaine's gaze.

"Prep, as in preparation? Because that seems a little fast. I don't usually put out on the *first* date," he winked at me, and I felt my blush growing even deeper. *Fuck.* If I was this tongue-tied just talking to him about it, how was I going to do this?

"But I might be convinced, see as how we have history and all. If you mean PrEP as in, 'pre-exposure prophylaxis,'" his voice rolled over me in a passable British accent. "I'm already on it."

"Wait, what?" I exclaimed. "You're on PrEP? Why—"

He shushed me with a finger to my lips.

"Why? Because I'm a gay man in his twenties? *Duh,*" He grinned as he teased me. "Not everyone is thoughtful about keeping cooties to

themselves. And I haven't exactly been celibate the last six years, Nicki. I... I've fooled around. A *lot*."

Kaine's face grew serious and an embarrassed glow flushed his cheeks.

"I know I wanted to wait, to find the right person. But after you left, I think I went... a little crazy for a while..." he said, his voice trailing off for a moment. "It was like I was trying fill in the Grand Canyon, one pebble at a time. I had this aching chasm inside me that no amount of sex would fill. I even had a steady boyfriend a couple of years ago, but he complained that I worked too much and he didn't get to see me enough."

"I can understand that. I know I haven't seen enough of you," I teased, waggling my eyebrows at him as I deliberately tried to lighten the mood.

"Really? Does that mean we've done enough talking for now?" he asked.

"I think we've been sufficiently adult-like for the evening. I'd like to just...*be*, for a while. Would that be okay?" I asked hesitantly.

"As long as I can just *be* with you," he whispered.

Kaine leaned into me, his hair falling down across his eyes, but he didn't bother pushing it back this time. I felt the satiny smoothness of his lips brush across my own, and I groaned as desire bubbled up from the core of my being. For so long I'd pushed all my feelings away, not even letting myself think about what life could have been like for us if things had been different. If I'd been able to love Kaine like I'd wanted.

I could feel Kaine's heartbeat pounding beneath my fingertips as I ran my hands over his chest, then under his shirt. His skin was hot and smooth, the brush of my touch causing goosebumps to rise up on his skin. I opened my mouth, my tongue flicking out to taste his lips, his tongue, caressing his mouth inside and out before nibbling along his jaw to his neck.

It was his turn to groan as I sucked a necklace of love bites along his chest before moving down to his nipples. I vaguely remembered him pulling his shirt off and tossing it aside as I began sucking at the honey-colored nubs. His body rippled under my touch, his defined abs contracting and relaxing as I caressed his body.

He tasted like summer heat and candle wax, like fire and first kisses. His touch was like coming home.

"Kaine…" I whispered, my hands clawing gently at the front of his jeans and the hardness I felt there. "I need… I need to see you…"

I looked up at him, realizing I was on the floor in front his bed. He was leaning back on his elbows, his eyes hooded as he watched me. His gaze caught mine, and I smiled knowingly at him. Keeping my eyes on his, I leaned forward and slid the zipper of his jeans down, my own positively painful erection. Fuck. I was so damn hard, but there was no way I was giving up a chance to get my hands, or mouth, on Kaine.

"Up," I commanded harshly as I tugged on his jeans. I saw an answering spark of fire in his eyes, but he didn't say anything, merely flexed his legs to raise his ass up off the bed far enough for me to slide his jeans and underwear down.

I pushed the offending denim down his legs and to the floor. Socks quickly followed, and I realized suddenly that I had an incredibly gorgeous godlike man on the bed in front of me, and he was all mine.

The thought almost made me come in my pants like a teenager, and I chuckled.

He cocked an eyebrow at me.

"I'm wondering if I should be offended," he said. "Here I am in all my bootylicious glory, and you're snickering at me…"

"I'm just appreciating the bounty laid out before me," I insisted, my eyes licking hungrily down his body. "And trying to figure out what I want to do first. Any requests?"

It was his turn to laugh.

"Nope, I'm just going to sit back and enjoy…" he said huskily. He grasped his fingers together and tucked them behind his head, his gorgeous green eyes glittering darkly at me. There was something perversely decadent about him being laid out naked on the bed in front of me while I was still fully clothed.

I trailed my fingers down his sides, causing even more goosebumps to pop up on his skin. I leaned in over his body and just inhaled the incredibly masculine scent of him. He smelled so goddamn good, his scent so familiar, but new and exciting at the same time. I inhaled deeply, smelling the cinnamon-y, musky smell of him.

I grasped his hips and buried my nose against him, my tongue darting out to lick along that spot where the leg and the hip meet.

Kaine groaned. "Fuck, Nicki..."

"I've waited my whole life to do this..." I whispered as I nuzzled the trimmed curls that nested at the base of his cock, just inhaling his scent. His cock was long and thick, the head a dusky red as I looked hungrily at him.

His eyes caught mine as I knelt in front of him. He'd grabbed a pillow to prop up his head so he could look down at me. His eyes were deep pools of mossy green, flecked with gold. I gazed into their depths for an eternity before looking back at his length. He looked almost painfully hard. A bead of pre-cum welled up from his slit and spilled over the edge of his cock, and I couldn't hold back any longer. My tongue flicked out, and the explosion of the taste of him made my eyes roll back in my head, and sent fireworks zinging off through my body.

I licked hungrily at him for more, my tongue dipping into his slit, then sucking all of him into my mouth.

"God, Kaine... You taste so fucking good..." I gasped in between sucks and licks.

I could feel him struggling under me, his body desperate to start thrusting against me. I realized my fingers were digging into his hips, holding him in place, so I deliberately loosened my grip to allow him to start to move.

His body flexed and bowed, rocking back and forth as he fucked my mouth.

"Fuck, Nicki... Fuck, I can't..." I heard the strain, then the warning as he struggled to hold back his release. But I didn't want him to hold back. I wanted him to give me all of him. I wanted to drink him down, suck away all the emptiness and darkness that had tried to take up residence inside of his heart and refill it with life and light and love.

Or maybe I just wanted his cum. Actually, I think I was good either way, and I was tired of Kaine giving and giving and giving and never taking what he needed. So I sucked and nipped, rolling his balls with one hand while stroking his cock with the other. His control was incredible, but I didn't want him in control. So I swiped a spit-slickened finger behind his balls and over his hole. I was rewarded in short order with the feel of him tensing beneath me, his hands flashing out to grasp my hair and hold me still as he fucked my mouth, his hips pistoning back and forth in a punishing rhythm.

"God, Nicki!" he yelled, his whole body spasming as he shot his release, hot and thick, down my throat.

16

KAINE

I'd heard the phrase "seeing stars" before, but I'd never known it could happen during an orgasm.

The feel of Nicki's mouth on my cock, his fingers playing with my balls while he stroked me had been mind-blowing, but when he'd brushed his slick finger over my hole, I'd exploded.

He looked up at me from where he knelt between my legs. Fuck, he still had all of his clothes on. We needed to change that, and quickly. He flashed me a small smile, a hint of nerves apparent in the way he nibbled on his lower lip.

"Was that... okay...?" he asked, his hesitation reminding me he'd never done this before.

"No, it was definitely not okay," I said, my voice racing forward as his face fell. "I definitely think you need work. Like, lots of practice. Lots. On me. And *only* me."

"Oh!" Was all he said, but I saw the smile that flashed across his face, chasing away his hesitation. "Glad to hear you're willing to take one for the team."

"Well, since it's for the betterment of humanity, sure..." I mumbled.

We both laughed, then he crawled his way up the bed to lie down next to me. I snuggled closer to him, my body just one big puddle of splooge. I hadn't felt this relaxed in, like, *ever*.

"Seriously, though, um... did you... is there anything you'd like me to change...?" he asked, his nerves still apparent in the press of his lips, the way his eyes darted around the room and avoided looking at me.

"Nicki..." I whispered. Something in the tone of my voice drew his gaze to me, and he looked up.

"*Kaine...*" he said, my name like a prayer on his lips.

"You are perfect, just the way you are..." I whispered, watching his red hair curl around his head like a fiery halo.

I couldn't stand us being even a millimeter apart any longer. I leaned into him, my slightly larger body leaning him backward across the bed. I ran my fingers through his hair, groaning at how good it felt under my touch.

I pressed my lips gently to his, the kiss almost chaste. Until it wasn't. I delved into his mouth, sucking and licking at him, tasting just a hint of my essence on his tongue. I ran my hands hungrily over his body. We'd already spent six years apart. I never wanted to spend another day apart from him, if I didn't have to.

His eyes gleamed in the light from my desk lamp, and I couldn't seem to look away from them.

"What?" he asked, finally. "Do I have cum on my face or something?"

He began running his hands over his face and hair in search of some evidence of our lovemaking. I chuckled and grabbed his hands, kissing his fingers one after another.

"Nope. I just... I can't believe you're here. I feel... God, I feel *giddy!*" I laughed. "I feel like if someone gave me a million dollars, there's nothing I'd want to spend it on, because I have everything I ever wanted, right here."

He smiled at me then, but it was a tolerant smile, one full of affection and knowing.

"Yeah, that would change *really* fast if someone put a mint condition X-Men #101 in front of you..." he teased.

"Hmmm… Nicki, or Phoenix? That's a hard one…" I teased. "But at least you're both redheads."

"Yes, it is. It's a *very* hard one…" He agreed, groaning as my hands passed over his crotch, pressing firmly against the hardness behind his zipper. I leaned in and captured his lips with mine, licking and sucking at his mouth. I gently nibbled his lower lip, as I soaked in the feel of him, his heat against my skin, the shudder he made when I squeezed his length through his jeans.

"*Fuck…*" he groaned.

I grinned and slid my fingers beneath his t-shirt, working my hands up his sides and sliding it over his head and flinging it aside.

He wasn't as muscled as I was, and was still on the thin side, but he'd definitely filled out since high school. A dusting of red hairs on his chest attested to being a natural redhead, and led to a happy trail that made me *very* happy indeed. I licked and nibbled his skin, sucking gently as I worshiped my way down his body. I didn't ignore the scars that traced around his sides, but didn't draw attention to them, either. We had time for that. We had a future now.

My lips paused and nibbled at the dusty pink nipples that begged for my attention. The first time I sucked on them he arched up off the bed.

"Holy *fuck*!" he exclaimed. I chuckled at him.

"Like that, do you?" I asked.

"Oh my god, that was insane!" he gasped. "Do it again!"

"Bossy…" I teased but complied. His body jerked against me as I sucked and laved the other nipple.

"That feels amazing!" he groaned.

"You've never had anyone do this…?" I asked before repeating my efforts.

He just shook his head and closed his eyes to concentrate on the sensation, and the thought of how alone he had been over the last six years saddened me. At least I'd had my family to support me, to encourage me. I'd been able to lose myself in perhaps too many bodies along the way. Nicki had only had Vivian, and she wouldn't have been able to give him this.

I continued my exploration of his body, and when I reached the waistband of his jeans, I paused, taking a moment to just appreciate what lay in store. My fingers traced the outline of his cock as it protested its denim confinement, a wet spot soaking through, further confirmation of his enjoyment.

"Kaine..." I heard him say my name and I glanced up to look at him. His eyes were half-lidded, arousal coursing through him. "Please god tell me you're not stopping..."

I shook my head.

"*Fuck*, no," I sighed. "Wild horses couldn't keep me away from you."

"Thank fuck..." he sighed, throwing his hand over his eyes dramatically.

I grinned at him, then leaned forward and mouthed him through his jeans, sucking on the thick material only to get a faint hint of his flavor.

"Fuck this..." he exclaimed when I paused for a moment, his hands flying between us to quickly remove his jeans and shove them down his legs.

"Someone's a bit impatient..." I teased.

"Well, it's only been six years..." he teased back.

My eyes roamed his naked body and I took my time to drink my fill of him. His cock wasn't quite as thick as mine, but it was longer and curved deliciously up from a nest of red curls. I could imagine the feel of that cock inside me, and almost moaned out loud. As kids there had only ever been those stolen locker-room glances, tantalizing glimpses of his body in wet swim trunks, or thin pajama pants. Now was so much better, because I could look all I wanted, and he was mine. *Mine.*

"Did you just *growl* at my cock?" he asked, laughing.

"Maybe..." I answered with a grin before leaning forward licking gently along the underside of his length.

"*Fuck!*" he gasped.

The wonder in his voice reminded me again that all of this was new to him.

"I want to do *so* many things with you, Nick," I said, my voice sounding about two octaves lower than normal. "This is just the beginning."

If I thought he had been hard before, now he could hammer nails. I'd read about people describing the skin of a man's cock feeling like hot silk under the touch, but hadn't really appreciated what that meant, until this moment.

I closed my lips around him, sucking gently at his tip as his flavor filled me. He was salty and sweet, and I couldn't get enough of him. I licked his cock eagerly, sucking him to the back of my throat. I heard him call my name and felt his hands flailing on the bed as his body bucked beneath me. I reached up to grasp his hand, then pulled it to my head, unwilling to release him to explain. He got the picture quickly, and his fingers twined in my hair. I felt the sting of his initial grip, but it eased rapidly and he began tugging me gently toward him.

I sucked him hungrily for a few moments, his hips rocking up to meet my lips.

"K-kaine—Close! So close!" he warned after a few moments, groaning and gasping as I fucked him with my mouth. The noises he made as he drove into me were making me insane. Even without the warning, I had known he was close.

I released him with a pop and he gasped.

"Wha—?"

"I want you inside me," I answered. He looked at me with a face that was lust-drunk and confused, and I knew he wasn't really tracking what I was saying.

"I— but—" he began, alarm crossing his face and I shushed him.

"I got this, baby," I answered, scrabbling at the bedside table, shoving aside the bubble gum to grab the bottle of lube and a strip of condoms. "I want to get tested before we decide whether to go without condoms. There are a lot of other nasty bugs out there besides HIV."

"But—but I haven't—you haven't—" he babbled, and I grinned at the panicked look on his face.

"You do this, I'll do that," I said, tossing the condom on his chest as

I slicked my fingers with lube and reached around to slide a lubed finger inside my hole.

He seemed to be regaining some of his brainpower, because he nodded and began to open the condom, but he had a hard time tearing his gaze from the sight of me beginning to stretch myself. I slid my lubed fingers in and out of my hole, groaning at the feel of it. Not just the physical feeling of it, but the elation that flooded me because it was Nicki's eyes on me, stroking his cock in time to my movements.

"I can't wait to be the one to do that," he said, his smile fled and his eyes grew dark with passion.

"Me neither. You'll be doing it soon enough, baby," I answered. "I just can't wait a minute longer to feel you inside of me."

I applied the excess lube to his latex-sheathed cock, then moved up the bed.

"How do you want—" he began.

"Stay there," I ordered.

"Now look who's being bossy," he said, the corner of his mouth ticking up.

"Hell, yes," I said, moving up the bed to capture his lips again while I seated myself across his hips.

His cock slid between my ass cheeks, teasing me with his hardness. I lifted my body, and Nicki reached between us, lining his dick up so it pressed gently against the wrinkled skin of my hole.

I froze for a moment, looking down at him, his brow adorably furrowed in concentration. He glanced up at me when I didn't move.

"What?" he asked. "Is something wrong? Should I—"

I stopped him with a kiss. "Nothing is wrong. I'm just enjoying this moment. We've waited so fucking long for this..."

A smile spread across his face. "We have, haven't we?"

I slowly lowered myself down, feeling the stretch and burn as his cock slowly slid inside me. I felt it slide past the first ring of muscles and took a deep breath. I'd learned about this, though, and expected it. I knew I had to pause for a moment to allow my body to become accustomed to the intrusion. I was just hoping the sharp pain would ease off soon.

"Fuck..." I whispered, sweat beading on my face.

"Oh *fuck*, Kaine..." Nicki whispered, his eyes closed as he concentrated on the feel. Suddenly his eyes flew open as the pain in my voice registered.

"*Fuck!* Have you ever done this before?" he demanded.

I managed a small smile through the pain.

"Not... not this. I've had lots of blow jobs and hand jobs. I just never... never really trusted anyone to do this," I answered.

Nicki looked up at me, his flame-like hair a tousled mess on my pillow, his concern for me evident on his face.

"Stop, we don't need to—" he began, but I leaned forward and kissed him again. The slight movement changed the angle of his cock inside me, and suddenly I was seeing stars.

"*Fuck!*" I exclaimed.

"*What?*" he demanded in alarm. "What's wrong?"

"Fuck, baby, I think you found my prostate," I gasped, grinning at him. I repeated the movement only to be rewarded by a repeat of the feeling. It was like lightning flashing through my body, but in the most pleasurable way imaginable.

"Oh! Okay, that's a *good* thing, then..." he chuckled, relaxing.

I slowly began rocking back and forth, feeling him sliding in and out of my body. *It. Was. Heaven.*

I understood now why so many men enjoyed bottoming. I picked up speed, continuing to kiss Nicki and brushing his length back and forth against that bundle of nerves inside me.

My erection had waned when he first entered me, but was back in full force a few moments after we discovered our perfect angle.

Nicki reached a hand between us, stroking my erection in time to the movements I was making on his cock. He moved in and out of me, brushing again and again against that bundle of nerves, his hips dancing up to meet my body as I tightened my grip on him almost automatically.

"Oh fuck! *Kaine!*" he exclaimed, his body rising up from the bed in harsh thrusts to meet my downward movements. I could feel the instant of his release, his cock spasming deep inside me as he unloaded into the condom. I followed him a moment later.

I had rocked back on my knees, my release painting Nicki's stomach, and felt like I was about to collapse, then I saw Nicki and froze.

The look on his face was pure bliss. His head was thrown back, his eyes closed. His hair was damp, plastered to his face in places, dark with sweat. The lamp on the bedside table threw long shadows across his face. Something inside me was terrified that someday he would leave me. Maybe he would decide I wasn't worth the bother, the drama. That he would decide I wasn't worth it. I desperately wanted to record that look, preserve it so I would never lose this moment, so I snagged the camera from the bedside table and snapped his picture.

His eyes flew open as I looked at him through the lens of the camera.

"Did you just... Seriously? Did you just take a picture of me coming?" he laughed.

I ducked my head, abashed, wanting to hide the camera behind my back like a kid caught stealing.

"Um, maybe...?" I answered.

"I want to see it," he said sleepily.

"Sec," I answered nervously. "Let's clean up first."

He held the condom while I moved off him and disposed of it in the trash can next to the bed.

"Stay here," he commanded.

I laughed again at his bossiness, but he disappeared out the bedroom door only to return a minute later with a wet washcloth and gently cleaned us both up.

I pulled the covers back and slid between the sheets as he threw the washcloth in the clothes hamper. He stood next to the bed a moment, looking down at me. I wanted to snap another picture of him, but figured I had pushed the limits far enough for one night.

"Are you... I mean, do you want me to— to stay?" he asked nervously.

"Of course," I answered. "I always want you to stay."

He smiled slowly, then crawled into bed next to me.

"Show me," he demanded.

I pulled the picture up on the video display of the camera.

"Wow..." he said, his eyes dancing over the screen. "That's an amazing shot."

I nodded.

"I don't think I'd want to share it, though," I said. He turned and looked at me. "You're mine. I'm not sharing you with anyone."

His smile warmed me to my toes.

17

NICKI

W<small>E SLEPT THAT NIGHT SPOONED TOGETHER,</small> K<small>AINE'S BODY WRAPPED</small> around mine. When I woke, it was to the feeling of him laying gentle kisses along my back. It took me a moment to realize that he was kissing each and every one of the scars my father had placed there over the years.

Tears filled my eyes at the feeling of him tracing each hurt with his lips. As he worked his way down my body, something inside me... eased... loosened. It was like the tangled web of hurt and loneliness that had bound my heart for so long was being clipped apart, set free by his touch, strand by ugly, painful strand.

His hand reached the swell of my ass, his fingers tracing the scars that dropped further down, sending a shiver through me.

"Good morning, Red," his hot breath whispered across my skin.

"I hate that nickname," I responded, only half-grumpily.

He slid back up my body and laid a gentle kiss on my lips.

"I know," he whispered, his tongue tickling the lips I was trying to keep pressed together in a pout. He laughed at my sullenness and kissed me again, his fingers tracing the curves and divots of my body.

I finally gave up my attempt at being a brat, and groaned.

"What?" he asked as I rolled over and looked up at him. "Something wrong?"

"Wrong? No, for once, everything seems juuuuust right..." I said, my fingers playing gently in his hair. "Except... I have to get to work."

He smiled. "No worries, Red. We've got all the time in the world."

He laid a final kiss on the tip of my nose, which sent butterflies winging through my stomach.

"Any word about the boys?" I asked as I sat up. Kaine swung his legs over the side of the bed and grabbed his phone.

"Mama D sent a text about an hour ago," he answered, scrolling through his notifications. "Everything is the same. They are keeping Hicks sedated for the time being, but Sonny is awake for short periods of time as the pain meds wear off."

"Do they have any idea who hit them?" I asked.

Kaine shook his head. "They didn't mention anything. Lee said the EMS guys who brought them in thought it might have been a hate crime."

"What?" I exclaimed. "In *Ohio*?"

"Unfortunately, it seems like it happens everywhere, now," he sighed.

"Any news on Mason? How is Lee doing?" I asked.

Kaine shrugged.

"Mama D didn't say anything in her text, and I just woke up about ten minutes before you did," he responded.

"Well, I *guess* I can forgive you for not being *all*-knowing," I teased.

Kaine laughed and went to stand, intent, I think, on grabbing some clothes from the dresser but I saw him freeze and wince.

"You okay?" I asked, concern squeezing my heart. I scrambled across the bed to sit next to him. Had I hurt him?

He flashed me a smile, a pink blush staining his cheeks. "Yeah, a little sore, but in all the best ways."

We kissed again, then took turns cleaning up in the bathroom. A joint shower might have been the very *best* way to wake up, but I would never have made it to work if we did

"I can drop you off at work," he offered. "I'm going to go hang out at the hospital for a while and give the 'rents a chance to get some sleep."

"Would you mind dropping me off at my apartment? I need to grab my uniform, and Viv will drop me off at work."

Kaine had just pulled a white t-shirt over his head that clung deliciously to his muscled chest. His blond hair was dark with the water from his shower, the short ends pointing up.

"What time do you get off work?" he asked.

"Should be around three," I responded, grabbing my phone to check my schedule. I noticed an email message notification and I clicked on it absently.

I froze, and it was his turn to look at me in concern.

"What is it?" he asked, his eyes dark with concern.

I stared at the screen, unmoving, until Kaine reached out and touched my shoulder, making me jump.

"Shit, sorry. The, um, the woman from the attorney's office just messaged me. She said my mom's attorney came back early and wanted to know if I could stop in to see him at five," I answered, turning off the phone and shoving it in my pocket.

"How do you feel about that?" he asked, his gaze intent on me.

I sighed.

"Anxious? Worried? I mean, I was supposed to have lunch with her, with Rhiannon, one day this week. She worked with my mom for a couple of years and knew her well. I was looking forward to the chance to find out a little of what Mom's life was like these last couple of years," I answered.

"Can't you still do that?" Kaine asked.

"I guess… it just seems… different? Like meeting with the attorney is a lot bigger deal than just meeting with a friend of my mom's. I just wasn't expecting it."

Kaine reached out and cupped my cheek with his hand.

"Do you want me to go with you?" he asked, concern furrowing his brow.

"You have your own shit to worry about," I began. "Your parents need you, what with your brothers…"

"One of the advantages to having a big family is there are *lots* of shoulders to help carry the load," he answered. "I can't do anything to help my brothers right now, but I *can* be there for *you.*"

I shook my head, then leaned in and laid a gentle kiss on his lips. I felt more than heard him groan as I licked at his mouth. His hands dropped the shirt he had been trying to button and wrapped around me instead.

"What did I do to deserve you?" I asked in wonderment.

"Pfft. Must have been a goddamn *saint* in another lifetime," he teased.

We both laughed. Kaine took me to my apartment where I changed into my work uniform, then he dropped me off at the restaurant.

The day dragged ridiculously. It was like a caricature of a long day. I'd get lost in a task, look up, and only minutes had gone by. Luckily, Erica wasn't there today, and I was beginning to feel semi-competent at my job.

Right before my lunch break, I felt my phone vibrate with an incoming text.

VIVIAN: So *someone* didn't come home last night...

ME: What did you do? Wait up for me?

VIVIAN: Well, for a while, at least... Are his brothers okay?

ME: It's still kinda touch and go, but they think they will be able to save Sonny's leg. Hick's is wait and see. He may have some memory problems.

VIVIAN: I'll keep sending good thoughts their way. How's your man?

ME: He's good... REALLY good... ;)

VIVIAN: OMG! You didn't!? I need deets!

ME: LOL Can't right now, but we can talk tonight?

VIVIAN: You want me to pick you up? You get off at 3 right?

ME: ... Kaine is picking me up. I've got an appointment at 4 to see the attorney handling mom's estate.

VIVIAN: /hugs. Do you want me to go with you?

ME: Kaine's coming. It seems like forever since I've seen you, though. Want to have dinner?

VIVIAN: You're on! Spaghetti a la Dunwoody! Say 7 p.m.? Bring Kaine!

By the time my shift ended, I was a nervous wreck. I had just cashed out and walked out the back when I saw Kaine drive up in his SUV.

"Hey, sexy," he called, rolling the window down as he approached.

"Hey!" I smiled, and gratefully opened the car door. On the seat was a long white box. I looked at Kaine in question.

"What did you do?" I asked.

"Get in, then open it," he said nervously, his finger tapping on the steering wheel.

I did as he said, stepping into the car and fastening my seatbelt before looking at the package again.

"What is it?" I asked.

"It's just… I saw it in the hospital gift shop, and it reminded me of you. Of us," he stammered.

I grinned, then opened the box.

Inside was an oblong ceramic container with a variety of succulents. Two of them had wound around each other, one with tiny yellow spines all over it's top, and the other with a bright red flower blooming on it.

A little card holder was angled so that it looked like the succulents were waving it, and it had the words "Better Together" on it.

It was adorable.

"I love it!" I exclaimed.

"You do? It's not too—" he began.

I silenced him with a kiss.

"It's perfect!" I announced. "I don't have to worry about forgetting to water it, and it's not going to die on me like cut flowers would. You are amazing…."

He grinned and ducked his head, a dark blush pinking his cheeks.

"I was hoping you'd like it…" he said.

"I do. Oh!" I exclaimed, suddenly remembering Vivian's text. "Are you free for dinner? Vivian wanted me to invite you over."

Kaine flashed that full-on smile of his.

"I'd love to!" he said.

The drive downtown went without incident. We seemed to be moving against the general flow of traffic, since everyone else was moving away from downtown at the end of the day.

I saw Kaine flashing me concerned glances out of the corner of his eye. I realized abruptly that I had chewed my nails down to the quick. *Shit.* I hadn't bitten my nails for years! I wiped my hands on my jeans guiltily.

Parking wasn't hard to find either, and before long we found ourselves inside an office building, standing outside doors that read "Alexander R. Young & Martin L. Zachary, Attorneys at Law".

"You okay?" Kaine asked, after he parked the car.

I nodded jerkily.

"No. *Really,*" he insisted, taking my hands in his own.

I sighed.

"Really?" I asked. "No, I'm not, but this is something I need to do."

Kaine glanced over at me, then reached his hand out to take mine.

"You can do this," he reassured me. I looked into his eyes for a moment, took a deep breath. I nodded, then opened the door.

The inside of the attorney's office wasn't what I was expecting. Sure, there was lots of mahogany and brass, but it had a touch of home, too. Small needlepoint throw pillows sat on the settee, and handmade doilies circled a plant on the glass top coffee table.

A woman sat behind the reception desk, her hair a premature silver. She was thin, and definitely older, but not old enough to warrant all the grey in her hair.

She looked up as we entered.

"Hello! How can I— *Nicki?*" she asked, her one eyebrow quirked at me. I saw her face go a little pale as she paused, her voice dropping almost to a whisper as she said my name.

"Rhiannon?" I asked.

"Oh, my goodness!" she exclaimed. I reached my hand out to her on instinct, but instead of a handshake, she moved from behind the counter and threw her arms around me. "You poor boy!"

She hugged me tightly and I stood there, feeling more than a bit awkward in her embrace. I didn't even know this woman. One of my hands was still caught in Kaine's grasp, the other tentatively patted the woman's shoulder. She seemed to sense my hesitation because she released me and backed away quickly.

"I'm so sorry! It's just... you look so much like— so much like Harley..." she said, her eyes bright.

Just then a tall, thin man with red hair shot with silver walked into the reception area, his head down as his eyes focused on a paper in his hand.

"Rhi, have you heard anything yet from—" he stopped suddenly and looked up, and I stared into my own eyes.

Okay, not *really* my own, of course, but... add twenty years, add some crow's feet at the corners of my eyes and some silver in my hair, and it was me.

"Who— who the fuck are *you*?" I snarled. It was like a jumbled lock suddenly clicked into place in my brain. Part of me needed to hear it aloud, to confirm what my heart already knew about this man.

He was frozen in his tracks as he stared at me, and I saw something... lost in the depths of his eyes. I saw something... *broken*... and *so* very sad as he looked at me. I saw grief. I saw anger. I saw regret. A whirlpool of emotions that threatened to suck me down.

"Nicki..." he whispered, his deep voice almost a rumble.

"Who *are* you?" I demanded again, realizing only a moment later that Kaine was holding my arms to keep me from grabbing the man and shaking some answers out of him.

"Dominick," Rhiannon began carefully. "Nicki... This—this is Alex Young. Alexander *Rowen* Young. He's... he's your biological father."

The world began to spin, and if not for Kaine's arms around me, I think I would have passed out.

Maybe I *did* actually black out for a minute, because the next thing I knew I was sitting on a chair in a conference room off the main office, my head between my legs and Kaine's comforting arm around me. Alex was sitting in a chair near us, and a man sat next to him. He was shorter, I think, than Alex, with neatly trimmed brown hair. Rhiannon was just walking into the room, a cold bottle of water in her hand.

"Here you go, dear," she said, handing me the water.

I took it numbly. Kaine tightened his grip on my shoulders and I nodded at him. I could do this.

I looked up at my biological father, still trying to wrap my mind around the idea. My father? How could he be... I saw the man next to him shift slightly, catching Kaine's attention.

"I'm not trying to be rude, but who are you?" Kaine asked, glancing at the gentleman who sat next to Alex.

"I'm Marty... Martin Zachary. I'm Alex's partner," he said.

"Law partner, or life partner?" Kaine growled, and I placed my hand on his knee.

Martin smiled calmly at Kaine's protective response and answered "Both."

I looked at Marty, my mind whirring, then back to Alex. My mind couldn't wrap itself around the situation. How could he be my father? Mom and Dad had been together for years, except...

"You were the one she had the affair with," I said, the pieces suddenly clicking into place. Those eyes that were so much like my own, winced at the accusation, but he nodded.

"Yes," he said. "Dominick... May I call you Nicki? Harley always called you Nicki, and it seems... wrong... somehow, to refer to you as Dominick."

I just nodded.

"Harley—your mom, and I... We were childhood sweethearts. We had been dating off and on since high school," he began, his fingers alternately crumpling and smoothing a tissue he held in his hands. The man beside him reached his hand out and gripped his shoulder, squeezing it in encouragement. Alex looked at him and allowed a small smile to reach the corner of his mouth. I watched the look pass between them and realized these two men cared a great deal for each other.

"We… we had a fight. A big one. I had been accepted into law school in New York, but she didn't want to leave Ohio," he began. "I saw it as a big chance for us to make something of ourselves. I thought Harley would have a better chance of getting published in New York, and I could work and go to school as well."

Alex's eyes got a faraway look as he continued. "Your mom was an amazing writer. She was able to really capture the heart and soul of people in her stories. She wanted to write for the big literary magazines, but her family wanted her to take a more… *traditional* route."

I vaguely remembered my grandparents on my mother's side. They had been stiff, formal people and I had never understood how they could have given birth to a free spirit like my mom. She hadn't been close to them, and I knew they had died when I was about seven or eight.

"Her parents lived in Ohio, and she didn't want to leave them. You grandfather had heart problems, and your grandmother had diabetes. Harley absolutely refused to go to New York with me. She seemed to think I was making a mistake by going, that we'd never be able to make it in the big city. I thought that if I left for a while she would cool off, and eventually see my side of the argument."

He grinned wryly at me. "I should have known better. Harley was damn stubborn when she wanted to be."

I nodded. My mom *had* been stubborn, which was one of the things she and Dad had fought about. When she got an idea in her head, you might as well give up then.

"Willis had always wanted your mother. More than that, he wanted the prestige marrying her could bring him. Her father was a well-known judge in the area, and Will saw Harley as a fast track for his career. He pursued her when I was away visiting the school in New York."

He shook his head.

"By the time I finished school, your mom had married Willis. Will and I had always been… rivals, I guess, for Harley's attention, but I never really thought she would marry him. I— was devastated, of course. I felt like I had lost the only thing that really mattered to me in the world," he said, staring blankly at the tabletop.

"Even though they struggled to understand her, family meant so much to her. Har wanted to stay in this area to take care of her parents, but right after they got married, Willis insisted that they moved to a county in Virginia where he had landed a position as Sheriff's deputy. He'd applied without telling her. Her parents told her that her place was with her husband, so she felt she didn't have much of a choice. They moved to Virginia. Her parents passed away about a year later."

Alex crumpled the tissues in his hands again.

"After they got married, I went... kind of crazy, for a while," he chuckled ruefully. "I was living in New York City, and everything, and everyone, was available, for a price. I tried to fill the hole she'd left in my heart with any substance or person I could find. I was not... not a good person."

Martin squeezed Alex's shoulder again, before leaning in and placing a kiss on his temple.

"That was a long time ago, baby," he whispered.

Alex nodded, though he seemed unsure, then looked back up at me.

"I was home on Christmas break my last year of law school. Your parents were having... problems," he sighed. "And I'm sure I didn't make them any better. Harley and I ran into each other at a Christmas party. She and Will had fought, and she'd gone to the party without him. Seeing her again... it was like someone had breathed life back into me. My world went from being black and white to having *color* again. We talked—and drank—for hours. We woke up the next morning in my hotel room."

Alex shook his head, then turned to look at me solemnly. "She didn't tell me about you, Nicki. Not at first. She and Will had been trying to have a baby for years, and they didn't know why they hadn't been able to."

"The first time I saw your baby pictures, I knew," Rhiannon said. "You had the same eyes Alex had when he was young. That same red hair… She didn't even have to say anything, I just knew Alex was your father, though she denied it, at first."

"With your birth, Harley and Will seemed to have worked out some of their problems. She refused to see me again for years," Alex continued. "I never knew… never knew I was positive, not until about six years ago. I started getting sick," Alex said, his voice dropping almost to a whisper. "I started losing weight. I had pneumonia three times one summer. I knew something was seriously wrong. I went to a specialist, and he diagnosed me with HIV. I don't know if I got it from having sex with the wrong person, or if it was from all the drugs I did when I was in college, but it didn't really matter where it came from. I had it, and I had passed it on to her, and— and you."

As he'd spoken, I couldn't stop the roil of emotions boiling through me. My mom had died because of this asshole, and I was likely to as well. I just shook my head, digging my fingers into my scalp as I tried to make sense of everything, anger, pain and grief mixing in my chest.

"So, Mom fooled around on my dad, and it ends up killing us both? *Great*! Just *fucking* great…" I said angrily.

"Nicki, that's not fair," Kaine began, but stopped as he noticed the faces of those around the table. They looked almost comical. Alex's face was white, but his eyes were wide in stunned surprise. Martin's mouth had dropped open into an O shape, and Rhiannon looked at me as if I'd grown two heads.

"Nicki, whatever are you talking about, dear?" she exclaimed. "Alex didn't have anything to do with your mother's death."

"You *know* what I'm talking about! Mom had AIDS, and she *died*!" I yelled.

"Oh, my dear, you didn't know?" Rhiannon asked, confusion apparent on her face.

"Know… what do you mean, '*know*'?" I demanded angrily. I'd had just about enough of these people and I stood, ready to walk out the door.

Rhiannon reached up from where she sat and took my hand gently in her own.

"Sweetheart, there has been some kind of horrible miscommunication. Harley didn't die from AIDS. She was killed by a drunk driver."

"What!" I exclaimed in surprise. "That's— What? She—"

Rhiannon opened a folder I hadn't realized was lying on the conference room table. Inside was a local news website printout with a news story dated about eight months ago with the headline "Local Woman Killed By Drunk Driver." My mother's photo was under the headline.

I stared at it for what seemed like hours. I didn't have many pictures of my mom, and in this one she was smiling and *happy.* I didn't realize how sad she had been, married to my father, until I saw true happiness on her face.

"You... you took this?" I asked, looking at Rhiannon. She smiled and nodded.

"It was about three years ago, I think. We'd just gotten some information she thought would help in a... a case... we were working on," she said.

"She worked here?" I asked. Rhiannon nodded again.

"She needed our help, Nicki," Alex said. "She was still trying to figure out how she could get you back from your dad. She fought every single day to find a way to get you back."

"Wait, that doesn't make any sense," Kaine interrupted. "Once he turned eighteen, his mom didn't have to *fight* his dad anymore. She could have just reached out to Nicki directly."

"She tried," Marty said. "Your dad is a very powerful man, Nicki. Based on your testimony during the custody hearings, he obtained a restraining order against your mother. He told her that the only way she would ever see you again was if she came back as his wife."

I shook my head, trying to reconcile what he was telling me with what I knew about my parents.

"Isn't that contradictory? A restraining order, but he wanted her back?" I asked.

"Your dad hasn't been a rational man in anything concerning your mother for many years," Alex said. "Your mom never gave up on getting you back in her life."

"Why... why would she *want* me back? After the lies... The things I said in court..." My voice trailed off, the sick coil of guilt wrapping around my midsection.

This time it was Alex who reached out and took my hand in his.

"You were her son, Nicki. She loved you. You need to listen to me and believe when I tell you this," he said, squeezing my hand. "Your Mom knew why you lied in court."

I looked up at him, startled.

"Your father—Willis—liked to gloat. He made sure she knew that those were *his* words you told the court. *His* lies. She just didn't have a way to *prove* that they were lies. You were a teenager, Nicki. You did what you had to, in order to survive," he said.

I shook my head, unwilling to be so quick to forgive myself.

"No! I should have found another way, done something else to stop him. To protect her..." I began. "We had an agreement!"

"What do you mean?" Kaine asked. "What kind of agreement?"

I looked up at him, wanting desperately to get lost in them and forget all of this. Anger and grief threatened to suck my soul into darkness, and I finally admitted out loud the cancer that had been eating at me.

"Dad... Dad was going to kill her. Me. The day she served the divorce papers," I whispered, my voice hoarse. "He held a gun to my head, and I promised... promised that if he let her live... I'd stay."

I heard the shocked silence in the room and felt the tears running down my face. I rubbed at them angrily. Tears weren't going to fix anything anymore. They never had.

"That's why you broke up with me..." Kaine whispered, realization hitting him.

I nodded, my head down. "He threatened you. He said if I didn't break up with you, stop all communication, he'd kill you, too."

"*Fuck*, Nicki..." he whispered, stricken. I looked at him.

"I'm so sorry, Kaine. I didn't want to leave you. I knew what it would do to you, but I had to," I answered. "I'm sorry, but I... I couldn't let him hurt you."

"It wasn't your fault, Nicki," Kaine insisted, wrapping me in a hug.

"You were a kid. Your father was insane. You were doing what you had to just to survive. I just wish... I just wish there had been a way for me to help you."

It felt so fucking good to have his arms around me, to have everything out in the open.

"Your mom *loved* you, Nicki," Marty said, his voice breaking slightly as he spoke. "She loved you so much. She knew you told the court those lies because you had to. She forgave you a long time ago."

"She— she wrote you something..." Rhiannon slid an envelope toward me. I looked up at her in surprise.

"Your mom knew that with her disease, there was no telling when it might... might claim her," she said. "She wrote you this and asked me to give it to you if— if the worst happened."

The envelope was long, the paper stiff under my fingers. I opened the seal and pulled out a couple of pages of unlined paper, filled with her handwriting.

My Darling Nicki,

When you read this, I will be gone. I am only hoping that it has occurred years after we have had a chance to rebuild a life together, you and I, far away from Will's influence.

I don't know what kind of an arrangement you made with your father, but I know that, somehow, I owe you for the fact that he granted me the divorce without a fight, much less a settlement and medical care. I know Will, and I know how he operates. He would never have let me go without getting something in return. My skin crawls at the thought that you paid for my freedom with your own flesh and blood. I would gladly have taken your place, but he wouldn't have let me. Will is an "all or nothing" kind of man.

I want you to know I didn't willingly leave you in your father's care. I was injured far worse than I let on. After Will beat me, I called Alex for help. He flew to Florida and stole me away from your father and hid me in a private hospital under an assumed name. I was in a coma for several weeks. Unfortunately, I had never told him about you, so he hadn't known to take you, too. By the time I woke, your father had already taken steps to keep us apart, and I have been heartbroken ever since. I'm so sorry that I left you alone to face him! It was never my intent.

As I ask you to forgive me for leaving you, please know I forgive you for the things you said in the court hearing. I know you had to lie to survive your life with Will. I do not blame you, and you should not blame yourself. We have all done things we had to do, to survive.

I am assuming that by now, you know that Willis Terhune is not your biological father. I could write pages about the wrongs that Will has done me, but I refuse to let him take up any more time in my thoughts or heart. Just know that there was a time when I genuinely thought we could build a life together. Will and I both made mistakes in our marriage, and I take responsibility for mine.

One of those mistakes I cannot bring myself to regret, though, because it brought me you. Your biological father is Alex Young. Rhiannon knows how to reach him, if you haven't spoken to him yet. Alex is one of the best men I've ever known, and is the man I should have spent the rest of my life with. If only I hadn't been so stupid and stubborn... I remember telling you once that people cheat for a variety reasons, and sometimes that reason is that they were never meant to be together in the first place. I feel that way about Willis. I should always have been with Alex. I never got to tell you about him, but I shared as much of him as I dared when I gave you your middle name. I hope you get a chance to know him and Marty. They have been incredibly kind to me, especially Marty. It takes an extremely gracious soul to allow a former love back into your partner's life without being eaten alive by jealousy. What Alex and I had is in the past, but these two men have become my family, and I hope they can become a family for you, too.

Being your Mother is the single best thing I've done with my life. I always prided myself on my ability to convey emotion in words, but I love you so very much that they fail me now. Please promise me that you won't let Will's jealousy, hate and anger infect your soul. You have an incredibly sensitive heart. I am confident that you will follow your dreams and let love and light grow in your heart instead darkness and hate.

I have had the wonderful fortune to love you and have you in my life, Nicki, and for that I will be forever grateful.

All my love,

Mom

I ran my thumb over her name, the loops and whorls of her hand-writing as familiar to me as my own. I gave up on trying to keep back the tears and let them roll down my cheeks unashamed.

She loved me. She forgave me. I sobbed and felt Kaine's strong arms wrap around me once more. He turned me so that he could hold me tight, and the tears washed my soul as I finally let go of the agony, the terror, the soul-numbing guilt.

After a while, I looked up from the letter. "There's... there's something I wanted to give you," Alex said, sliding a folder of papers to me. I glanced down at them, then back up. I felt Kaine's hand at the small of my back, reassuring me, and I started turning over pages from the folder.

Inside were photos...of me. From the time I was fifteen until just about six months ago. Some were me at school, others outside our house. One was of me at work at the restaurant, tell-tale bruises peeking out of the collar of my shirt.

One photo was super grainy, like it had been enlarged repeatedly. It was a photo of my father heading toward the shed in our backyard. He had my arm in a vise-like grip as he dragged me across the yard, my reluctance apparent even in the still photo. Another photo followed it, taken a short while later, if the shadows showed the passage of time. It was a picture of him leaving the barn, peeling red-smeared gloves off his hands. The picture was dark, the only light coming from inside the barn. A shadow played on the one wall, a silhouette of me, hanging by my arms, clearly visible.

I didn't recall that night in particular. It could have been any one of a hundred nights just like it. A drop of moisture fell on the photos and I hastily brushed it off. It took me a moment to realize it was my own tears.

"That's how she knew," he said, tapping the photo.

"Who...?" I asked, struggling to get the words out as I remembered the terror of those nights.

"I hired a private detective in Tampa to keep an eye on you. He sent us those only a few days before your mother died," Alex said, his eyes grave.

"Did my father...Did he...?" I tried to ask but couldn't get the words out. Alex seemed to understand anyway.

"As far as we can tell, he had nothing to do with your Mother's death," Alex said, his eyes narrowing. "It was...a tragic accident. An elderly gentleman with twenty-two DUI's on his record went left of center and struck her car, killing them both instantly."

I nodded, still trying to process everything. Somehow, knowing my Mom had died from a drunk driver was both better and worse than having her die from AIDS. Better in that it wasn't a long wasting death. Worse in that it could have been prevented.

"I know it probably doesn't matter to you right now, but we sued the driver's estate on behalf of your Mom's estate," Alex said. "It will take a while, but you should see money from her estate. Enough to let you go to school or start a business. Whatever you want to do with your life."

The thought of being able to go to school was a good one. One I knew my Mom would have loved. But he was right, money was the *last* thing I was thinking of at that point.

"Did he...did he have a family?" I asked. Regardless of what he'd done, I couldn't see taking away someone's legacy from their kids.

"The driver?" Alex asked. I nodded.

"No. His first two wives had predeceased him, and he didn't have any children," he answered.

"Do you have any other questions for us, right now?" Marty asked.

"Where...where is my Mom buried?" I asked.

"She's at Rose Park Cemetery," Rhiannon answered. "I can take you there if you want."

I nodded again. If I kept this up, I might as well be a bobble head doll. I shoved the inane thoughts down. It was all just...too much. Too much to take in, too much to process.

"I...I need some time. I need to try and figure all this..." I gestured at the file. "...out."

It was their turn to nod. Kaine was still by my side, and Alex still sat there, tears running down his own face. He thrust a box of tissues at me and I took some thankfully. I tried to fix my face as much as possible, but I knew I was a mess.

"So…you're my Dad, huh?" I asked, sniffling.

"Appears that way," he answered.

"You loved her?" I questioned.

"So very much," he replied. He dropped his head into his hands, and I saw his shoulders heave once, twice, before lifting his face back up and snagging some more tissues to wipe the tears that matched my own. Marty squeezed his shoulder in a move reminiscent of Kaine's.

I studied Alex for a minute. There were tiny lines on his face and I couldn't help but feel for him. We'd both loved my mother and had both lost her. At least I'd had her most of my life. He'd only had her for a few years.

"I'm glad she had someone else who loved her, too," I finally said.

He nodded then looked at me.

"Nicki… Can I… Can I hug you?" he asked. "Because I could really use a hug right now, so I figure you could, too."

I nodded, and before I knew it, I was enveloped in his strong embrace.

"I'm so glad you're here… son," he whispered.

With that simple acknowledgment, my heart seemed to overflow. In those encircling arms I felt protected, loved and accepted, something my father—Willis—had denied me. Alex didn't see anything wrong with me, or my life, because it was very similar to him and his.

We separated after a few moments, with more sniffling and throat clearing.

"We…we understand you need time. I'm willing to give you all the time you need," he began. "…but I'd like you to know something."

"Nicki, after I lost your mother, I never thought I'd have a chance at love again, much less a family," he said, glancing over at Marty. "But I found love with Marty, and suddenly, I have a son in front of me who is the spitting image of his mother. I hope… I hope you give me the chance to get to know you, to maybe be a better father to you than the one you had the first time around."

I stared into those eyes, eyes so much like my own. I knew what my Mom would have wanted.

I nodded.

"...At least you couldn't be worse..." I teased.

It took a moment for Alex to realize I wasn't serious, but when he did, he laughed, a sharp bark of sound reminiscent of my own. After we'd stopped laughing, he said, "I can see who you get your sense of humor from. I look forward to getting to know you, son," he said.

"Me, too," I said in the same whisper, hugging him back. "I just... I don't think I can call you Dad, yet? Is it okay if I just call you Alex?"

He nodded and squeezed me tightly once more before letting me go.

"You can just call me Marty..." his partner said, when I looked at him.

"I'm... I'm your aunt, Nicki," Rhiannon said, smiling gently at me.

I looked at her and Alex.

"Your older and *much* more beautiful aunt," she insisted saucily. "I also have much better choice in men."

She sniffed in Marty's direction. Instead of being offended, Marty dished it right back at her.

"Keep it up, you old bat. I get to choose what nursing home you go to!" he taunted.

"Pffft! As if I'd leave my care in *your* hands!" she exclaimed.

We'd left with smiles on everyone's faces. The drive home was quiet. I stared at the pictures as he drove, lost in thought. When he pulled into the lot next to the apartment building, Kaine finally broke the silence and asked, "Nicki, are you okay?"

I thought for a moment.

Was I okay?

"I think so," I whispered, looking at him. Kaine ducked his head, gripping the steering wheel tightly. When he looked up, his eyes were shimmering with unshed tears. I lifted a finger up to brush his cheek, and they overflowed.

"What's wrong?" I asked, as my thumb brushed away his tears.

"*Fuck*, Nicki. I should have been there. I should have *stopped* him..." Kaine growled, slamming his palm against the steering wheel.

"You had no way of knowing," I answered, pulling him close. He wrapped his arms around me in a death grip, and for a moment I just let myself melt into his embrace. I let go of all the grief, and fear, and pain, and just felt his love enfold me. It was almost like I could feel it soaking into my very pores. I was a sponge. A love sponge.

An unbidden vision of SpongeBob popped into my head, and I snorted a laugh.

"...Nicki?" Kaine asked, raising an eyebrow at me in question.

"I'll tell you later..." I whispered, before placing a gentle kiss on his lips.

18

KAINE

WE GOT OUT OF THE CAR, HEARTS BOTH HEAVIER AND LIGHTER THAN they had been before the trip.

I was glad, for Nicki's sake, that he had some closure with his mom. I knew how much she meant to him. He had literally shed his blood for her. The thought of anyone laying hands on Nicki still made me so angry that I couldn't see straight, but I struggled to tamp down the rage inside me. Now was not the time.

I walked around the front of the car and held my hand out to Nicki.

"You hungry for some spaghetti?" he asked as he took my hand.

I pulled him in to me, then dragged his hand to my mouth. I laid gentle, nibbling kisses on each of his fingers.

"I'm hungry for something..." I said, waggling my eyebrows salaciously. I figured we'd had enough of tears for a while, a little humor was overdue.

"You are in*satiable!*" he exclaimed, laughing. It was so good to see him laugh. He deserved all the joy I could give him.

"Hey! I've got six years to make up for!" I answered. I leaned close to him, ghosting my fingers up his sides until my hands gently cupped his face. "...and all the time in the world to do it in..." I breathed, then pressed our lips together gently, my tongue teasing his mouth until he opened for me. I slid inside his delicious mouth and began sucking and nibbling on any part of him I could reach. Our tongues danced back and forth until I relented and let him start to explore my mouth.

My hands slid down his back and cupped his ass. One of Nicki's hands had slid up my shirt and was gripping my back, the other hand sliding down beneath my waistband, his long, thin fingers sliding between my ass cheeks.

"Fuck..." I gasped, grinding our cocks together through our jeans.

"I second that colorful metaphor," he whispered.

"Hey, you two! Knock it off!" A voice yelled. "I don't want to have to take you in for public indecency!"

We jumped apart like kids caught making out at a school dance until we realized it was Micah.

"Fuck you, Asano!" I yelled, flipping him the bird.

Nicki pulled me closer and snuggled in my arms.

"You're just jealous!" Nicki yelled back.

"Hell, yeah, I'm jealous!" Micah answered as he walked toward us, swinging his leather jacket over his shoulders. The grin on his face belied his words. "It's not fair to have two gorgeous men making out in front of me, and I have to go to work!"

We each shook his hand.

"Well, I have a whole house full of gay men in my family. Lee's the only one taken..." I laughed, letting my voice trail off.

Micah seemed to consider my offer for a moment. "Lee's the military one, right?"

I nodded.

"Yeah, but he and Mason are pretty hot and heavy. I don't think they even realize anyone else is in the room, most days," I laughed.

Micah grinned at me sardonically, then shook his head. "Nah, I've had my fill of Devereaux's, thank you very much."

We said goodbye, then headed inside. We walked up the concrete stairs to the building and Nicki unlocked the door. As we walked up the hall, I could smell the wonderful aroma of spaghetti wafting through the hall, but smelled a hint of something burning, as well.

"Wait until you try this!" he exclaimed. "You will not believe the Dunwoody secret ingredient!"

"As long as it's not sardines, I think I can handle it!" I teased. Nicki made a face.

"Ew! No, no sardines. They actually use coffee in their spaghetti sauce. Coffee!" he exclaimed.

"Bishop would be scandalized!" I answered, laughing.

"Scandalized, or enamored, one or the other..." he said.

As we walked up the stairs I noticed the door to the apartment was standing open.

"Uh, oh, looks like Viv burned the bread again," Nicki said, his lips twitching. "You've got to promise not to tease her. She had our oven have a hate-hate relationship."

"Hey Viv! Everything okay?" He called as we walked into the apartment. He turned around to look at me, and all I saw was a flash of surprise and alarm on his face, then something slammed into the back of my head and darkness descended.

19

NICKI

I HADN'T EVEN GOTTEN A WARNING OUT BEFORE MY FATHER BROUGHT the butt of his gun down on Kaine's head, and my lover dropped like a stone.

"Kaine!" I'd lunged forward trying to catch him, only to find myself staring down the barrel of my father's gun. Again. I was getting pretty damn tired of this.

"Where is she?" My father demanded, his face red with fury.

"Where is who?" I responded, frozen in horror as blood started to pool around Kaine's head.

"You know goddamn well *who!*" My dad screamed. "Where's your *mother?*"

I looked at him, stunned. He didn't know? How could he not know? He always seemed to know everything that happened, sometimes before it even happened! He had informants everywhere. Surely one of them had told him about my Mom's accident?

"She's not here, Dad!" I yelled back. "She's dead! She was hit by a car months ago!"

"You lying piece of shit!" he yelled, backhanding me. "I'm not falling for your lies again! You *promised* me! 'I'll stay' you said! 'No matter what!' you said! You're a fucking liar, just like that goddamn whore of a mother of yours!"

My hand flew to my mouth and came away smeared with blood. I looked at the man I'd called Dad my whole life, and I could only stare at him in sadness and confusion.

A distant part of my mind wondered what had happened to the man I used to love and respect. He had always seemed so much larger than life, an honest-to-God superhero. I remembered him, but as I looked at my father now, I realized that the man who had taught me to ride a bike, to drive a car, to hook a fish... was gone. All that remained was a small, angry man, whose impotent rage lashed out at everyone around him. I was sick of being the target of his rage.

I straightened up and watched with a growing, icy calm as he held the gun pointed at me, a plan beginning to formulate in my mind. My eyes narrowed in fury.

He must have seen some change in my posture, something in my face that challenged him, because the next thing I knew, I was doubled over on the floor, struggling to scrape oxygen into my lungs after a second, savage blow to my midsection.

My eyes fell on Kaine's form as I tried to breathe, and I saw his eyes twitch and snap open, then close again quickly. I doubled over on top of his body in the hopes my father wouldn't notice his movement.

"Don't you fuck with me, boy. I brought you into this world, and I sure as *fuck* will take you out!" he yelled. "Where is she?"

My automatic response was to duck from his blows, my mother's voice whispering in my ear. *Don't rile him. Don't rile him. Don't rile him.*

I loved my mother, but I had three words for that voice my ear.

Fuck.

That.

Shit.

I drew a ragged breath as I looked up at my father—at *Willis*—as I knelt over Kaine's prone form, fury burning away the sadness I'd felt at the loss of the only father I'd known... until today. Alex had shown me more compassion, more concern, more *love* in one day than this man had shown me in the last six *years*. He was right in one way, though. For good, or ill, he'd helped make me who I was. Even if he wasn't my biological father, he had molded me through pain, and anguish, and suffering. It was about time he got a taste of his own goddamn medicine.

I mumbled something under my breath, deliberately keeping it low so he would lean close to me.

"What?" he growled, looking at me angrily, his eyes focusing on me.

I mumbled it again, just a little bit louder this time as I stood to my feet. He leaned in to listen.

"What? Speak up, *boy*! I can't hear you!" he yelled, his gun wavering slightly as he pointed it at me.

I raised my head and looked him in the eye.

"Count," I whispered.

He looked at me in confusion, then my fist was flying out to connect with his stomach.

"*One*," I growled as he doubled over, his gun going off as it fell past my ear and the sound exploding in the small apartment.

"*Two*," I growled, bringing my knee up to connect solidly with his nose.

"*Three*," I heard Kaine's voice say as his foot flashed, swiping Willis' feet out from under him, his body landing on the floor with a thud, his head snapping back against the hardwood floor and his form going limp.

"Go team Devereaux!" I said, a sad smile on my face as I held my hand out to Kaine and helped him to his feet.

His hand was pressed to the back of his head, the blood darkening his blond highlights. I peered at it in concern. It was bleeding freely, and he might need some stitches, but it didn't look *too* serious. I helped him stand and grabbed a dishtowel from the kitchen to press against the cut.

I pulled out my phone and dialed nine one one, and shakily told the dispatcher what had happened, then went back to check on Kaine.

My lover had just stood and walked over to kick the gun out of my father's reach. I looked at him and raised an eyebrow at the practiced move. "Somebody's been watching too many crime shows," I muttered. Kaine just grinned at me incorrigibly.

"*Somebody* got me hooked on them before he moved to Florida," he responded. "I had to have *something* to do for the last six years."

I chuckled and leaned in to kiss him, then remembered I had a split lip.

"Fuck..." I whispered, annoyed.

Kaine seemed to understand my thoughts as he grinned wryly at me.

"Don't worry, I'm sure we'll manage to find *some* way to pass the time until your mouth heals," he said, waggling his eyebrows at me salaciously.

We both laughed, and he pulled me close to him.

"I was so scared for you..." I began, ghosting my fingers over his jaw.

"Me? Why me? It's you he was after! I was just an afterthought," he argued.

"I don't know, I think maybe we were both afterthoughts," I murmured, my eyes fixed on my father's still form. He hadn't moved since Kaine had swiped his feet out from under him and frankly I couldn't have cared less.

A thought occurred to me, though, and I spun around.

"Fuck! Vivian!" I yelped. "Where's Vivian?"

We searched the apartment quickly. When we didn't find her, I made Kaine stay in the apartment to keep an eye on my dad and ran out to the parking lot.

None of the cars looked like any my dad had owned in the past, but I did see one with Florida plates. I knocked hesitantly on the trunk, only to hear a muffled "thud thud" in response, and some noises that sounded like muffled swearing in a voice that was distinctly Vivian-esque.

The car door was locked, but rather than try and find the keys I picked up a large rock from the landscaped area around the apartment and slammed it into the driver's side window. The glass shattered beautifully. They could bill me.

I found the trunk release and hustled around to the back and threw open the trunk. To my relief, Vivian was lying there, unharmed, but mad as a hornet. I helped her out of the trunk and to her feet. Fortunately, her feet weren't bound, but the duct tape in her hair was awful. I was able to peel the edges away from her mouth far enough to get rid of the rags my Dad had used to secure it and let her speak, but I wasn't able to get her hair untangled from the sticky mess.

"Nicki!" she exclaimed, throwing her arms around me once I got her hands released. "Are you okay? What happened? Where's your dad?"

"Kaine's got him under control," I reassured her. "The police are on their way. He's in the living room."

We walked back into the apartment, where Kaine was still keeping pressure on his head wound and my father still lay, unmoving. Vivian went in the bathroom to try and free her hair, and I went to check on Kaine.

"He's still breathing," Kaine reassured me when I walked over to him.

"I don't really care about him. How are *you* doing?" I asked as I forced him to take a seat. He looked up at me and winced as I pulled the towel away from his head to get a look at the cut.

"It's starting to hurt more, now that the adrenaline is wearing off," he admitted.

"Yeah, and it's still bleeding. As soon as the cops get here, we should probably take you to the ER to get it stitched up," I said, pressing the makeshift bandage back against the wound.

"My *hair's* gonna need an ER visit!" Vivian called as she walked out of bathroom. "I had to cut it to—*shit*, Nicki! *Lookout!*" she called, her eyes widening in alarm.

At the same time, I heard Micah's voice yell, *"Akron Police!* Drop the weapon!"

It was one of those moments you see in movies, when everything seems to move in slow motion. I spun around, catching a glimpse of the detective standing in the open doorway, his weapon raised. Behind Kaine, I saw my father rising up off the floor like some kind of horror movie villain, hunting knife in hand. Without thought, I shoved Kaine to the ground, putting myself between him and my father.

Dad's right arm wrapped around me, his face an angry snarl. I felt him punch my side over and over and felt a strange tugging, tearing sensation in my belly button as we locked gazes. His eyes were bloodshot and enraged, his lips pulled back from his teeth as he thrust his knife into my side.

Then a gunshot exploded in the apartment and my Dad flew backward, the knife he'd held in his hand spinning off into the air.

After that, nothing seemed to make sense. I was worried that the knife would break something when it landed or get stuck in the wall. I'd seen blood on the edge. How would I ever explain that to the landlord? "Oh yeah! That was the time my dad tried to kill me..." It bothered me for some reason that there was blood on the blade, but I couldn't seem to think why...

Then something seemed to pop, and everything sped back up and became a blur of sound and lights and people.

"Nicki? *Nicki!*" I heard Kaine scream my name as he scrambled to his feet. I tried to reassure him, because he sounded *so* frightened, but nothing seemed to come out. I tried to clear my throat as my legs suddenly got super heavy and coughed into my hand. I was alarmed when I pulled it away from my mouth and saw blood spattered across it.

Blood? There was something about blood I was always supposed to remember. I stared at my hand in confusion, the watery red spittle revolting as it dribbled down my wrist and over the plus sign tattooed on my wrist.

Plus sign. Positive. Shit! My *blood!* I couldn't let anyone touch my blood!

I tried to push Kaine away from me, but all the strength seemed to drain out of my legs at once. I fell to my knees as activity exploded around me. My ears were still ringing with the sounds of the gunshots. I blinked, and suddenly it seemed like we had dozens of people in the room.

"Hold on, Nicki! The ambulance is almost here," Kaine reassured me. Why was he reassuring me? Why was I lying on the ground? When had that happened? I could see Vivian in the kitchen, her hands covering her mouth as tears streaked down her cheeks.

"Wh-what…" I managed to get out, as I tried to ask why she was crying, but the more I tried to talk, the more I felt like I was choking. Vivian shouldn't cry. Vivian was wonderful.

"Just be quiet, Nicki, it's going to be okay," I heard Micah saying as he lifted my feet up onto the coffee table. Vivian didn't like feet on the coffee table. I tried to tell him so, but nothing came out but a few gurgling gasps.

Where was Kaine? He was here just a second ago, but I had blinked, and he had disappeared. That scared me more than anything else, more than the gunshots, more than the blood. Kaine would never leave me. I looked around the room wildly. Kaine should be *here*, right? He belonged with me.

Then I saw him sprinting back to the room and he knelt down beside me, pressing some bath towels against my stomach. That hurt enough for me to cry out and crying out made me start coughing again.

My head began to swim, the dizziness almost too much.

"Stay with me, Nicki! *Please*, God, don't leave me!" I heard Kaine whisper into my ear. I felt something warm and wet land in my ear. I hated getting water in my ears. I tried to tell Kaine I wasn't going anywhere, and that he needed to stop crying in my ears, but suddenly my head was too heavy to move. My sudden weakness left my head lying to the side, line of sight giving me a view past where Kaine knelt next to me, and directly at the side of my father's head. Right where the bullet had entered it.

I tried to reassure Kaine that I would never leave him, not ever… but then everything went dark.

KAINE

MY FAMILY HAD BEEN SPENDING ENTIRELY TOO MUCH TIME IN HOSPITALS lately.

The beep of the monitors attached to Nicki's poor, battered body was only tolerable because it let me know that he was still alive, just unconscious. I sat by his bed in the hospital room in the surgical ward, my hand covering his, my head on his arm, just like it had for the last several hours. Mama K and Mama D were curled up in one recliner on the other side of the bed, and Alex and Marty had somehow folded their tall frames together into another one.

Nicki lay in the hospital bed, his face almost the same shade of white as the bedsheets, his normally flame-colored hair looking a subdued auburn in the dim fluorescent lighting of the hospital room.

Willis Terhune had known what he was doing when he stabbed his son. His first attack hadn't been that deep, but his subsequent strikes had sliced into Nicki's liver. The surgeon told us that if his aim hadn't been knocked off by Micah's shot, he probably would have severed an artery, and Nicki would have bled out in seconds. I owed that man my life, because he had saved the man who was my heart.

Micah was still at the police station where he was answering questions in the shooting of Nicki's father. He was being ably represented, though, by the firm of Young & Zachary, attorneys at law. Alex said there was nothing to worry about and that they'd be releasing him soon, but one cop shooting another, even if they were from different states, was bound to raise eyebrows.

Alex had stormed into the hospital like an avenging angel, his silver and red hair blazing around his head. I think if Willis Terhune hadn't already been dead, Alex would have killed him. Come to think of it, the way he'd looked, if necromancy was a thing, he would have resurrected Willis just so he could kill him again...

A detective I didn't recognize had taken statements from Vivian and me in the emergency room, because we'd refused to leave Nicki's side. What did it say about my family that we were beginning to know the members of the Akron Police Department by name?

Of course, being a Devereaux, my whole clan had shown up at the hospital within a matter of minutes. Weaver had just convinced Vivian to head back to the house to get some rest about an hour ago. Lee was hanging out with Sonny on the orthopedics floor, and Bishop was with Hicks.

The detective told us that Willis had gotten a neighbor to let him into the building pretending to be a new tenant. He had broken into Vivian and Nicki's apartment and threatened Vivian with his gun. Once she was in the trunk of the car, all he'd had to do was wait for Nicki and me to arrive.

I shuddered again at the thought of how close I'd come to losing Nicki again, after having spent so many years apart... He'd been in surgery for a few hours after we'd arrived and had required a transfusion, but the doctors said he was going to make a full recovery.

I felt his fingers tighten on mine, and my eyes shot to his face. His gorgeous, beautiful, perfect face that was now awake and aware.

"Hey, sexy..." I whispered, getting to my feet and moving to the head of the bed so I could lean over and place a gentle kiss on Nicki's forehead.

"H-he... Hey..." he managed to gasp, his voice dry and raspy.

"Here, wait..." I said. I reached for a pitcher of water that was on the tray table and poured him a glass, popping the straw into the water and tilting it so he could drink.

"Go slow," I said, guiding the straw between his lips. The nurses had said he should drink as much water as possible to help replace some of the fluids he'd lost. He had an IV running and an oxygen cannula in his nose, and but they'd said he'd probably have a dry, sore throat when he woke up because they'd had to intubate him for the surgery to repair the damage his father had caused.

Nicki nodded slightly when he'd had enough, and I set the cup down on the tray table.

"Hey there..." He managed to whisper, a ghost of a smile forming at the corner of his mouth.

"Do you... do you remember what happened, Nicki?" I asked.

His eyebrows drew together and made an adorable divot above his nose, then I saw the memory return. He scrunched his eyes closed in pain, then opened them and managed to nod.

"My... dad...?" he got out.

"I'm sorry, Nicki," I whispered, all the concern and love that Nicki had for his father—even after all he'd been put through—so apparent on his face. "He didn't make it," I whispered.

He closed his eyes and nodded again, this time tears leaked from the corners of his eyes. I put my hands on both sides of his face, his eyes opening. I swiped my thumbs sideways, brushing away his tears.

"S-stupid..." He managed as he brought the hand that didn't have the IV in it up to rub his eyes.

"B-but... he was my dad..." he whispered. After a minute he continued, "Did anyone... b-blood...?"

"No, Micah had gloves on him," I reassured him. "The cops and medics were prepared, too. There was some damage to your liver, but they were able to repair it. Doc said you'll be good as new in a few days."

He looked at me, then glanced upward, to a space right above my left ear.

"You... Okay? Vivian?" he rasped, his voice already getting stronger

I grinned and nodded.

"I'm going to have a *rakishly* good-looking scar, but nothing my hair won't cover," I teased. "As well as a hell of a story to tell about how my boyfriend saved my life. Viv is going to be sporting a fabulous new hair style in a day or two, but no lasting damage."

He grinned weakly, a slight blush adding some color to his cheeks.

"...Good..." he managed, his eyes closing for a moment.

"Do you want anything? How's the pain?" I asked.

"M'kay. Sleepy..." he said.

I placed another kiss on his forehead.

"Get some rest, baby," I insisted. "The sooner you get better, the sooner I can get you out of here and take you home."

Nicki closed his eyes and drifted off to sleep, but this time there was a touch of a smile on his lips.

21

NICKI

<small>THE NEXT FEW WEEKS PASSED IN A BLUR.</small>

After I was released from the hospital, the Devereaux fam refused to let me go back to our second story apartment, for which I was grateful. I didn't think I could have done the stairs on a regular basis.

Micah had put us in touch with an industrial cleaning crew who had managed to take care of all the blood and bits from the shooting, but none of us wanted to deal with the shadow of my father's death on a daily basis.

The landlord was more than willing to let us out of our lease—I think his lawyers had told him he could be held liable for not having a better security system in place—but as luck would have it, he had another property that he was willing to offer us at a very reasonable rate. It was a three-bedroom house that wasn't far from the Devereaux Den. It had an attached, two-car garage and a small yard.

There hadn't even been any major discussion, Vivian and I had just included Kaine when we started planning the move.

Alex, Marty and Rhiannon were slowly becoming a major part of my life. Kaine and I typically spent Saturday afternoons or evenings with them, and I'd found my biological father to be an extremely intelligent, sensitive man. Marty had a wicked sense of humor, and he and Rhiannon had an ongoing pretend dislike of each other that was hilarious to watch.

One of my favorite things was to just to sit on the couch with Kaine's arm around me, sipping a glass of wine while they reminisced about some of the crazy things they and my mom had done when they were younger—bearing in mind, "when they were younger," was all of two years ago.

I never asked, because it wasn't really my business, but it sounded to me as if she, Marty, and Alex had been a thruple, and a very happy one.

I loved hearing stories about my mom and the family she had chosen. It warmed something deep in my heart that she had found love and happiness, even if it had been incomplete because we were separated.

Speaking of family, Viv had been hanging out at the Devereaux home a lot lately, especially on the days when a certain red-headed sister was in town. No one had said anything yet, but I had heard some muffled moaning coming from Vivian's bedroom late one night, and found some red hair in our new bathroom that was way too long to have been mine... I hadn't said anything to Viv, because it still seemed really new, but I didn't think I'd ever seen her happier than she was when she was with Weaver.

Her parents had come up for Thanksgiving, and introducing them to the entire clan had been a head-spinning experience. Dr. and Mrs. Dunwoody had adored the Devereauxs and had become fast friends with Alex, Marty, and Rhiannon. Mrs. Dunwoody had even spoken about possibly moving to Ohio to be closer to Vivian.

I was sitting on the couch in our living room one afternoon a few days before Christmas waiting on Kaine to get home. Christmas break was just beginning and I was looking forward to some quality time with my man.

Kaine had cut back significantly on both his work hours and his school schedule. He claimed that now that he had something more worthwhile to spend his time on, he didn't feel quite so much of a need to keep busy all the time.

It might also have helped that he had decided to change from engineering to a fine arts major. He wasn't quite sure if he wanted to open his own photography business, or work for someone else, but I had a feeling we'd be seeing a "Kaine's Photography" sign in the near future.

Things had started to move forward quickly for me, as well. I'd gotten a job at a call center in the area selling mobile phone services. The pay was decent, though the hours sucked. Still, I couldn't complain. It not only provided great medical benefits but would also give me five thousand dollars a year toward my college education. I was continuing my internet classes for this semester but had applied to the University of Akron from Spring session. In the meantime, I had started a blog, and had begun doing freelance copywriting work in my spare time.

Huh. A photographer and a copywriter. What kind of trouble could we get into, I wondered?

Kaine walked through the door, pulling his knit hat off his head, his gloved hands full of mail as he brushed snowflakes off the shoulders of his coat.

"Hey, sexy!" I called, looking up at him from the article I was working on at the kitchen table. I could have worked in the area we had designated as "the office," where we each had a desk and computers set up, but the view from the kitchen table was so much prettier. I had forgotten how much I had loved the snow when I was a kid. Years spent in Florida hadn't dimmed my love of the changing seasons, or the colder weather.

Kaine smiled at me as he came over and wrapped his arms around me.

"Hey sexy, yourself," he rumbled, placing a gentle kiss on my lips. "You about ready to go?"

I glanced back at the laptop, a document open with a couple of bulleted lists.

"Yeah, I was just putting together some ideas for the blog," I answered, shutting the laptop so I could turn around and give Kaine my undivided attention.

I stood and wrapped my arms around him, ignoring the slight

dampness on his coat from the falling snow. I pressed our lips together and savored the taste of him. He tasted like marshmallows and hot chocolate, and his breath smelled like cinnamon.

"Mmmmm... you've been drinking Mama K's hot chocolate again, haven't you?" I asked accusingly.

He grinned and kissed me again, his lips cold and soft against mine.

"Mayyybe..." he drawled teasingly.

"How *could* you! You *beast!*" I exclaimed, jokingly punching his shoulder. "You know how much I love Mama K's hot chocolate!"

He grinned at me unrepentantly.

"Am I still a beast if I tell you I've got a thermos of it in the car waiting on you?" he asked.

My eyes went wide and I grabbed the hunter-green scarf off the back of my chair that Mama D had knitted me.

"Why didn't you say so!" I exclaimed as I snagged my coat from the closet. "Let's get going!"

He chuckled at my sudden speed as I made my way out to the car. It was well known in the family that the way to my heart was through hot chocolate. Mama D used real chocolate for hers, not some fake powder. She also used the full size marshmallows and added just a touch of cinnamon when it was all done. It. Was. Perfect.

Kaine was taking me to the cemetery to take some pictures of me at my mother's grave. Mom had loved the seasons in Ohio, and Christmas had been one of her favorite holidays. She had always gone nuts for the family at Christmas, insisting on stockings, and Santa cookies, and the whole nine yards.

I missed her so much at this time of year, but the pain had softened now. It was becoming more of an ache than the sharp, biting thing it had been initially. Alex and Marty had helped me learn so much more about her than I ever had before, and I knew she'd built a good life for herself back in Ohio.

As we parked and got out of the car at Rose Park Cemetery, I paused for a moment just to take in the view.

There was a fresh blanket of snow on the ground from the night before. The sky was a brilliant winter blue, dotted with just a few fluffy white clouds.

Kaine had insisted on bringing his tripod to take some pictures of us together and he was setting up while I waited. Her grave was at the top of a low hill, underneath a huge maple tree. During the fall, the leaves had been a vibrant, gorgeous red. Now, the tree stood empty of leaves, its dark branches silhouetted against the winter sky.

I took my gloves off, ignoring the chill as I ran my fingers over the rough bark. Even though there was no apparent life right now, there was still so much potential within that strong tree.

My mother's gravestone was at the foot of the tree. It simply read, "Harley Phillips Terhune. Beloved Wife, Mother and Friend. Taken from us too soon."

My fingers stroked over it lovingly, brushing the snow away from the top of the monument. My fingers played across the carved words.

I looked up from where I knelt and saw the carving in the side of the tree. It was a heart that said "Harley plus Alex" inside. Marty's name had been added on a bit later, and a second heart was added around it to include all three names.

"I was really nervous when she came back to Akron," Marty had told me the fall day when I'd first come with him and Alex to visit my mother's grave.

"I was so afraid, and so jealous of their relationship," he explained. "Alex and I hadn't been together that long before she came back and I was afraid that the return of his childhood sweetheart spelled the end for us."

Alex had smiled sweetly at Marty and kissed him gently, then traced the outline of the larger heart.

"When Marty finally admitted his fears to her, Harley brought the three of us up here. She took out a pocketknife and added Marty's name to the tree. She drew the larger heart around it and said 'Love's always got room. Love's the only thing you can get more of by giving it away.'"

I admit, there had been lots of tears at that visit.

Elsewhere in the graveyard, but not within sight, was a small monument for my father. It didn't hold his body, though. We had been able to donate his organs and give new life to eight different people. His heart would beat for someone else, his eyes would see for them. His tissue would give new hope to others, and I'd donated the rest of his body to science.

I didn't understand what had driven my father to be the way he was, to cause the pain he'd caused, but I was glad that I had been able to bring some good out of his life.

"You okay, baby?" I heard Kaine ask and I nodded as I turned around. I'd heard the telltale shutter sound of his camera taking photos as I'd touched the tree. The sound was becoming the backdrop of our lives together and I loved it.

He took one more look through the viewfinder of the camera on the tripod, then pressed a button and stepped forward until we were standing together against the tree, He leaned toward me, capturing my lips with his, and the feel of his arms around me made me sigh. The winter sun made us cast long shadows, and when he finally released my lips I was breathless.

"So, I came up here last week to have a talk with your mom," Kaine said, a bit sheepishly.

I looked at him in confusion. I often came up here to talk to her, but I didn't know he had come up alone before.

"We had a long talk about you, about how much I love you," Kaine continued, the winter sunlight making his blond highlights look even more golden than normal. "I told her that if I had the chance, I would give you the moon."

He reached into his pocket and knelt down on one knee in the snow.

"She told me the moon would be kind of hard to keep in our bedroom, so maybe I should give you this instead," he said. In his hand was a small dark box, and as he opened it, my hand flew to my mouth in shock.

Inside the box was a thin platinum band.

"Dominick Rowen Terhune, you are one of the strongest, most determined men I have ever met. You protect the ones you love and you *never* give up without a fight. Would you do me the lifelong honor of becoming my husband?" He asked, his eyes glowing in the sunlight.

I stared at him in shock, trying to comprehend what was happening. Husband? Me?

I must have been more stunned than I realized, because Kaine looked around after a minute, then ran his hand along the back of his neck.

"Red, you're making me a little worried here..." he said.

"Yes!" I finally managed to get out, laughter bubbling through me as I pulled him to his feet and kissed him soundly before continuing, *"Hell, yes*! My answer to you, Kaine Devereaux will *always* be yes!"

ABOUT THE AUTHOR

Mellanie Rourke lives in Akron, Ohio with her husband, two kids, three cats, a dog, and two ferrets.

Join my newsletter for news of upcoming events here: http://bit.ly/MellanieRourkeNewsletter

For up-to-date info, stop by my Facebook site "Mel's Misfits & Malcontents."

If this is your first introduction to the Devereaux's, check out my first book, "Mason's Run" available on Kindle Unlimited!

facebook.com/mellanie.rourke